# THE RACKHAM FILES

**BAEN BOOKS by DEAN ING**

Firefight Y2K

Houses of the Kzinti
*(created by Larry Niven,*
*with Jerry Pournelle & S.M. Stirling)*

# THE RACKHAM FILES

DEAN ING

THE RACKHAM FILES



A Baen Books Original Megabook

Baen Publishing Enterprises
P.O. Box 1403
Riverdale, NY 10471
www.baen.com

ISBN: 0-7434-7183-0

Cover art by Stephen Hickman

First printing, February 2004

Library of Congress Cataloging-in-Publication Data

Ing, Dean.
The Rackham files / by Dean Ing.
p. cm.
"A Baen Books original megabook"—T.p. verso.
ISBN 0-7434-7183-0 (HC)
1. Automobile racing drivers—Fiction. 2. Bounty hunters—Fiction. 3. Survivalism—Fiction. 4. California—Fiction. 5. Forgers—Fiction. I. Title.

PS3559.N37R33 2004
813'.54—dc22 2003022164

Distributed by Simon & Schuster
1230 Avenue of the Americas
New York, NY 10020

Production by Windhaven Press, Auburn, NH
Printed in the United States of America

10 9 8 7 6 5 4 3 2 1

# CONTENTS

# Introduction

by Larry Niven

Once upon a time, my wife Marilyn and I went to England for a World Science Fiction Convention. On return, the Customs official scanned my passport and said, "Larry Niven the writer? *Lucifer's Hammer*?"

I said, "Right. You're a science fiction fan?"

"No," he said, and lifted the magazine he was reading. It was a publication for survivalists.

*Lucifer's Hammer* (written with Jerry Pournelle) was, at that time, being used as a survivalist text. Several of the surviving characters in that book are of that stamp: determined to make themselves self-sufficient and ready for anything the universe or the Soviet Union might throw at them.

The survivalists in *Lucifer's Hammer* weren't just ready for the collapse of civilization. They were eager. Dr. Forrester was an exception. He was a diabetic. He needed to find a group that would find him worth saving. Dr. Forrester's preparations were given in nitpicking detail. Dr. Pournelle researched them thoroughly, and that's what got the attention of the survivalists.

There are more survivalists than you think. Their ideal is self-sufficiency.

I raise the subject because Dean Ing is one of those. From my viewpoint it seems he can do anything with his hands. He designs and builds cars and planes and other tools, sometimes to leave a clean environment, sometimes to win races, sometimes—as in the Rackham stories—to weave a plausible near-future.

I'm not one of these myself: not good with my hands. I sometimes wonder if people like Dean Ing know how I see them. They're the original model for Motie Engineers (as in *A Mote in God's Eye.*) A better model might be Dr. Zarkhov from the Flash Gordon comic strip. He knows enough about anything to make the tool that fits.

This tool building talent is the most human of traits, but some of us have more of it than others.

Dean Ing wants you to survive, if you're smart enough to read his books.

He's a muscular guy, not spectacularly tall, who weighs no more than he should. In this respect he's quite different from his character Rackham. But Rackham is another Zarkhov: he can make a tool on the spot. The difference is that you will understand the tool. You'll be able to make it yourself.

The Rackham stories date from the Cold War. That's okay. The laws of physics and engineering haven't changed.

My favorite of his novels is *Soft Targets.* If I tried to describe the premise, you wouldn't believe me. It's up-to-the-minute relevant. I just can't quite believe it would work.

—Larry Niven
September 2003

# INSIDE JOB

# One

"The longer I live, the more I realize the less I know for sure." That's what my friend Quentin Kim used to mutter to me and curvy little Dana Martin in our Public Safety classes at San Jose State. Dana would frown because she revered conventional wisdom. I'd always chuckle, because I thought Quent was kidding. But that was years ago, and I was older then.

I mean, I thought I knew it all. "Public Safety" is genteel academic code for cop coursework, and while Quent had already built himself an enviable rep as a licensed P.I. in the Bay Area, he hadn't been a big-city cop. I went on to become one, until I got fed up with the cold war between guys on the take and guys in Internal Affairs, both sides angling for recruits. I tried hard to avoid getting their crap on my size thirteen brogans while I lost track of Dana, saw Quent infrequently, and served the City of Oakland's plainclothes detail in the name of public safety.

So much for stepping carefully in such a barnyard. At least I got out with honor after a few years, and I still had contacts around Oakland on both sides of the law. Make that several sides; and to an investigator that's worth more than diamonds. It would've taken a better man than Harve Rackham to let those contacts go to waste, which is why I became the private kind of investigator, aka gumshoe, peeper, or just plain Rackham, P.I.

Early success can destroy you faster than a palmed ice pick, especially if it comes through luck you thought was skill. A year into my new career, I talked my way into a seam job—a kidnapping within a disintegrating family. The kidnapped boy's father, a Sunnyvale software genius, wanted the kid back badly enough to throw serious money at his problem. After a few days of frustration, I shot my big mouth off about it to my sister's husband, Ernie.

It was a lucky shot, though. Ernie was with NASA at Moffett Field and by sheer coincidence he knew a certain Canadian physicist. I'd picked up a rumor that the physicist had been playing footsie with the boy's vanished mother.

The physicist had a Quebecois accent, Ernie recalled, and had spoken longingly about a teaching career. The man had already given notice at NASA without a forwarding address. He was Catholic. A little digging told me that might place him at the University of Montreal, a Catholic school which gives instruction in French. I caught a Boeing 787 and got there before he did, and guess who was waiting with her five-year-old boy in the Montreal apartment the physicist had leased.

I knew better than to dig very far into the reasons why Mama took Kiddie and left Papa. It was enough that she'd fled the country illegally. The check I cashed was so much more than enough that I bought a decaying farmhouse twenty miles and a hundred years from Oakland.

Spending so much time away, I figured I'd need to fence the five acres of peaches and grapes, but the smithy was what sold me. "The smith, a mighty man was he, with large and sinewy," et cetera. Romantic bullshit, sure, but as I said, I knew it all then. And I wanted to build an off-road racer, one of the diesel-electric hybrids that were just becoming popular. I couldn't imagine a better life than peeping around the Port of Oakland for money, and hiding out on my acreage whenever I had some time off, building my big lightning-on-wheels toy.

And God knows, I had plenty of time off after that! Didn't

the word get out that I was hot stuff? Weren't more rich guys clamoring for my expensive services? Wasn't I slated for greatness?

In three words: no, no, and no. I didn't even invest in a slick Web site while I still had the money, with only a line in the yellow pages, so I didn't get many calls. I was grunting beneath my old gasoline-fueled Toyota pickup one April afternoon, chasing an oil leak because I couldn't afford to have someone else do it, when my cell phone warbled.

Quentin Kim; I was grinning in an instant. "I thought I was good, but it's humbling when I can't find something as big as you," he bitched.

I squoze my hundred kilos from under the Toyota. "You mean you're looking for me now? Today?"

"I have driven that country road three times, Harvey. My GP mapper's no help. Where the devil are you?"

Even his cussing was conservative. When Quent used my full given name, he was a quart low on patience. I told him to try the road again and I'd flag him down, and he did, and twenty minutes later I guided his Volvo Electrabout up the lane to my place.

He emerged looking fit, a few grey hairs but the almond eyes still raven-bright, the smile mellow, unchanged. I ignored the limp; maybe his shoes pinched. From force of habit and ethnic Korean good manners, Quent avoided staring around him, but I knew he would miss very little as I invited him through the squinchy old screen door into my authentic 1910 kitchen with its woodstove. He didn't relax until we continued to the basement, the fluorescents obediently flickering on along the stairs.

"You had me worried for a minute," he said, now with a frankly approving glance at my office. As *fin de siècle* as the house was from the foundation up, I'd fixed it all Frank Gehry and Starship *Enterprise* below. He perched his butt carefully on the stool at my drafting carrel; ran his hand along the flat catatonic stare of my Magnascreen. "But you must be doing all right for yourself. Some of this has got to be expensive stuff, Harve."

"Pure sweat equity, most of it." I shrugged. "I do adhesive bonding, some welding, cabinetry—oh, I was a whiz in shop, back in high school."

"Don't try to imply that you missed your real calling. I notice you're working under your own license since a year ago. Can people with budgets still afford you?"

"I won't shit you, Quent, but don't spread this around. Way things are right now, anybody can afford me."

It had been over a year since we'd watched World Cup soccer matches together, and while we caught each other up on recent events, I brewed tea for him in my six-cup glass rig with its flash boiler.

He didn't make me ask about the limp. "You know how those old alleyway fire-escape ladders get rickety after sixty years or so," he told me, shifting his leg. "A few months ago I was closing on a bail-jumper who'd been living on a roof in Alameda, and the ladder came loose on us." Shy smile, to forestall sympathy. "He hit the bricks. I bounced off a Dumpster." Shrug.

"Bring him in?"

"The paramedics brought us both in, but I got my fee," he said. "I don't have to tell you how an HMO views our work, and I'm not indigent. Fixing this hip cost me a lot more than I made, and legwork will never be my forte again, I'm afraid."

I folded my arms and attended to the beep of my tea rig. "You're telling me you were bounty hunting," I said. It wasn't exactly an accusation, but most P.I.s won't work for bail bondsmen. It's pretty demanding work, though the money can be good when you negotiate a fifteen percent fee and then bring in some scuffler who's worth fifty large.

While we sipped tea, we swapped sob stories, maintaining a light touch because nobody had forced either of us into the peeper business. You hear a lot about P.I.s being churlish to each other. Mostly a myth, beyond some healthy competition. "I suppose I couldn't resist the challenge," said Quent. "You know me, always trying to expand my education. As a bounty hunter you learn a lot, pretty quickly."

"Like, don't trust old fire escapes," I said.

"Like that," he agreed. "But it also brings you to the attention of a different class of client. It might surprise even you that some Fed agencies will subcontract an investigation, given special circumstances."

It surprised me less when he said that the present circumstances required someone who spoke Hangul, the Korean language, and knew the dockside world around Oakland. Someone the Federal Bureau of Investigation could trust.

"Those guys," I said, "frost my *cojones.* It's been my experience that they'll let metro cops take most of the chances and zero percent of the credit."

"Credit is what you buy groceries with, Harve," he said. "What do we care, so long as the Feds will hire us again?"

"Whoa. What's that word again? *Us,* as in you and me?"

"If you'll take it. I need an extra set of feet—hips, if you insist—and it doesn't hurt that you carry the air of plainclothes cop with you. And with your size, you can handle yourself, which is something I might need."

He mentioned a fee, including a daily rate, and I managed not to whistle. "I need to know more. This gonna be something like a bodyguard detail, Quent? I don't speak Hangul, beyond a few phrases you taught me."

"That's only part of it. Most people we'll interview speak plain American; record checks, for example. The case involves a marine engineer missing from the tramp motorship *Ras Ormara*, which is tied up for round-the-clock refitting at a Richmond wharf. He's Korean. Coast Guard and FBI would both like to find him, without their being identified."

There's an old cop saying about Richmond, California: it's vampire turf. Safe enough in daylight, but watch your neck at night. "I suppose you've already tried Missing Persons."

Quent served me a "give me a break" look. "I don't have to tell you the metro force budget is petty cash, Harve. They're overloaded with domestic cases. The Feds know it, which is where we come in—if you want in."

"Got me over a barrel. You want the truth, I'm practically wearing the goddamn barrel. Any idea how long the case will last?"

Quent knew I was really asking how many days' pay it might involve. "It evaporates the day the *Ras Ormara* leaves port;

perhaps a week. That doesn't give us as much time as I'd like, but every case sets its own pace."

That was another old Quentism, and I'd come to learn it was true. This would be a hot pace, so no wonder gimpy Quentin Kim was offering to share the workload. Instead of doping out his selfish motives, I should be thanking him, so I did. I added, "You don't know it, but you're offering me a bundle of chrome-moly racer frame tubing and a few rolls of cyclone fence. An offer I can't refuse, but I'd like to get a dossier on this Korean engineer right away."

"I can do better than that," said Quent, "and it'll come with a free supper tonight, courtesy of the Feds."

"They're buying? Now, *that* is impressive as hell."

"I have not begun to impress," Quent said, again with the shy smile. "Coast Guard Lieutenant Reuben Medler is fairly impressive, but the FBI liaison will strain your belief system."

"Never happen," I said. "They still look like IBM salesmen."

"Not this one. Trust me." Now Quent was grinning.

"You're wrong," I insisted.

"What do you think happened to the third of our classroom musketeers, Harve, and why do you think this case was dropped in my lap? The Feebie is Dana Martin," he said.

I kept my jaw from sagging with some effort. "You were right," I said.

Until the fight started, I assumed Quent had chosen Original Joe's in San Jose because we—Dana included—had downed many an abalone supreme there in earlier times. If some of the clientele were reputedly Connected with a capital C, that only kept folks polite. Quent and I met there and copped a booth, though our old habit had been to take seats at the counter where we could watch chefs with wrists of steel handle forty-centimeter skillets over three-alarm gas burners. I was halfway through a bottle of Anchor Steam when a well-built specimen in a crewneck sweater, trim Dockers, and tasseled loafers ushered his date in. He carried himself as if hiding a small flagpole in the back of his sweater. I looked away, denying my envy. How is it some guys never put on an ounce while guys like me outgrow our belts?

Then I did a double take. The guy had to be Lieutenant Medler because the small, tanned, sharp-eyed confection in mid-heels and severely tailored suit was Dana Martin, no longer an overconfident kid. I think I said "wow" silently as we stood up.

After the introductions Medler let us babble about how long it had been. For me, the measure of elapsed time was that little Miz Martin had developed a sense of reserve. Then while we decided what we wanted to eat, Medler explained why shoreline poachers had taken abalone off the Original Joe menu. Mindful of who was picking up the tab, I ordered the latest fad entree: Nebraska longhorn T-bone, lean as ostrich and just as spendy. Dana's lip pursed but she kept it buttoned, cordial, impersonal. I decided she'd bought into her career and its image. Damn, but I hated that . . .

Over the salads, Medler gave his story without editorializing, deferential to us, more so to Dana, in a soft baritone all the more masculine for discarding machismo. "The *Ras Ormara* is a C-1 motorship under Liberian registry," he said, "chartered by the Sonmiani Tramp Service of Karachi, Pakistan." He recited carefully, as if speaking for a recorder. Which he was, though I didn't say so. What the hell, people forget things.

"Some of these multinational vessels just beg for close inspection, the current foreign political situation being what it is," Medler went on. He didn't need to mention the nuke found by a French airport security team the previous month, on an Arab prince's Learjet at Charles De Gaulle terminal. "We did a walk-through. The vessel was out of Lima with a cargo of balsa logs and nontoxic plant extract slurry, bound for Richmond. Crew was the usual polyglot bunch, in this case chiefly Pakis and Koreans. They stay aboard in port unless they have the right papers."

At this point Medler abruptly began talking about how abalone poachers work, a second before the waitress arrived to serve our entrees. Quent nodded appreciatively and I toasted Medler's coolth with my beer.

Once we'd attacked our meals he resumed. Maybe the editorial came with the main course. "You know about Asian working-class people and eye contact—with apologies, Mr. Kim. But one young Korean in the crew was boring holes in my corneas. I decided to interview three men, one at a time, on the fo'c'sle deck. At random, naturally."

"Random as loaded dice." I winked.

"With their skipper right there? Affirmative, and I started with the ship's medic. When I escorted this young third engineer, Park Soon, on deck the poor guy was shaking. His English wasn't that fluent, and he didn't say much, even to direct questions, but he did say we had to talk ashore. 'Must talk,' was the phrase. He had his papers to go ashore.

"I gave him a time and place later that day, a coffeehouse in Berkeley every taxi driver knows. I thought he was going to cry with relief, but he went back to the *Ras Ormara*'s bridge with his jaw set like he was marching toward a firing squad. I went belowdecks.

"A lot of tramps look pretty trampy, but it actually just means it's not a regularly scheduled vessel. This one was spitshine spotless, and I found no reason to doubt the manifest or squawk about conditions in the holds.

"Fast forward to roughly sixteen hundred hours. Park shows at the coffeehouse, jumpy as Kermit, but now he's full of dire warnings. He doesn't know exactly what's wrong about the *Ras Ormara*, but he knows he's aboard only for window dressing. The reason he shipped on at Lima was, Park had met the previous third engineer in Lima at a dockside bar, some Chinese who spoke enough English to say he was afraid to go back aboard. Park was on the beach, as they say, and he wangled the job for himself."

Quent stopped shoveling spicy sausage in, and asked, "The Chinese was afraid? Of what?"

"According to Park, the man's exact English words were 'Death ship.' Park thought he had misunderstood at first and put the Chinese engineer's fear down to superstition. But a day or so en route here, he began to get spooked."

"Every culture has its superstitions," Quent said. "And crew members must pass them on. I'm told an old ship can carry enough legends to sink it." When Medler frowned, Quent said, "Remember Joseph Conrad's story, 'The Brute'? The *Apse Family* was a death ship. Well, it was just a story," he said, seeing Dana's look of abused patience.

Medler again: "A classic. Who hasn't read it?" Dana gave a knowing nod. Pissed me off; I hadn't read it. "But I doubt anyone aboard told sea stories to Park. He implied they all seemed to be appreciating some vast, unspoken serious joke. No one would talk to him at all except for his duties. And he didn't have a lot to do because the ship was a dream, he said. She had been converted somewhere to cargo from a small fast transport, so the crew accommodations were nifty. She displaces maybe two thousand tons, twenty-four knots. Fast," he said again. "Originally she must've been someone's decommissioned D.E.—destroyer escort. Not at all like a lot of those rustbuckets in tramp service."

Quent toyed with his food. "It's fairly common, isn't it, for several conversions to be made over the life of a ship?"

"Exigencies of trade." Medler nodded. "Hard to say where it was done, but Pakistan has a shipbreaking industry and rerolling mills in Karachi." He shook his head and grinned. "I think they could cobble you up a new ship from the stuff they salvage. We've refused to allow some old buckets into the bay; they're rusted out so far, you step in the wrong place on deck and your foot will go right through. But not the *Ras Ormara*; I'd serve on her myself, if her bottom's anything like her topside."

"I thought you did an, uh, inspection," said Dana.

"Walk-through. We didn't do it as thoroughly as we might if we'd found anything abovedecks. She's so clean I understand why Park became nervous. Barring the military—one of our cutters, for instance—you just don't find that kind of sterile environment in maritime service. Not even a converted D.E."

"No," Dana insisted, and made a delicate twirl with her fork. "I meant afterward."

Medler blinked. "If you want to talk about it, go ahead. I can't. You know that."

Dana, whom I'd once thought of as a teen mascot, patted

his forearm like a den mother. I didn't know which of them I wanted more to kick under the table. "I go way back with these two, Reuben, and they're under contract with confidentiality. But this may not be the place."

I was already under contract? Well, only if I were working under Quent's license, and if he'd told her so. Still, I was getting fed up with how little I knew. "For God's sake," I said, "just the short form, okay?"

"For twenty years we've had ways to search sea floors for aircraft flight recorders," Dana told me. "Don't you think the Coast Guard might have similar gadgets to look at a hull?"

"For what?"

"Whatever," Medler replied, uneasy about it. "I ordered it after the Park interview. When you know how Hughes built the CIA's *Glomar Explorer*, you know a ship can have a lot of purposes that aren't obvious at the waterline. Figure it out for yourself," he urged.

That spook ship Hughes's people built had been designed to be flooded and to float vertically, sticking up from the water like a fisherman's bobbin. Even the tabloids had exploited it. I thought about secret hatches for underwater demolition teams, torpedo tubes—"Got it," I said. "Any and every unfriendly use I can dream up. Can I ask what they found?"

"Not a blessed thing," said Reuben Medler. "If it weren't for D—Agent Martin here, I'd be writing reports on why I insisted."

"He insisted because the Bureau did," Dana put in. "We've had some vague tips about a major event, planned by nice folks with the same traditions as those who, uh, bugged Tel Aviv."

The Tel Aviv Bug had been anthrax. If the woman who'd smuggled it into Israel hadn't somehow flunked basic hygiene and collapsed with a skinful of the damned bacilli, it would've caused more deaths than it did. "So you found nothing, but you want a follow-up with this Park guy. He's probably catting around and will show up with a hangover when the ship's ready to sail," I said. "I thought crew members had to keep in touch with the charter service."

"They do," said Dana. "And with a full complement of two

dozen, only a few of the crew went ashore. But Park has vanished. Sonmiani claims they'll have still another third engineer when the slurry tanks are cleaned and the new cargo's pumped aboard."

"And we'd prefer they didn't sail before we have another long talk with Park," Medler said. "I'm told the FBI has equipment like an unobtrusive lie detector."

"Voice-stress analyzer," Dana corrected. "Old hardware, new twists. But chiefly, we're on edge because Park has dropped out of sight."

Quent: "But I thought he told you why."

"He told me why he was worried," Medler agreed. "But he also said the *Ras Ormara* will be bound for Pusan with California-manufactured industrial chemicals, a nice tractable cargo, to his own homeport. He was determined to stay with it, worried or not. Of course it's possible he simply changed his mind."

"But we'd like to know," Dana said. "We want to know sufficiently that—well." She looked past us toward the ceiling as if an idea had just occurred to her. Suuure. "Sometimes things happen. Longshoremen's strike—" She saw my sudden glance, and she'd always been alert to nuance. "No, we haven't, but little unforeseen problems arise. Sonmiani is already dealing with a couple of them. Assuming they don't have the clout to build a fire under someone at the ambassador level, there could be one or two more if we find a solid reason. Or if you do."

"I take it Harve and I can move overtly on this," Quent said, "so long as we're not connected to government."

Medler looked at Dana, who said, "Exactly. Low-profile, showing your private investigator's I.D. if necessary. You're known well enough that anyone checking on you would be satisfied you're not us. Of course you've got to have a client of record, so we're furnishing one."

I noticed that Quent seemed interested in something across the room, but he refocused on Dana Martin. "As licensed privateers, we aren't required to name a client or divulge any other details of the case. Normally it would be shaving an ethical guideline."

"But you wouldn't be," Dana said. "You'd be giving up a few

details of a cover story. Nothing very dramatic, just imply that our missing man is a prodigal son. Park Soon's father in Pusan would be unlikely to know he's put you on retainer."

Quent: "Because he can't afford us?"

Dana, with the shadow of a smile: "Because he's been deceased for years. I'll give you the details on that tomorrow, Quent. Uhm, Quent?"

But my pal, whose attention had been wandering again, was now leaning toward me with an unQuentish grin. "Harve," he said softly, "third counter stool from the front, late twenties, blond curls, Yamaha cycle jacket. Could be packing."

"Several guys in here probably are," I said.

"But I'm not carrying certified copies of their bail bonds, and I do have one for Robert Rooney, bail jumper. That's Bobby."

Dana and Medler both looked toward the counter, at me, and at Quent, but let their expressions complain.

"You wouldn't," I said.

"It's my bleeding job," said Quent. "Wait outside. I'll flush him out gently, and if gentle doesn't work, don't let him reach into that jacket."

I was already standing up. "Back shortly, folks. Don't forget my pie à la mode."

"I don't believe this," I heard Medler say as I moved toward the old-fashioned revolving door.

"Santa Clara County Jail is on Hedding, less than a mile from here. We'll be back before you know it," Quent soothed, still seated, giving me time to evaporate.

I saw the bail-jumper watching me in a window reflection, but I gave him no reason to jump. I would soon learn he was just naturally jumpy, pun intended. Can't say it was really that long a fight, though. I pushed through the door and into the San Jose night, realizing we could jam Rooney in it if he tried to run out. And have him start shooting through heavy glass partitions, maybe; sometimes my first impulses are subject to modest criticism.

Outside near the entrance, melding with evening shadow, I listened to the buzz and snap of Joe's old neon sign. I could still see our quarry, and now Quent was strolling behind diners at the counter, apparently intent on watching the chef toss a blazing skilletful of mushrooms. Quent reached inside his coat; brought out a folded paper, his face innocent of stress. Then he said something to the seated Rooney.

Rooney turned only his head, very slowly, nodded, shrugged, and let his stool swivel to face Quent. He grinned.

It's not easy to get leverage with only your buns against a low seat back, but Rooney managed it, lashing both feet out to Quent's legs, his arms windmilling as he bulled past my pal. I heard a shout, then a clamor of voices as Quent staggered against a woman seated at the nearest table. I stepped farther out of sight as Bobby Rooney hurled himself against the inertia of that big revolving door.

He used both hands, and he was sturdier than he had looked, bursting outside an arm's length from me. Exactly an arm's length, because without moving my feet, just as one Irishman to another I clotheslined him under the chin. He went down absolutely horizontal, his head making a nice bonk on the sidewalk, and if he'd had any brains they would've rattled like castanets. He didn't even pause, bringing up both legs, then doing a gymnast's kick so that he was suddenly on his feet in a squat, one arm flailing at me. The other hand snaked into his jacket pocket before I could close on him.

What came out of his right-hand pocket was very small, but it had twin barrels on one end and as he leaped up, Rooney's arm swung toward me. Meanwhile I'd taken two steps forward, and I snatched at his wrist. I caught only his sleeve, but when I heaved upward on it, his hand and the little derringer pocketgun disappeared into the sleeve. A derringer is double-barreled, the barrel's so short its muzzle blast is considerable, and confined in that sleeve it flash-burnt his hand while muffling the sound. The slug headed skyward. Bobby Rooney headed down San Carlos Avenue, hopping along crabwise because I had held on to that sleeve long enough that when he jerked away, his elbow was caught halfway out.

I'm not much of a distance runner, but for fifty meters I can move out at what I imagined was a brisk pace. Why Bobby didn't just stop and fire point-blank through that sleeve I don't know; I kept waiting for it, and one thing I never learned to do was make myself a small target. Half a block later he was still flailing his arm to dislodge the sleeve, and I was still three long steps behind, and that's when a conservative dress suit passed me. Quentin Kim was wearing it at the time, outpacing me despite that limp. He simply spun Bobby Rooney down, standing on his jacket which pinned him down on his back at the mouth of an alley.

I grabbed a handful of blond curls, knelt on Bobby's right sleeve because his gun hand was still in it, and made the back of his head tap the sidewalk. "Harder every time," I said, blowing like a whale. "How many times—before you relax?" Another tap. "Take your time. I can do this—for hours."

As quickly as Bobby Rooney had decided to fight, he reconsidered, his whole body going limp, eyes closed.

"Get that little shooter—out of his sleeve," I said to Quent, who wasn't even winded but rubbed his upper thigh, muttering to himself.

Quent took the derringer, flicked his key-ring Maglite, then brought that wrinkled paper out of his inside coat pocket and shook it open. "Robert Rooney," he intoned.

Still holding on to Rooney's hair, I gazed up. "What the hell? Is this some kind of new Miranda bullshit, Quent?"

"No, it's not required. It's just something I do that clarifies a relationship."

"Relationship? This isn't a relationship, this is a war."

"Not mutually exclusive. You've never been married, have you," Quent said. He began again: "Robert Rooney, acting as agent for the hereafter-named person putting up bail . . ."

I squatted there until Quent had finished explaining that Rooney was, by God, the property of the bondsman named and could be pursued even into his own toilet without a warrant, and that his physical condition upon delivery to the appropriate county jail depended entirely on his temperament. When Quent was done I said, "He may not even hear you."

"He probably does, but it doesn't matter. I hear me," Quent said mildly. A bounty hunter with liberal scruples was one for the books, but I guess Quent wrote his own book.

"How far is your car?"

"Two blocks. Here," Quent said, and handed me the derringer with one unfired chamber. I knew what he said next was for Rooney's ears more than mine. "You can shoot him, just try not to kill him right away. That's only if he tries to run again."

"If he does," I said, "I'll still have his scalp for an elephant's merkin."

Quent laughed as he hurried away, not even limping. "Now there's an image I won't visit twice," he said.

Twenty minutes later we returned from the county lockup with a receipt, and to this day I don't know what Bobby Rooney's voice sounds like. The reason why those kicks hadn't ruined Quent's legs was that, under his suit pants, my pal wore soccer pro FlexArmor over his knees and shins for bounty hunting. He'd suggested Original Joe's to Dana because, among other good reasons, Rooney's ex-girlfriend claimed he hung out there a lot. Since Rooney was dumb as an ax handle, Quent figured the chances of a connection were good. He could combine business with pleasure, and show a pair of Feds how efficient we were. Matter of fact, I was so efficient I wound up with a derringer in my pocket. Fortunes of war, not that I was going to brag about it to the Feds.

Dana and Reuben Medler were still holding down the booth when we returned, Medler half-resigned, half-amused. Dana was neither. "I hope your victim got away," she said. If she'd been a cat, her fur would've been standing on end.

Quent flashed our receipt for Rooney's delivery and eased into the booth. "A simple commercial transaction, Agent Martin," he said, ignoring her hostility. "My apologies."

She wasn't quite satisfied. "Can I expect this to happen again?"

"Not tonight," Quent said equably.

It must've been that smile of his that disarmed her because Dana subsided over coffee and dessert. When it became clear that Quent would take the San Francisco side—it has a sizable Korean population—while I worked the Oakland side of the bay,

Reuben Medler told me where I'd find the *Ras Ormara*, moored on the edge of Richmond near a gaggle of chemical production facilities.

Eventually Dana handed Quent a list of the crew with temporary addresses for the few who went ashore. "Sonmiani's California rep keeps tabs on their crews," she explained. "I got this from Customs."

Medler put in, "Customs has a standard excuse for wanting the documentation; cargo manifest, tonnage certificate, stowage plan, and other records."

"But not you," I said to Dana.

She shook her head. "Even if we did, the Bureau wouldn't step forward to Sonmiani. We leave that to you, although Sonmiani's man in Oakland, ah, Norman Goldman by name, has a clean sheet and appears to be clean. We feel direct contacts of that sort should be made as—what did you call it, Quentin? A simple commercial transaction. Civilians like to talk. If Goldman happened to mention us to the wrong person, the ship's captain for example, someone might abort whatever they're up to. If they see you rooting around, they'll assume it's just part of a routine private investigation."

Maybe I was still pissed that our teen mascot had become our boss. "Implying sloth and incompetence," I murmured.

"You said it, not I," she replied sweetly. "At least Mr. Goldman seems well enough educated that he would never mistake you for an agent."

"You've run a check on him, then," said Quent.

"Of course. Majored in business at Michigan, early promotion, young man on the way up. And I suspect Sonmiani's Islamic crew members will watch their steps around a bright Jewish guy," she added, looking over the check.

Quent drained his teacup. "We'll try to keep it simple; Park Soon could show up tomorrow. Then we'll see whether we need to talk with this Goldman. Is that suitable?"

Quent asked with genuine deference, and Dana paused before she nodded. It struck me then that Quent was making a point of showing obedience to his boss. And his quick glance at me suggested that I might try it sometime.

I knew he was right, but it would have to be some other time. I shook hands again with Reuben Medler, exchanged cards with him, and turned to Dana. "Thanks for the feed. Maybe next time we can avoid a floor show."

She looked at Medler and shook her head, and I left without remarking that she had a lot of seasoning ahead of her.

# Two

It was Quent's suggestion that I case the location of the *Ras Ormara* itself, herself, whatever. Meanwhile he made initial inquiries across the bay alone in his natural camouflage, in the area everyone calls Chinatown though it was home to several Asiatic colonies. It was my idea to bring my StudyGirl to record a look at this shipshape ship we'd heard so much about, and Quent suggested I do it without making any personal contacts that required I.D.

StudyGirls were new then, cleverly named so that kids who wanted the spendy toys—meaning all kids—would have leverage with Dad and Mom. Even the early versions were pocket-sized and would take a two-inch *Britannica* floppy, but they would also put TV broadcasts on the rollout screen or play mini-CDs and action games, and make video recordings as well. It was already common practice to paint over the indicator lights so nobody knew when you were videorecording. I'll bet a few kids actually used them for schoolwork, too.

I took the freeway as far as Richmond, got off at Carlson Boulevard, and puzzled my way through the waterfront's industrial montage. Blank-fronted metal buildings with ramped loading docks meant warehousing of imports and exports, and somewhere in there were a few boxcarloads of Peruvian balsa logs. Composite panels of carbon fiber and balsa sandwich were much in demand at that time among builders of off-road racers for their light weight and stiffness. I enjoyed a moment of déjà future vu at the thought that I might be using some of the *Ras Ormara*'s balsa for my project in a few months.

Unless my woolgathering got me squashed like a bug underfoot. I had to dodge thrumming diesel-electric rigs that outclamored the cries of gulls and ignored my pickup as unworthy of notice. Hey, they were making a buck, and this was their turf.

In a few blocks-long stretches, the warehouses gave way to fencing topped with razor wire, enforced isolation for the kind of small-time chemical processing plants that looked like brightly painted guts of the biggest dinosaurs ever. Now and then I could spot the distant San Rafael Bridge through the tanks, reactor vessels, piping, and catwalks that loomed like little skeletal skyscrapers, throwing early shadows across the street. You knew without a glance when you were passing warehouses because of the echoes and the sour, last-week's-fast-food odor that drew those scavenging gulls. The chemical production plants no longer stank so much since the City of Richmond got serious about its air. And beyond all this at an isolated wharf, berthed next to a container ship like a racehorse beside a Clydesdale, the *Ras Ormara* gleamed in morning light. I wondered why a ship like that was called a "she" when it had such racy muscular lines, overlaid by spidery cargo cranes and punctuated by the gleam of glass. I pointedly focused on the nearby container vessel, walking past an untended gate onto the dock, avoiding flatbed trucks that galumphed in and out. I had my StudyGirl in hand for videotaping, neither flourishing nor hiding it. In semishorts, argyle socks, and short sleeves, I hoped I looked like a typical Midwestern tourist agog over, golly gee, these great big boats. If challenged I could always choose whether to brazen it out with my I.D.

I strolled back, paying casual attention to the *Ras Ormara*, listening to the sounds of engine-driven pressure washers and recording the logos on two trucks with hoses that snaked up and back to big tanks mounted behind the truck cabs. I could see men operating the chassis-mounted truck consoles, wearing headsets. Somehow I'd expected more noise and melodrama in cleaning the ship's big cargo tanks.

Words like "big" and "little" are inadequate where a cargo vessel, even one considered small, is concerned. I guess that's what numbers are for. The *Ras Ormara* was almost three hundred feet stem to stern, the length of a football field, and where bare metal showed it appeared to be stainless steel. All that cleaning was concentrated ahead of the ship's glassed bridge, where a half dozen metal domes, each five yards across, stood in ranks well above the deck level. Two rows of three each; and the truck hoses entered the domes through open access ports big enough to drop a truck tire through. Or a man. Welded ladders implied that men might do just that.

I suppose I could have climbed one of the gangways up to the ship's deck. It was tempting, but Quent had told me—couched as a suggestion—not to. It is simply amazing how obedient I can be to a boss who is not overbearing. I moseyed along, hoping I stayed mostly out of sight behind those servicing trucks without seeming to try. From an open window behind the *Ras Ormara*'s bridge came faint strains of someone's music, probably from a CD. It sounded like hootchie-kootchie scored for three tambourines and a parrot, and I thought it might be Egyptian or some such.

Meanwhile, a bulky yellow extraterrestrial climbed from one of those domes trailing smaller hoses, and made his way carefully down the service ladder. When he levered back his helmet and left it with its hoses on deck, I could see it was just a guy with hair sweat-plastered to his forehead, wearing a protective suit you couldn't miss on a moonless midnight. My luck was holding; he continued down the gangway to the nearest truck. Meanwhile I ambled back in his direction, stowing away my StudyGirl.

The space-suited guy, his suit smeared with fluid, was talking with the truck's console operator, both standing next to the chassis as they shared a cigarette. Even then smoking was illegal in public, but give a guy a break. . . .

They broke off their conversation as I drew near, and the console man nodded. "Help you?"

I shrugged pleasantly and remembered to talk high in my throat because guys my size are evidently less threatening as tenors. "Just sightseeing. Never see anything like this in Omaha." I grinned.

"Don't see much of this anywhere, thank God," said the sweaty one, and they laughed together. "Thirsty work. Not for the claustrophobe, either."

"Is this how you fill 'er up?" I hoped this was naive enough without being idiotic. I think I flunked because they laughed again. The sweaty one said, "Would I be smoking?" When I looked abashed, he relented. "We're scouring those stainless tanks. Got to be pharmaceutically free of a vegetable slurry before they pump in the next cargo."

"Those domes sitting on deck," I guessed.

"Hell, that's just the hemispherical closures," said the console man.

"The tanks go clear down into the hold," said his sweaty friend.

I blinked. "Twenty feet down?"

"More like forty," he said.

The console man glanced at his wristwatch, gave a meaningful look to his friend; took the cigarette back. "And we got a special eco-directive on flushing these after this phase. We have to double soak and agitate with filterable solvent, right to the brim, fifty-two thousand gallons apiece. Pain in the ass."

"Must take a lot of time," I said, thinking about Dana Martin's ability to make people jump through additional hoops on short notice, without showing her hand.

"Twice what we'd figured," said Consoleman. "I thought the charter-service rep would scream bloody murder, but he didn't even haggle. Offered a bonus for early completion, in fact. Speaking of which," he said, and fixed Sweatman with a wry smile.

"Yeah, yeah," said his colleague, and turned toward the *Ras Ormara.* "For us, time really is money. But that ten-minute break is in the standard contract. Anyhow, without my support hoses it's getting hot as hell in this outfit."

"Hold still, it's gonna dribble," I said. I found an old Kleenex in my pocket, and used it to wipe around the chin plate of Sweatman's suit, then put it back in my pocket.

"Guess I'm lucky to be in the wrought-iron biz," I said. With a smithy for a hobby, I could fake my way through that if necessary.

"My regards to Omaha," said Consoleman. "And by the way, you really shouldn't be here without authorization. Those guys are an antsy lot," he said, jerking his head toward the bridge. It was as nice a "buzz off, pal" request as I'd ever had.

I didn't look up. I'd seen faces staring down in our direction, some with their heads swathed in white. "Okay, thanks. Just seeing this has been an education," I said.

"If the skipper unlimbers his tongue on you, I hope your education isn't in languages," Consoleman joked.

I laughed, waved, and took my time walking back to the gate, stopping on the way to gaze at the much larger container ship as if my attention span played no favorites.

When I got back to my Toyota I rummaged in the glove box and found my stash of quart-sized evidence baggies. Then I carefully sealed that soggy old Kleenex inside one and scribbled the date and the specimen's provenance. I'd seen Sweatman climb out of a cargo tank of the *Ras Ormara* and that fluid had come out with him. Quent might not do handsprings, but the Feebs got off on stuff like that.

I took a brief cell call from Quent shortly before noon, while I was stoking up at one of the better restaurants off Jack London Square. The maître d' had sighed when he saw my tourist getup. Quent sighed, too, when I told him where I was. "Look, the Feds are paying, and I keep receipts," I reminded him.

He said he was striking out in Chinatown, just as he had in hospitals and clinics, but the Oakland side had its own ethnic neighborhoods. "I thought you might want to ride with me this afternoon," he said.

"Where do we meet? I have something off the ship you might want Dana to have analyzed," I said.

"You went aboard? Harve—oh well. Just eat slowly. It's not that far across the Bay Bridge," he replied.

"Gotcha. And I didn't go aboard, bossman, but I think I have a sample of what was actually in the *Ras Ormara*'s tanks, whatever the records might say. You'll be proud of your humble apprentice, but right now my rack of lamb calls. Don't hurry," I said, and put away my phone.

Quent arrived in time for my coffee and ordered tea. I let him play back my StudyGirl video recording as far as it went, and took the evidence baggie from my shirt pocket as I reported the rest. "We have the name of the pressure-washing firm. No doubt they can tell some curious Fed what cleaning chemicals they use. What's left should be traces of what those tanks really carried," I said.

Quent said Dana's people had already analyzed samples of the stuff provided by Customs. "But they'll be glad to have it confirmed this way. Nice going." He pocketed the baggie and pretended not to notice that I made a proper notation on my lunch receipt. We walked out into what was rapidly becoming a furry overcast, and I took the passenger's seat in his Volvo.

Quent said we'd try an Oakland rooming house run by a Korean family. From the list we had, he knew a pair of the *Ras Ormara*'s crew were staying there. "You, uh, might want to draft your report while I go in," he said as he turned off the Embarcadero. "Shouldn't be long."

"I thought you wanted me with you."

"I did. Then I saw how you're dressed."

"I'm a tourist!"

"You're a joke with pale shins. I can't do a serious interview with a foreign national if you're visible; how can I have his full attention when he's wondering whether Bluto is going to start juggling plates behind me?"

I saw his point and promised to bring a change of clothes next time. Quent found the place, in a row of transient quarters an Oakland beat cop would call flophouses. Without a place to park, he turned the Volvo over to me. "I'll call when I'm done," he said, and disappeared into the three-story stucco place.

I did find a parking spot eventually. My printer was at home, but I stored my morning's case report on StudyBint. Quent called not long afterward and, because he wore a frown only when puzzling things out, I hardly gave him time to take the wheel. "Something already?"

He thought about it a moment before replying. "Not on Park. Not directly, at any rate. But I'm starting to understand why our missing engineer was uneasy." When giving Park's name he had mentioned the ship to the rooming-house proprietor, who said she hadn't heard of Park but named the two crew members who were there. The Korean, Hong Chee, she described as taller than average, late thirties. The second man, one Ali Ghaffar, was older; perhaps Indian. Pretending surprise at this lucky accident, Quent asked to speak with them.

Hong Chee was out, but Quent found his roommate Ghaffar in the room, preternaturally quiet and alert. Ghaffar, a middle-aged Paki, was a studious-looking sort wearing one of those white cloth doodads wound around his head, who had evidently been reading one of two well-thumbed leather-bound books. Quent couldn't read even the titles though he got the impression they might be religious tomes.

Ghaffar spoke fair English. He showed some interest in the fact that an Asian speaking perfect American English was hoping to trace the movements of an engineer off the *Ras Ormara.* Quent explained that Park's family was concerned enough to hire private investigators, blah-blah, merely wanted assurance that Park hadn't met with foul play, et cetera.

Ghaffar said he had only a nodding acquaintance with Park. He couldn't, or more likely wouldn't, say whether Park had made any friends aboard ship, and had no idea whether Park had friends in the Bay Area. Ghaffar and Hong Chee had seen the engineer, he thought, the day before in some Richmond bar, and Park was looking fit, but they hadn't talked. That's when Quent noticed the wastebasket's contents. He began pacing around, stroking his chin, trying to scan everything in the room without being obvious while doing it.

Personal articles were aligned on lamp tables as if neatness counted, beds made, nothing out of place. Quent took his nail clippers out and began idly tossing them in one hand as he dreamed up more questions, and he just happened to drop his clippers into the wastebasket, apologizing as he fished them out with slow gropes of bogus clumsiness.

Quent realized that Ghaffar was waiting with endless calm for this ten-thumbed gumshoe to go away, volunteering little, responding carefully. Quent said he'd like to talk with Hong Chee sometime if possible and passed his cell-phone card to Ghaffar, who accepted it solemnly, and then Quent left and called me to be picked up.

"So I ask you," Quent said rhetorically: "What would a devout Moslem, who adheres to correct practices alone in his room, have been doing in a gin mill, with or without his buddy? Not likely. I don't think he saw Park, I think he wanted me to think Park was healthy. And you haven't asked me about the trash basket."

"Didn't want to interrupt. What'd you see?"

"Candy wrappers and an empty plastic pop bottle. Oh, yes," he added with studied neglect, "and an airline ticket. I didn't have time to read it closely, but I caught an Asian name—not Hong Chee's—Oakland International, and a departure date." He paused before he specified it.

"Christ, that's tomorrow," I said.

"I'm not through. Ghaffar is on the crew list as the ship's machinist. You ever see a machinist's hands?"

"Sure, like a blacksmith's. Like he force-feeds cactus to Rottweilers for kicks."

"Well, at the least they're callused and scarred. Not Ali Ghaffar. He may know how to use a lathe, but I'd bet against it."

"Then who's the real machinist? Ships have to have one."

"Do they? From what Medler and you tell me, and from what I saw on your video, the *Ras Ormara* might go a year without needing that kind of attention."

He checked some notes and drove silently across town like he knew where he was going. Presently he said, as if to himself: "So Hong Chee has dumped what looks like a perfectly good airline ticket for somebody out of Oakland. Wish I'd seen where to. More particularly, I wish I knew how he could afford to junk it. And why he knows to junk it the day before the flight."

"Me, teacher," I said, putting up a hand and waving it. "Call on me."

"Tell the class, Master Rackham," he said, going along with it.

"Somebody else is funding him better than most, and he's changed his departure plans because La Martin and company have put the brakes on whatever he had in mind."

"Take your seat, you've left the heart of my question untouched. Is he worried for the same reasons as Park?"

"Suppose we give him a chance to tell us," I said.

"Maybe we'll do that. But I'm not sure he's making plans for his own departure. Another Asian?"

"At a guess, I'd say the name is unimportant. How many sets of I.D. might he have, Quent?"

After a long pause, he exhaled for what seemed like forever. "Harve, you are definitely paranoid—I'm happy to say. Now you've torn the lid off this little box with a missing engineer in it, and I find a much bigger box inside, so to speak. And there wasn't a second ticket there—so Ghaffar may still intend to go back aboard. Or not. But I'll tell you this: Our machinist is no machinist, and he certainly isn't spending his time ashore as if he had the usual things in mind."

I couldn't fault his reasoning. "So where are we headed?"

"Korean social club. Maybe we'll find Hong Chee there."

"And not Park Soon?" All I got was a shrug and a glance, and I didn't like the glance. Quent found a slot for the Volvo in a neighborhood of shops with signs in English and the odd squiggles that weren't quite Chinese characters; Hangul has a script all its own. "You might try calling Dana while I'm inside," Quent said. "Let her know we've got a gooey Kleenex for her."

So I did, and was told she was in the field, and I tried her cell phone. She sounded like she was in a salt mine and none too pleased about it. She perked up slightly at my offer of the evidence. "I'll pick it up when we're through here," she said, and sneezed. "I thought the incoming cargo might be dirty, but the spectral analyzer says no. A few pallets are too heavy, though. My God, but wood dust is pervasive!"

"You're in a warehouse," I said, glad that she couldn't see me grinning. Climbing around on pallets of logs probably hadn't been high on her list of adventures when she joined up. "I haven't seen the stuff, but if it's that dusty maybe it's not plain logs. Probably rough-sawn, right?"

She said it was. "What would you know about it?"

"I've seen how balsa is used in high-tech panels. The stuff is graded by weight per cubic meter and it varies from featherweight, which is highly prized, to the density of pine. In other words, pallets could vary by a factor of three or so."

"Well, damn it to hell," she said. "Excuse me. Scratch one criterion. What's the significance of its being sawn?"

"Just that it may make it easier for you to see whether some of it's been cut lengthwise with a very fine kerf and glued back."

"What's a kerf?"

"The slot made by a saw. Balsa can be slitted with a very thin saw-blade. It occurs to me that it might be the lighter timbers you should be checking for hollowed interiors. Bags of white powder aren't that heavy, Dana."

I think she cussed again before she sneezed. She said, "Thanks," as if it were squeezed out of her.

"But I don't think you'll find anything," I said.

She demanded, "Why not?" the way a kid says it when told she can't ride behind the nice stranger on his Superninja bike.

"I just feel like whatever's being delivered, if anything, hasn't been. The monkey wrench your people threw into their schedule didn't delay those pallets—*gesundheit*—but they're behaving as if you did delay something. They're waiting, apparently with patience."

She said she'd get back to me and snapped off. To kill time, I played back our conversation on StudyBabe. Dana had a spectral analyzer with her? I had thought they were big lab gadgets. Right, and computers were room-sized—once upon a time.

While I was still muttering "Duhh" and thinking about

possible uses of Dana's gadgetry, Quent came down out of a stairwell in a hurry. He motioned for me to drive, pocketing his phone. "You love to drive like there's no tomorrow, and I don't. Please don't bend the Volvo," he begged. "Just get us across the bridge to Jackson and Taylor."

While I drove, he filled me in on his fresh lead. He'd struck out again upstairs, but had just taken a call on his cell phone from Ali Ghaffar. His buddy Hong, said the Paki, had returned. Ghaffar had asked about Park. Oh, said Hong, that was easy; back at the gin mill, Park Soon had said he was considering a move to a nice room in San Francisco for the rest of his time ashore. Corner of Jackson and Taylor.

"Smack-dab middle of Chinatown. Didn't say which corner, I suppose," I said, overtaking a taxi on the right.

"No such luck. But there can't be more than a half dozen places with upscale rooms on or near that corner. We can canvass them all in twenty minutes."

I tossed a look at Quent. "You speak directly to Hong?"

"Watch the road, for Christ's sweet sake," he gritted. "I asked, but Ali said he was gone again. Very handy."

"That's what I was thinking," I said, swerving to miss a pothole on the way to the Bay Bridge on-ramp.

Quent closed his eyes. "Just tell me when we get there."

To calm him down I played my conversation with Dana. It pacified him somewhat, and I turned down the Volvo's wick nearing Chinatown, which was a traffic nightmare long before the twenty-first century.

I chose a pricey parking lot near Broadway, and we jostled our way through the sidewalk chaos together. By agreement, Quent peeled off to take the two west corners of the intersection. Because some of the nicer little Chinatown hotels aren't obvious, I had to ask a restaurant cashier. When she hesitated, I said I had a job offer for an Asian gent and knew only that he'd taken a nice room thereabouts. I said I hadn't understood him very well.

Evidently, Asiatics have their own privately printed local phone books, but she didn't hand it over and I couldn't have read what I saw anyhow. She gave me five addresses, and three of them were on Quent's side. I tipped her, hoping I'd remember to jot it down, and found the first address almost next door.

If there's a small Chinatown hotel on a street floor, it's one I never saw. I climbed three narrow flights before I saw what proved to be a tiny lobby through a bead curtain. A young Asiatic greeted me, very courteously, his speech and dress yuppily American. He heard my brief tale sympathetically. Sorry, he said, but no young person of either gender had registered in several days. Would I mind describing the employment I had to offer?

I said it was a marine engineer's job, and I swear he said, "Aw shit, and me a journalism major," before he wished me good day, no longer interested in my problems.

I crossed the street and began to search for the second address when my phone clucked. "Bingo," Quent said with no preliminaries. "But no joy. Meet me at the car in ten. Until then you don't know me." No way I could mistake the implication.

He didn't sound happy, and when I saw him on the street he had turned away, heading down Jackson. It's a one-way street, and he walked counter to the traffic flow, something you do when you suspect someone may be trying to tail you in a car.

So I did the same on Taylor, which is also one-way, doubling back after a long block to approach Quent's car on Jones—again counter to one-way traffic. If anyone followed me on foot, he was too good for me to make him.

I had paid the lot's fee and was waiting in the Volvo when Quent appeared. "Oakland it is," he said, racking his seat back to disappear below the windowsill. As I sought an on-ramp he said, "A man calling himself Park Soon rented a room for a week, not two hours ago; one flight up, quiet, expensive. Told the concierge he might be staying with a friend for a night or so but please to hold his messages and take names."

"He's not hard up for cash," I said.

"He's also about my height and age," said Quent, who was five-eight, pushing forty.

I'd had Park's description. "The hell he is," I said.

"The man who rented that room with a cash advance is," Quent said. "Unless the lady was pulling my leg. And why would she if she wanted me to think it was Park? Park Soon is five-three. What's wrong with this picture, Harve?"

"I might know if I got a look inside that room."

"That was my thought, but it's a risky tactic in a subculture that's understandably wary, so I didn't even try. The Feds can do it if they want to. They know how to lean on people to, ah, I think the phrase is, 'compel acquiescence.'"

"Our own little Ministry of Fear," I observed.

"Everybody's got 'em, Harve. I even have one," he said with a half smile, and pointed a finger at my breast. "And if I had to choose between Uncle's and the ones run by people who call him the Great Satan, I choose Uncle.

"Meanwhile, we don't know who's pushing our buttons, waiting for us to show up, and watching us flail around all over hell. But I'd bet someone is, and I'd just as soon they didn't pin a tail on us."

I nodded, pointing the Volvo onto the Bay Bridge. "You don't think Park could somehow be in on this," I suggested.

"Not in any way he'd like. I don't think Park is where anyone will find him anytime soon," Quent replied grimly. "Whoever tried to create a fresh trail for him would probably be pretty confident he's not leaving his own trail of crumbs. I really don't like that idea, Harve. Well, maybe I'm wrong. I hope so."

"When are we gonna drop that one on Dana?"

He levered himself and his seat erect; opened his phone. "Right away. She's probably still in the field. I will bet you a day's expenses Mr. Ghaffar knows who took that room for Park; the description fits Hong, of course."

I nodded. "Should we go back and have a talk with him now?"

"Not yet, I want to be very calm for that, and at the moment I am peeved. I am provoked."

"You are royally pissed," I supplied. He nodded. "Me too," I added, as he punched Dana's number.

It was nearing rush hour by that time, but with a few extra twists and turns, I managed to satisfy myself that we weren't tailed while Quent spoke with our pet Feeb. She said she'd meet us in twenty at the boathouse on Lake Merritt, in residential Oakland.

She was as good as her word, looking as frazzled as she'd sounded earlier but even more interesting, which irked me. No Feeb had the right to look that good. She took the perimeter footpath and we caught up to her, two visitors hitting on a cutie. When we found a park bench, she plopped her shoulder bag next to me. "If that specimen's bagged, stuff it in here," she said.

"And if not, where do I stuff it?"

She simply looked toward my partner. "While he figures out the answer to his own question, Quent: We've still drawn blanks at every bus terminal, airport and rail connection between Vallejo and Santa Clara. What's your best guess on Park?"

Quent told her while I put my evidence in her bag. At his bidding I let her review the video I'd made. He described the timing of the connections we'd made and blunted the conclusions he and I had reached together. "Wherever Park is, and for whatever reason, I just have a suspicion he won't surface again in the Bay Area," he said. Then he described the Chinatown lead and told her flatly why he believed it was fugazi, a false trail.

She turned to me. "You're uncharacteristically silent. What do you think?"

"Much the same. And I think Quent ought to borrow your spectral analyzer, if it's small enough to put in a Bianchi rig."

"Mine won't fit in any shoulder holster I've seen," she said, "but some will. The covert units are slower, though. Encryption-linked to a lab in Sunnyvale, which is why they can be so small. I've seen one implanted in a LOC-8. And they are very, very expensive," she added. A LOC-8 was one of the second-generation GPS units with two-way comm and a memory just in case you wondered where you'd been. Combined with a linked-up analyzer it would be worth a new Volvo.

"You want me to ship out on the *Ras Ormara* or something," Quent said to me, amused.

Dana turned to him again. "Better you than King Kong here. You look the part, and you could talk with the crew more easily."

Quent: "You're not serious."

Dana: "Not actually shipping out, but you might try getting

aboard while the new cargo is being loaded. A spectral analyzer needs no more than a whiff to do its job, and I'd hate to try to guess all the ways a cargo can be falsified."

Quent was silent for a time. Then, "I'd never get aboard without the rep's authorization, or the captain's. There goes one layer of our deniability but yes, I could try it. Or Harve could, in a pinch."

We kicked the idea around a bit, and then she excused herself and walked off a ways to use her phone while Quent and I watched boats slice the lake's surface under psychedelic bubbles of sail. When she turned back, she was nodding. "You'll need to learn how to use it," she said.

Quent said if it was anything like the one she carried, she could show us using the specimen I'd collected. She simpered for him and said she should've thought of that herself. We found a picnic table and, sandwiched between me and Quent, Dana pulled a grey, keyboard-faced polymer brick from her bag and opened my evidence baggie next to it.

She stuck her forefinger into a depression labeled CRUCIBLE in the brick and pressed the CRU key. When she withdrew her finger its tip was covered by a filmy shroud, which she quickly stuck into my soggy tissue. Then she pushed the fingertip into another depression and pressed SAMPLE, and the brick whirred very faintly for an instant. Dana withdrew her finger, stripped the film off, and let it drop to the tabletop, an insubstantial wisp. Then after a silence, the brick's little screen began to print gibberish at a rate too fast to follow.

"Essentially, a carbon ribbon wipes a bit of the specimen off the film—don't ask me why it's called a crucible—and analyzes it," Dana murmured.

"What if you're testing the air," Quent asked.

"Wave your finger around for a moment. They say the crucible has microscopic pores on its surface," she explained.

"And how many of those little mouse condoms are inside," I asked, unrolling the discarded wisp for a better look.

"Rackham, you are a piece of work," she said under her breath. Then more loudly, "A hundred or so. By that time the battery needs replacing." When the little screen quit printing

Martian, it showed a line with several numbered pips of varied height. She showed us how to query each number, which could be shown as chemical symbols or in words.

The biggest pip was for water, the next was for a ketone solvent, then cellulose, then something called Biopol.

I put my finger out and touched the screen. "Bad actor?"

"No. A polymer from genetically altered canola," she said.

"How in the hell would you know that," I demanded.

She let me stew for a moment. Then, "Customs. Biopol was the plant extract on the manifest. Quent would've figured that out and told you anyway," she added grudgingly.

The trace of $C_{10}H_{18}O$, according to the screen, was eucalyptol. Dana pointed out that the heavily aromatic tree hanging over us was a eucalyptus. "So you see it's pretty accurate."

I said no it wasn't, or it would've told us what the little condom was made of. She said yes it was and positively beamed, explaining that the analyzer knew to ignore the crucible's signature. I gave up. The damned thing was pretty smart at that.

"At least we know the cargo was as advertised," Quent said.

Dana nodded. "Including those pallets of wood. We 'scoped enough of it. So now we focus on the next cargo because no one has come ashore with sizable contraband, and the incoming cargo was clean."

"Unless they'd already pumped it out into those trucks I saw," I said.

"They didn't," said Dana. "One of the cleanout crew is one of ours. You don't need to know which one. The *Ras Ormara* crew are watching him carefully enough to make us even more suspicious."

"I wasted my time then," I said.

"You proved the wharf isn't all that secure," Quent mused, and checked his wrist. "If you're going to spring for a couple of those analyzers, ma'am, we should get to it."

She reminded him that it was a loan, and there'd be only one. Thinking ahead as usual, he said as long as we were going to show our hand overtly as a P.I. team, he'd feel better going aboard if I went along. That meant I could contact the Sonmiani rep myself for the authorization and save some time.

"If you drop me off at my Toyota right away," I said, "I might catch this Goldman guy before he leaves his office."

We quick-marched back to the Volvo and Dana agreed to meet Quent back at the Sunnyvale lab in the South Bay.

I knew I was cutting it close for normal working hours but StudyBimbo found the Sonmiani number while Quent drove me to my pickup. I was in luck; better luck than Quent would find. One Mike Kaplan answered for Sonmiani Shipping, and put me through without rigamarole. That's how my brief platonic fling began with my friend, Norman Goldman.

# Three

When you first meet someone of your own sex that you like right away, no matter how hetero you are, you tend to go through something resembling courtship. When the other guy is equally outgoing, ordinary things sink into a temporary limbo: time, previous appointments, even mealtimes.

That's how it had been with me and Quent, and it happened again with Norm. The reason he and his staff assistant had still been at the office was that the Goldman suite and Sonmiani's office were over-and-under, in one of the smaller of those old Alameda buildings respiffed in the style they call Elerath Post-Industrial. I guessed that Sonmiani did a healthy business because the whole two-story structure was theirs.

It was a few minutes after five, but Goldman had said he'd leave the front door unlocked. Following the signs, I moved down a hallway formed by partitioning off a strip from the offices, which I could see through the glassed partition. One man was still in there, wearing a headset and facing a big flat screen. He looked up and waved, and I waved back, and he motioned for me to continue.

The place must have once doubled as a warehouse to judge from the vintage—now trendy again and clean as a cat's fang—

freight elevator. I obeyed its sign, tugging up on a barrier which met its descending twin at breastbone height. It whirred to life on its own, a bit shaky after all those years of service, and a moment later I saw a pair of soft Bally sandals come into view under nicely creased allosuede slacks. A pale yellow dress shirt with open collar followed, and finally I saw a tanned, well-chiseled face looking at mine. Hands on hips, he grinned. I couldn't blame him; I'd forgotten how I was dressed.

We introduced ourselves before he jerked a thumb toward the glass door of what might have been an office, but turned out to be his digs. "Sorry about the time," I said, as he ushered me into a big airy room with an eclectic furniture mix: futon, modern couch, inflatable chairs, and a wet bar. And some guy-type pictures, one of which had nothing to do with ships. I thought it would stand a closer look if I got the time. "I tend to forget other people keep regular hours," I added.

"Couldn't resist your opening," he said, with a wave of his hand that suggested I could sit anyplace, and I chose the couch. "Anyone looking for the same crew member I'm looking for, is someone I want to meet. Besides, I've never met a real live—ah, is 'pee-eye' an acceptable buzz phrase?" He had heavy expressive brows that showed honest concern at the question, and big dark eyes that danced with lively interest. "And if it's not, would some sour mash repair the damage?" His accent was Northeast, I guessed New York, and in Big Apple tempo.

"Maybe later," I said. "But P.I. is a term always in vogue."

"As long as I'm on Goldman time, I'll have a beer," he said, and bounced up like a man who played a lot of tennis. He uncapped a Pilsener Urquell from a cooler behind the bar, dipped its neck toward me, then took a swig of the brew before sitting down again. "We've about given up on Park, by the way. Do you suppose the dumb slope has gotten himself in some kind of trouble?"

I admitted I didn't know. "That's what the client wants us to find out. At this point, we're hoping his personal effects aboard ship might point us in some direction. With your authorization, of course, Mr. Goldman. That's what we had in mind."

He nodded abstractedly. "Don't know why not. And hey, my father is Mr. Goldman, God forbid you should mix us up." His grin was quick and infectious. "It's Norm; okay?"

I'd intended to keep this on a semiformal level but with Norm it was simply not possible. I insisted on "Harve," and asked him if he ever felt ill at ease dealing with Moslem skippers. He got a kick from that; a ship's captain might be Allah on the high seas, said Norm, but they knew who signed their checks. "No, it's the poor ragheads who aren't all that easy about me." He laughed. "But Sonmiani's directors include some pretty canny guys. As long as I keep cargoes coming and going better than the last rep, what's to kvetch about?

"Actually the skipper probably will anyway. Gent with a beard, named something-Nadwi. A surly lot, Harve, especially when they're behind schedule." He stopped himself suddenly, shot a quick glance at me. "I don't suppose it's my bosses who put you onto our man's trail. Nobody's told me, but they don't always tell the left hand what its thumb is doing. In a way I hope it is them."

"Against my charter to identify a client, but let's just say it's someone worried about a young guy who's a long way from home," I said. A hint that broad was, as Quent had said, bending the rules a bit but that wasn't why I felt a wisp of guilt. I felt it because I knew our real client wasn't a deceased Korean.

Norm was understanding. He said he'd seen Park Soon exactly once, and that, while he was making his own inquiries, a couple of the crew who had their papers had claimed they saw the engineer in a bar. "They may have been mistaken. Or—hell, I don't know. You couldn't pick a more suspicious mix than we have on the *Ras Ormara.* Schmucks will lie just for practice. You can't entirely blame them, you know. Some skippers skim company food allowances intended for the crews, though I don't believe Nadwi does. I won't have it, by God, and our skippers know it. There's a backhander or two that I can't avoid in half the foreign ports. A lot of their manning agencies are corrupt—"

"Backhander?"

"Kickback, bribe. It's just part of doing business in some ports, and the poor ragheads know it, but they never get a dime of the action. Same-old, same-old," he chanted, shook his head, and took another slug of Urquell.

His shirt pocket warbled, and he tapped it without looking. "Goldman," he said, not bothering to keep the conversation private from me. I was struck by the openness of everything, the offices, Norm's apartment, his dealings with people.

"I'm about squared away here, guv," said a voice with a faint Brit flavor. "Thought I'd nip out for a bite."

"Why not? You've been on Kaplan time for," Norm consulted a very nice Omega on his wrist, "a half hour. Oh! Mike, would you mind running up here a minute first? Gentleman in an unusual business here I want you to meet."

The voice agreed, sounding slightly put-upon, and after he rang off I realized it must be the man I'd seen in the office. It was obvious that Norm Goldman had the same view of formalities that I did, but something about his decisive manner said he might crack a whip if need be. I decided he was older than I'd first thought; maybe forty, but a very hip forty.

Then I took a closer look at that framed picture on his wall, a colorful numbered print showing one formula car overtaking another as a third slid helplessly toward a tire barrier. It was the Grand Prix of Israel, Norm said, adding that he was a hopeless fan. I said I shared his failing; worse, that I had half the bits and pieces of an off-road single-seater in my workshop awaiting the chassis I'd build. He crossed his arms and sighed and, beaming at me, said he might have known.

A quick two-beat knock, and Mike Kaplan entered without waiting. He was swarthy and slim, with very close-cropped dark hair and a nose old-time cartoonists used to draw as a sort of Jewish I.D. His forearms said he'd done a lot of hard work in his time. I got up. Norm didn't, waving a hand from one of us to the other as we shook hands. "Mike Kaplan, Harve Rackham. Mike's my second, and when we're both out of the office, our young tomcat Ira Meltzer holds down the fort. Ira's not in his rooms—where the hell is Ira—as if it were any of my effing business," Norm added with a smile.

Mike said how would he know, and Norm shrugged it off. "Let me guess," Mike said to me. "Wrestler on the telly?"

"That's me," I said, and pulled up my pants. "Harve, the Terrible Tourist."

"Come on," Mike said, because Norm was chuckling.

"I didn't know they existed anymore, Mike, but you are looking at a private eye. In disguise, I hope," said his boss, enjoying the moment. When Mike didn't react, he said, "As in, private investigator. You know: Sam Spade."

Mike Kaplan's face lit up then, and his second glance at me was more appraising and held a lot more friendly interest. "Personally, I'd be inclined to tell him whatever he wants to know," he said to Norm. I must have outweighed him by fifty kilos.

"If you knew, you might. But that would more likely be the job of the *Ras Ormara*'s skipper," Norm replied. "You're better at those names than I am."

Mike shook his head in mock censure. "If you worked at it as I do, you'd get along better with them," he said. "Captain Hassan al-Nadwi, you mean." As Norm nodded, Mike Kaplan went on, "And what do we need from that worthy?"

I told him, and admitted we needed to look at the engineer's effects as soon as possible—meaning the next day.

Mike allowed as how al-Nadwi would put up a pro forma bitch, but it shouldn't really be a problem if I didn't mind a lot of silent stares, and people on board who suddenly seemed to know no English at all. He said he'd call the skipper, stroke him a little, lean on him a little. Al-Nadwi knew who held the face cards. Piece of cake, he said.

Norm said he gathered I wasn't working alone, and I told him about Quentin Kim, apologizing for the oversight. "If Park Soon left any notes in Hangul," I said, "it'd be Quent who could read them. He speaks Korean, of course; that's probably why he got the case. I'd be just as useful chasing down other leads."

Norm donated a quizzical look. "I didn't realize there were other leads."

New friend or not, there are times when you see you're about to step over the line. That can reach around and bite you or your friend sometimes in ways you can't predict. I said, "There may not be. If there were, I couldn't discuss them. 'Course, if Quent stumbled on one, it wouldn't surprise me if you got wind of it later." I let my expression say, *the game's a bastard but rules are rules.*

"I respect that. Can't say I understand it, but I respect it," said Norm.

"Good," I said. "So for all I know, Quent may come alone to the ship and send me off in another direction."

Norm's reaction warmed my heart. "But—I was going to go along because you were," he said. "Spring for lunch, pick your brains about racing—uh-unh; you've got to go along, Harve."

"I'll try, but it's Quent's call. He's my boss," I said.

A sly half smile, and one lifted brow, from Norm. "Well," he said softly, reasonably, "just tell him the real call is Norm Goldman's. And Goldman is an unreasonable asshole."

Mike Kaplan laughed out loud and jerked his head toward Norm while looking at me. "I've been saying that for ages," he said.

After Kaplan promised to set up a visit to the ship for me and Quent, he left us. I told Norm that just about cleared my decks for the day, and said I'd take one of those Czech beers if the offer was still open. We jawed about our tastes in racing—I couldn't see his fascination with dragsters; he thought karts were kid stuff. He showed me around his place while we discussed Norm's good luck in falling heir to a floor of rooms that split so nicely into three apartments. Whatever Sonmiani paid their seamen, Norm and his staff obviously were in no fiscal pain. Finally, we bonded a little closer over the fact that both of us placed high value in working with people we liked.

I promised Norm he'd like Quent because they shared a subdued sense of humor, though he might find my old pal oddly conservative considering the career he chose. That was the chief way, I said, that Quent's ethnicity showed.

Norm said believe it or not, I'd find Kaplan had a touch of the prude. He added that it couldn't be the man's Liverpool upbringing, so maybe it was the Sephardic Jew surfacing in him. It was a comfort, he said, to know he could be gone a week and feel confident that the office was secure in the hands of Mike Kaplan. I'd find Ira Meltzer a frank Manhattan skirt-chaser, he said, which could get a bit wearing but Ira was a real *mensch* for hard work.

I tried to call Quent about the good news, but got his tape. I didn't call Dana Martin because I didn't want to seem secretive, and I sure wasn't going to talk with a Fed in front of Norm.

And when he suggested we go looking for dinner—on him, or rather on Sonmiani, he reminded me—I said it might be better if we called a pizza in because I was tired of people looking at me funny. I was catching on to his dry humor by then, and laughed when he said with a straight face that he couldn't imagine why they might.

"Pizza's a good idea," he said, "but we could order it from anywhere. How about from your workshop?"

He was as serious about it as most race-car freaks, and the idea of a forty-minute drive didn't dismay him. It was long odds against a deliveryman finding my place, I said, but we could pick that pizza up on the way. He'd be driving back alone for the first few miles on dark country roads, I cautioned. He said he had a decent Sony mapper, so he was up for it if I was, but if I had any objection we could do it another time.

Objection? Hell, this would be the first time I could recall that I'd had two guests in one week, and I said as much while we rode the rocking old elevator down.

Eventually, using our phones while he followed me out of town in his enviable, cherried-out classic black Porsche Turbo, I suggested we save time by my cobbling up a couple of reubens on my woodstove. He agreed, and when we hit the country roads I tried Quent again without success.

Now I could call our pet Feeb, who sounded slightly impressed that I was still at work. She liked it even better that Sonmiani's people were receptive to our private search and would help us snoop aboard ship, the next day.

Quent, she said, had taken the LOC-8 with its hidden spectral analyzer after playing with it under lab tutelage. She thought he might be cruising around Richmond trying to find crewman Hong Chee. Reception, especially in some of the popular basement dives, wasn't all that reliable. I told myself Quent could cruise the ethnic bars better as a singleton and besides, I was working in a way, schmoozing with a guy who could hinder or help us. No doubt Quent would call me when he was ready.

Dana wasn't so happy with my suggestion that the Feds canvass airline reservation lists scheduled for the next few days, just to see if they got any hits on the *Ras Ormara*'s crewlist. Did she think it was pointless? Maybe not entirely, she admitted, before she hung up. I still think Dana was simply pissed because she hadn't already gotten around to it.

No need to worry about Norm Goldman's ability to keep my pickup in sight. He stayed glued to my back bumper, perhaps to prove that he had a racer's soul. But Jesus! A Pooch Turbo tailing an old Toyota trash hauler? My sister Shar could've done it. Even so, he must've bottomed his pan following me up the lane to my place. A moment later my phone chirped.

I hoped it was Quent, but, "Harve? Is this a gag? How much farther is it," asked a slightly subdued Norm.

I asked if he could spot the old white clapboard farmhouse past the orchard ahead, and he said yes. "That's it. We're on my acreage now," I said. With hindsight, I think he had started to wonder whether his new friend had something unfriendly in mind for him.

My workshop was still more than half smithy then, a short walk from the house, and we parked beside it. I toggled a key-ring button that unlocked the side door, and its sensor lit the shop up for us as I approached.

Norm stepped inside with the diffidence of an acolyte in a cathedral, ready to be awed by a genuine racing-car shop. It may have been a disappointment. The most significant stuff I had on hand was the specialized running gear, protectively bagged in inert argon gas, but he spent more time studying my half-sized chassis drawings and the swoopy lines I had lofted to show the body shells I hadn't molded yet. When I saw him rubbing his upper arms I realized it was chilly for him. "You might enjoy looking at some recent off-road race videos," I said, "while I get the kitchen stove warmed. Or you could sit on top of the stove," I cracked. "Takes about ten minutes to get that cast-iron woodhog of mine up to correct temperature."

So we closed up the shop and I used my century-old key

to get us past the kitchen door. I explained my conceit, keeping the upstairs part of the house turn-of-another-century except for a few sensible improvements: media center, smoke and particulate detectors, a deionizer built into a squat wooden 1920s icebox. I couldn't recall whether I'd left any notes on my desk or screen downstairs, so I didn't mention my setup there.

I showed Norm to the media center in my parlor, swore to him that the couch wouldn't collapse, and left him with a holocube of the recent Sears Point Grand Prix. I'd be lying if I said I was worried about Quent, but while rustling up the corned beef, cheese, and other munchables necessary to a reuben I kept expecting him to call. I thought he might wind up his day by driving out, and we could all schmooze together. I thought wrong.

Just for the hell of it, I opened a bottle of Oregon early muscat for our sandwiches. A bit on the sweet side, but, to make a point, I reminded Norm that Catalonians serve it to special guests and I admired their style.

After supper we skimmed more holocubes and played some old CDs, and I was yarning about the time I had to evade a biker bunch when I heard my phone. It had to be Quent, I thought; and in a way it was. I said, "Sorry, you never know," to Norm, went into the back bedroom, and answered.

It was Dana, terse and angry. "You won't like this any better than I do," she warned me, and asked where I was.

I told her, and added, "I sure don't like it when I don't know what's up, boss lady. Tell me."

She did, and a flush of prickly heat spread from the back of my neck down my arms. I only half heard the essentials, but every word would replay itself in my mind during my drive back to Richmond.

"Give me a half hour," I said. "The Sonmiani rep is here with me. He might be some help tracing some of the crew's movements if there's a connection."

"Say nothing tonight; Sonmiani might be one of those firms that demand advocacy no matter what."

"Firms like yours," I said grimly, and regretted it in the same moment. "Forgive me, I'm—I need to go out and slug a tree. See you in thirty."

Norm must have been sensitive to body language because he stood up as I stumped through the parlor door. I told him I had to drive back into town as soon as I changed clothes. To his question I said it wasn't anything he could help with; just a case that had taken a new turn. He asked whether my Korean boss let me go along on the *Ras Ormara* thing. I replied that there wasn't much doubt I'd make it, and promised to give him an early-morning call. Then I hurried into my bedroom for a quick change, my hands shaking.

As I slapped the closures on my sneakers I heard the Porsche start up, and Norm was long gone when my tires hit country-road macadam. Not so long gone that I didn't almost catch him nearing Concord. I hung back enough to let him find the freeway before me. After all, there wasn't any need for breaking records now; hard driving was simply the only way I could use up all that adrenaline before I met the Feds off the freeway in East Richmond, near the foothills. I kept thinking that from downtown Richmond to some very steep ravines was only five minutes or so. And wondering whether my buddy Quent had still been alive during the trip.

Linked to Dana by phone, I found the location a block off the main drag, a long neon strip of used-car lots and commercial garages. Evidently Dana's people had shooed the locals away, though a pair of uniformed cops still hung around waiting to control the nonexistent crowd, and I seemed to be it. The guys doing the real work wore identical, reversible dark jackets. I knew that "F B I" would be printed on the inner surfaces of those jacket backs and, when Dana waved me forward, a strobe flash made me blink.

I saw the chalk outline before I spotted the partially blanketed figure on a foldable gurney in the extrawide unmarked van. The chalk lines revealed that Quent had been found with his legs in the street, torso in the gutter, head and one arm up on the curb. The stain at the head oval looked black, but it wouldn't in daylight.

We said nothing until I followed Dana into the van, sitting on jump seats barely out of the way of a forensics woman who was monitoring instruments while she murmured into her headset. The gadget she occasionally used looked like my StudyFrail but probably cost ten times as much. I leaned forward, saw the misshapen contours of a face I had known well. I knew better than to touch him. I think I moaned, "Awww, Quent."

"He was deceased before he struck the curb, if it's any consolation," said Dana. "Long enough before, that he lost very little blood on impact. Presumption is that someone dropped him from a moving vehicle."

I couldn't help wondering what I'd been doing at the time. Nodding toward the forensics tech, I managed to mutter, "Got a time of death?"

Dana said, "Ninety minutes, give or take." I would've been licking my fingers right about then. "We thought it might have been accidental at first."

"For about ten seconds," said the tech dryly. She wasn't missing anything. Her gloved hand lifted Quentin Kim's lifeless wrist. It was abraded and bruised. She pointed delicately with her pinkie at the bluish fingertips. The nails of the smallest two fingers were missing. The cuticles around the other nails were swollen and rimmed with faint bloodstains, and the ends of the nails had been roughened as if chewed by some tiny animal. "He still had a heartbeat when this was done," she added.

"Pliers," I said, and she grunted assent. "Somebody wanted something out of him. But how could pulling out fingernails be lethal," I asked, shuddering by reflex as I tried to imagine the agony of my close friend, a friend who had originally hired me for physical backup. Fat lot of good I had done him. . . .

The tech didn't answer until she glanced at Dana, who nodded without a word. "Barring a coronary, it couldn't. But repeated zaps of a hundred thousand volts will give you that coronary. Zappers that powerful are illegal, but I believe Indonesian riot control used them for a while. The fingernails told me to look for something else. Nipples, privates, lips, other sites densely packed with nerve endings."

"I'll take your word for it," I said. She was implying torture by people who were good at it, and I lacked the objectivity to view the evidence.

"But that's not where I found the trauma," said the tech. "It showed up as electrical burn marks in a half dozen places where a pair of contact points had been pressed at the base of the skull, under the hair. Not too hard to locate if you know what you're looking for. The brain stem handles your most basic life support; breathing, that sort of thing. Electrocute it hard, several times, and it's all over."

"It's not over," I growled.

"It is for him," the woman said, then looked into my eyes and blinked at whatever she saw. "Got it," she mumbled, going back to her work.

"Under the circumstances," Dana said, not unkindly, "you may want to break this one off without prejudice. Even though there may be no connection between this and the particular case you're working. Quentin had other active cases, and we know he's not above working two at once, don't we?"

"I resent that word 'above.' We also know how we'd bet, if we were betting," I said.

"You *are* betting, Rackham. And stakes don't go much higher than this."

Neither of us could have dreamed how wrong she was, but I could dream about avenging my pal. I said, "I'm feeling lucky. Where's that LOC-8 with the analyzer? I'll learn to use it by tomorrow. Maybe Norm Goldman can divert some people's attention. He'll be with me."

She said she'd be glad to, if she knew where it was. "It might be in Quentin's Volvo; the Richmond force is on it, too. It could turn up at any time," she said.

She led me out of the van again and into its nightshadow. "There's not much point in going aboard that ship until we find you an analyzer. Preferably the one Quent had. Don't contact Goldman's people again until we do."

"He might call me. We hit it off pretty well, and he could be an asset," I said.

"He may be, at that," she said as if to herself, then sighed and shifted her mental gears with an almost audible clash. "You may as well go home, there's nothing you can do here. I called you in only because I knew you two were close." A pause. "You'd have told me if Quentin had called you tonight. Wouldn't you?"

"About what?"

"About anything. Answer my question," she demanded.

Before that tart riposte was fully out of her mouth I said, "Of course I'd tell you! What is this, anyway?" When she only shook her head, I went on, "I kept my phone on me at all times because I kept hoping he'd call. I was getting uncomfortable because, normally, he'd have called just for routine's sake. I called *him* a couple of times, that's easy enough for you to check. I'd like to know where you're going with this."

"So you don't feel just a touch of, well, like you'd let him down, left him waiting? A little guilty?"

Her tone was gentle. In another woman I might've called it wheedling. And that told me a lot. "Goddamned right I feel guilty! I did let him down, but not because I put him off when he called. He never called, Martin. Why don't you just say 'dereliction of duty' and be done with it? And be glad you're half my size when you say it."

I turned and stalked off before she could make me any madder, wondering how I was going to get any sleep, wishing Quent had called in so I'd know where he'd gone. Wishing I had that LOC-8 so I'd have a reason to go aboard the *Ras Ormara*. And suddenly I realized how important it was that I find the gadget for its everyday use. Hadn't Dana said she'd be glad to lend me the damn thing if she knew where it was?

I was pretty sure where it would be: in the breakaway panel of the driver's side door in the Volvo. Quent had padded the pocket so he could keep a sidearm or special evidence of a case literally at hand.

But the Volvo was missing. If it were downtown, it should already have been spotted. If it was a Fed priority, the Highway Patrol would have picked it up five minutes after it hit a freeway. Very likely someone had hidden it, maybe after using it to dump poor Quent along Used Car Row. Maybe it was in the bay. Maybe parked in a quiet neighborhood, where it might not be noticed for a day or so. Maybe in a chop shop someplace, already being dismantled for parts for other used cars. . . .

Used Car Row! What better place to dump an upscale used car? I fired up my Toyota and drove slowly past the nearest lot, noting that a steel cable stretched at thigh height from light pole to light pole, with cars parked so that no one could cruise through the lot or hot-wire a heap and cruise out with it. Or dump a stolen car there.

Several long blocks later I lucked out, not in a car lot but at the end of a row of cars outside a body-and-fender shop. I hadn't remembered the license; it was that inside rearview of Quent's that stretched halfway across the windshield just like mine did, one of those after-market gimmicks every P.I. needs during a stakeout or traffic surveillance.

Pulling on gloves, I parked the pickup out of sight and flicked my pocket flash against the Volvo's steering column. The keys were in the ignition. Knowing Quent as I did, I avoided touching the door plate. In fact, though the racket should have brought every cop in town, I didn't touch the car until, on my fourth try, the old bent wheel rim I'd scrounged managed to cave in the driver's side window, scattering little cubes of glass everywhere.

By that time the alarm's *threep, threep, whooeeeet, wheeeoot* parodied a mockingbird from hell and for about thirty seconds I expected to see gentlemen of the public safety persuasion descending on the scene. Only after I got the keys out and unlocked the driver's side door did the alarm run out of birdseed and blessed silence overtook the place once more.

Fed forensics are better than most folks think, so while I intended to tell Dana what I'd done, I wanted it to be at a time of my choosing. That's why I didn't climb inside the car. I just opened the driver's door and checked the spring-loaded door panel.

And good old Quent, following his procedures as always, had squirreled away the Feds' tricky little LOC-8 right where it would be handy, and whoever had left the Volvo there hadn't suspected the breakaway panel. I pocketed the gadget, left the keys in the ignition again, and drove like a sober citizen back to the freeway and home. I could hardly wait to check out the LOC-8's memory. Every centimeter of its movements through the whole evening would have been recorded—unless Quent or someone else had erased it.

The normal functions of the LOC-8's little screen hadn't been compromised, so I was able to scroll through its travels beginning with Quent's departure from the Sunnyvale lab early in the evening. I brewed strong Java and sipped as I made longhand notes with pen on paper at my kitchen table. Say what you will about old-fashioned methods, nothing helps me assemble thoughts like notes on paper.

Quent had driven back via the Bay Bridge to Richmond at his ordinary sedate pace, and the Volvo had stopped for two minutes or so halfway down a block in the neighborhood where he had spoken earlier in the day with the so-called machinist. If he hadn't found a parking slot, I guessed he had double-parked.

Next he had driven half a mile, and here the LOC-8 had stayed for over an hour. At max magnification it showed he must have used a parking lot because the Volvo had been well off the street. I noted the location so I could interview the parking attendant, if any. From the locale, I figured Quent had been cruising the ethnic bars and game palaces, maybe looking for our missing engineer or, still more likely, the machinist's roomie. Then the car had left its spot, found the freeway, and headed south through Oakland to the Alameda, not in any special hurry.

But when the Volvo's trail traversed a long block for the second time, I checked the intersections. There was no mistake: Quent had circled the Sonmiani offices a couple of times, then parked in an adjacent alleyway, the same one Norm used for his Porsche as access to the garage entrance of the first-floor offices. As well as I could recall, I hadn't been gone from there long when Quent arrived to do his usual careful survey of the whole layout before committing himself. That would fit if he'd intended to meet someone like Mike Kaplan or the other guy I hadn't met—Meltzer. Someone whose phone number he didn't have. Maybe he had been confident I was still there.

But if he had been trying to contact me, why hadn't he just

grabbed his phone? Obviously he hadn't thought it was necessary. That meant he wasn't worried about his safety, because Quent had told me up front that he'd rented me, as it were, by the pound of gristle. And, like most P.I.s, Quent worked on the premise that discretion was the better part, et cetera. The P.I. species is often bred from insurance investigators, a few lawyers, ex-military types, and ex-cops. Guess which ones are most willing to throw discretion in the dumper. . . .

Despite the lateness of the hour, my first impulse was to call Norm and ask him a few questions about what, or whom, Quent might have met there. But what would he know? He'd been tailgating me out past Mt. Diablo at that time. Another thing: Nearing my place I had called Quent to no avail. Had he gone inside by then? Or he could have met someone in another car. Illegal entry wasn't Quent's style. I decided that if he had been looking for me, he'd have called before parking there. The car had stayed there for about five minutes and then its location cursor virtually disappeared, but not quite. With its signal greatly diminished, it said the Volvo had been driven into Norm's garage. There it had stayed for about an hour.

Then when the cursor suddenly appeared with a strong satellite signal, the Volvo went squirting through the Alameda as if someone were chasing it. It would've been dark by then as the cursor traced its way up the Nimitz Freeway to the Eastshore route, taking a turnoff near Richmond. I was feeling prickly heat as I keyed the screen back and forth between real time and fast-forward, because in real time Quent never drove with that kind of vigor.

I concluded he hadn't been driving by then. The Volvo had gone some distance up Wildcat Canyon near Richmond's outskirts, now driving more slowly, at times too slowly, then picking up the pace as it turned back toward the commercial district. There was no doubt in my mind where this jaunt would end, and for once I nailed it. The Volvo sizzled past the spot where a chalk outline now climbed a boulevard curb, turned off the main drag, and doubled back and forth on a service road before it stopped. The site was approximately where I had found the Volvo.

The screen said more than two hours passed before the cursor headed toward my place, duly recording the moment when I stole the gadget—recovered it, I mean; Dana had clearly said she wished she could lend it to me. Had she been lying? Probably, but it didn't matter. I had the gimmicked LOC-8 and I had time to fiddle with its hidden functions, having watched while Dana showed another one off while sitting on a park bench between me and Quent.

And I had something else: a cold hard knot of certainty that someone working for my new friend Norm Goldman was no friend of Quent's. Or of mine.

# Four

I did sleep, after all. Worry keeps me awake but firm resolve has a way of grinding worry underfoot. I woke up mad as hell before I even remembered why, and then I sat on the edge of my bed and shed the tears I never let anyone see.

Then I dressed for a tour of the *Ras Ormara.* I'm told that the Cheyennes used to gather before a war party and ritually purge their bellies. They believed it sharpened their hunting instincts, and I know for a fact that if you expect a reasonable likelihood of serious injury, your chances of surviving surgery are better on an empty stomach. For breakfast I brewed tea, and nothing else, in memory of my friend.

Around nine, I called Norm Goldman and asked if my visit was on. He said yes, and asked if my Korean boss would be coming, too. I told him I hadn't been able to raise Quent, before I realized the grisly double entendre of my reply. We agreed to meet at the slip at ten-thirty. I went downstairs and made a weapons check. Assuming the guys who took Quent down were connected with the ship—and I did assume it—somehow it just seemed a natural progression for them to make a run on me on what was their turf. Especially if Quent, in his agony, had admitted who was running the two of us.

I ignored my phone's bleat because its readout didn't identify the caller and there was no message, and I figured it might be my Feebie boss with new orders I didn't want to follow.

With my StudyChick in one jacket pocket, the LOC-8 in the other, my Glock auto in its breakaway Bianchi against my left armpit and the ex-Bobby Rooney derringer taped into the hollow of my right armpit, I felt like the six-million-gadget man. My phone chortled at me as I drove into town. Still no ident for the caller, and I didn't reply, but this time there was a message and it was clearly Dana's voice on the messager.

She was careful with her phrasing. "The car's been found, but not our property. Whoever has it is asking for a grand theft indictment. But the real news is, someone with political pull back East has complained at ministerial level about the, and I quote, unconscionable interference with Pacific Rim commerce. We're now obeying a new directive. Absent some solid evidence of illegal activity by the maritime entity—and nothing ironclad is present—we're terminating the operation. Of course last night's felony will be pursued by the metro force.

"I want you to report to me immediately. After what's happened, it makes me nervous not to know whether you're still pursuing the operation. If I knew, it would probably make me even more nervous. Just ask yourself how much your license is worth." No cheery good-byes, no nothing else.

I wanted to answer that last one, though not enough to call her back. While my license was worth a lot to me, it wasn't worth Quentin Kim's life. She might not know it, but I could make a decent living as a temp working under someone else's license. If Dana Martin's people dropped out, whatever the Richmond homicide detail found they'd almost certainly discover that their suspects had sailed on the *Ras Ormara.* Good luck, Sergeant, here's a ticket to Pusan and the damnedest bilingual dictionary you ever saw . . .

I played the recording back again, trying to listen between the lines. If Dana had been thinking how her message would sound when replayed for her local SAC, she'd have said just about what she did say. Did she suspect the Volvo's window had been busted by clumsy ol' Harve, who had the LOC-8 and was now en route to the docks? If so, she evidently wasn't going to share that suspicion with her office.

She had also made it plain that I'd have bupkis for backup, leaving an implication that until I got her message, I was still on the case. Or I could just be reading into it what I wanted to read.

What I wanted to read at the moment were my notes, not an easy task in what had now become city traffic.

With twenty minutes to burn, I pulled over beside a warehouse near the wharf and scrolled over my notes hoping to identify the next cargo. The stuff Sonmiani wanted to load was something called paraglycidyl ether, a resin thinner. Quent had checked a hazmat book on the off chance that it might be really hazardous material.

The classic historic screwup along that line had been the burning shipload of ammonium nitrate in 1947 that was identified only by its actual intended use as fertilizer. However, Quent had found that this cargo wasn't a very mean puppy though it was flammable; certainly not like the old ethyl ether that puts your lights out after a few sniffs.

When I checked the manufacturing location I found that the liquid was synthesized right there, not merely there in Richmond but in one of the fenced-off chemical plants with an address off the boulevard facing me. I drove on and found a maze of chemical processing towers, reactor tanks, pipes, and catwalks a half mile past the *Ras Ormara.* A gate was open to accept a whopping big diesel Freightliner rig that was backing in among the storage tanks, carrying smaller tanks of its own like grain hoppers. For a moment I thought the driver would bend a yellow guide barrier of welded pipe and wipe out the prefab plastic shed that stood within inches of the pipe. Near the shed stood a vertically aligned bank of bright red tanks the size of torpedoes. I recognized the color coding, and I didn't want to be anywhere near if that shed got graunched.

The driver stopped in time, though. He was no expert, concentrating on operating his rearview video instead of using a stooge to damned well direct him, and I thought he looked straight at me when he was only concentrating on an external mirror directly in front of him. He didn't see me any more than he would've seen a gull in the far background.

It was Mike Kaplan.

I couldn't be wrong about that. Same caricature of a beak, same severe brush cut and intense features. And why shouldn't it be him? Okay, using a desk jockey to drive a rig might be unusual, and I had thought Kaplan was slated to take the ship tour with me. But if the Fed-erected barriers to Pacific Rim commerce had come tumbling down during the morning as Dana claimed, an aggressive bunch of local reps might be pitching in to make up for lost time.

I wondered what, if anything, Kaplan might be able to tell me about what had happened in that office building early on the previous night. He had left before Norm and I did, but how did I know when he had come back? The third guy—Seltzer? Meltzer!—was one I hadn't met, but without any positive evidence I had already made a tentative reservation for him on my shit list.

It was only a short drive back to the gate that served the *Ras Ormara.* This time the gate was manned, but Norm Goldman, in a ritzy black-leather jacket, leaned with a skinny frizzle-haired guy against the fender of his Turbo Porsche, just outside the fencing. Norm recognized me with a wave and called something to the two guys at the gate as I parked beside the swoopy coupe.

The skinny guy with Norm turned out to be Ira Meltzer, who spoke very softly and had a handshake that was too passive for his work-hardened hands, and wore a denim jacket that exaggerated his shoulders. When Meltzer asked where my partner was, I said he hadn't answered my calls, so I figured he wasn't coming.

Neither of them seemed to find anything odd about that. If Meltzer knew *why* Quent wasn't coming, it was possible that Norm might know. I didn't like that train of thought; if true, it made me the prize patsy of all time. And if they had learned from Quent who it was that had been giving him orders, they would assume I already knew what had happened to him. While

I thought about these things, the three of us stood there and smiled at one another.

Then Meltzer said, "By the way, aboard ship it's the captain's little kingdom—except for government agencies. And you're private, am I right?"

I agreed.

"Then if I were you, I wouldn't try to go aboard with a concealed weapon." His smile broadened. "Or any other kind."

He didn't actually say I was carrying, and it took a practiced eye to spot the slight bulge of my Glock, but I didn't need an argument with the honcho on board. "Glad you told me," I said, and popped the little black convincer from its holster. I unlocked the Toyota and shut my main weapon in the glove box. "I carry my GPS mapper; it's a LOC-8. And I've got a StudyGirl for notes. That a problem?"

Meltzer looked at Norm, who made a wry grimace. "Shit, Ira, why would it be? In fact, you might carry one of 'em openly in your hand, Harve. I'll do the same with the other, and I'll give it back once we're aboard. I don't think al-Nadwi will get his shorts in a wad. I'm supposed to carry a little weight around here, even with these ragheads."

Meltzer said he supposed so, and I handed over StudySkirt, carrying the LOC-8 in one hand. We left our vehicles near the gate and walked in side by side toward the *Ras Ormara.*

The commercial cleanup outfit I had previously seen on the wharf was finally leaving, a bright yellow hazmat suit visibly untenanted in a niche near the truck's external console. I recognized two of the three guys in the truck's cab, and Consoleman, now the driver, waved. When Sweatman, the guy who had worn the suit, pretended he didn't notice us I knew which of them the Feds had co-opted on the job. I would've given a lot to talk with him alone right then.

Norm waved back, his good spirits irksome to me though I couldn't very well bitch about it. He kept looking around at the skyline and the wheeling gulls, taking big breaths of mud-flavored waterfront air that I didn't find all that enticing. Wonderful day, he said, and I nodded.

As we walked up the broad metal-surfaced ramp leading to

the ship, Norm made a casual half salute toward the men who stood high above on deck to meet us. Other men in work clothes were shouting words I couldn't understand as they routed flexible metal-clad hoses around forward of the bridge. A couple of them wore white head wraps.

The skipper took Norm's hand in his in a handshake that seemed clumsily forced, but he shook mine readily enough, unsmiling, as Norm made formal introductions.

Captain Hassan al-Nadwi had a full beard and an old sailor's rawhide skin, bald forward of his ears, but with chest hairs curling up from the throat of his work shirt. He wore no socks, and the soles of his sandals must have been an inch thick.

He spoke fair English. "You want see engineer quarters? Go. Much much work now," he said, friendly enough though shooing me with gestures. He gave an order to one of the two men, evidently officers, who stood behind him, then turned away to watch his work crew.

"You come, okay. I show where Park, eh, sleep," said the Asian, a hard-looking sort whose age I couldn't guess. He led us quickly through a portal, Norm giving me an "after you" wave, and down a passageway sunlit by sealed portholes. Another doorway took us through a room dominated by a long table surrounded by swiveling chairs that seemed bolted in place. Finally, we negotiated another passage with several closed doors, and as the crewman opened the last door I had a view of the skyline through the room's portholes.

The Asian stood back to let us in, pointing to one of three bunks in the room. "Park, okay," he said, and paused, with a sideways tilt of his head. Somewhere in the ship a low thrumm had started, and I could feel a hum through the soles of my shoes. He seemed to talk a bit faster now as he stepped quickly to a bunk with a half-filled sea bag on it. "Park, okay," he said, then moved to a table secured to the metal. Wall? Bulkhead? Whatever. "Park, okay," he said again. I recalled Quent saying once that all Korean kids took English courses. I figured maybe this guy had cheated on his exams.

I pulled out the table's single drawer, which was so completely empty in a room shared by three guys that it fairly screamed "total cleanout job." "Okay," I said. At my reply the crewman turned on his heel, obviously in a hurry to be off. "Wait," I said. The crewman kept going.

Ira Meltzer said something singsong. The crewman stopped in the doorway, not pleased about it. Meltzer looked at me.

"Ask him if there was any other place Park kept any of his personal effects," I suggested.

"I'll try," he said, and then said something longer. The crewman said something else. Meltzer said, "*Nae,*" which was damn near all the Korean I knew, meaning "yes."

The man said something else; glanced at Norm as if fearing eye contact; then, when Meltzer nodded, left hurriedly. "He doesn't know of any. I guess this is all," he said, and nodded at the bunk.

As I unlatched the hasp that closed the sea bag, I could hear quick footfalls of a running man in the corridor. Norm laughed. "Skipper keeps the crew on a tight leash," he commented.

"I don't doubt it," I said. I knew he was explaining the Korean crewman's hellacious hurry to me. And I wasn't sure if that was the best explanation. In fact, I sat down on the bunk so that I wouldn't have my back to my trusty guides while I carefully pulled out the contents of the bag to inspect them, one by one.

A small cheap zippered bag held toilet articles, soap, and a prescription bottle of pills with instructions in Spanish. After that, a pair of worn Avia cross-trainers; socks; a set of tan work clothes, and a stained nylon windbreaker. A heavy hooded rainproof coat; a couple of girlie mags; two pairs of work gloves, one pair well worn. A small, pre-palmtop book full of engineering tables, which I flipped through without finding any handwritten notes.

I saw Meltzer take a peek at his watch, so I decided to use up some more time. "Norm, you have that StudyGirl of mine?"

He handed it over. "You find something?" In answer I shook my head. He squatted for a closer look and, I figured, to see what notes I might make.

I used the audio function, first citing the date and location. As I placed each item back in the big bag I described it, and asked if Norm could translate the label on the pill bottle.

He couldn't, but Meltzer could. While I spelled out "methacarbamol," he said, "Muscle relaxant," practically running his words together.

I announced for the audio that this was my complete audit of Park Soon's effects left aboard ship. I added, in traditional P.I. third-person reportage, "The investigator found nothing more to suggest the subject's itinerary ashore, or whether he intended to return. In the investigator's opinion, the value of the bag's contents would not exceed a hundred dollars." By the time I'd latched the bag and placed it back on the bunk, the combined silences of Norm and Meltzer hung like smoke in the little room. They were being nice, but clearly they wanted me the hell out of there.

And just as badly, I wanted to stick around. I hadn't found anything suspicious to use the analyzer on, and in any case these guys were right at my elbow. Norm stepped into the corridor and waited expectantly.

"Just one more thing," I said, following him into the corridor. "I wonder if the captain would let me see Park's workstation. You never know what he might've left lying around."

Meltzer exhaled heavily as we retraced our steps. Norm shot me a pained smile. "I'll ask. In case you're wondering, they just got their clearance this morning, so they're hoping to get under way today. I'd like to see them do it, Harve."

"Message received," I said. "I guess that's why Mike Kaplan isn't with us."

"He's doing three men's work in the office this morning," said Norm.

And as I tried to read Norm's expression, Meltzer saw my glance and chimed in, "It's always like this at the last minute. He isn't even taking calls."

*So he lies and you swear to it,* I thought. Aloud I said, "I promise to keep out of the way. I just need to cover all the bases." *And one base is the discovery that my new friend may not be that good a friend.*

We found our way back on deck. A faint, musky odor lay on the breeze, reminding me of rancid soy protein. The rushing thrum in the ship's innards was more pronounced as we neared the bridge. It seemed to be coming from those big cargo tank domes that protruded from the forward deck plates. "Wait here," said Norm.

Meltzer stopped when I did. He pulled out a cigarette and, as he lit it, I could see that his hands trembled. It wasn't fear, I decided; not a chill, either, because of the way he was smiling to himself.

It was suppressed excitement.

And when the phone in my pocket gave a blurt, Ira Meltzer jumped as if I'd goosed him. "It's probably Quent," I said. "Let me take it over here." By now I was virtually certain he knew Quentin Kim would not be making any more phone calls. But maybe he didn't know that I knew.

I walked back far enough for privacy, unfolding my phone, casually holding my StudyWench at my side so that its video recorded Meltzer. "Rackham," I said. I didn't want to pull the LOC-8 out until I could make it look like a response to this call. I'd lugged the damn thing aboard to no purpose.

"Your location is known," said Dana Martin. Sweatman had evidently done me a favor. "Are we clean?" Meaning, "is our conversation secure?"

Meltzer was watching my face. "More or less. Our Mr. Park didn't leave anything aboard that might tell us—" I said.

Until her interruption I had never heard her speak with a note of controlled panic. "Get out of there aysap. A.T.F. liaison tells us that ether compound can be converted in the tank to a component of a ternary agent. Do you understand?"

I smiled for Meltzer. "Not exactly. Where are you?"

"Sunnyvale. We have to arrive in force, and that could take an hour. *Listen to me!* Binary nerve gas isn't deadly 'til two components are mixed. A ternary agent takes three. A relatively small proportion of an ether derivative is one. Our other asset just confirmed that the second component is already aboard. No telling how much is there, but to be effective, it's needed in far greater amounts than the ether derivative."

The rushing noise aboard the *Ras Ormara* and the deep vibrations abruptly resolved themselves in my mind into a humongous pump, dumping something into those newly cleaned cargo tanks. A hell of a lot of something. "Does it stink like bad tofu?"

"Wait one."

"Make it quick," I muttered with a smile for Meltzer, seeing Norm as he walked back toward me, a sad little smile on his face.

I was still waiting when Norm showed me a big shrug and headshake. "I'm sorry. Park didn't even have a particular workstation anyway," he said.

On the heels of this came Dana's breathless, "That's what you're smelling, Rackham. Judging from the order form for ether, and assuming they intend to convert it to another compound, we predict an amount of ternary agent that is—my God, it staggers the imagination. Component three is a tiny amount of catalyst, easy to hide. If they have it, you're on a floating doomsday machine."

Norm Goldman now stood beside me. "Copy that," I said, with a comradely pat on Norm's shoulder to show him there were no hard feelings. "Hell of a secretary you are if you don't even know where Quent is. Look, I expect I'll be having lunch with a friend. I'll call in later." With that, I folded my phone away.

Norm took my arm, but very gently. "Part of my job is knowing when not to bug the troops, Harve. Sorry." We moved toward the gangway ramp.

Somewhere in the distance, the double-tone beeps of police vehicles dopplered off to inaudibility. I hoped the audio track of my StudyBroad was picking up the sound of whatever it was that surged into those huge tanks, and then I released the button and pocketed my gadget. If the ether component was still being loaded for transfer, or if its conversion was complicated, there might be some way to slow them down. "About lunch," I began, as Meltzer followed us down to the wharf.

"Hey, listen, I'll have to take a rain check on that," said Norm, as if answering my prayer. "Mike will need help in the office. Before the clearance came through I even had a lunch reservation for a nice place where I run a tab, up in San Rafael.

Promise me you'll do lunch there today anyway. My treat. Just give 'em this," he said, fishing a business card from his wallet, scribbling a Mission Avenue address in San Rafael on the back of the card. "Have a few drinks on me. Promise me you'll do that."

"It's a promise," I said, as we walked toward our vehicles. Hey, if he had lied to me I could lie to him. . . .

Because San Rafael lay to the northwest, I gave a cheery wave and drove off as if keeping my promise, tugging on my driving gloves. Then I reached over and retrieved my Glock as I doubled back toward the place where I'd seen Mike Kaplan loading up. Minutes later, while I redlined the Toyota along the boulevard, I managed to call Dana. "I'm circling around to where they're loading ether into a big rig," I said over the caterwaul of my pickup. "Why not call the Richmond force and get them to meet me there until you show up? Someone should've already thought of that."

"They have casualty situations in both high schools at the other end of town, called in almost simultaneously ten minutes ago. Perps are adults with automatic weapons. It's already on the news and traffic is wall-to-wall there. And we're having trouble getting compliance with metro liaison staff."

That was weasel-talk for getting stonewalled by city cops who have had their noses rubbed in their inferiority by Fed elitists too many times and who might not believe how serious the Mayday was. I didn't take time to say, "what goes around comes around." Of course that sort of rivalry was stupid. It was also predictable.

I growled, "I'll give odds those perps are decoys to draw SWAT teams away from here. Bring somebody fast. Strafe the goddamn ship if you have to; I'll try to delay the load of ether. Am I sanctioned to fire first?"

A two-beat pause. "You know I can't authorize that. Let me check with our SAC," she said.

I made a one-word comment, dropped the phone in my pocket, and swung wide to make it through the open gate.

Fifty feet inside was the nose of the Freightliner, and behind it two guys in coveralls and respirator masks stood on its trailer fooling with transfer hoses. A guy in street clothes stood near the gate, jacket over his arm, and it barely registered in my mind that the guy was Ira Meltzer. The yellow-pipe barrier, protection for that long utility shed, ran from beside the rig almost to the gate. I made a decision that I might not have made if I'd had time to think.

My Toyota weighed something over a ton, and was still doing maybe thirty miles an hour. The Freightliner with its load might've weighed over twenty tons, but it wasn't in motion. I figured on moving it a little, probably starting a fire. I popped the lever into neutral as my pickup blew past the openmouthed gate guard, then tried to hit the pavement running. Meanwhile my Toyota screeched headlong down the guide barrier, which kept nudging my vehicle straight ahead. Straight toward the nose of the towering Freightliner.

The scrape of my pickup's steel fender mixed with shouts from the gate man, and I lost my balance and went over in a shoulder roll. Inertia brought me back to my feet and nearly over again, and I heard a series of reports behind me just before my poor old pickup slammed into the left fender of the Freightliner with an earsplitting *wham* that was almost an animal scream.

Guttural little whines told me someone's ricochets were hitting distant metal, and I somehow managed to clear that knee-high barrier of four-inch pipe without slowing. I ducked—actually I tripped and fell—behind the utility shed, and saw the common old lock on its door. I was in full view of the diesel rig and turned toward it, drawing my Glock.

I had expected an instant fireball, but I was wrong. Big rigs have flame-resistant fiberglass fenders these days, and only one fat tire on each side up front. The Toyota's entire front end was crammed up into the splintered shreds of truck fender, and the cab leaned in the direction of my four-wheeled sacrifice. With a deflated front wheel, that Freightliner wasn't going anywhere very fast.

And the reason why nobody was shooting at me from the truck was that the Toyota's impact had shoved the entire rig back, not by much, but enough to crimp the already tight fit of transfer hoses. The guys in respirators were wrestling with a hose and shouting, though I couldn't understand a word. As I stood unprotected in the shadow of the shed Meltzer pounded up, an Ingram burp gun in hand. I guess he didn't expect me to be standing so close in plain sight as he rounded the shed.

Because Meltzer was six feet away when he pivoted toward me, it was an execution of sorts. The truth is, we both hesitated; but my earlier suspicions about his dealings with Quent must have given me an edge. Meltzer took my first round in the chest with a jolt that made dust leap from his shirt, and went down backward after my second round into his throat, and I risked darting farther into the open because I needed his weapon.

A burst of three or four rounds grooved the pavement as I leaped back. I saw a familiar face above a black-leather jacket, almost hidden behind the remains of the Freightliner's fender, holding another of those murderous little Ingrams one-handed. I fired once, but only sent particles of fiberglass flying, and Norm Goldman's face disappeared.

He called, "Majub!"

I heard running footsteps, and whirled to the shed's metal-faced door before they could flank me. With those big red tanks standing nearby I had a good idea what was in the shed, so I put the muzzle of my Glock near the hasp and angled it so it *might* not send a round flying around inside. The footsteps halted with my first round, maybe because the guy thought I could see him. I had to fire twice more before the hasp's loop failed, and took some scratches through my glove from shrapnel, but by the time I knew that, I was inside the shed fumbling with two weapons. A drumming rattle on the shed didn't sound promising.

From behind the Freightliner's bulk, Norm's voice: "You couldn't leave it alone, could you?"

I didn't answer. I was scanning the shed's interior, which was lit by a skylight bubble. About half of the machinery there was familiar stuff to me: big battery-powered industrial grinders and drills, a hefty Airco gas-welding outfit, a long worktable with insulated top, a resistance-welding transformer, and tubes with various kinds of wire protruding, welding and brazing rod. Above the table were ranks of wrenches, fittings, bolts, a paint sprayer—the hardware needed to repair or revise an industrial facility.

And I could hear Norm shouting, and voices answering. Simultaneous with gunshots from outside, several sets of holes appeared in both sides of the shed at roughly waist height.

Norm yelled again, this time in English. "Goddammit, Majub, don't waste it!"

And the response in another slightly familiar voice and genuinely English English: "Sorry, guv. We do have the long magazines." So Mike Kaplan's name was also Majub. *What's in a name? Protective coloration,* I thought. Noises like the tearing of old canvas came from somewhere near. I squatted and lined up one eye with a bullet hole, but not too near the hole. By moving around, I caught sight of my wrecked Toyota. Norm and a guy in coveralls were ripping the fiberglass away as best they could. It might take them ten minutes to change that tire if I let them.

I darted to the end of the shed nearest the action and put a blind short burst from the Ingram through the wall, with only a fair guess at my targets. Because I stood three feet from the plastic wall, I didn't get perforated when an answering burst tore a hole the size of my fist in the wall.

I had taken out one man and there were several more. They seemed partial to Ingrams, about thirty rounds apiece, meaning I was in deep shit. And when I heard the hiss of gas under pressure, the hair stood up on my nape. Those big red torpedoes just outside were painted to indicate acetylene. I hadn't noticed where the oxygen tanks were, but they had to be near because of the long twinned red and black hoses screwed into the welding torch.

And acetylene, escaping inside that shed from a bullet-nicked hose, could blow that entire structure halfway to Sunnyvale the next time I fired, or when an incoming round struck a spark. I darted toward the hiss, wondering if I could repair the damage with tape, and saw that it was the black oxygen hose, not the red one, which had been cut. A slightly oxy-rich atmosphere wasn't a problem, but if I'd had any idea of using a torch somehow, it was no longer an option.

Outside, angry jabbers and furious pounding suggested that Goldman's crew was jacking up the Freightliner's left front for a tire change. It would be only a matter of minutes before they managed it, and another round through the shed reminded me that Kaplan was deployed to keep me busy. From the shafts of sunlight that suddenly appeared inside when he fired, I could tell he was slowly circling the shed, clockwise.

That long workbench with its insulated top must have weighed five hundred pounds, but only its weight anchored it down. If I could tip it over, it should stop anything short of a rifle bullet if and when Kaplan tried to rush the door, and I could fire back from cover. Maybe.

I took off my jacket to free my shoulders and tried to tip the table quietly, but when I had the damn thing halfway over, another round from Kaplan whapped the tabletop a foot from me and I flinched like a weenie. The muted slam of the tabletop's edge was like a wrecking ball against the concrete floor. My shirt tore away under the arms so badly that only the leather straps of my Bianchi holster kept it from hanging off like a cape.

Then I scurried behind the table and tried to visualize where Kaplan might be. Ten seconds later another round ricocheted off a vise bolted to the tabletop. But I saw the hole where the slug had entered, made a rough judgment of its path, and recalled that Kaplan was still moving clockwise. He had fired from about my seven o'clock position, so I used Meltzer's Ingram and squeezed off three rounds toward seven-thirty. The astonished thunderstorm of his curses that followed was Wagnerian opera to me, but his real reply was a hysterical burst of almost a dozen rounds. A whole shelf of hardware cascaded to the floor behind me, and I crouched on the concrete.

Maybe I hadn't hurt Kaplan badly, but he didn't fire again for a full minute. A handful of taps, dies, and brass fittings rolled underfoot, the kind of fittings that were used for flammable gases because brass won't spark. I stood up and found that I could see through the nearest bullet hole toward the Freightliner. My good buddy Norm was barely visible, wrestling a new tire into position. I thought I could puncture it, too, then recalled that late-model tires would reseal themselves after anything less than an outright collision. Then I noticed that the end of that four-inch railing of brightly painted yellow pipe was within a foot of the truck. The pipe was capped; one of those extra precautions metalworkers take to prevent interior corrosion in a salt-air environment.

And that made me rush to another hole at the end of the shed to see if the other end was capped.

It was.

Which meant, if there weren't any holes in the rail of pipe, I just—might—be able to use it as a very long pressure tank.

I duck-walked back behind the overturned table and routed the hoses with the welding torch along the floor, where they couldn't be struck again. Among all the stuff underfoot were fittings sized to match those that screwed the hoses into the torch, and taps intended to create threads in drilled holes of a dozen sizes. Five minutes before, they'd all been neatly arranged, but now I had to scavenge among the scattered hardware. Not a lot different, I admitted to myself, from the chaos I sometimes faced in my own workshop. My best guess was that I'd never face it again.

Another round from Kaplan struck within inches of the big battery-powered drill I was about to grab, and the new shaft of sunlight sparkled off a set of long drill bits, and I gave unspoken thanks to Mike-Majub while promising myself I would kill him.

I knelt and used a half dozen rounds from the Ingram to blow a ragged hole in the wall at shin height, hearing a couple of ricochets. My Glock wasn't all that big, but its grip gouged me as I wallowed around on my right side, so I laid the weapon on the floor where it would still be handy.

Lying on my side, I could see the near face of the pipe rail in sunlight six inches away, with bright new bullet scars in its yellow paint. Like the big acetylene tanks outside, its steel was too thick to be penetrated by anything less than armor-piercing rounds. That's what carbide-tipped drill bits are for.

One of the scars was deep enough to let me start the drill bit I eyeballed as a match for the correct brass fitting, and while

I was chucking the long bit that was the thickness of my pinkie, I heard Mike-Majub yelling about the "bloody helo." A moment later I understood, and for a few seconds I allowed myself to hope I wouldn't have to continue what seemed likely to become my own personal mass murder-and-suicide project. The yelling was all about the rapid *thwock-thwock-thwock-thwock-thwock* of an approaching helicopter.

It quickly became so loud the shed reverberated with the racket from overhead, so loud that dust sifted from the ceiling, so loud I couldn't even hear the song of the drill as it chewed, too slowly, through the side of the pipe rail just inches outside the shed wall. Someone was shouting again, in English I thought, though I couldn't make out more than a few words. A few single rounds were fired from different directions and then the catastrophic whack of rotor blades faded a bit and I could understand, and my heart sank.

". . . Telling you news crews don't carry fucking weapons, look at the fucking logo! Don't waste any more ammunition on it," Norm yelled angrily.

So it was only some TV station's eye in the sky; lots of cameras, but no arms. As a cop I used to wish those guys were forbidden to listen to police frequencies. This time, as the noise of the circling newsgeek continued in the distance, I gave thanks for the diversion and hoped they'd at least get a close-up of me as I rose past them.

The bit suddenly cut through and I hauled it back, burning my wrist with the hot drill bit in my haste to fumble the hardened steel tap into place. Of course I couldn't twist the tap in with my fingers, but in my near panic, that's what I tried.

Another round hit the shed, and this time the steel-faced door opened a few inches. Bad news, because now the shooter could see inside a little. I wriggled to my knees and looked around for the special holder that grips a tap for leverage. No such luck. But another round spanged off the door, and in the increased daylight I spotted that bad seed among good tools, a pair of common pliers. They would have to do.

Because I was on my knees at the end of the overturned table and reaching for the pliers when Mike-Majub rushed the door,

I only had time to grovel as he kicked the door open and raked the place with fire. I don't think he even saw me, and he didn't seem to care, emptying his magazine and then, grinning like a madman, grabbing a handgun from his belt as he dropped the useless Ingram.

Meanwhile, I had fumbled at my Bianchi and then realized the Glock lay on the floor, fifteen feet behind me. But I was sweating like a horse, and the irritant in my right armpit was now hanging loose, and the tatters of my shirt didn't impede my grasp of Bobby Rooney's tiny palmful of bad news. Tape and all, it came away in my hand as I rolled onto my back, and the grinning wide-eyed maniac in the doorway spied my movement. We fired together.

Though chips of concrete spattered my face, he missed. I didn't. He folded from the waist and went forward onto his knees, then his face. The top of his head was an arm's length from me and I had made a silent promise to him ten minutes previous and now, with the other barrel, I honored it.

Blinking specks of concrete from my vision, eyes streaming, I grabbed the pliers, stood up, vaulted over the tabletop, and kicked the door shut before scrambling back to the mess I had made. Pliers are an awful tool for inserting a steel tap, but they'll do the job. Chasing a thread—cutting it into the material—requires care and, usually, backing the tap out every turn or so. I wondered who was moaning softly until I realized it was me, and I quit the backing-out routine when I heard the Freightliner's starter growl.

Then Norm Goldman called out: "Let him go, Majub, it won't matter."

The tap rotated freely now. I backed it out quickly. "If he answers, I'll blow his head off," I shouted, and managed to start the little brass fitting by feel, into the threaded hole I had made. When it was finger-tight I forced it another turn with the pliers. Then I pulled the torch to me with its twinned slender snakes of hose, one of them still hissing. To keep Norm talking so I'd know where he was: "Some Jews you turned out to be," I complained. "Who am I really talking to?"

The Freightliner snicked into gear, revved up, and an almighty screech of rending metal followed. The engine idled again while Norm shouted some kind of gabble. Then, while someone strained at the wreckage and I adjusted the pliers at the butt of the torch: "I am called Daud al-Sadiq, my friend, but my true name is revenge."

"Love your camouflage," I called back. Now a louder hiss as the acetylene fitting loosened at the torch while I continued to untwist it. With the sudden unmistakable perfume of acetone came a rush of acetylene, which has no true odor of its own. The fitting came loose in my hands and I shoved the hose through the hole, to fumble blindly for the fitting. "I especially like that 'my friend' bullshit" I called.

"In my twenty years of life in the bowels of Satan I have been a true friend to many," Norm-Daud called back in a tone of reproach, everything in his voice more formal, more rhetorical than usual. Now it became faintly whimsical. "Including Jews. You'd be surprised."

"No I wouldn't," I called, knowing that if a hot round came through now it would turn me into a Roman candle. My own voice boomed and bellowed in the shed. "How else could you learn to pass yourself off as your own enemy?" I tried to mate the fittings without being able to see them. Cross-threaded them; felt sweat running into my eyes; realized some of it was blood; got the damned fittings apart and began anew.

The Freightliner's engine revved again. Norm-Daud called, "Not the real enemy. Western ways are the enemy, but I could be your friend. Heaven awaits those of us who die in the struggle; do you hear me, Majub? What can this man do but send you to your glory an hour sooner?"

I knew he was goading his buddy into trying to jump me or to run. "He's just sitting here with the whites of his eyes showing," I lied, to piss my friend-enemy off. The sigh of escaping acetylene became a thin hiss, then went silent. In its place, a hollow whoosh of gas rushing unimpeded into an empty pipe fifty feet long, starting slowly but inevitably—if the bank of supply tanks was full enough, and if there weren't any serious leaks—to fill that four-inch-diameter pipe that was now a pressure tank.

"We will all find judgment when I reach the *Ras Ormara*," Norm-Daud called happily.

"The Feds know about your ternary agent, pal, and they're on the way. That tub isn't going anyplace," I called.

That set his laughter off. "So you've worked that out? Fine. I agree. And no one else will be going anyplace, downwind, from the Golden Gate to San Jose. What, two million dead? Three? It's a start," he said, trying to sound modest.

Then the Freightliner's engine roared, and the rending of metal intensified. The big rig was shoving debris that had been my Toyota backward. I didn't know how fast my jury-rigged tank was filling, and if I misjudged, it wouldn't matter. I grabbed up my Glock and the burp gun and darted to the door I had kicked shut.

I had jammed it hopelessly.

I began to put rounds through the wall, emptying my Glock in a pattern that covered a fourth of an oval the size of a manhole cover. When I'd used that up I continued with the Ingram until it was empty. The oval wasn't complete. That's when I went slightly berserk.

I kicked, screamed, cursed and pounded, and the oval of insulated wall panel began to disintegrate along the dotted line. With insulation flying around me, the Freightliner grinding its way toward the boulevard in a paroxysm of screaming metal, I saw the oval begin to fail. I could claim it wasn't hysteria that made me intensify my assault, but my very existence had focused down to shredding that panel. When it bent outward, still connected at the bottom like the lid of a huge tin can, I hurled myself into the hole.

For an endless moment I was caught halfway through, my head and shoulders in bright sunlight, an immovable target for anyone within sight. But I was on the opposite side of the shed from the big rig, and when the wall panel failed I found myself on hands and knees, free but without a weapon.

Twenty feet away stood a huge inverted cone on steel supports, and beyond that a forest of braces and piping. As I staggered away behind the pipes one of Norm-Daud's helpers saw me and cut loose in my direction, ricochets flying like hornets.

Meanwhile the Freightliner moved inexorably toward the open gate, the Toyota's wreckage shoved aside, the massive trailer trundling its cargo of megadeath along with less than a half mile to go. I hadn't so much as a stone left to hurl at it.

But I didn't need one. Funny thing about a concussion wave: when that fifty-foot pipe detonated alongside the trailer, I didn't actually hear it. Protected by all that thicket of metal, I felt a numbing sensation of pressure, seemingly from all directions. My next sensation was of lying on my side in a fetal curl, a thin whistling in my head. Beyond that I couldn't hear a thing.

I must have been unconscious for less than half a minute because unidentifiable bits of stuff lay here and there around me, some of it smoking. The trailer leaned drunkenly toward the side where my bomb had exploded, every tire on that side shredded, and gouts of liquid poured out of its cargo tanks from half a hundred punctures. Still addled by concussion, I steadied my progress out of the metal forest by leaning on pipes and supports. I figured that if anyone on the truck had survived, I'd hear him. It hadn't yet occurred to me that I was virtually stone deaf for the moment.

Not until I saw the blood-smeared figure shambling like a wino around to my side of the trailer, wearing the remnant of an expensive black-leather jacket. He was weaponless. One shoe was missing. He threw his head back, arms spread, and I saw his throat work as he opened his mouth wide. Then he fell on his knees in a runnel of liquid chemical beside the trailer, and on his face was an unspeakable agony.

A better man than I might have felt a shred of pity. What I felt was elation. As I stalked nearer I could see a headless body slumped at the window of the shrapnel-peppered Freightliner cab. Now, too, I could hear, though faintly as from a great distance, a man screaming. It was the man on his knees before me.

Standing three feet behind him, I shouted, "Hey!" I heard that, but apparently he didn't. I put my foot on his back and he fell forward, then rolled to his knees again. I would have hung one on him just for good measure then, but one look at his face told me that nothing I could do would increase his suffering. Even though his bloody hair and wide-open eyes made him look like a lunatic, a kind of sanity returned in his gaze as he recognized me.

Still on his knees, he started to say something, then tried again, shouting. "What did this?"

I pointed a thumb at my breast. "Gas in a pipe. Boom," I shouted. He looked around and saw the long shallow trench that now ran along the pavement. The entire length of the shed wall nearest the pipe rail had been cut as if by some enormous jagged saw, and of course the pipe itself was nowhere. Or rather, it was everywhere, in little chunks, evidence of a fragmentation grenade fifty feet long.

He looked up at me with the beginnings of understanding. "How?"

I could hear him a little better now. "Acetylene is an explosive all by itself," I shouted. "Can you hear me?" He nodded. "You store it under pressure by dissolving it in acetone. Pump it into a dry tank and it doesn't need any prompting. As soon as it gets up to fifteen or twenty pounds pressure—like I said: boom," I finished, with gestures.

He showed his teeth and closed his eyes; tears began to flow afresh. "Primitive stuff, but you would know that," he accused in a voice hoarse with exhaustion.

I nodded. "The new model of Islamic warrior," I accused back, "so all you know is plastique. Ternary agent. The murder of a million innocents."

"There are no innocents," said the man who had been, however briefly, my friend. Why argue with a man who says such things? I just looked at him. "There are many more like me, more than there are of men like you," he said, the words rekindling something fervid in his eyes. "The new model, you said. Wait for us. We are coming."

My eyes stung from the tons of flammable liquid around us. When I reached out to help him up, he shook his torso, fumbling in his pockets. "Get away," he said. "Run."

Only when I saw that he had pulled a lighter from his pocket did I realize what he meant. I scrambled away. An instant later, the whole area was ablaze, and for all I knew the tanks on the trailer might explode. Daud-al-Sadiq, alias Norm Goldman, knelt deeply and prostrated himself in the inferno as though facing east in prayer as the flames climbed toward his warrior's heaven.

The metro cops got to the scene before anyone else, and after that came the paramedic van. Aside from cuts on my face and arms and the fact that the whistle would remain in my head for hours, I had lucked out. I could even hear ordinary speech, though it sounded thin and lacked resonance.

Captain Hassan al-Nadwi and several of his crew weren't so lucky in my view but, in their own view, I suppose they found the ultimate good luck. Using automatic weapons, they had tried to prevent a boarding party. One competence the Feds do have is marksmanship. No wonder the remaining crew were so hyperactive that morning; they were going to heaven, and they were going *now.*

Dana Martin pointed out to me after I handed over her cracked, useless LOC-8 gadget an hour later, that there had probably never been any intention on the part of the holy warriors to sail beyond the Golden Gate again. Their intent was evidently to start up their enormous doomsday machine and, if possible, set it in motion toward San Francisco's crowded Fisherman's Wharf. The crew would all be dead by the time the *Ras Ormara* grounded; dead, and attended by compliant lovelies in Islamic heaven while men, women, kids, pets, and birds in flight died by the millions around San Francisco Bay.

Dana said, "We came to that conclusion after we found that all the Korean crew members but one had reservations of one kind or another to clear out of the area," she told me. "They knew what was coming. Once we realized how much of the major component they must have to react with all that stuff on the trailer, we knew they were using the ship itself as a tank. An external hull inspection wouldn't pick that up."

"You lost me," I said.

"You know that most ships are double-hulled? Well, the *Ras Ormara* is triple-hulled, thanks to a rebuild by the Pakistanis. The main component of the ternary agent was brought in using the volume between the hulls as a huge cargo tank. I think Park

Soon must have found the transfer pipes, and they couldn't take a chance on him."

"Three hulls," I muttered. "Talk about your basic inside job. You think the entire crew knew?"

"Hard to say, but they wouldn't have to. It doesn't take but a few crewmen to pull away from the slip. The North Koreans helped set the stage, but most of them don't believe Allah is going to snatch them up to the highest heaven," she said wryly.

"I don't get it. Which one of them did," I prompted.

"The one who was an Indonesian Moslem," she said. "He was on the truck crew with the perp who passed himself off as Norman Goldman."

"Then he's a clinker over there." I nodded across the boulevard toward the still smoking ruin. "Really keen of you people, assuring me what a great guy Norm Goldman was. Who did your background checks: Frank and Ernest?"

She didn't want to talk about that. Journalists had a field day later, second-guessing the Feds who failed to penetrate the "legends," the false bona fides, of men who had inserted themselves into mythical backgrounds twenty years before. And in twenty years a smart terrorist can make his legend damned near perfect.

Dana Martin preferred to concentrate on what I had done. I had already set her straight on the carnage at the chemical plant. She had it in her noggin that I had started the fire. The truth was, that's exactly what I would have done first thing off, if I'd had the chance. I didn't say that.

"I still don't see exactly how you detonated your bomb," she said. I responded, a bit tersely, by telling her I didn't have to detonate the damned thing. Acetylene doesn't like to be crowded in a dry tank, and when you try, a little bit of pressure makes it disassociate like TNT.

"I'm no chemist," she said, "but that sounds like you're, ah, prevaricating."

"Ask a welder, if the FBI has any. If he doesn't know, don't let him do any gas welding. End of discussion."

Her big beautiful eyes widened, not even remotely friendly. I knew she thought I'd been carrying some kind of incendiary device, which has been a sore point with Feds for many years, ever since the Waco screw-up. She kept looking hard at me. Well, the hell with her—and that's what I said next.

"You're under contract to us," she reminded me.

"You offered to cut me loose early today," replied. "I accepted, whether you heard me or not. Keep your effing money if you don't believe me. Oh, don't worry about sweeping up," I said into her astonished frown. "I'll testify in all this; I've got nothing to hide."

And while she was still talking, I walked away from there with as much dignity as a man can muster when his clothes are in tatters and his only vehicle lies in smoking shreds.

Actually I did have something to hide: gratitude. I didn't want to try explaining to Dana Martin how I felt about the brilliant, savage, personable, murderous Daud. I wasn't sure I could if I tried.

There was only one reason why he would've made me promise to drive the miles to San Rafael for lunch: to make certain I wouldn't be a victim of that enormous, lethal cloud of nerve gas that would be boiling up from the *Ras Ormara.* And while he could have grabbed my ankles when he set himself alight, he didn't. He told me to run for it.

He would kill millions of people he had never seen, yet he felt something special for a guy who had befriended him for only a few hours. I didn't understand that kind of thinking then, and I still don't.

I do understand this: A man must never trust his buns to anyone, however intelligent and friendly, who believes there's a bright future in suicide. And as long as I live, I will be haunted by what Daud said, moments before he died. There are more of us, he said. Wait for us. We are coming.

Well, I believe they'll come, so I'm waiting. But I'm not waiting in a population center with folded hands. I'm recounting the last words of Daud al-Sadiq to everyone who'll listen. I'm also erecting a cyclone fence around my acreage, and I'm in the process of obtaining a captive breeding permit. That's the prerequisite for a guard animal no dog can ever match.

# VITAL SIGNS

Before July, it promised to be an off-year. Not an election year, nor especially a war year—either of which seems to enrich bail-bondsmen. Early in the summer I was ready to remember it as the year I bought the off-road Porsche and they started serving couscous Maroc at Original Joe's. But it was in mid-July when I learned that the Hunter had been misnamed, and that made it everybody's bad year. It had been one of those muggy days in Oakland with no breeze off the bay to cool a sweaty brow. And I sweat easily since, as a doctor friend keeps telling me, I carry maybe fifty pounds too many. I'm six-two, one-eighty-eight centimeters if you insist, and I tell him I need the extra weight as well as height in my business, but that's bullshit and we both know it. It's my hobbies, not my business, that make me seem a not-so-jolly fat man. My principal pastimes are good food and blacksmithy, both just about extinct. My business is becoming extinct, too. My name's Harve Rackham, and I'm a bounty hunter.

I had rousted a check-kiting, bail-jumping, smalltime scuffler from an Alameda poolroom and delivered him, meek as mice, to the authorities after only a day's legwork. I suppose it was too hot for him to bother running for it. Wouldn't've done him much good anyhow; for a hundred yards, until my breath gives out, I can sprint with the best of 'em.

I took my cut from the bail-bondsman and squeezed into my Porsche. Through the Berkeley tunnel and out into Contra Costa County it was cooler, without the Bay Area haze. Before taking the cutoff toward home I stopped in Antioch. Actually I stopped twice, first to pick up a four-quart butter churn the antique shop had been promising me for weeks and then for ground horsemeat. Spot keeps fit enough on the cheap farina mix, but he loves his horsemeat. It was the least I could do for the best damn' watchcat in California.

Later, some prettyboy TV newsman tried to get me to say I'd had a premonition by then. No way: I'd read a piece in the *Examiner* about a meteorite off the central coast, but what could that possibly have to do with me? I didn't even have a mobile phone in the Porsche, so I had no idea the Feebies had a job for me until I got home to my playback unit. The FBI purely hates to subcontract a job, anyway. Especially to me. I don't fit their image.

My place is only a short drive from Antioch, a white two-story frame farmhouse built in 1903 in the shadow of Mount Diablo. When I bought it, I couldn't just stop the restoration at the roof; by the time I'd furnished it in genuine 1910 I'd also become a zealot for the blacksmith shop out back. By now I had most of my money tied up in functional antiques like my Model C folding Brownie camera, my hurricane lamps with polished reading reflectors, swage sets for the smithy, even Cumberland coal for the forge and a cannonball tuyere. I had no one else to spend my money on but before I got Spot, I worried a lot. While I was tracking down bail-jumpers, some thief might've done a black-bag job on the place. With Spot around, the swagman would have to run more than seventy miles an hour.

If I'd had more than five acres, I couldn't've paid for the cyclone fence. And if I'd had less, there wouldn't've been room for Spot to run. The fence doesn't keep Spot in; it keeps sensible folks out. Anybody who ignores the CHEETAH ON PATROL signs will have a hard time ignoring Spot, who won't take any food or any shit from any stranger. I'm a one-cat man, and Spot is a one-man cat.

I saw him caper along the fence as he heard the guttural whoosh of the Porsche fans. I levered the car into boost mode, which brings its skirts down for vastly greater air-cushion effect. Just for the hell of it, I jumped the fence.

An off-road Porsche is built to take a Baja run, with reversible pitch auxiliary fans that can suck the car down for high cornering force on its wheels, or support it on an air cushion for brief spurts. But I'd seen Feero on film, tricking his own Baja Porsche into bouncing on its air cushion so it'd clear an eight-foot obstacle. You can't know how much fun it was for me to learn that unless you weigh as much as I do.

Of course, Spot smelled the horsemeat and I had to toss him a sample before he'd quit pestering me. After we sniffed each other around the ears—don't ask me why, but Spot regards that as a kind of back-slap—I went to the basement and checked Spot's automatic feeder. My office is in the basement, too, along with all my other contemporary stuff. From ground level up, it's *fin-de-siècle* time at my place, but the basement is all business.

My phone playback had only two messages. The first didn't matter, because the last was from Dana Martin in Stockton. "We have an eighty-eight fugitive and we need a beard," her voice stroked me; softly annealed on the surface, straw-tempered iron beneath. "My SAC insists you're our man. What can I say?" She could've said, whatever her Special Agent in Charge thought in Sacramento, she hated the sight of me. She didn't need to: ours was an old estrangement. "I can come to your place if you'll chain that saber-toothed animal. And if you don't call back by five P.M. Friday, forget it. I wish they'd pay me like they'll pay you, Rackham." Click.

My minicomputer terminal told me it was four-forty-six. I dialed a Stockton number, wondering why the FBI needed a disguising ploy to hunt a fugitive fleeing from prosecution. It could mean he'd be one of the shoot-first types who can spot a Feebie around a corner. I can get close to those types but I'm too easy to target. The hell of it was, I needed the money. Nobody pays like the Feebies for the kind of work I do.

Miz Martin was out mailing blueprints but was expected shortly. I left word that I'd rassle the sabertooth if she wanted a souffle at my place, and hung up chuckling at the young architect's confusion over my message. Time was, brick agents didn't have to hold down cover jobs. Dana did architectural drafting when she wasn't on assignment for her area SAC, who's in Sacramento.

I took a fresh block of ice from the basement freezer and put it in my honest-to-God icebox upstairs. I had nearly a dozen fertile eggs and plenty of cream, and worked up a sweat all over again playing with my new butter churn until I'd collected a quarter-pound of the frothy cream-yellow stuff. It smelled too good to use for cooking, which meant it was just right. After firing up the wood stove, I went outside for coolth and companionship.

I'd nearly decided La Martin wouldn't show and was playing "fetch" with my best friend when, far down the graveltop road, I heard a government car. When you hear the hum of electrics under the thump of a diesel, it's either a conservation nut or a government man. Or woman, which Dana Martin most assuredly is.

Spot sulked but obeyed, stalking pipe-legged into the smithy as I remoted the automatic gate. Dana decanted herself from the sedan with the elegance of a debutante, careless in her self-assurance, and stared at my belt buckle. "It's a wonder your heart can take it," she sniffed. Dana could well afford to twit me for my shape. She's a petite blonde with the face of a littlest angel and a mind like a meat cleaver. One of those exquisite-bodied little charmers you want to protect when it's the other guy who needs protection.

I knew she worked hard to keep in shape and had a fastidious turn of mind so, "We can't all have your tapeworm," I said.

I thought she was going to climb back into the car, but she only hauled a briefcase from it. "Spare me your ripostes," she said; "people are dying while you wax clever. You have an hour to decide about this job."

Another slur, I thought; when had I ever turned down Feebie

money? I let "no comment" be mine, waved her to my kitchen, poked at the fire in the stove. Adjusting the damper is an art, and art tends to draw off irritation like a poultice. I started separating the eggs, giving Dana the cheese to grate.

She could've shredded Parmesan on her attitude. "I can brief you," she began, "only after you establish an oral commitment. My personal advice is, don't. It needs an agile man."

"Hand me the butter," I said.

She did, shrugging. "All I can tell you beforehand, is that the fugitive isn't human."

"Spoken like a true believer, Dana. As soon as somebody breaks enough laws, you redefine him as an unperson."

Relishing it: "I'm being literal, Rackham. He's a big, nocturnal animal that's killed several people. The Bureau can't capture him for political reasons; you'll be working alone for the most part; and it is absolutely necessary to take him alive."

"Pass the flour. But he won't be anxious to take *me* alive; is that it?"

"In a nutshell. And he is much more important than you are. If you screw it up, you may rate a nasty adjective or two in history books—and I've said too much already," she muttered.

I stirred my supper and my thoughts, adding cayenne to both. Obviously in Bureau files, my dealings with animals hadn't gone unnoticed. They knew I'd turned a dozen gopher snakes loose to eliminate the varmints under my lawn. They knew about my ferret that kept rats away. They knew Spot. I'd taken a Kodiak once, and they knew that, too. But true enough, I was slower now. I postulated a Cape Buffalo, escaped while some South Africans were presenting it to a zoo worth its weight in Krugerrands to antsy politicians. "I think I'll give this one a 'bye," I sighed and, as afterthought; "but what was the fee for taking it *à la* Frank Buck?"

"Who the devil is Frank Buck?"

"Never mind. How much?"

"A hundred thousand," she said, unwilling.

I nearly dropped the dry mustard. For that, I could find Spot a consort and dine on escargot every night. "I'm in," I said quickly. "Nobody lives forever."

* * *

While the souffle baked, Dana revealed how far afield my guess had gone. I fed her flimsy disc into my office computer downstairs and let her do the rest. The display showed a map of Central California, with a line arching in from offshore. She pointed to the line with a light pencil. "That's the path of the so-called meteorite last Saturday night. Point Reyes radar gave us this data." Now the display magicked out a ream of figures. "Initial velocity was over fifteen thousand meters per second at roughly a hundred klicks altitude, too straight and too fast for a ballistic trajectory."

"Would you mind putting that into good old feet and miles? I'm from the old school, in case you hadn't noticed," I grinned.

"You're a goddamn dinosaur," she agreed. "Okay: we picked up an apparent meteorite coming in at roughly a forty-five degree angle, apparent mass um, fifty tons or so, hitting the atmosphere at a speed of about—fifty thousand feet per second. Accounting for drag, it should've still impacted offshore within a few seconds, sending out a seismometer blip, not to mention a local tsunami. It didn't.

"It decelerated at a steady hundred and forty g's and described a neat arc that must've brought it horizontal near sea-level."

I whistled. "Hundred and forty's way above human tolerance."

"The operative word is 'steady.' It came in so hot it made the air glow, and it was smart—I mean, it didn't behave as though purely subject to outside forces. That kind of momentum change took a lot of energy under precise control, they tell me. Well, about eleven seconds after deceleration began it had disappeared, too low on the horizon for coverage, and loafing along at sub-mach speed just off the water."

"Russians," I guessed.

"They know about it, but it wasn't them. Don't they wish? It wasn't anybody human. The vehicle came in over the Sonoma coast and hedge-hopped as far as Lake Berryessa northwest of Sacramento. That's where the UFO hotline folks got their last report and wouldn't you know it, witnesses claimed the usual round shape and funny lights."

I sprinted for the stairs, Spot-footed across the kitchen floor, snuck a look into the oven. "Just in time," I called, as Dana emerged from below.

She glanced at the golden trifle I held in my pot-holder, then inhaled, smiling in spite of herself. "You may have your uses at that."

"Getting up here so fast without jolting the souffle?"

"No, cooking anything that smells this good," she said, and preceded me to the dining room. "I don't think you have the chance of a cardiac case on this hunt, and I said as much to Scott King."

She told me why over dinner. The scrambled interceptors from Travis and Beale found nothing, but a Moffett patrol craft full of sensor equipment sniffed over the area and found traces of titanium dioxide in the atmosphere. Silicon and nox, too, but those could be explained away.

You couldn't explain away the creature trapped by college students near the lake on Sunday evening. Dana passed me a photo, and my first shock was one of recognition. The short spotted fur and erect short ears of the quadruped, the heavy shoulders and bonecrunching muzzle, all reminded me of a dappled bear cub. It could have been a terrestrial animal wearing a woven metallic harness but for its eyes, small and lowset near the muzzle. It looked dead, and it was.

"The pictures were taken after it escaped from a cage on the Cal campus at Davis and electrocuted itself, biting through an autoclave power line. It was evidently a pet," Dana said, indicating studs on the harness, "since it couldn't reach behind to unlock this webbing, and it wasn't very bright. But it didn't need to be, Harve. It was the size of a Saint Bernard. Guess its weight."

I studied the burly, brawny lines of the thing. "Two hundred."

"Three. That's in kilos," Dana said. "Nearly seven hundred pounds. If it hadn't got mired in mud near a student beer-bust, I don't know how they'd have taken it. It went through lassos as if they were cheese, using this."

Another photo. Above each forepaw, which seemed to have thumbs on each side, was an ivorylike blade, something like a dewclaw. One was much larger than the other, like the asymmetry of a fiddler crab. It didn't seem capable of nipping; slashing, maybe. I rolled down my sleeves; it wouldn't help if Dana Martin saw the hairs standing on my forearms. "So how'd they get it to the Ag people at Cal-Davis?"

"Some bright lad made a lasso from a tow cable. While the animal was snarling and screeching and biting the cable, they towed it out of the mud with a camper. It promptly chased one nincompoop into the camper and the guy got out through the sliding glass plate upfront—but he lost both legs above the ankle; it seems the creature ate them.

"The Yolo County Sheriff actually drove the camper to Davis with that thing fighting its way through the cab in the middle of the night." Dana smiled wistfully. "Wish I could've seen him drive into that empty water purification tank, it was a good move. The animal couldn't climb out, the Sheriff pulled the ladder up, and a few hours later we were brought into it and clamped the lid down tight."

"Extraterrestrial contact," I breathed, testing the sound of a phrase that had always sounded absurd to me. The remains of my souffle were lost in the metallic taste of my excitement—okay, maybe "excitement" wasn't quite the right word. "If that's the kind of pets they keep, what must *they* be like?"

"Think of Shere Khan out there," Dana jerked a thumb toward a window, "and ask what *you're* like."

Why waste time explaining the difference between a pet and a friend? "Maybe they're a race of bounty hunters," I cracked lamely.

"The best guess is that the animal's owner is hunting, all right. Here's what we have on the big one," she said, selecting another glossy. "Four men and a woman weren't as lucky as the fellow who lost his feet."

I gazed at an eight-by-ten of a plaster cast, dirt-flecked, that stood next to a meter stick on a table. Something really big, with a paw like a beclawed rhino, had left pugmarks a foot deep. It might have been a species similar to the dead pet, I thought, and said so. "Where'd this cast come from?"

"Near the place where the beer-bust was busted. They're taking more casts now at the Sacramento State University campus. If the hunter's on all-fours, it may weigh only a few tons."

"Davis campus; Sac State—fill it in, will you?"

It made a kind of sense. Once inside a chilled-steel cage, the captive pet had quieted down for ethologists at Davis. They used tongs to fumble a little plastic puck from a clip on the harness, and sent it to Sacramento State for analysis, thinking it might be some kind of an owner tag. It turned out to be a bug, an AM/FM signal generator—and they hadn't kept it shielded. The owner must have monitored the transmitter and followed it to Sacramento. More guesswork: its vehicle had traveled in the American River to a point near the Sac State labs where the plastic puck was kept.

And late Tuesday evening, something big as a two-car garage had left a depression on the sand of an island in the river; and something mad as hell itself had come up over the levee and along a concrete path to the lab.

A professor, a research assistant, a top-clearance physicist brought in from nearby Aerojet, and an FBI field agent had seen the hunter come through a pumice block wall into the lab with them, but most of the information they had was secure.

Permanently.

Dana Martin didn't offer photos to prove they'd been dismembered, but I took her word for it. "So your hunter got its signal generator back," I prompted, "and split."

"No, no, and yes. It's *your* hunter, and our man had left the transmitter wrapped in foil in the next room, where we found it. But yes, the hunter's gone again."

"To Davis?"

"We doubt it. Up the river a few klicks; there's an area where a huge gold dredge used to spit its tailings out. A fly-fisher led us to remains in the tailings near the riverbank yesterday. A mighty nimrod type who'd told his wife he was going to sight in his nice new rifle at the river. That's a misdemeanor, but he got capital punishment. His rifle had been fired before something bent its barrel into a vee and—get this—embedded the muzzle in the man's side like you'd bait a hook."

"That's hard to believe. Whatever could do that, could handle a gorilla like an organ grinder's monkey."

"Dead right, Rackham—and it's loose in the dredge tailings."

Well, she'd warned me. I knew the tailings area from my own fishing trips. They stretch for miles on both sides of the American River, vast high cairns of smooth stones coughed up by a barge that had once worked in from the river. The barge had chewed a path ahead of it, making its own lake, digesting only the gold as it wandered back and forth near the river. Seen from the air, the tailings made snaky patterns curling back to the river again.

This savage rape of good soil had been committed long ago and to date the area was useless. It was like a maze of gravel piles, most of the gravel starting at grapefruit size and progressing to some like oval steamer trunks. A few trees had found purchase there; weeds; a whole specialized ecology of small animals in the steep slopes. The more I thought about it, the more it seemed like perfect turf for some monstrous predator.

I took a long breath, crossed my arms, rubbed them briskly and stared across the table at Dana Martin. "You haven't given me much to go on," I accused.

"There's more on the recording," she said softly.

I guessed from her tone: "All bad."

Shrug: "Some bad. Some useful."

I let her lead me downstairs. She had an audio-tape salvaged from the lab wreckage, and played me the last few minutes of it.

A reedy male expounded on the alien signal generator. "We might take it apart undamaged," he ended, sounding wistful and worried.

"The Bureau can't let you chance it," said another male, equally worried.

A third man, evidently the Aerojet physicist, doubted the wisdom of reproducing the ar-eff signals since what looked like junk on a scope might be salient data on an alien receiver. He offered the use of Aerojet's X-ray inspection equipment. A young woman—the research assistant—thought that was a good idea at first. "But I don't know," she said, and you could almost hear her smile: "it looks kinda neat the way it is."

The woman's sudden voice shift stressed her non sequitur. It sounded idiotic. I tossed a questing frown at Dana and positively gaped as the recording continued.

The Feebie again: "I suppose I could ask Scott King to let you disassemble it. Hell, it's harmless," he drawled easily in a sudden about-face. King, as I knew, was his—and Dana Martin's—SAC in the region.

The reedy older voice was chuckling now. "That's more like it; aren't we worrying over trifles?"

The physicist laughed outright. "My sentiments exactly." Under his on-mike mirth I could hear the others joining in.

And then the speaker overloaded its bass response in a thunderous crash. Several voices shouted as the second slam was followed by clatters of glass and stone. Clear, then: "Scotty, whatthehell—" ending in a scream; three screams. From somewhere came a furious clicking, then an almost subsonic growling *whuffff.* Abrupt silence. Posterity had been spared the rest.

I glowered at Dana Martin. "What's good about that?"

"Forewarning. Our man wasn't the sort to vacillate, and the professor was known as a sourball. It's barely possible that they all were being gassed somehow, to hallucinate during the attack."

"Maybe," I said. "That would explain why your man thought he saw Scotty King coming through the wall. Ah—look, Dana, this just about tears it. You need a covey of hoverchoppers to find this, this hunter of yours. I get a picture of something that could simply stroll up to me while I grinned at it, and nothing short of a submarine net could stop it. Won't I even have a brick agent to help?"

"Every hovercraft we can spare is quartering the Berryessa region. And so are a lot of chartered craft," she said softly, "carrying consular people from Britain, France, the Soviets, and the United Chinese Republics. *They know,* Rackham, and they intend to be on hand from the first moment of friendly contact."

"Some friendly contact," I snorted. I realized now that the air activity over Lake Berryessa was a deliberate decoy. "Surely we have the power to ground the rest of these guys . . ."

"The instant our government makes contact, we are committed by treaty to sharing that confrontation with the rest of the nuclear club," Dana said wearily. "It's an agreement the Soviets thought up last year, of which we have been forcibly reminded in the past days."

I showed her my palms.

"*You're not government,*" she hissed. "We're a laissez faire democracy; we can't help it if a private U.S. citizen does the first honors. Could we help it if he should dynamite the spacecraft in perfectly understandable panic?"

"Destroy a diamond-mine of information? Are you nuts?" For the first time my voice was getting out of hand.

"Perfectly sane. We've got a kit for you to record the experience if you can get into the craft—maybe remove anything that looks portable, and hide it. We don't want you to totally wreck the vehicle, just make it a hangar queen until another civilian friend has studied the power plants and weaponry, and then he might blow it to confetti."

I was beginning to see the plan. Even if it worked it was lousy politics. I told her that.

"This country," she said, "has an edge in communications and power plants at the moment. We'd a whole lot rather keep that edge, and learn a few things to fatten it, then take a chance that everybody—including Libya—might get into an equal technological footing with us overnight. *Now* will you drop the matter?"

"I may as well. Am I supposed to ask the damn' hunter for some thermite so I can burn his ailerons a little?"

"We've sunk a cache of sixty per cent dynamite in the river shallows for you—common stuff you could buy commercially. We've marked it here on a USGS map. Best of all, you'll have a weapon."

I brightened, but only for a moment. It was a gimmicked Smith & Wesson automatic, a bit like a Belgian Browning. Dana took it from her briefcase with reverence and explained why the special magazine carried only seven fat rounds. I could almost get my pinkie in the muzzle: sixty calibre at least. It was strictly a short-range item rigged with soluble slugs. Working with the dead pet and guessing a lot, Cal's veterinary science wizards had rendered some of its tissues for tallow and molded slugs full of drugs. They might stop the hunter.

On the other hand, they might not.

If I couldn't make friends with it I would be permitted to shoot for what, in my wisdom, I might consider noncritical spots on its body.

Finally, *if* I hadn't been marmaladed and *if* I had it stunned, I was to punch a guarded stud on the surveillance kit which looked like an amateur's microvid unit with a digital watch embedded in its side. At that point I could expect some other co-opted civilian to "happen" onto me with his Hoverover.

I wondered out loud how much money the other guy was getting for his part in this, and Dana reminded me that it was none of my damned business. Nor should I worry too much about what would happen after the beast was trussed up in a steel net and taken away. It would be cared for, and in a few days the Feebies would "discover" what the meddling civilians had done, and the rest of the world could pay it homage and raise all the hell they liked about prior agreements which, so far as anyone might prove, would not have been violated. It was sharp practice. It stank. It paid one hundred thousand dollars.

I collected the pitifully small assortment of data and equipment, making it a small pile. "And with this, you expect me to set out?"

"I really expect you to *crap* out," she said sweetly, "in which case you can expect to be iced down for awhile. We can do it, you know."

I knew. I also knew she had the extra pleasure of having told me not to commit myself. There was one more item. "What if I find more than one hunter?"

"We only need to bag one. For reasons I'm not too clear on, we don't think there's more. Something about desperation tactics, I gather." She frowned across the stuff at me. "What's so funny—or are you just trembling?"

I shook my head, waved her toward the stairs. "Go home, Dana. I was just thinking: it's our tactics that smack of desperation."

She swayed up the stairs, carrying her empty case, talking as she went. It was no consolation to hear that nobody would be watching me. The little foil-wrapped AM/FM bug would be my only bait, and of course they'd be monitoring that; but it was essential that I dangle the bait only in some remote location. Lovely.

Spot ambled out as he heard my automatic gate energize, chose to frisk alongside Dana Martin's sedan as she drove away. I called him back, closed the gate, and felt Spot's raspy tongue on the back of my hand. I shouted at him and he paced away with injured dignity, his ears back at half-mast. How could I explain it to him? I knew he was enjoying the salt taste of sweat that ran down my arm in defiance of the breeze off Mount Diablo. It might have been worse: some guys get migraines. I'd known one—a good one, too, in my business—who'd developed spastic colon. All I do is sweat, without apologizing. You can't explain fear to a cheetah . . .

I spent the next hour selecting my own kit. In any dangerous business, a man's brains and his equipment are of roughly equal quality. Nobody has yet worked out a handier field ration than "gorp," the dry mix of nuts, fruit bits and carob I kept—but I tossed in a few slabs of pemmican, too. Water, spare socks, a McPhee paperback, and my usual stock of pills, including the lecithin and choline.

I considered my own handguns for a long time, hefting the Colt Python in a personal debate, then locked the cabinet again and came away empty-handed. In extremis, my own Colt would've been too great a temptation—and I already had a weapon. Whether it would work was something else again.

When the Porsche was loaded I spent another hour in my office. The maps refreshed my memory, corrected it in a few cases. A new bridge over the American River connected Sacramento's northeast suburb of Orangevale with Highway Fifty, cutting through the dredge tailings. Gooseflesh returned as I imagined the scene at that moment. Dark as a hunter's thoughts, not enough moon to help, the innocent romantic gleam of riffles on water between the tailings to the south and the low cliffs on the north side. More tailings on the other side too, upriver near Orangevale. This night—and maybe others—it would be approximately as quiet, as inviting, as a cobra pit. I pitied anyone in that area, but not enough to strike out for it in the dark. I needed a full day of reconnaissance before setting out my bait, and a good night's sleep wouldn't hurt.

Usually, sleep is no problem. That night it was a special knack. And while I slept, a pair of youthful lovers lay on a blanket near the river, too near the Sac State campus, and very nearly died.

Saturday morning traffic was light on the cutoff to Interstate Five. I refueled just south of Sacramento, then drove across to the El Dorado Freeway and fought the temptation to follow it all the way to Lake Tahoe. A part of my mind kept telling me I should've brought Spot along for his nose and ears, but I liked him too much to risk him.

I left the freeway east of the city and cruised slowly toward the river, renewing auld acquaintance as I spotted the river parkway. Nice: hiking and bridle trails paralleled the drive, flowing in and out of trees that flanked the river. I didn't wonder why the area was deserted until I saw the road crew lounging near their barricade. The flagman detoured me to a road that led me to a shopping center. I checked a map, took an arterial across the river, spotted more barricades and flagmen barring access to the drive along the north bank of the river as well.

That flagman's khakis had been creased; and who irons work khakis these days? Also, he'd been too pale for a guy who did that every day. I found a grocery store and called Stockton from there, cursing.

Dana Martin answered on the first ring, bright and bubbly as near beer and twice as full of false promise. "Hi, you ol' dumplin'," she cascaded past, after my first three words. I stammered and fell silent. "I won't be able to make it today, but you have Wanda's address; she's really dynamite. Why don't you call on her, shug, say around noonish, give or take an hour? Would you mind just terribly?"

I'd worked with Dana enough to know that the vaguer she sounded, the exacter she meant. Wanda at twelve on the dot, then—except that I didn't know the lady or her address. "Uh, yeah, sure; noonish more or less. But I've mislaid her address. You got her phone number?"

Slow, saccharine: "She hasn't got a phone, honeybuns. Must you have a map for such a dynamite lady?"

Map. Dynamite. Ahhh, shee-it, but I was dull. "Right; I must have it somewhere. The things I do for love," I sighed.

Dana cooed that she had just oodles of work to do, and hung up before I could object that the whole goddamn river area was crawling with fuzz in false clothing.

I went back to the Porsche and studied my map. The explosive cache was fairly near a dead-end road, only a few miles downriver. I found the road led me past a few expensive homes to a turnaround in sight of the river. No barricades or khakiclads that I could see, but the damned dredge had committed some of its ancient crimes nearby. I guessed there were so many dead-end roads near the river it would take an army to patrol them all. It was nearly two hours before noon and it occurred to me that the time might best be spent checking available routes to and from the tailings areas.

Shortly before noon I hauled ass from a bumpy road near Folsom and headed for my tryst with Wanda. I'd marked several routes on the map, where I could get very near tailings or sandbars from Sacto to Folsom. It was the sort of data the Feebies couldn't have given me, since they didn't really know what the Porsche could do.

At eleven fifty-three I realized I was going to be late if I kept to the boulevards. I checked my route, turned right, zipped on squalling tires to a dead end, and shifted to air cushion mode. A moment later the Porsche was whooshing over the lawn of some wealthy citizen, scattering dandelion puffs but leaving no tracks as it took me downslope and over a low decorative fence.

Using the air cushion there's always the danger of overspeeding the Porsche's primary turbo, but I kept well below redline as I turned downriver just above the ripples. In air cushion mode, the legendary quick response of a Porsche is merely a myth. The car comes about like a big windjammer and tends to wander with sidewinds, so I had my hands full. But I navigated five miles of river in four minutes flat.

Triangulating between bridges, eyeballing the map, I estimated that the cache of dynamite was at the foot of a bush-capped stone outcrop that loomed over the river. I slowed, eased onto a sandbar, let the car settle and left the turbo idling. At exactly noon by my watch, I stood over a swirl of bubbly river slime as long and broad as my kitchen. It had sticks and crud in it, and reminded me of the biggest pizza in town, which made my belly rumble. Junk food has its points too.

I was thirty feet from the Porsche, and past my grumbling gut and the turbo whistle I could hear the burbling hiss of the river. Nothing else. It was high noon on a sandbar on a hot Saturday in the edge of Sacrabloodymento, perfect for a meal and a snooze, and there I stood feeling properly unnerved, waiting for a woman to tell, or bring, or ask me something. I put one hand to my jacket, feeling the automatic in my waistband for cold-steel comfort, and to nobody at all I shook my head in disgust and said, "Wanda."

"Mister Rackham," said the voice above me, and I damned near jumped into the river. He was decked out in waders and an old fishing vest of exactly the right shades to blend with the terrain. He had a short spinning rig, and behind the nonglint sunglasses he was grinning. He'd sat inside those bushes atop that jumble of rocks and watched me from above the whole time, getting his jollies. I'd busted my hump to be punctual but judging from this guy's demeanor, fifteen minutes one way or the other wouldn't've mattered. No wonder people learn to scoff at government orders!

He'd done nothing for my mood, or my confidence. I cleared my throat. "Would you mind telling me—" I trailed off.

"I'm Agent Wanda. And there can't be two car-and-mercenary combos like you, *anywhere.*" He didn't climb down but made a longish cast into the river; began to reel in. "New developments," he said casually. "Fortunately all the white noise around us should raise hob with any shotgun mikes across the water."

I waited until he'd reeled in, changed his spinner for another lure, and flashed me the I. D. in his lure wallet as though by accident. Wanda explained that while the decoy action at Lake

Berryessa still seemed to be working on the foreign nationals, some of that cover might be wearing thin. The night before, a lovestruck couple had been thoroughly engaged—even connected, one might infer—near the river when something, surely not boredom, added a religious touch to their experience. According to the girl it seemed to be a great guardian angel, suddenly transformed into a moving rock of ages wielding a terrible swift sword.

Agent Wanda broke off to tell me the girl was a devout fundamentalist, evidently a newcomer to the oldest sport, who'd been overcome by her sense of the rightness and safety of it all—until a huge boulder nearby became a winged angel, gave a mighty chuff, flashed a scimitar in the faint moonlight, and glided into the river like a stone again to sink from sight. It left pugmarks. It probably weighed five tons.

To the girl it had been a powerful visitation. To her boyfriend, who also got a set of confused images of the thing, it had been a derailment. But the girl was the niece of the Sacramento County Sheriff who had—and here fisherman Wanda drawled acid—not been told of the security blanket. The girl trusted her uncle, called him in hysterics. He knew an explosion had taken its toll at a campus lab, and had heard from Yolo County where his counterpart had delivered a wild woolly package to another campus, and like any good lawman he put some things together. By now, elements of the city, county, state and United States were gradually withdrawing the cordon of bozos he had deputized and strung along the river. It was quick action, but far too obvious to suit the feds. Worse still, the campus radio station at Sac State had already got an exclusive from the young man.

School media, Wanda told me, have their own news stringers and an alternative network in National Public Radio. When KERS-FM ran its little hair-raiser on Saturday morning, it scooped the whole country including the FBI. The Feebies had only managed by minutes to quash a follow-up story which, in its usual ballsy aggressive way, NPR's network headquarters in Washington had accepted from Sacramento. It described a huge version of the dead specimen, complete with silvery harness and flaming sword. As a dog-days item for summer consumption, it had almost been aired coast-to-coast over NPR. It would have blown the government's cover from hell to lunch. As it was, KERS had already aired too much of the truth in Sacramento but with TV, Wanda sighed, fortunately almost nobody listens to NPR.

I resolved, in the future, to pay more attention to National Public Radio; it was my kind of network. Meanwhile, the national government was drawing off the protective net along the river, to avoid tipping our hand to other governments—while casually allowing hundreds of nature lovers to wander into harm's way. When officialdom up and down the line conspires to endanger a thousand people, I reasoned, it must be balancing them against a whole lot more. Millions, maybe. It was a minimax ploy: risk a little, save a lot. I began to feel small, like the lure on the end of Wanda's monofilament line: hurled into deep water and very, very expendable.

I watched Wanda cast again, the line taking a detour into the deepest part of the channel. "I expect my explosives are under all that crap," I said, jerking a palm toward the slowly wheeling green pizza in the lee of the stone outcrop.

"Sure is. Looks natural, doesn't it? Just grab the edge and pull it in when you need it. It's anchored on a swivel to a weighted canvas bag. And you know what's in the bag."

I stared at the spinning pizza, and damned if it wasn't a work of plastic camouflage. Real debris, polyurethane slime and bubbles, gyrating in an eddy. I said, "Never know what's real along the river, I guess."

"That's the point," Wanda replied, pulling against a snag almost below him. "The hunter was in plain sight last night, not ten meters from those kids, and the girl claims she never felt so safe. Even thought she saw an approving angel for a few seconds."

"Like your man thought he saw his SAC coming through that wall on the campus?"

"Could be," he nodded. "We thought you should know that, and the part about your quarry being at home in the water."

He frowned at the river; his rod bent double until he gave it slack. I touched my sidearm for luck as his line moved sideways, then began a stately upstream progression. "Jesus, I must have a salmon," he said, his face betraying a genuine angler's excitement.

With the bright July sun and the clear sierra water, I saw a dark sinuous shape far below the surface and grinned. I knew what it was; it wasn't salmon time, and salmon don't move with the inexorable pace of a finned log moving upstream. "No, you have a problem," I said. "And so do I, if a gaggle of Soviet tourists come snooping around here in copters."

"Just keep it in mind," said Wanda, scrambling up, reluctantly letting more line out. "Play it safe and don't have a higher profile than necessary." Then, plaintively, as I turned to go: "What the hell do I have here?"

"Sturgeon."

Pause as the upstream movement paused. Then, "How do I land it?"

I nodded toward the plastic pizza. "Try some sixty per cent dynamite. Or wait him out. Some of 'em get to be over ten feet long; don't worry, they're domestic."

He called to me as I trudged to my Porsche: "Domestic, *schmomestic;* what's that got to do with it?"

I called back: "I mean it's not a Soviet sturgeon. At least you needn't worry about catching an alien."

When I drove away he was still crouching there, a perfect metaphor of the decent little guy in a big government, jerking on his rod and muttering helplessly. I kept the Porsche inches off the water en route downriver as far as the county park and thrilled a bunch of sporty car freaks as I hovered to the perimeter road, trying to let the good feeling last. It wouldn't; all the Feebie had to do was cut his line and he'd be free of his problem. All I had to do was unwrap an alien transmitter and my problem would come to me in a hurry. Maybe.

For sure, I wasn't about to do it in full view of a dozen picnickers. I hadn't yet seen a piece of ground that looked right for me, and I'd covered a lot of river. To regain the low profile I drove twenty miles back upriver on the freeway without being tailed, and to exercise my sense of the symbolic I demolished a pizza in Folsom. Thus fortified, I found a secondhand store in the restored Gay Nineties section of Folsom and bought somebody's maltreated casting rig with an automatic rewind. Wanda had been right to use fishing as a cover activity. I was beginning to grow paranoid at the idea of foreign nationals watching me—and drawing sensible conclusions.

I drove from Folsom to a bluff that overlooked the river and let my paranoia have its head as I studied the scene. Somewhere, evidently downriver, lay my quarry. I'd assumed it was nocturnal simply because it hadn't shown in daylight. But for an instant, just before I caught a glimpse of that sturgeon, I'd realized the hunting beast might have been on the other end of Wanda's line. Truly nocturnal? Not proven . . .

I'd also assumed, without thinking it out, that the hunter was strictly a land animal. Scratch another assumption; it apparently could stroll underwater like a hippo. Gills? Scuba?

The report about the sword led me to a still more worrisome train of thought. A saber was hardly the weapon I'd expect from an intelligent alien. What other, more potent, weapons did it carry? Its harness might hold anything from laser weapons to poison gas—unless, like the smaller animal, it too was a pet. Yet there had been no evidence of modern weapons against humans. The fact was, I hadn't the foggiest idea what range of weapons I might run up against.

Finally there was the encounter with the lovers, sacrificial lambs who weren't slaughtered after all. Why? They could hardly have been more vulnerable. Maybe because they were mating; maybe, for that matter, because they *were* vulnerable. All I could conclude was that the hunter did discriminate.

One thing sure: he knew how to keep a low profile with his own vehicle. So where do you hide a fifty-ton spacecraft? Surely not where it can be spotted from the air. The likeliest place seemed to be in the river itself, but I could think of a dozen reasons why that might not be smart. And if the Feebies couldn't track it by satellite from Berryessa to Sacramento, the hunter was either damned smart, or goddamn lucky.

I decided to make some luck on my own by being halfway smart, and eased the Porsche down to the river. It takes less fuel to hover on the water if you're not in a big hurry, and I cruised downstream slowly enough to wave at anglers. Mainly, I was looking for a likely place to spend the night.

A glint from the bluffs told me someone was up there among the trees in heavy cover. Birdwatcher, maybe. From the British Embassy, maybe. I swept across to a banana-shaped island in plain sight and parked, then unlimbered my spinning rig and tried a few casts. I never glanced toward the bluffs and I still don't know if it was perfidious Albion or paranoia that motivated me. But while sitting on a grassy hummock I realized that I couldn't choose a better stakeout than one of these islands.

It required a special effort for me to scrunch through the sand at the water's edge. If I'd weighed five tons it should slow me a lot more. Even a torpedo doesn't move through water very fast; if I chose an island with extensive shallows and a commanding view, I'd have plenty of warning. Well, that was the theory . . .

By the time I'd found my island, the sun was nearing trees that softened the line of bluffs to the west, and dark shadows crept along the river to make navigation chancy. It's no joke if the Porsche's front skirts nose into white water, especially if the turbo intake swallows much of it. I floated upslope past clumps of brush and cut power as my Porsche nosed into tall weeds at the low crest. I stretched my legs, taking the fishing equipment along for protective coloration, and confirmed my earlier decision. It was the best site available.

The island was maybe two hundred yards long; half that in width. Tailings stretched away along both sides of the river. Sand and gravel flanked the island on all sides and the Porsche squatted some twenty feet above the waterline. The nearest shallows were thirty yards from me and, accounting for the lousy traction, I figured Spot might cover the distance in four or five seconds. Surely, surely the hunter would be slower: In that time I could jump the Porsche to safety and put several rounds into a pursuer.

Then I bounced my hand off my forehead and made a quick calculation. If I hoped to be ready for damnall at any second,

I absolutely *must not* let the turbo cool down. It takes roughly twelve seconds before the Porsche can go from dead cold to operational temperature, but if I kept it idling I'd be okay. Fuel consumption at idle: ten quarts an hour. I sighed and trudged back to the car, and went back to Folsom and refueled. Oh, all right: and had Oysters Hangtown with too much garlic and synthetic bacon. Hell; a guy's gotta eat.

I cruised back to the island again by way of the tailings. I'd been half afraid the air cushion wouldn't work along those steep piles of river-rounded stone. Now I was all the way afraid, because it only half worked. You can't depend on ground effect pressure when the "ground" is full of holes and long slopes. It was like roller-coasting over an open cell sponge; controlling it was a now-you-have-it, now-you-don't feeling. As sport it could be great fun. As serious pursuit it could be suicide.

Back among the tall weeds atop the island, I let the Porsche idle as I walked the perimeter again, casting with my pitiful used rig now and then for the sake of form. How any trout could be so naive as to hit my rusty spinner I will never know; I played the poor bastard until he finally threw the hook. Ordinarily I would've taken him home for an Almondine. But they spoil fast, and I wasn't planning on any fires, and if Providence was watching maybe it would give me a good-guy point. God knows I hadn't amassed many.

There were no pugmarks or prints in the sand but mine, and the tic tac toeprints of waterbirds. I returned to the Porsche and unwrapped the foil shielding from the rounded gray disc that had already cost too many lives. It was smaller than a hockey puck, featureless but for a mounting nipple. It didn't rattle, hum, or shine in the lengthening shadows, but it had been manufactured by some nonhuman intelligence, and it damned well gave me indigestion. I knew it was broadcasting as it lay in my hand even if I couldn't detect it: calling like unto like, alien to alien, a message of—what? Distress? Vengeance? Or simply a call to the hunt? I imagined the hunter, responding to the call by cruising upriver in its own interstellar Porsche, as it were, and got busy with an idea that seemed primitive even to me, while the light was still good enough to work by.

I cut a pocket from my jacket, a little bag of aramon fiber that held the alien transmitter easily. Then, using a fishhook as a needle, I sewed the bag shut and tied it, judging the monofilament line to be twenty pound test. Finally I jammed the rod into the crotch of a low shrub, took the bag, and walked down the gentle slope kicking potential snags out of the way. I laid the bag in the open, hidden by weeds fifteen yards from the waters edge, and eyeballed my field of fire from the Porsche that whined softly to me from above. It was ready to jump. So was I.

A light overcast began to shoulder the sun over the horizon, softening the shadows, making the transition to darkness imperceptible. I retreated to the car, grumbling. I knew there were special gadgets that Dana Martin's puppeteers could have offered me. Night-vision glasses, mass-detector bugs to spread around, constant two-way tightband TV between yours truly and the feds—the list became a scroll in my head. The trouble was, it *was* all special, the kind of equipment that isn't available to private citizens. The microvid was standard hardware for any TV stringer and its "mayday" module could be removed in an instant. If I wound up as a morgue statistic surrounded by superspy gadgetry, my government connection would be obvious. I didn't know how Dana's SAC would explain the alien hockey puck, but I knew they'd have a scenario for it. They always do.

I cursed myself for retreating down that mental trail, practically assuming failure, which could become a self-fulfilling prophecy. Night birds called in the distance, and told me the whispering whine of my turbo was loud only in my imagination. I released the folding floptop on the Porsche and let it settle noiselessly behind me, something I should have done earlier. I might be more vulnerable sitting in the open, but my eyes and ears were less restricted. My panoramic rearview commanded the upriver sweep, the big-bore automatic was in my hand, and the Porsche's tanks were full—well, nearly full. What was I worried about?

I was worried about that standing ripple a stone's throw off; hadn't it moved? I was spooked by the occasional splash and plop of feeding trout; were they really trout? I was antsy as hell over the idea that I might spend the next eight hours this way, nervous as a frog on a hot skillet, strumming my own nerves like a first-timer on a fruitless stakeout.

Recalling other vigils, days and nights of boredom relieved only by paperbacks and the passing human zoo with its infinitely varied specimens, I began to relax. The trout became just trout, the ripple merely a ripple, the faint billiard-crack of stones across the channel to my left, only a foraging raccoon. Soon afterward, another series of dislodged stones drew my interest. I decided my 'coon was a deer, and split my attention between the tailings and the innocent channel to my right. I'd been foxed once or twice by scufflers who melted away while I was concentrating on a spider or a housecat.

A third muffled cascade of stones, directly across on my left, no more than fifty yards away across the narrow channel. With it came a faint odor, something like a wet dog, more like tobacco. I hoped to see a deer and that's what I saw, the biggest damn buck I'd ever seen in those parts. It relieved me tremendously as it picked its way down toward the water. Though they're actually pretty stupid, deer know enough to stay well clear of predators. The buck that moved to the shoreline hadn't got that big by carelessness, I figured, which meant that the alien hunter almost certainly couldn't be nearby.

Well, I said "almost." In the back of my mind I'd been hoping to see something like that big buck; some evidence that the locale was safe for the likes of me. He picked his way along the shore, staring across in my general direction. As part of the dark mass of the Porsche among the scrub and weeds, I moved nothing but my eyes, happy to have him for a sentry on my left, and alert for anything that might be moving through the channel to my right.

It took the animal perhaps a minute to disappear up a ravine in the tailings—but long before that I began to feel a creeping dread. It came on with a rush as I strained to see the path of the buck along the water's edge. Where the "buck" had made his stately promenade there was a new trail that gleamed wet in the overcast's reflection from the city, and instead of dainty hoof-prints I saw deep pugmarks in the patches of sand. They seemed the size of dinner plates. I had wanted to see something safe, and I had seen it, and somewhere up in the tailings a fresh rumble told me the alien hunter was not far off.

I let the adrenal chill come, balled my fists and shuddered hard. If I couldn't trust my eyes or instincts, whatthehell *could* I trust? My ears; the hallucination had been visual, my eldritch buck larger than life, the clatter of stones a danger sign I had chosen to misinterpret.

I knew that my hunter—and the deadly semantics of that phrase implied "the one who hunted me"—would make another approach. I didn't know when or how. Damning the soft whistle of the turbo, I fought an urge to put my foot to the floor, idly wondering what my traitor eyes would offer next as a talisman of safety. I'd made some new decisions in the past minutes: one, that the first thing I saw coming toward me would get seven rounds of heavy artillery as fast as I could pull the trigger.

I waited. I heard a swirl of water to my right, thought hard of trout, expected a shark-sized rainbow to present itself. Nothing. Nothing visual, at least—but in the distance was an almost inaudible hollow slurp as if someone had pulled a fencepost from muck. I opened my mouth wide, taking long silent breaths to fuel the thump between my lungs, and made ready to hit the rewind stud that would reel in the transmitting bait a few feet. I was leaning slightly over the doorsill, the spinning rig in one hand, the Smith & Wesson in the other, staring toward the dim outlines of weeds near my lure. I saw nothing move.

I could hear a distant labored breathing, could feel an errant breeze fan the cold sweat on my forehead, yet the stillness seemed complete. A cool and faintly amused corner of my mind began to tease me for my terror at nothing.

The truth telegraphed itself to the tip of my spinning rod; the gentlest of tugs, the strike of a hatchery fingerling, and in a silent thunderclap of certainty I realized that despite the breeze I had not seen the high grass move either, was hallucinating the visual tableau. To see nothing was to see safety. Not only that: I felt safe, so safe I was smiling. So safe there was no danger in squeezing a trigger.

I fired straight along the fishing line. Yes, goddammit; blindly, since my surest instinct told me it was harmless fun.

When firing single rounds at night, you're wise to fire blindly anyway. I mean, blink as you squeeze; the muzzle flash blinds anyone who's looking toward it and by timing your blinks, you can maintain your night vision to some extent. In this case, I heard a hell of a lot, thought it all hilariously silly, but still I saw nothing move until after my second blink and the round I sent with it.

The second round hit something important because my vision and my sense of vulnerability returned in a flicker. Straight ahead of me, a great dark silvery-banded shape rolled aside with a mewling growl and crunch of brush, and I knew it would be on me in seconds. I floored the accelerator, hit the reel rewind stud, let the Porsche have its head for an instant holding the steering wheel steady with my knee.

Subjectively it seemed that the car took forever to gain momentum, pushing downslope through that rank tobacconist's odor. I dropped the automatic in my lap to steer one-handed, desperately hoping to recover the tiny transmitter.

As my Porsche whooshed to the water's edge I saw the hunter's bulk from the tail of my eye, its snuffling growl louder than its passage through the brush. I was twenty feet out from the shore when it reached the water and surged into the shallows after me. Only the downward slope of the channel saved me in that moment as the hunter submerged. A flash of something ivory-white, scimitar-curved, and the Porsche's body panel drummed just behind the left front wheel skirt. Then I scooted for the far shore.

I turned upstream at the water's edge, grasping the spinning rig, unwilling to admit that the spring-loaded rewind mechanism had reeled in nothing but bare line. The hunter had taken my lure; now I had no bait but myself. At the moment, I seemed to be enough.

Furious at my own panic, I spun the Porsche slowly so that it backed across the shallows. Apparently I could outrun the hunter, but it wasn't giving up yet. A monstrous bow wave paced me now, a huge mass just below the water. It was within range of my handgun but you can't expect a slug to penetrate anything after passing through a foot of water. I took my bearings again, seeing a sandbar behind me, and hovered toward it.

I saw massive humped shoulders cleave the bow wave, grabbed for my weapon, fired two more rounds that could not have missed, marveled at the hunter's change of pace as it retreated into deeper water. There was nothing for me to shoot at now, no indication of the hunter's line of travel. I angled out across the channel, knowing my pursuer was far too heavy to float and hoping "deep" was deep enough. Every instant I had the feeling that something would lash up through the Porsche's bellypan until I heard the heavy snort from fifty yards downstream. I'd been afraid the damned thing could breathe underwater, but apparently it had to surface for breath just like any mammal. Chalk up one for my side.

Moving far across the sandbar, I settled the car and let it idle, waiting for the next charge, straining to hear anything that might approach. Under the whirl of possibilities in my head lay the realization that the hunter had lost or abandoned its habit of fooling me; since my second shot, my vision and hearing had agreed during its attacks. All the same, I didn't entirely believe my senses when the hunter splashed ashore a hundred yards downriver, bowling over a copse of saplings to disappear into the darkness.

The overcast was my ally, since it reflected the city's glow enough to reveal the terrain. I wondered where the hunter was going, then decided I might follow its wet trail if I had the guts. And since I didn't, that was when I thought of backtracking its spoor.

I traversed the river, guided my car up a tailings slope, cut power to a whisper. Standing to gaze over the windshield I could see where the "deer" had moved over the tailings, leaving a dull dark gleam of moist trail on the stones. In a few minutes the stones would be dry. I spotted more damp stones just below the crest of the tailings ravine and followed.

Hardly half a mile downstream the tail petered out, the stones absorbing or losing their surface moisture. But the trail led me toward a bend in the river, and I could see a set of monster pugmarks emerging from the shallows.

I guessed I'd find more pugmarks directly across the river, but I didn't want to bet my life on it. The hunter could be anywhere, on either side of the river. I estimated that the brute couldn't travel more than thirty miles an hour over such terrain, and knew it had been within fifteen minutes of me when I unwrapped the transmitter. A seven-mile stretch? No, wait: I'd heard its original approach over a period of a minute or two, so it had been moving slowly, cautiously. My hunter had probably been holed up within a couple of miles of me—perhaps in its own vehicle somewhere deep in the river.

The Porsche was not responding well and, climbing out with my weapon ready, I inspected the car for damage. There was only one battle scar on it, but that one was a beaut: a clean slice down through the plastic shell, starting as a puncture the size of a pickax tip. It allowed the air cushion skirt to flap a bit behind the wheel well, and it told me that the stories about the hunter's sword hadn't been hogwash.

I tested my footing carefully, moved off from my idling machine, then squatted below the hillock crest so I could hear something besides the turbo. Again there came the lulling murmur of the river, a rustle of leaves applauding a fidget of breeze. No clatter of stones, no sign of stealthy approach. I wondered if I had been outdistanced. Or outsmarted.

A subtle movement in the tailings across the river drew my attention. I wasn't sure, but thought I'd caught sight of stones sliding toward the river. Why hadn't I heard it? Perhaps because it was two hundred yards away, or perhaps because it suggested safety. I obeyed the hackles on my neck and slipped back to the Porsche.

As I was oozing over the doorsill I saw above the rockslide and watched a small tree topple on the dim skyline. An instant later came the snap of tortured green wood; I judged that the hunter was more hurried than cautious. Its wet trail would be fresh. I applied half throttle down the slope, passed across the river near enough to spot telltale moisture climbing the tailings, and gunned the turbo.

* * *

Twice I felt the car's flexible skirts brush protruding stones as I moved up the adjoining pile of tailings. I was trying to see everything at once: clear escape routes, dark sinister masses of trees poking up through the stones, my alien adversary making its rush over treacherous footing. When the Porsche dipped into the vast depression I nearly lost control, fought it away from the steep downward glide toward a hidden pool. I wasn't quite quick enough and my vehicle slapped the water hard before shuddering across the surface. I tried to accelerate, felt the vibration through my butt and knew I'd drawn water into the air cushion fans. I'd bent or lost a fan blade—the last thing I needed now. Traveling on wheels was out of the question in this terrain; walking wasn't much better, and if I tried to move upslope again the unbalanced fan might come apart like a grenade.

I brought the Porsche to a stop hovering over water, checking my position. I'd found a big water pocket, one of those places where a rockslide shuts off a small valley in the tailings and, over the years, becomes a dead lake. The tarn was fifty yards or so long, thirty yards wide; the water came up within fifteen yards of the crest. That was a hell of a lot higher than the river, I thought. The stones around the water's edge were darker for a foot or so above the water—whether from old stain or fresh inundation, I couldn't tell. Yet.

I felt horribly vulnerable, trapped there at the bottom of a sloping stone pit, knowing I couldn't be far from an alien hunter. The fan warning light glowed, an angry ruby eye on the dashboard. I let the car settle until its skirts flung a gentle spray in all directions, trying to stay afloat with minimum fan speed. If the fans quit, my Porsche would sink—and if I tried to rush upslope I would blow that fan, sure as hell. Nor could I keep hovering all night. Idle, yes; hover, no.

My own machine was making so much racket, I couldn't immediately identify the commotion coming from somewhere beyond my trap. Then, briefly, came a hard white swath of light through treetops that were just visible over the lip of the pit. A hovering 'copter—and a big one, judging from the *whock-whock* of its main rotors—was passing downriver with a searchlight.

The big machine lent momentum to the hunter: the huge beast came tearing over the lip of my pit in a sudden avalanche of stones large and small, twisting to lie flat, watching back toward a new enemy that shouted its way downriver.

The hunter was simply awesome, a quadruped the size of a shortlegged polar bear with the big flat head of an outsize badger. Around its vast middle, crossing over the piledriving shoulders, ran broad belts that could have been woven metal. They held purses big as saddlebags on the hunter's flanks. The beast's weight was so tremendous that the stones beneath it shifted like sand when it moved suddenly; so powerful that it had plowed a furrow through the tailings crest in its haste to find shelter. But with such a mass it couldn't travel in this terrain fast unless it made a big noise and a furrow to match. It hadn't, until now. Once again I revised my estimate of its den, or vehicle. The hunter couldn't have started toward me from any great distance.

I had a clear field of fire as the searchlight swept my horizon again, but the hunter was fifty yards away; too far to risk wasting a single round. It was intent on the big 'copter and hadn't seen me yet. I gunned the Porsche directly across the water, intending to make one irrevocable pass before angling upslope on my damaged fans toward the river. There should be time for me to empty the Smith & Wesson.

There should have been, but there wasn't.

Alerted by the scream of the turbo and the squall of galled fan bearings, the hunter rolled onto its back, sliding down in my direction, forepaws stretched wide. I saw a great ivory blade slide from one waving forepaw, a retractable dewclaw as long as my forearm, curved and tapered. The hunter scrambled onto its hind legs, off-balance on the shifting stones but ready for battle.

I wrenched the wheel hard, trying to change direction. Crabbing sideways, the Porsche slid directly toward certain destruction as the hunter hurled a stone the size of my head. I was already struggling upright, trying to jump, when the stone penetrated body panels and cannoned into the chassis.

I think it was the edge of my rollbar that caught me along the left breast as the Porsche shuddered to a stop under the staggering impact. That was when the forward fan disintegrated and I fell backward into the pool. Blinding pain in my left shoulder made me gasp. I shipped stagnant water, also lost my grip on the weapon in my right hand, but surfaced a few yards from the great beast. It was at the pool's edge as I raised the Smith & Wesson, but the convulsion of my spluttering cough made me duck instead of firing.

The hunter had another stone now, could have pulped me with it, but poised motionless over me; immeasurably powerful, looming too near to miss if it chose to try. I jerked a glance toward the Porsche, which had slowly spun on its aft fan cushion toward deeper water before settling into the stuff. My car began to sink, nose tilted down, and the hunter emitted a series of loud grinding clicks as it watched my car settle. It didn't seem to like my car sinking any better than I did.

Since I'd originally intended to simply immobilize the brute, why didn't I fire again? Probably because it would've been suicide. The hunter held one very deliberate forepaw out, its palm vertical, then lobbed the stone behind me. It was clearly a threat, not an attack; another stone, easily the size of a basketball, was tossed and caught for my edification. When the dewclawed paw waved me nearer, I came. There was really no choice. The effort to swim made my shoulder hurt all the way down to my belly, and the grating of bone ends told me I had a bad fracture.

The damned shoulder hurt more every second and, standing in the shallows now, I eased my left hand into my belt to help support my useless left arm. No good. Without releasing the drenched Smith & Wesson which might or might not fire when wet, I ripped a button from my shirt and let the gap become a sling. Not much better, but some. The hunter towered so near I was blanketed by the rank bull durham odor, could actually feel the heat of its body on my face.

Again the hunter slowly extended both forepaws, digits extended, palms vertical. There was enough cloud reflection for me to see a pair of flat opposable thumbs on each paw, giving the beast manipulation skills without impeding the ripping function of those terrible middle digits.

I stuck the pistol in my belt and held up my right hand, and not all of my trembling was from pain. But I'd got it right: my enemy had signaled me to wait. I was willing enough. Just how much depended on that mutual agreement, I couldn't have imagined at that moment; I figured it was only my life.

Still moving with care and deliberation, the hunter retracted the swordlike dewclaw and fumbled in a saddlebag, bringing forth a wadded oval the thickness of a throw rug. It glowed a dim scarlet as it unfolded and became rigid, two feet across and not as flimsy as it had looked. Around the flat plate were narrow detents like a segmented border. I squinted at it, then at the bulk of the hunter.

The glow improved my vision considerably; I could see three smallish lumps through the bristly scant fur of the hunter's abdomen, and a greatly distended one, the thickness and length of my thigh, ending in a pouch near the hind legs. I took it to be a rearward-oriented sex organ. In a way, I was right.

The hunter sat back with a soft grunt, still looming over me, watching with big eyes set behind sphincter-like lids. I didn't make a move, discounting the sway when I yielded to a wave of pain.

The hunter propped the glowing plate against one hind leg and ran its right "hand"—obviously too adroit to be merely a paw—along the edge of the plate. I saw a slow rerun of myself squinting into my own face, looking away, trying not to fall over. It made me look like a helpless, waterlogged fat man.

Then the display showed a static view of me, overlaid by others, as a series of heavy clicks came from the plate. The picture became a cartoonish outline of me. After more manipulation by the hunter, the cartoon jerkily folded into a sitting position. The hunter looked at me, thumbed the margin of the plate again. The cartoon sat down again. So did I.

The hunter placed its left "hand" to its chest and made a big production of letting its eyelids iris shut.

"What the hell does that mean," I said.

Instantly the eyes were open, the dewclaw extended and waving away in what I took to be a slashing negation.

I knew one sign: "wait." I raised my empty hand, palm out, and thought hard. Humans have a lot of agreed-upon gestures that seem to be based on natural outcomes of our bodies and their maintenance. But we're omnivores. Pure predators, carnivorous like the great cats, have different gestural signs. I didn't *know* the hunter was in either category but you've got to start somewhere.

I cudgeled my memory for what I'd read of the ethologists, people like Tinbergen and van Iersel and Lopez, whose books had helped me live with a cheetah. The slashing motion was probably a mimed move of hostility, a rejection. Maybe it was hunterese for "no."

To test the notion, I made an obvious and slow gesture of reaching for the automatic in my belt. The eyes irised, the dewclaw slashed the air again as easily as it could have slashed me. I started to say something, suddenly suspected that the hunter didn't want me to talk. I remembered something about speech interfering with gestural language, then pointed to the weapon with my finger and made a throwing-away gesture of my own.

Distinctly and slowly in the red glow, the hunter folded its left hand to its breast and closed its eyes in a long blink. I brought my good hand to my breastbone and blinked in return. It made sense: if an intelligent predator closes its eyes and withdraws its natural weapon from sight, that compound gesture should be the opposite of hostility. Unless I was hopelessly—maybe fatally—wrong, I had signs for "no" and "yes" in addition to "wait."

The hunter's next attempt with the display took longer, with several evidently botched inputs. It seemed to breathe through a single sphinctered nostril in its muzzle, and the snuffling growl of its breath was irregular. I began to wonder if any of those drugged bullets was having an effect; tried not to cough as I watched. My chest hurt, too—not with the spectacular throb of my collarbone but enough to make me short of breath.

The dimness of the display suggested that the hunter could see infrared, including the heat signatures of prey, better than I could. That display was now showing a cartoon of the hunter and of me, gesturing, while clouds of little dots migrated from each head to the other. Germs? Were we infecting each other?

The hunter pointed a thumb at the display. Sign: yes. Then the display, under the hunter's guidance, stopped the gestures and the dots flowing from my side. The next cartoon was pellucid and coldblooded, as the figure of the hunter slashed out at the me-figure. The human part of the display disintegrated into a shapeless mass of dots. The hunter tapped the display plate and signed, no.

If the hunter wanted those dots to pass between us, they must mean something useful. If not germs, then what? If I stopped gesturing, the dots stopped. Uh-huh! The dots were communications; messages. There was an assumption built into the display sequence: it assumed that our brains were in our heads. For all I'd known, the hunter's brain might've been in its keester.

So I was being warned to cooperate, to talk or I'd be dead meat. I signed "yes" twice and coughed once, tasting salt in my mouth.

The display went blank, then showed the hunter sketch without me. Not alone, because from its bulging pouch a small hunter's head protruded, biting on the prominent sex organ of the big beast. Not until then did I harbor a terrible surmise. I pointed from the display to the hunter, and I was close enough that I could point specifically at the big swollen organ.

She lifted the long dribbling teat from her pouch, and she signed, "yes."

She. Oh sweet shit. The hunter was a huntress, a female with a suckling babe, and I'd mistaken the lone functioning teat for a male organ. But she had no suckling babe, as she indicated by patting the empty pouch. No, and she wouldn't ever have it again. The little one had been an infant, not a pet. It hadn't been entirely our fault but I felt we, the human race, stumblebums of the known universe, had killed it. Or let it kill itself, which was almost as bad.

My fear of the revenge she might take—and a pang of empathy for a mourning mother of any species—conspired to make me groan. That brought on a cough, and I ducked my head trying to control the spasm because it hurt so goddamn much to cough. I wasn't very successful. Luckily.

When I looked up again, the huntress was staring at me, her head cocked sideways in a pose that was almost human. Then she spread the short fur away from her belly with both hands and I saw a thick ooze of fluid that matted the fur there. When she pointed at the weapon in my belt, then at the puncture wound, I knew at least one slug had penetrated her flesh. But it might have been from the guy she'd met with the new rifle. Not likely: she had specifically indicated my weapon. When she ducked her head and grunted, I cocked my own head, waiting. She repeated the charade, complete with the series of coughing grunts and ducked head, as if imitating me.

By God, she *was* imitating me. It didn't take a Konrad Lorenz to know when an animal is in pain, and she was generating a sign for "hurt" that was based on my own behavior.

I signed "yes." Staring at the woven belt that bandoliered over her shoulders, I saw that another slug had been deflected by a flat package with detent studs—pushbuttons for a big thumb. The studs were mashed, probably deformed by the slug's impact, and while I may never know for sure, I suspect that little package had been responsible for the hallucinations before I put it out of commission.

The huntress was punching in a new display. Images fled across the screen until she had the one she wanted, a high-resolution moving image. Somehow I knew instantly it was a family photo, my huntress lounging on a sort of inflated couch while another of her species, slightly smaller and with no pouch, stood beside her leaning on a truly monstrous dewclaw like a diplomat on his umbrella. Proud father? I think so. He—is—was looking toward the infant that suckled in her protective custody.

The huntress pointed at her breast, then at the image to assure me that the image was indeed of her.

I gave a "yes," managing to avoid another cough which could have been misinterpreted. I was beginning to feel cold; on hindsight I suppose it was mild shock. If I fainted, I'd stop communicating. The huntress had made it very clear what would happen if I stopped communicating.

From a saddlebag she drew the little transmitter she'd stolen back from me, still in the sewn-up pocket. She developed a cartoon of the disc, gestured to show it represented the real one, adjusted the display. The disc image floated across the display to the now-still-shot of the infant. She stared at me, unmoving.

Of course I understood. I signed "yes."

She patted her empty pouch, held both hands out, drew them toward her. In any language, a bereft mother was imploring me for the return of her baby.

I signed "no," then gritted my teeth against the fit of coughing that overtook me, and this time I knew the salt taste was blood in my throat. When I looked up, I knew the cough had saved my life; the dewclaw was an inch from my belly, and she was dribbling something like dark saliva from her fanged mouth while she insisted "yes," and "yes" again.

I ducked my head and formally grunted. I was hurt, I was sorry. I pointed to the image of the infant hunter, made the negative sign again, again the sign for my pain. Anguish can be mental, too; we seemed to agree on that.

She withdrew the threatening scythe, wiped her mouth, changed the display again. Now it was an image of the infant with an image of me. Expectant stare.

I denied it, pointing off in the distance. She quickly multiplied the image of me, made them more slender. Other men had her baby? I agreed.

She showed another swarm of dots moving between her baby and the men's images, waited for my answer.

Negative. Her baby wasn't communicating with us. I don't know why I told the truth, but I did. Eventually she'd get around to the crucial question. If I lied she might take me hostage. If I told the truth she might mince me. She sat for a long moment, swaying, staring at me and, if the dark runnel meant what I think it did, sobbing. I also think she was as nearly unconscious as I was.

At last she fumbled the display into a single outline of her baby, then—with evident reluctance—made an adjustment. The image collapsed into shapeless fragments.

I started to make the "pain" sign, but it developed into the real thing before I could recover. Then I signed "yes." Her baby was dead.

She tucked her muzzle into forearms crossed high, soft grinding clicks emanating from—I think—some head cavity, swayed and snuffled. Not a message to me or anyone else. A deeply private agony at her loss.

My next cough brought enough blood that I had to spit, and I put one hand out blindly as I bowed to the pain. I felt a vast enveloping alien hand cover my own, astonishingly hot to the touch, and looked up to find her bending near me. Her tobaccolike exhalation wasn't unpleasant. What scared me was the sense of numbness as I tried to get my breath. I slumped there as she withdrew her big consoling hand, watched dully as she pointed to the image of the infant's remains.

She motioned that she wanted the body. I thought if I stood up, I could breathe. I signed "yes" and "no" alternately, then tried an open-handed shrug as I struggled to my feet. It helped, but even as I was making the sign for her to wait, she kept insisting. Yes, yes, give me my baby. The big dewclaw came out. I couldn't blame her.

But the way I could get her baby back was by calling a mayday, and my microvid with its transmitter was in the sunken Porsche. As I turned, intending to gesture into the pool, I saw that the Porsche hadn't completely sunk after all, was floating still. Maybe I could find the microvid. I stumbled backward as the huntress lurched up to stop me, signing negation with murderous slashes.

She came as far as the shallows, erect, signing for me to wait as I kicked hard in the best one-armed sidestroke I could manage. I was giddy, short of breath, felt I wasn't going to make it; felt the grating in my collarbone, told myself I *had* to, and did.

My next problem was getting into the car and, as my feet sank, they touched something smooth below the car. My mind whirled, rejecting the idea that the bottom was only two feet down. But a faint booming vibration told me the bottom was hollow. Then I knew where the huntress kept her vehicle. My Porsche had settled squarely atop an alien ship, hidden beneath the surface of that stagnant pool.

I got the door open, sloshed inside, managed to find the

microvid with my feet and brought it up from the floorboards with my good hand, coughing a little blood and a lot of water. The car's running lights worked even if the headlights were under water, and I found the mayday button before I aimed the gadget toward the huntress. She had staggered back to shore, dimly lit by the glow of the Porsche's rear safety lights, and was gesturing furiously.

As near as I could tell, she was waving me off with great back-handed armsweeps. She pointed down into the pool, made an arc with her dewclaw that ended in a vertical stab. I could barely see her but thought I understood; it wouldn't be healthy for me to stay there when she lifted off. I agreed and signed it, hoping her night vision could cope with my message, showing her my microvid and signing for her to wait.

The last I saw of her, the huntress was slowly advancing into the depths of the pool. She was signing, "No! Clear out."

I wanted to leave, but couldn't make my muscles obey. I was cold, freezing cold; bone-shivering, mind-numbing cold, and when I collapsed I lost the microvid over the side.

Not far out from the Porsche, a huge bubble broke the surface, a scent of moldy cavendish that must have come from an alien airlock. *They aren't really all that different from us,* I thought, and *I wish I could've told somebody that and ohjesus I can feel a vibration through the chassis. Here we go . . .*

Olfactory messages have got to be more basic than sight or sound. By the smell of starch and disinfectant, I could tell I was in a hospital long before I could make sense of the muttered conversation, or recognize that the buttercup yellow smear was featureless ceiling. In any case, I didn't feel like getting up right then.

Just outside my private room in the hall, a soft authoritative female voice insisted that she would not be pressured into administering stimulants at this time, exclamation point. Rackham had bled a lot internally from his punctured lung, and the ten-centimeter incision she'd made to reposition that rib was a further shock to his system, and for God's sake give the man a chance.

Other voices, one female, argued in the name of the national interest. If the good doctor watched newscasts, she knew Harve Rackham was in a unique position vis-a-vis the human race.

The doctor replied that Rackham's position was flat on his arse, with a figure-eight strap holding his clavicle together and a pleurovac tube through his chest wall. If Miz Martin was so anxious to get stimulants into Rackham, she could do it herself by an old-fashioned method. Evidently the doctor had Dana Martin pegged; that was the first time I ever knew that caffeine can be administered as a coffee enema.

A vaguely familiar male cadence reminded the doctor that Rackham was a robust sort, and surely there was no real risk if his vital signs were good.

The doctor corrected him. Vital signs were only good considering Rackham's condition when the chopper brought him in. His heartrate and respiration were high, blood pressure still depressed. If he carried twenty less kilos of meat on him—at least she didn't say "flab"—he'd be recovering better. But the man was her patient, and she'd work with what she had, and if security agencies wanted to use Rackham up they'd have to do it after changing physicians. Then she left. I liked her, and I hadn't even seen her.

Dana Martin's trim little bod popped into view before I could close my eyes; she saw I was awake. "Harve, you've given us some anxious hours," she scolded cutely.

I'd heard some of that anxiety, I said, and flooded her with questions like the time of which day, how long would I be down, where was the alien, did they know it was a female.

"Hold on; one thing at a time, fella." Scott King stepped near, smiling, welcoming me back as if he meant it. Scotty, Dana's area SAC, was an ex-linebacker with brains. I'd met him years before; not a bad sort, but one who went by the book. And sometimes the book got switched on him. From his cautious manner I gathered he was thumbing through some new pages as he introduced me to Señor Hernan Ybarra, one of the nonpermanent members of the U.N. Security Council. Ybarra, a somber little man in a pearl-gray summer suit that must have cost a fortune, showed me a dolorous smile but was barely civil to the two Feebies, managing to convey that there was nothing personal about it. He just didn't approve of the things they did for a living.

I put my free hand out, took Ybarra's. I said, "Security Council? Glad to meet a man with real clout."

The eyes lidded past a moment's wry amusement. "A relative term," he assured me. "Our charter is to investigate, conciliate, recommend adjustments, and—" one corner of his mouth tried to rebel at the last phrase, "—enforce settlements."

"What's wrong with enforcement, *per se?* I've been in the business myself."

With softly accented exactness: "It is an egregious arrogance to speak of *our* enforcing a Sacramento settlement."

"The clout is with the hunting people," Dana chimed in, patting my hand, not letting it go. Her sex-appeal pumps were on overdrive, which meant she was on the defensive.

I let her think I was fooled. "Hunting people? You've found more, then?"

"They found us," King corrected me, "while we were draining that sinkhole in the middle of the night. Smart move, immobilizing that shuttle craft by parking on it. We owe you one."

I thought about that. "The huntress didn't lift off, then," I said, looking at King for confirmation.

A one-beat hesitation. "No. Paramedics realized you were lodged on top of something when they found you. The most important thing, right now, is whether you had any peaceful contact with the female hunter before you zapped each other."

"Is anybody taping us now?"

Ybarra and King both indicated their lapel units with cables snaking into coat pockets. "Rest assured," King said laconically.

I told them I'd managed a couple of lucky hits with the medicated slugs. When I mentioned that the visual hallucinations and the shallow whatthehell feeling stopped after I hit a piece of the huntress's equipment, a sharp glance passed between Ybarra and King.

"So: it would seem not to be an organic talent," Ybarra mused with relief. "Go on."

I gave a quick synopsis. The hovercraft that passed downriver—chartered by Chinese, Ybarra told me—the way I'd managed to get myself walloped when falling from my Porsche, my sloppy sign language with the huntress, my despairing retreat to the half-sunken car to find my microvid.

"So you made no recording until you were safely distant," Ybarra muttered sadly, sounding like a man trying to avoid placing blame. "But still you were making sign language?"

"Mostly the huntress was doing that. She wanted me the hell out of there. I wanted to, believe me."

King, in hissing insistence: "*But where is the microvid unit?*"

"You'll find it in the pool somewhere," I said. The shrug hurt.

King shook his head. "No we won't. Maybe the hunting people will." At my glance he went on: "Pumping out the pool must have given them a fix. They came straight down like a meteorite and shooed us away before dawn this morning. No point in face-to-face negotiation; anybody that close, acts like he's on laughing gas. But they've been studying us a while, it seems."

"How'd they tell you that?"

"Clever system they have," Ybarra put in; "a computer-developed animation display that anyone can receive on VHF television. The hunting people make it clear that they view us as pugnacious little boys. The question before them, as we understand it, is whether we are truly malign children."

"You can ask the huntress. She's reasonable."

"That is what we cannot do," Ybarra said. "They acknowledge that the female came here mentally unbalanced."

Scotty King broke in, waving his hand as if disposing of a familiar mosquito: "Spoiled young base commander's wife; serious family argument. She takes their kid, steals a jeep, rushes off into cannibal country. Kid wanders off; distraught mother searches. Soap opera stuff, Harve. The point is, they admit she was nuts."

"With her baby dead from cannibal incompetence," I added, spinning out the analogy. "Who *wouldn't* be half crazy? By the way, what base do they command?"

King looked at Ybarra, who answered. "Lunar farside; the Soviets believe their site is just beyond the libration limit in the Cordillera chain. The hunting people are exceedingly tough organisms and could probably use lunar mass to hide a fast final approach before soft-landing there."

"You don't have to tell me how tough they are," I said, "or that we reacted like savages—me included."

"It is absolutely vital," Ybarra said quietly, "that we show the hunting people some sign that we attempted a friendly interchange. If we cannot, our behavior is uniformly bad in their view. Some recording of your sign talk is vital," he said again.

"Find the microvid. Or bring me face to face with the huntress, since she didn't lift off after all." I brightened momentarily, trying to be clever. "The vital signs are hers, after all."

Silence. Stolid glances, as Dana withdrew her hand.

"You may as well tell him," Ybarra husked.

"I wouldn't," Dana warned. She knew me pretty well.

Scotty King: "It took a half-hour to find you after your mayday, Harve; and two hours more to pump the water down to airlock level. The female had turned on some equipment but she never tried to lift off. There were no vital signs when we reached her."

Dana Martin cut through the bullshit. "She's dead, Rackham. We don't know exactly why, but we learned that much before their second ship came barreling in."

I made fists, somehow pleased at the fresh stabbing twinge through my left shoulder. "So I killed her. No wonder you're afraid of a global housecleaning."

King: "Not much doubt they could do it."

"And they might exercise that option," Ybarra added, "without a recording to verify your story."

Dana Martin sought my gaze and my hand. "Now you see our position, and yours," she said, all the stops out on her Wurlitzer of charm.

I pulled my hand away. "Better than you do," I growled. "You people have taped this little debriefing. And the flexible display the huntress used seemed to have videotape capability, or it couldn't have developed an animation of me on the spot. She was taping, too, out there on the rockpile."

King, staccato: "Where is her recording?"

"Ask the hunting people." My voice began to rise despite my better judgment. "But don't ask anything more from *me*, goddamn you! Take your effing debrief tape and run it for the hunting people. Or don't. Just get out and leave me alone."

Scott King cleared his throat and came to attention. "We are prepared, of course, to offer you a very, very attractive retainer on behalf of the State Department—"

"So you can pull more strings, hide more dynamite, slip me another weapon? Get laid, Scotty! I've had a gutful of your bloody mismanagement. My briefings were totally inadequate; your motives were short-sighted; the whole operation was half-assed, venal and corrupt."

Dana abandoned the cutesypie role; now she only looked small and cold and hard. "How about your own motives and venality?"

"Why d'you think I'm shouting," I shouted.

King became stiffly proper. "Let me get this straight for the record. You won't lift a hand for the human race because you're afraid to face the hunting people again."

"Don't you understand *any*thing, asshole? I'm not afraid: I'm *ashamed*! That grief-stricken predator showed more respect for life processes than all of us put together. In the most basic, vital way—the huntress was my friend. You might say yes when your friend says no, but once you've agreed to defer a selfish act you've committed a friendly one."

Ybarra had his mouth ready. "Don't interrupt," I barked. "The first agreement we made was to hold back, to confer; to wait. I know a cheetah named Spot who wouldn't waste a second thought on me if he thought I'd had anything to do with killing one of his kits. He'd just put me through Johnny Rubeck's machine. And I wouldn't blame him."

Ybarra's face revealed nothing, but King's was flushed. "You're inhuman," he said.

"Jesus, I hope so," I said, and jerked my thumb toward the door.

Well, I've had a few hours to think about it, mostly alone. What hurts a lot more than my collarbone is the suspicion that the huntress waited for me to clear out before she would move her ship. Okay, so she'd wasted some lives in her single-minded desperation to recover her child. In their ignorance those killed had been asking for it. Me? I was begging for it! It was no fur off her nose if I died too, and she was lapsing into a coma because I'd shot her full of drugs that may have poisoned her, and other humans had used her own baby's tissues to fashion weapons against her. And there she sat, for no better reason than an uncommon decency, waiting. And it killed her.

It's bad enough to get killed by enmity; it's worse to get it through friendship. In my friend's place, I know what I'd have done, and I don't like thinking about that either. When you're weak, waiting is smart. When you're strong, it's compassion. Compassion can kill you.

As soon as I get out of here I'm going into my smithy in the shadow of Mount Diablo and pound plowshares for a few weeks, and talk to Spot, and mull it over.

*If* I get out of here. Nobody seems very anxious to stick to the hospital routines; they're all watching the newscasts, essentially doing what I'm doing.

What the hunting people are doing.

Waiting.

[illegible]

[illegible]

[illegible]

[illegible]

[illegible]

# MILLENNIAL POSTSCRIPT

Today, Harve would have a cell phone, a GPS unit, and night vision goggles. The nuclear club has no Soviets as such; they're Russians again. And the club members include India, Pakistan, and others too depressing to mention.

That new bridge from Orangevale to the Interstate? It was only a good idea when I wrote about it, but it's in place as of this writing. No predictions: in California, you never know what next week's temblor will bring.

Harve's Porsche is still a pipe dream because, as car freaks get dumber, even Porsches get heavier. We may not see real improvements until fuel gets truly pricey or—a worse scenario but more likely—laws penalize grossly overpowered cars.

About that alien base on the lunar farside: if it's there, we should find evidence of it before this edition goes to press. Before the Lunar Prospector finally impacts the moon it will be making passes for six months only 25km above the moon. Our SR-71 recon aircraft fly that high above earth, and on a good day they can read a license plate. That's not what the LP is for, but anything like an outpost for spacecraft will tip its hand to the LP's sensors unless it is buried very deep and gives no anomalous readings that we can interpret.

# PULLING THROUGH

*For*
*Dave Shumway*
*. . . who has pulled me through*
*more than once.*

## I. Doomsday

I found her thirty miles north of Oakland at Sears Point—the international raceway, to be exact, where headstrong car freaks of all sexes liked to hang out before the war. She looked smaller than eighteen. Also older. I had no trouble recognizing her from mug shots and, from the bail bondsman, glossies from her days as a teen model. But the glossies were before she'd gone pro in the worst sense, the sense that brought me into it. My name's Harve Rackham; I was a bounty hunter.

My first problem was isolating her from the quiet machos who ran Sears Point on autumn weekdays, teaching chauffeurs evasive driving and making a show of unconcern to the pit popsies—or whatever they called wistful jailbait in those days. I hadn't kept up on pit jargon since my weight climbed into the two-fifty range and I let my competition license lapse. You can't give away sixty pounds to other drivers when you drive the little cars. My Lotus Cellular wasn't tiny, but it weighed next to nothing; just the thing to drive when some bail jumper tried to sideswipe you, because the air-cushion fans could literally jump you over the big bad Buicks. And the plastic chassis cells in an off-road Lotus would absorb a handgun slug as—but I was talking about the girl. Like most sportscar nuts, she could be hypnotized by certain phrases: my Ferrari, my Lotus, my classic DeLorean; but you had to be ready to put up or shut up.

The girl had a very direct way about her, and in five minutes while I watched she was left standing at the Armco pit barrier twice by guys who didn't need whatever she was offering. She was making it easy for me.

Instead of sidling up to her—ever see anybody six foot two *sidle*? Ridiculous . . . I waved her back, adopting a proprietary air. "These are private practice sessions, miss. And you're in a bad spot; if one of these four-door Bimmers kisses the Armco barrier it'll be spitting hunks of mag all down the pit apron." It wasn't likely, but it sounded good.

Her voice was a surprise, as sunny blonde as her Mediterranean features were dark. "I wasn't thinking," she said, "thanks. Uh—d'you know if any of those big limos," she paused, drowned out as a long BMW limousine howled around the last turn and then accelerated up the straight with a muted *thrummm*, "will be going home today or tomorrow?"

"A couple," I said, just as if I had the foggiest idea. "Why?"

I could see *what's it to you* in her sultry, too-experienced young face, but she erased it after a moment's thought. "I've never copped a ride in fifty thousand bucks' worth of limo," she said with a shrug.

By God, but she had cute ideas! Chauffeurs trained in the limos they drove from Denver or L. A., and the evasive training took a week. So an enterprising wench on the run might cop a ride out of the Bay Area without showing her lush tush at bus depots or freeway on-ramps, where some plainclothesman might recognize her. And she could pay off in the oldest coin of all.

A big Jag sedan sailed past, its Pirellis squalling. Its plate prefixes told me it was from L.A.; in my business you memorized that kind of trivia for the times when it might not be trivial. "He'll be heading for Pasadena," I said into the ensuing quiet—it might even be true—"and I expect I'll beat him there by two hours in my Cellular."

Quick, suspicious: "You're taking a Lotus to Pasadena?"

"Nope. To Palm Springs," I lied, and sighed a rich man's self-indulgent sigh. "A limo's okay, but they always put me to sleep." I pulled my Frisbee-size pocket watch out, though I already knew the time. A wrist chrono hangs up on clothing sometimes, and my ancient eighteen-jewel Hamilton was rugged as hell. It also carried the same false hint of money as a Rolex. I flipped the Hamilton's protective cover up, studied the dial, sighed again, put the thing away. "Enjoy your trip," I said and turned away.

For an instant I thought she had spurned the bait. Then, "I don't believe it," she said to my back.

I turned my head. "Shall I hover and wave?"

She hurried to catch up. "You just don't look like a man who drives superlight cars," she said brightly. "A Lotus Cellular? Can it really outrun the Porsches?"

"Outjump, yes. Outrun? No," I said truthfully. Now we approached the glass-walled anterooms where staff members made their low-key pitches to interested execs.

She was so intent on peering through the glass to spot my car in the parking lot, she didn't notice much else. Two young men stood in the anteroom in much-laundered driving coveralls labeled "Mitch" and "Jerry." I'd never seen either of them before. "See you next time, Jer," I rumbled on my way out, for the girl's benefit. Every little scam helps.

When she saw my car, her suspicion fled. I slid the half-door aside, shoehorned my gut in with me. She ran her hand along the sand-tinted door sill opposite. "Feels rubbery," she said.

"Stealth coating. Plays hell with fuzz radar," I said, winked, fired up the engine, and made an unnecessary check of the system's digitals.

She had to talk louder, so she did. "My name's Kathy." I knew it was Kate Gallo. "You really going to Palm Springs? Right now?"

One good lie deserves another. "Right now," I said, and let the hover fans burp a puff of dust from beneath the Cellular's skirts.

"Aren't you even going to ask me if I want a ride?"

"Nope. Haven't time for you to collect luggage. And young girls are trouble." I blipped the engine.

She held up her shoulder bag, the kind that you could swing a cat in; the kind that alerts shopkeepers. "I travel light. And I'm free and twenty-one." She licked her lips, forced a desperate smile: "And I can be very friendly."

"I'll settle for repartee that keeps me awake on Interstate Five," I replied and waved her in as if already regretting my bigheartedness.

She piled in with a goodly flash of leg; levered her torso safety cushion into place as I backed in wheel-mode onto macadam. No sense in leaving a ground-effects dust pall behind. Then I eased onto the highway, ran the Lotus up through her gears manually and cut in the fans again for that lovely up-and-over sensation, nosing upward until we could have soared over anything but a big semi rig, before I settled us down again to a legal pace on wheels. All to give Kathy-Kate a wee thrill. It was the least I could do; she didn't know I'd locked her torso restraint. She couldn't get out if she wanted to, and that would've given her something entirely different. A wiwi thrill.

So far it had been so easy I was ashamed of myself. I hadn't needed cuffs on her. She didn't even know my name, or that she was headed for the Oakland jug—and she wasn't, but *I* didn't know *that*, of course. I got my first inkling of it as we passed the new bridge that led to Mare Island Shipyard.

Mare Island wasn't just fenced off: it boasted two men in civvies carrying Ingrams with the tubular stocks extended and thirty-round magazines. No suppressors. Those guys commanded real respect; not even an armored Mercedes could get past them, much less fat Harve with his puddle-jumping Lotus. But I intended to pass them by anyhow, over the Carquinez bridge and down to Oakland before rush hour with my unsuspecting "suspect."

So much for my intentions. Carquinez bridge was closed to southerly traffic—and patrolled. I didn't understand until, diverted toward the Martinez bridge some miles away, I noted the wall-to-wall traffic heading north from the Oakland area. I pulled up near a uniformed Vallejo officer who was directing traffic. I bawled, "What's the trouble over Carquinez?"

He looked at me as though I were an idiot. "You must be

kidding," he called, but saw from my expression that I wasn't. "You got a radio in that thing?" I nodded. "Use it. And if you're thinking of heading south, think again," he shouted, and jumped at the dull gong of a minor collision behind him.

I punched the radio on and exchanged shrugs with the girl. In my rearview I could see the officer waving the fender-benders aside with no effort to ascertain injuries or to take videotapes. It was a bad intersection, already littered with glass and fluids from other recent collisions. Evidently the officer had special orders to keep the roadway clear at all costs.

"Okay," I said to myself as much as to the girl, "we'll detour east to Martinez," and squirted the Lotus ahead at a speed that should've put a black-and-white on my tail.

But long before I reached the Martinez bridge, the radio had told me why that was wishful thinking. A nervous announcer was saying, ". . . at the request of the White House, to participate in the Emergency Broadcast System. During this emergency most stations will remain on the air, broadcasting news and official information to the public in assigned areas. This is Station KCBS, San Francisco; we will remain on the air to serve the San Francisco County area. If you are not in this area, you should tune to other stations until you hear one broadcasting news and information in your area.

"You are listening to the Emergency Broadcast System serving the San Francisco County area. Do not use your telephone. The telephone lines should be kept open for emergency use. The Emergency Broadcast System has been activated—" Flick. The girl beat me to it, seeking another station.

". . . is Station KABL, Oakland. This station will broadcast news, official information and instruction for the Alameda County area—" Flick. This time I made the change.

I got KWUN, a Concord station. The girl couldn't have known it, but Concord was within ten miles of my place and by now I had no other goal but that fenced five-acre plot of mine on the backside of Mount Diablo. The announcer seemed disbelieving of his own news. "Radio Damascus claims that the Syrian attack on elements of the US Sixth Fleet was a legitimate response to violations of Syria's air space by our carrier-based aircraft. In Washington the Secretary of Defense defended the policy of hot pursuit against the bases from which Soviet-built Syrian fighter-bombers sank the US tender *Bloomsbury* about fifty miles west of Beirut early this morning. There has been no official response from Washington to the Syrian claim that the supercarrier *Nimitz* lies capsized in the Mediterranean after a nuclear near-miss by a Syrian cruise missile—"

"Oh shit," the girl and I said simultaneously.

We soon learned that most stations were simply repeating the prefabricated EBS messages we'd heard earlier, awaiting an official White House announcement. Little KWUN soon fell back on the same script as the others, but it had already told me enough. Syria's cruise birds were Soviet-made; her nukes probably Libyan. It no longer mattered whether the Soviets had known that Syria could screw nuclear tips onto those weapons. Far more important was the battle raging between our Sixth Fleet and the fast Soviet hoverships we had engaged as they poured from the Black Sea into the Aegean. I figured the *Nimitz* for a supercasualty, and I was right; once the Navy lost that big vulnerable beauty they'd be shooting at everything that moved. Our media weren't telling us, yet, that things were moving toward West Germany, too, on clanking caterpillar treads.

We found the Martinez bridge blocked, its southbound lanes choked with the solid stream of northbound traffic. Cursing, I took the road past the old Benicia historical monument because I knew it led to the water. "I hope you can swim, Kate," I called over the wail of the engine, "in case we get a malf halfway across Suisun Bay."

"Stop this thing," she screamed. I did. "We'd never make Palm Springs in traffic like this," she said, her dark eyes very round and smokily Sicilian. "*And why did you call me Kate?*"

"I know all my property," I said. "Legally, Kate Gallo, you are my temporary chattel property by California law. I can slap you around if I need to, or put you in handcuffs and gag you."

Her eyes became almost circular. "Bounty hunter," she accused.

"You got it, and it's got you. But I'm not taking you back

to Oakland now, Kate. I'm heading for my home in Contra Costa County, which has a nice deep basement and all of Mount Diablo to protect us against whatever ails the Bay Area." She was struggling against her torso restraint. "Are you listening?"

In answer she turned toward me with claws flashing; raked my jacket sleeve in lightning swipes that almost drew blood through the Dacron; shifted her aim toward my face. It was not a move calculated to bring out my gentlemanly instincts.

I cuffed her with my gloved hand, lightly, twice—just enough to make her draw back to protect those lovely strong cheekbones. "You can go," I said, and repeated it as she gazed at me through defensive hands. I triggered the release on the torso restraint and, while she surged up from the seat, I added, "While you lie dying, remember I gave you a chance."

She hadn't panicked because she was still thinking ahead. She paused astraddle the door sill. "A Berkeley whizkid told me once that the only smart way out of Oakland, in an evacuation, was north along the coast. I'll make it."

"So will a million others." I jerked my head back toward the clogged arterials. "Did he also mention that you might starve? Did he mention the very few people there who might be willing to share food and drinkable water? I may take chances, Kate, but I haven't been stupid."

While she stood there undecided, for all I knew, heavyweight Soviet rockets might've been thundering up from Semipalatinsk—and from Nevada, for that matter. I jazzed the engine. "I asked if you can swim, Kate."

"Damn right," she shot back, and twinkletoed back into my Lotus. "You just make sure I don't have to haul *your* fat ass ashore."

And that was how I chose to spend Doomsday with a beautiful felon.

If I'd had a true unfettered choice, I'd have chosen someone other than Kate Gallo for a nuclear survival companion. And I probably would've chosen worse; Kate was no survivalist, but a born survivor—as I learned. As for Doomsday: you can't split a planet with a few gigatons of explosive, but you can sure doom a lot of its inhabitants.

I muttered something to that effect while keeping the Lotus above small, languid whitecaps in Suisun Bay. Kate Gallo stayed scrunched down, scanning the October sky as if by sheer willpower she could keep it clear of hostile weapons. Halfway across the two-mile stretch of water she showed optimistic colors. "So what do you do with me if this turns out to be a false alarm?"

"Hadn't thought about it," I said, shouting to compete with the fan noises. "Let you give yourself up, maybe, if you can convince me you're through making dumb decisions. But don't count on—oh, *Jeez-us,*" I finished, glancing to my left toward the soaring bridge structure a mile distant.

Near the bridge center, vaulting the rail of concrete and steel, a tiny oblong of four-door sedan climbed aloft, etched on a hard sapphire sky, propelled from behind by a determined eighteen-wheeler. Shards of concrete and metal sparkled. A minuscule firebloom trailed the sedan as it cartwheeled nearly two hundred feet to the water. When the big rig jackknifed, its trailer found the same hole in the rail and (okay, admit it, Rackham) I had the satisfaction of seeing the bully ooze through the gap and begin a one-and-a-half pike into the bay. The rig moved so slowly that I saw its driver, ant-size from my view, leap to the safety of the bridge. However small his chances, they were better than those of anybody a few miles behind him in Oakland.

I guessed that the bridge incident was being multiplied by drivers made mindless by terror from San Jose to Norfolk. We couldn't hear the truck caterwaul past the railing, nor even its splash, and our distance somehow insulated us. In minutes we'd be nosing into the reality of waterfront chaos in Martinez.

The dashboard map display reminded me we'd have to cross one major arterial, then skirt the Concord NavWep station en route to the winding roads near my place. With traffic like we were seeing, those odds had no appeal whatever. Our chances would be better with the bay itself as our conduit—but not if I kept the Lotus's engine near redline for much longer. "Don't worry if you feel water," I called to Kate Gallo, and eased back on the pedal while turning the wheel.

The worry was all mine. I passed under the highway bridge heading up the bay, fully aware that an errant wave could toss a gallon of water into the fan intakes and send us skating like a flat rock; a rock that would disintegrate before it sank, at the speed we were crossing. A dozen big powerboats and twice that many smaller ones crisscrossed the bay, creating a nightmarish chop that slapped our bottom. Twice I heard strangled surges as bits of spray entered the fan intakes. I'd destroyed an off-road Porsche that way once, and my sphincter didn't unpucker until we droned up the mouth of the San Joaquin River.

I took the first boat ramp that wasn't clogged, which was on the outskirts of tatty little Pittsburg, and ignored the outraged yells of folks who were trying to clog it as the Lotus wheels found purchase. We fled from the waterfront, eastward through town, between rows of Pittsburg's down-at-the-heel date palms that, like the tall, rawboned strippers in Vallejo, promised a lot but never put out much.

Kate called to me between gear changes: "Why is the traffic so light here?"

"Just guessing," I replied, "but Pittsburg and Antioch have been small towns so long, they don't realize how near they are to ground zero." I still don't know if that's the right answer. I just know a hell of a lot of nice folks died thinking a nuclear strike was a respecter of city limits.

At the outskirts of Antioch, with the brush-dotted hump of Mount Diablo looming nearly a mile high ahead of us, I turned south and passed wrecks at several intersections before turning onto Lone Tree Way. The power lines hadn't yet fallen across this broad boulevard, but some poor bastard's old highwing Luscombe was hung up like a bat on a clothesline between two highline towers, smoking and sparking as it dribbled molten aluminum ninety feet to the dry grass below. To wrench Kate's attention from the grisly clinkers that jerked in the cockpit, I pointed ahead. "Just past the airport we hit Deer Valley Road. No more towns now." I pulled the phone from under the dash, coded a number, gave the handset to Kate. "I need both hands; this road becomes a gymkhana up ahead. See if you can get through."

"We're not supposed to use the phone," she said. "Your wife?"

"My sister Sharon, in a San Jose suburb. If I'm any judge, she and Ernie and the kids'll be at my place before we are." Which just goes to show I'm a lousy judge.

Relaxing too soon can be suicide. In the years since the '81 depression, when I lucked into some cash and bought my country place, I'd driven the Deer Valley-Marsh Creek route a thousand times—before this always enjoying the extravagant curlicues of two-lane blacktop winding between slopes so steep they hid the major bulk of Mount Diablo. I hadn't met a single car since turning onto the creek road; I knew every ripple on the road shoulder; and I was so near home that I'd begun to worry about Shar, taking my own safety for granted. That was when the old black Lincoln slewed around a blind bend, fishtailing toward us.

My midbrain made its subconscious guess. If we were lucky, the Continental would regain enough traction to lurch back so that we could pass on the shoulder.

We weren't lucky. Neither was he. This was no gimmicked limo with tuned shocks and suspension but your truly classic two-ton turd, and it began to spin at us just past the bend. But a mass that size does everything in slow motion; by the time its overlong rump swung around, my hand was on the fan lever.

The trick to a Cellular's jackrabbit leap is in slapping the gear selector to neutral a split second before you engage the fans, so that all the engine's torque is available to energize those big air impellers inside the body shell. It doesn't halt your forward motion; in fact, removing your tires from macadam, it relinquishes all braking and steering control to the fan vents, so you can't obtain any strong side forces. With fans moaning, we soared over the trunk of the Lincoln by a two-foot margin, only to sideswipe the branches of a pinoak that showered us with twigs as my airborne Lotus tilted and veered back over the road. I kept my foot off the brake, let the fan vents remedy the tilt, chopped back on the impellers and didn't engage third gear until I felt the tires touch the road. After that I kept busy getting through the bend and decided to slow down a bit.

"Aren't we going to stop?" Kate was white-faced, her neck craned backward.

I hadn't risked a backward glance. "What for?"

"He rolled and hit a big sycamore next to the creek!"

I slowed while thinking it over, then let my biases show and pressed on. "If he was driving that kind of fat-cat barge with that kind of disregard," I growled, "the hell with him."

She started to reply, then gave me a judgmental headshake and tried the phone again. But communication lines, like other traffic, had become overloaded to the point of paralysis. When I ducked off the macadam onto the gravel access road to my place, the girl was still trying Shar's number fruitlessly.

I remoted the gate in the cyclone fence surrounding my place as we approached and caught sight of my friend Spot, whose ears could always discriminate between the sounds of my Lotus and any other machine. Kate studied the sign on the eight-foot fence, one of several around my five-acre spread that proclaimed:

CHEETAH ON PATROL

and she gave me a smirk as the gate swung shut behind us. "You don't expect anyone to believe that," she chided.

I drove slowly toward the garage, a partly converted smithy behind the house, and smirked right back. "Just so long as *he* believes it," I said, and jerked my thumb toward her door sill.

Kate's brow furrowed and then she turned and stared full into the dappled half-feline face of Spot, whose lanky stride kept his blunt muzzle almost even with hers. Her whole bod stiffened. Then she faced straight ahead, swallowed convulsively, and slid far down into her seat. Her knuckles on the torso restraint were bone-white, but, tough little bimbo that she was, Kate never whimpered.

I drove into the garage and killed the engine and delivered a long sigh, then traded obligatory ear sniffs with Spot while my head was still level with his. His yellow eyes kept straying to my passenger, more a question than a warning; I rarely brought nonfamily guests to my place. "Company, Spot," I said, and reached over to scratch Kate behind the ear.

She sat rigid. "Does that mean I'm one of your pets, too?"

"It means you're his peer; he'll let you take the first swipe. But Spot's no pet; he's my friend and a damn good watchcat. My Captive Breeding Permit from the Department of the Interior says I own him—but nobody's told *him* that."

"So how do I behave? No sudden moves?" I caught the tremor in her voice.

"Neither of us could possibly make a move he'd consider sudden," I said, and proved it by pushing my door aside abruptly. Spot, of course, pulled back untouched as I grunted my way out of the Lotus and waved for Kate to do the same.

But: "Don't leopards turn against people sometimes?"

"I wouldn't know. Spot isn't a leopard; he's a male cheetah in his prime and he stays healthy on farina mix and horsemeat. He's the nearest thing to a link between cats and dogs; his claws aren't fully retractile and he wasn't born with the usual feline hunting instincts. Even has coarse hair like a dog, as you'll find out when you pat him."

"Fat chance." At least she was getting out of the car.

"Or you can panic and run wild and wave your arms and scream," I said, "and he'll frisk circles around you and laugh at the funny lady. Come on, I need to check my incoming messages," I added, and let them both follow me to the tunnel while she stared at my house.

My white clapboard two-story house, I told her, was a basket case when I bought it. I reroofed it, then found myself shopping for antique wallpaper patterns and reflectors for kerosene lamps, and ended with an outlay of fifty thou and two hundred gallons of sweat only when the house was furnished à la 1910 from the foundation up. The basement and part of the old smithy were something else again: you can't maintain a Cellular, or an automated cheetah feeder, or a bounty hunter's hardware, amid dust and mildew.

I led Kate past gray shreds of wooden doors that led to my root cellar. The doors lay agape on an earth mound, flanking the dark stairs fifty feet from my back door. "Let there be light," I said on the stairs, and there was light. I could've said "Keep it dark," and the tunnel lights would've come on anyway. It was my voiceprint, and Shar's and Ern's, that the system reacted to. It didn't recognize Spot's sound effects. For all his wolfen ways, Spot had a purr like God's stomach rumbling. Plus a dozen other calls, from a tabby's meow to yips and even a ludicrous birdy chirp.

Kate Gallo negotiated the turn behind me. "Curiouser and curiouser, cried Alice," she gibed. "I can't decide whether you're behind the times or ahead of 'em, Mr. Rackham."

It was my turn to register surprise, and I stopped. So did she. "You didn't lift my wallet, so how'd you know my name?"

"You told me."

I merely shook my head, very slowly. Smiling.

"Okay, if your ego needs stroking: most people on the scam in the Bay Area know about you. You're seven feet tall and weigh four hundred pounds and leap tall buildings, et cetera, and inside that rough exterior beats a heart of pure granite. You've got no friends, no family, no home, and anybody who tries to negotiate with you had better do it with silver bullets. I suspect you invented some of that crap yourself. Satisfied?"

"Eminently," I said and laughed. "So why didn't you peel off when you first saw me?"

"Lots of fa—uh, heavyset men around," she amended, glancing at my backlit paneling. "Let's just say I'm stupid."

"Not me. You've suckered too many bright solid citizens into the badger game for me to make that mistake, Kate." She just grinned an impudent grin and, for good measure, deliberately laid her hand on Spot's patient head. I pressed on: "I know your family has money. Why'd you do it?"

"*Because* of my family—and because I damn well like making men squirm. If you knew my mother you wouldn't have to ask."

I nodded. Raised in a strict household where females were expected to keep the Sabbath holy, the pasta tender, and the men on pedestals, Kate Gallo had learned too much about the rest of the world; had cast aside her illusions and her virginity before reflecting that both had their good points; had decided she would make the system pay. And men ran the system, so-o-o. . . . "Ever meet a male who didn't undervalue your gender?" I asked.

"A few."

"Well, you've just met another one. Two, if you count him," I said, nodding at Spot. Who just sat there with his tongue showing in a doggy leer. "Time's awasting, Kate; and quit laughing, you skinny sonofabitch," I said to Spot.

Long before I'd asked Ern McKay to critique my ideas on "the place"—we seldom called my fenced homestead anything else. With twenty years at NASA's Ames wind tunnel in the south Bay Area, master modeler Ernest McKay was what the Navy called a mustang engineer; no degree, but bagsful of expertise. Ern had taught me about parsimony, i.e., keeping it simple. Why require two codes for my tunnel lights and basement door lock when a unique voiceprint was the key to both functions? It was my idea to hang the steel-faced door into my underground office so that gravity swung it open, and Ern's dictum to avoid an automatic door closer. That would've required a selenium cell, pressure plate, or capacitance switch—all fallible—when all I needed, quoth ol' Ern, was a handle. While helping me convert a basement into a livable modern apartment and office, Ern had briefed me on a lot of NASA's design philosophy.

The result was a subterranean Bauhaus living area without many partitions, where everything worked with a minimum of bells and whistles—and when something didn't work, like a clogged drain, it was easy to get at. You can carp all you like about exposed, color-coded conduits, but I liked knowing which plastic pipes were air vents and which one led from my basement john to my septic tank down the hill. *You* guess which was painted a rich brown.

Kate Gallo stepped onto the linolamat of my office and gawked while I heaved the door shut. "Up those stairs"—I pointed to the freestanding steel steps that melded into old-fashioned wooden stairs halfway up—"is the kitchen, and just off the kitchen is a screen porch. Grab the antique galvanized tub off the porch wall and all the pans in the kitchen, bring 'em down here to the john, and fill 'em with water."

I strode around the apartment divider, a rough masonry interior wall that served as a central crossbeam under the floor above, grabbed my remotable comm system handset from my computer carrel, and headed for the john while querying for incoming messages. In the back of my head was envy for Kate, who was evidently slender enough that she didn't make those top stairs squeak on her way upstairs.

The first message was from a bail bondsman, who assured me positively that Kate Gallo had run to Sacramento. I muttered an anatomical instruction for him under my breath while readying my oversize bathtub for filling; started back to my office as the second message pinged; stopped dead as I saw why Signorina Katerina hadn't made squeaky music on my stairs. She was still standing on my linolamat, arms crossed in defiance. We traded hard stares as the message began, and Spot's ears twitched in recognition of the voice from my speaker.

"We're on the way, Harve, at—uh, eleven fifteen or so. Ernie and Cammie are putting bikes in the vanwagon and Lance is clearing out the freezer. I dumped our medicines and toilet things into a box and I'm checking off everything, and we'll take the Livermore route to avoid freewayitis. In case you haven't heard, Ernie says tell you somebody at Ames got word from Satellite Test Center at Lockheed: they're monitoring evacuation out of Leningrad and Moscow . . ."

Then we caught part of a McKay tradition in the background, young Lance throwing one of his patented tantrums. " . . . but he's not taking mine and he *knows* I gotta have it, he can fix it, I know it, Iknowitiknowit—" and then a slam of something. I knew it wasn't the impact of Shar's palm on Lance's butt; that was beyond reasonable hope.

My sis again: "Poor Lance, his bike is broken so he's been using Cammie's in spite of everything we've—well, Ernie isn't packing it so of course the child is broken up," she went on quickly, ending with a breezy, "Well, we'll cope. We always do. Oh! You said to be specific, so: we're taking Route Six-Eighty toward Livermore, then the old Morgan Road to your place. Don't worry, bubba, we should be at your place by three pee-em unless we have to fire the second-stage. Coming, hon," she called to someone, and then the line went dead.

"Poor Lance," I snarled, tossing my handset control and

catching it instead of hurling it against a wall. "Little bastard beats the bejeezus out of his bike, too lazy to fix it, and now that he realizes why Ern nagged him to keep it in shape it's too late, so he takes his frustration out on everybody else. And why the fuck aren't you collecting water containers," I shot at Kate.

"Because the fuck," she said, sweetly enunciating it to extract its maximum gross-out potential, "I didn't relish being ordered around like a servant. What was all that stuff in the garage about peers, mister?"

I took two long breaths; stared at my reproduction of Bierstadt's *Rocky Mountains* near the stairwell for solace. "I believe I said you're Spot's peer, Kate. Not a pet but a working part. He keeps the place free of swagmen and rabbits, and if he didn't, he wouldn't have any place here. I'll be as democratic as I can—which means not very, when it's my place and I know the drill and you don't, and since there has to be a leader it is going to be the one who knows what must be done.

"That was my sister Shar, on tape. They're two hours late and I don't like wondering why, and if you think I'm stuck with you here, you should know that you are exactly one more smart-ass refusal away from getting tossed over my cyclone fence." My one office window gave me a view of Mount Diablo and, reluctantly, I cranked its wire-reinforced outer panels closed. I hated the thought of shoveling dirt against those panels, since it would block off the only natural light into my basement. But that was part of the original drill we'd worked out long ago, after Shar inexplicably signed up for an urban survival course at a community college.

I went back to the john and shut off the water, painfully aware that I'd given the girl a galling choice; also aware that I meant every word. When I glanced at her again she had aged astonishingly, arms hanging loosely, no longer the pert rebel—maybe ever again. "All right," she choked, and went up the stairs. "You know I don't have any choice."

Following her, I said, "Neither do I. I hope you can be part of the solution, Kate—and I can't afford you as part of my problem. Cheer up, kid, maybe this is all just—"

"Please," she said, looking around her at my turn-of-the-century kitchen, "just leave me alone. Please?" Then, spotting the squat bulk of my cast-iron wood stove, she allowed a piece of a chuckle to escape as she passed it. "Boy, you are really weird—don't do that," she added suddenly.

I removed the hand I'd put on her shoulder, intending to convey something—hope, camaraderie, understanding; hell, I don't know what—but obviously I *didn't* understand her. "Right," I mumbled, and sloped outside to get a shovel. Swinging up in a long arc from Travis AFB was one of our new heavies under rocket boost. I heard several more while digging, and while I didn't stop to watch them, I wondered what they were up to. I don't wonder anymore.

Working up a fast sweat, I shoveled a ramp of turf against my office window until it almost matched the slope of the earthen ramp that surrounded the house about to the level of the first floor. I tried not to tally the minutes by which Shar and Ern and the kids were overdue. The tally came unbidden, since it was nearly five pee-em, two hours past Shar's estimate. Muted thunks and sloshes reached me as Kate filled my kitchenware with water. I was ruminating along the lines of, *Even if this false alarm costs a thousand lives, it may eventually save fifty million,* when a vast white light filled the sky, more pitiless than any summer noon, and did not fade for many seconds.

In my hurry, I hadn't followed my own drill; hadn't kept two radios tuned to different stations; and so I didn't hear the President's brief, self-serving spiel that called for crisis relocation and, by implication, admitted that we could expect a "limited" nuclear response to the tactical weapons we were unleashing on the wave of Soviet tanks that had lashed across the border into West Germany. "Crisis relocation" was an old weasel phrase for "evacuation"; our Office of Technology Assessment and think-tanks like the Hudson Institute had solemnly agreed that Americans would have between twenty-four and seventy-two hours of warning before any crisis developed into a nuclear exchange.

Actually, from the moment our Navy engaged Russkis in the Aegean until the first wave of nuke-tipped MIRVs streaked up from Soviet hard sites, we'd had about fifteen hours. It might've been halfway adequate if we'd planned for it as Soviet-bloc countries had done—or even as one solitary local government had done in Lane County, Oregon.

Everybody joked about the jog-crazy, mist-maddened tokers around the University of Oregon in Eugene, so the media had its fun upon learning that city and county officials there were serious about evac—I mean, crisis relocation. Some poly sci professor, in a lecture about legal diversion of funds, pointed out that most federal funding for crisis relocation was turned over to emergency-services groups in sheriffs' departments. And that those funds—all over the country, not just in Oregon—were being diverted by perfectly legal means to other uses. The overall plan for a quarter-million people in the Eugene area was orderly movement to the touristy strip along the coast.

Then an undergrad checked out the routes and nervously reported that the wildest optimist wouldn't believe that many people could drive out of firestorm range in two days' time through a bottleneck consisting of a solitary two-lane highway and a pair of unimproved hold-your-breath gravel roads. County maps showed several more old roads. They hadn't existed for thirty years.

Firestorm in Eugene bloody *Orygun*? A strong possibility, since the Southern Pacific's main switching yards in the coastal Northwest sprawled out along the little city's outskirts. No prime target, certainly, but all too likely as a secondary or tertiary strike victim. In a county commission meeting, some citizen asked, Why worry? We'll just get on the capacious Interstate 5 freeway and drive south.

The hell you will, replied a state patrol official. We have orders to keep that corridor clear for special traffic running south from Portland and the state capital. There'll be riot guns at the barricades; sorry 'bout that, but Eugeneans were scheduled to the coast and if they didn't like that, they could stay home and watch the firestorm from inside it, har har.

When local politicos realized how many feisty folks in the Eugene-Springfield area were clamoring for a solution, one of them hit on a rationale that couldn't be faulted. Eugene could be a target because the railroad had such tremendous load-carrying capacity, right?

Right. And SP's rolling stock, flatcars for milled lumber and boxcars slated for Portland and Seattle, often sat waiting on sidings all over the place, right?

Right. And the SP had a branch railway straight to the coast and a small yard for turnarounds only two hours away by slow freight. A hastily assembled train could haul fifty thousand people and all the survival gear each could lift from Eugene in a single trip, then return for more.

And that was right, too. With public subscriptions helping to fund their studies, SP troubleshooters found that they could make up such a train in about twelve hours. They even tried it once, billed as an outing for subscribers who'd paid SP to do the groundwork, and though two drunks were injured falling off a flatcar, it made a lighthearted tag end to the eleven o'clock news across the nation. That had been two years ago.

Eugene's solitary preparations flashed through my head as, groveling flat on my belly, shouting into the eerie silence and seemingly endless flashbulb glare, I protected my eyes and called to Kate to do the same. I'd always thought an enemy would choose, as ground zero, the Alameda naval facility to my west. Ern had said STC, the satellite control nexus south of me in Sunnyvale, would be the spot. Occasional news pieces had suggested Travis AFB, a reactivated base twenty-five miles north of me; or Hamilton AFB, thirty-five miles northeast.

And we were all absolutely correct. The ghastly efficiency of a MIRV lay in each big missile's handful of warheads, and each warhead could be aimed at a different target. Travis disappeared in a ground burst, perhaps to take out our bombers and deep-stored nukes there. That was the deadly flower that blossomed first in hellish silence over the hills north of my place. The others were only moments behind.

When the light through my eyelids dwindled to something like normal afternoon brightness, I heaved myself up and pounded back into the house. On my way downstairs I saw my dining room wallpaper reflect another actinic dazzle from the windows, coming from the low airburst over Hamilton to our west. The fluorescents in my office below seemed pale for a moment. "Come on," I called, unable to find Kate. "Our best protection is in the tunnel!"

She rolled from beneath my desk; yelped, "Don't *do* that," as Spot darted ahead of her while *she* was darting ahead of *me.* I shut the big door, slapping the light plate to keep the tunnel lit, and sat down on the tough yielding linolamat.

"Spot, come," I said as his languid trot carried him toward the root cellar entrance. Another burst of energy lit the root cellar from the distant entrance, making Spot wheel back quickly.

"That's three," I said. But I was wrong, having missed the light show of Alameda's airburst. We were seeing cloud reflections of the ground-pounder that took out Sunnyvale, Palo Alto, and much of San Jose.

In a very small voice Kate said, "The air is bad in here," and slumped against the wall. Spot nuzzled her ear as I got down on one knee and propped her into a sitting position.

Her breath was quick and shallow, pulse racing but strong, and Spot wasn't sneezing or showing any of the discomfort he shows in foul air. She wasn't shocky cold either, and suddenly I realized she'd been hyperventilating—not the deliberate deep whiffs of a free diver but the slow oxygen starvation you could experience when quiet panic and rigid self-control made a battleground of your hindbrain. "Head between your knees, Kate," I murmured to her trembles. "Try breathing slowly; all the way out, then all the way in."

At that moment a sharp rumble whacked the house and my ears, not very hard. But a softer rumble continued for what seemed a full minute; the Travis shock wave and its retinue of thunders. Spot's white-tipped tail flicked, his ears at half-mast. He showed his teeth in a hiss at the doorjamb, which was buzzing in sympathy with a vibration that shook the earth remorselessly.

When the second shock came it hit sharply, with a clatter of my fine Bavarian china as obbligato upstairs.

The third jolt hit five seconds later, the one from Alameda. A freak shock front raced through Concord, making lethal Frisbees of every glass pane and marble false-front in town. My western windows blew in and, with a pistol's report, one of my sturdy old roof beams ended nearly a century of usefulness. My ears popped with a faint pressure change; popped again. I could hear bricks falling from my chimney onto the roof, sliding off, but couldn't at first identify the snap-crack that came more and more rapidly until it became a guttural rising groan. It had to be my handsome old water tower, though, because that was what toppled near my kitchen, splintering porch stairs as it struck.

My electric pump was probably whining furiously to refill it, but I couldn't shut it off right then, thanks. The tank, strap-bound like a wine cask, had held several hundred gallons of water twenty feet in the air for gravity flow—probably the only overloaded structure on my place.

Well, it was overloaded no longer. One of Ern's old NASA bromides was that highly stressed structures have a way of unstressing themselves for you—but wouldn't you really rather do it yourself?

The last shock wave, from Sunnyvale near San Jose, was almost negligible for us in the lee of Mount Diablo. I tried to recall the crucial time sequences: the initial long flash that distributed heat and hard radiation at the speed of light and could have temporarily flash-blinded me if I'd had a line-of-sight view of the initial moment; the shock waves, one through the ground and a slower one through air that pulverized concrete near ground zero; a momentary underpressure a moment later near the blast that could suck lungs or houses apart: another machwave that could flatten a forest or a skyscraper. Fires and cave-ins were my most likely failure modes during those first long moments. If we came through all that alive, *then* it was time to worry about the fallout that could destroy live tissue through a brick wall.

Yet Shar's classroom work had taught us something vital, something most of the doomsday books ignored: *if you were twenty miles or so from ground zero, you got several hours of "king's X" between blast and fallout.*

My tunnel lights were still on, and we hadn't felt any suction after the blast waves. That suggested the nearest detonation had been many miles distant. According to Shar's texts, the fallout of deadly radioactive ash and grit moved upward into the stem of the mushroom cloud to an altitude of several miles within ten minutes, then more slowly upward and laterally with the wind. Usually the wind speed was fifteen to forty miles an hour. While it was cooling, the stuff fell heavily from the mushroom cloud, which, at first, moved laterally at great speed. But if you were directly beneath that initial cloud you would've already taken enough thermal and shock damage so that only a miracle or a deep, hermetically sealed hideyhole would've made it of any interest to you.

I didn't know where the blasts had occurred. If they had been more than fifteen miles away, I'd probably have a few hours in which to assess damage, fight fires, or pray before the slowly descending ashfall dropped several miles downward to begin frying everything it fell on.

Kate seemed to be improving. "We made it through the first round," I told her, huffing to my feet: "Now we've gotta make sure the place isn't burning up or falling down. You up to it?"

Her olive skin was sallow but, "We'll know if I keel over," she said, and let me help her up.

I led her back to my office, touched my liquor cabinet where I'd hidden the detent, swung back the bottle-laden shelf. I fingered the detent for her to see. "Just a simple pressure latch. Always keep it shut when you're not using what's in here. And never pick up anything you don't know how to use."

"*Jesu bambino,*" she breathed, goggling at the tools of my trade: "I thought alcohol and firearms didn't mix. Is all that stuff legal?"

"Perfectly," I lied, and pointed out the few things she might need. "Malonitrile spray up here—better than Mace; the target pistol over here, the twenty-two longs for its magazine down there," I pointed among the ammo boxes. The extra sunglasses and thin leather gloves were self-explanatory. I'm always losing the damn things so I keep a dozen pairs of each on hand.

"What on earth is that thing in the middle, a cannon?"

"Near enough," I grunted, swinging the liquor shelf back. She'd seen my heavyweight, the sawed-off twelve-gauge auto shotgun with two pistol grips and a vertical magazine as thick as a two-by-four. That fat magazine held sixteen cartridges filled with double-ought buckshot, and the thoroughly illegal twelve-inch barrel fired a pattern that couldn't miss at ten yards. I could also hide it inside a coat front. Frankly, I didn't like the thing and had flashed it only once, at a man whose own emm-oh included concealable shotguns. He had just blinked and then had gone down on his face without a word. "That's one of the gadgets you *don't* want to pick up," I told her. "If you weigh under two hundred pounds it'll knock you on your can."

"I'll take your word for it." She put on her glasses and we went upstairs.

I first studied the kitchen ceiling and walls, which showed no cracks or wrinkles, and then bobbed my head up to window level for a fast glance outside, taking care with the splinters of glass on the floor. I saw nothing unusual, but the nearby hills impeded my view. "Sweep up this stuff before it dices us, will you?" I crunched my way into the spacious old dining room, mourning the shambles where window glass had speared into my glass-fronted china cabinet. The living room seemed undamaged and I saw no sign of danger through the intact multipaned north and east windows. The parlor windows had held, too. They revealed a sky innocent of intent to kill. I took the stairs two at a time to check on the second floor.

My first glance out the splinter-framed bathroom window upstairs made me duck by reflex action. Boiling into the stratosphere many miles north, an enormous dirty ball of cloud writhed on the skyline above my neighboring hilltops, showing streaks of red, like blood oozing out through crevices in burned fat. I risked another look; realized the target had been either the old mothball fleet anchored in Suisun Bay or Travis AFB, twice as far away. For all its agonized motion, the top of that cloud did not seem to be climbing very quickly, but from all reports it *had* to be. That meant it must be twenty miles or so away from us, and the prevailing winds were west to east. That hideous maelstrom of consumed rock and organic matter—including ash that had been trees, homes, human flesh—would scatter downwind for hundreds of miles but might miss us entirely. Given a direction and approximate distance, I knew the target had been Travis.

In retrospect I keep juggling ideas about preparation and luck. The Travis bomb was a ground-pounder which vaporized a million tons of dirt and, irradiating it in the cloud stem, lifted it to be flung in a lethal plume beyond Sacramento into the Sierra. Bad luck for anyone in that plume, my good luck to be out of its path. Nor could I have affected some Russki decision to kill Hamilton AFB and Alameda with low airbursts, which started vast firestorms but scooped up relatively little debris to add to their fallout plumes. From my view, that was all luck.

Yet our understanding wasn't luck; it was the result of Shar's classwork and Ern's inside knowledge. I knew it was likely that a ground-pounder was more likely to be used against hardened targets: missile silos, underground munitions, control centers under concrete and bedrock. And I knew what else I needed to find out, such as the locations of those other detonations and the extent of the damage to my roof. I climbed the attic stairs, pushed the door aside, and let my flashbeam play across an immediate problem.

My central roof beam, a rough-sawn timber supported by A-frames, had buckled halfway between its slanting supports. No telling how soon it might completely collapse without a jury-rigged support, but I couldn't see light through the roof and wanted it to stay that way. An intact roof would keep fallout particles from drifting down into the attic—a little more distance between our heads and hard radiation. I had laid fiberglass batts between the attic joists for insulation, but it wasn't much protection against fallout; too fluffy and porous.

I called for Kate to accompany me and puffed out to the garage, pausing on the screen porch to snap the circuit breaker to my water pump. The garage and smithy hadn't come through unscathed. A pressure wave had slanted the clapboard west wall, taking the window out. I had two things in mind: checking for damage to the structure lest it fall on the Lotus, and collecting tools to dismantle the child's swing set I'd erected outside, years before, for Cammie and Lance. The tubular A-frame of the swing set was rusty but ideal for propping up that broken beam in my attic. Now a dozen other problems intervened, each clamoring for top priority.

I stopped and looked around, breathing hard. Some things Kate could do alone—I hoped. But she didn't know where I kept my tools, so I'd have to collect things. Rummaging for my necessaries, I explained. "Kate, in the root cellar are two rolls of clear polyethylene wrap, about knee-high, the kind of plastic you can unwrap and nail over broken windows. It may have a brand name on it—Visqueen, I think. One roll is two-mil—uh, too flimsy. Get the ten-mil stuff and haul it out here. It's eight feet wide when you unfold it. Cut a piece and stretch it across outside this broken window, and then do the same on all the house windows, upstairs and down, okay?"

She was already sprinting for the root cellar. I found the short, big-headed roofing nails and hammer, placed snips next to them, then snatched up penetrating oil, wrenches, and my other hammer and hauled my freight into the yard. I met Kate on the way, toting her milk-white roll of plastic film. I pointed to her tools and then attacked the swing set's rusty bolts with oil.

Kate looked into the sky—wishing, I supposed, for an umbrella. "Why not nail the plastic over the windows from the inside?" she asked.

"Makes a better seal on the outside," I hollered, more snappish than I intended. "You're trying to keep the wind from blowing tiny particles of radioactive ash indoors. If a breeze slaps a plastic sheet that's on the outside, it'll only make the edges hug tighter instead of bulging open between the nails."

I found it hard to explain one thing while doing another, and it made me clumsy. Naturally I ripped my sleeve while detaching the chains of the two little swings. It occurred to me that those sturdy chains could serve as guy wires if I drove nails into the links, so I piled the chains where I wouldn't forget. And forgot. One bolt hung up, and I was in the act of swinging the hammer when I recalled that if I put one little dent in the tube, most of its stiffness would be lost. I managed to ease the blow, and with that, the whole tubular framework squealed and collapsed, and I bundled the pieces so I could carry them over my shoulders.

Kate was spacing her nails only at the corners. "You need a nail head every six inches," I shouted.

"I've been thinking about the way people use this stuff on unfinished houses," she called back. "They nail strips of wood all the way around the edges."

She was right. "I don't have any furring strips," I began, then remembered. "Yes I do! Some old strips of wooden molding on the floor against the smithy wall. Break 'em up as you need 'em and go to it! If you need more, just—just use the hammer's claw and pull the molding loose in the rooms upstairs." That hurt; I'd mashed many a finger installing the stuff. I carried the tubing up to the attic, wondering how much of my place we'd have to cannibalize while securing its basement.

In my haste I'd removed bolts I hadn't needed to remove, wasting time instead of thinking it through. It was hot work in the attic without much light, and only when I'd reassembled the A-frames did I notice that they were too long by a foot. And I'd need those chains, and big twenty-penny nails to help anchor the tubular legs and the chains. What I needed most was another set of hands and a heaping dose of calm. I was starting to act suspiciously like a panic-stricken klutz.

Okay, so I might have to cut the ends of the tubes off. My list of hardware lengthened: swings with chains attached, hacksaw, nails, battery-powered lamp (my three-way emergency flasher from the Lotus would do), and stubs of two-by-four. If the steel A-frames simply didn't work, I might have to break into an upstairs interior wall for wooden supports. That meant I'd need a pry-bar and wood saw. Dashing downstairs and outside, I called to Kate: "Great; neater than I'd have done it!" She had woman-handled my telescoping ladder from the garage and was stretching a sheet of poly film across my kitchen window.

I dumped trash from a hefty cardboard box in the garage; placed nails, pry-bar, and saws inside; then simply swept an array of hand tools from their places over my workbench and added them to the load. I grabbed my flasher lamp from the Lotus and grinned in spite of everything as Spot plopped down in the passenger seat with a little falsetto yawp. It was his way of begging a ride. Poor fool cat, he was infected by all this hurry and could think of nothing more exciting than a nice little rip down the road. Which was the last thing in the world I intended to do. Or was it?

"Sorry, fella," I told him, returning with the box to get the chains. Kate was trying to lengthen the ladder, having finished with the broken first-floor windows. I parked my load on the screen porch and helped her.

"I'll have to steal that molding upstairs," she said, hoisting her shoulder bag by its sling. Bright girl: she'd dumped her bag and used it now to tote hammer and nails up the ladder. The scissors she was using to slit the plastic weren't mine; a matched set of stilettos so sharp she didn't need to snip with them. I wondered how near I'd been to getting them between my ribs earlier in the day, then thought again about her ability to fend for herself. Kate was street-smart; more so than my sis and her family.

"Kate, it's five thirty, roughly a half-hour since the bombs. More could hit any minute and you know where to take cover if they do. Judging by those clouds," I stabbed a finger to the west, then north, "we may have only a few hours before fine gritty ash starts falling here."

"Tell me later," she grunted with another fine leg show as she leaned out to my upstairs bathroom window.

"I may not be here later." She stopped, frowned down at me, her brows asking her question, so I answered it. "I intended to bring all my tools and stored fuel from the garage to the tunnel, but I can't do that and check on my sis, too. If I hadn't listened to Shar, I wouldn't be any better prepared for this than your average bozo. Her family is somewhere out there," I nodded at the southern skyline, "and you can see parts of the road from where I'm going. Believe me, I intend to be back soon, but I've got to do this. I've *got* to," I repeated as though arguing with somebody, which I was: my own sense of self-preservation. I started to give her more instructions but there would be no end to them, so I shut my trap and turned away toward the garage.

"It's only fair to tell you," she called after me. "When I lock myself up in that basement without you, it won't be with a full-grown cheetah."

A clutch of scenarios fled past me as I headed for the garage with Spot at my side. Each scene led to some innocent act on Kate's part that would cause Spot to show her a modest warning. Not that his threats are loud, as big cats go, but a raised ruff and an ears-back show of *his* front scissors will scare the piss out of a Doberman pinscher. Who would blame Kate for unlimbering my target pistol against him the instant his spinal ridge fur came erect?

For that matter, I wasn't sure how well Spot could accept a week of confinement, and I worried about that as I fired up the Lotus and eased it from the garage. I told Spot to stay, sizzled toward the closed gate, then shouted, "Spot: *come,*" before engaging the fans to leap the fence. I was twenty yards ahead of him when I called out. Would you believe the lanky bugger beat my Cellular over an eight-foot fence?

It had been a silly stunt, I saw, as Spot's half-canine claws raked the paint of my rear deck. But I was only doing thirty-five at the moment—half-speed for him across open ground. Spot scrabbled into the seat and placed a forepaw against the dash, settling his chin onto the door sill, sniffing the air. I hurled the Lotus along an access path leading to the fire lane up the mountain.

Every few years a brush fire proved the wisdom of fire lanes, bulldozed paths along ridge tops that cleared away brush and grass as a barrier against wildfire. A four-wheel-drive vehicle or a ground-effects car like my Cellular could follow a fire lane all the way to the top, if you avoided the occasional boulder. And the new obstacles that I should've counted on, but hadn't. People.

For the first five minutes I had to dodge only a farmer and his cream-yellow Charolais cattle along the lower slopes. The man didn't even disfavor me with a glance. Whatever errand took me over his property, the responsibility for his dairy herd made him single-minded. I hoped he could keep them all under a roof for many days since (Shar had told me) cattle and dogs aren't as resistant to radiation as, say, swine and poultry.

Then a middle-aged man passed me on a scrambler bike at a suicidal pace, bounding down from the fire lane. Jesus, but he was good! The *burrrp* and *snarlll* of his engine vied with my Lotus for only a moment, making me realize how much noise I was making on my way up. Spot's senses beggared mine; the quick jerk of his head revealed a young fellow who was evidently prying debris from the drive chain of his bike. Then a girl Kate's age slithered and slewed downhill on a trail motorbike, hair flying, riding point for a half-dozen others who were taking their half of the fire lane right down the middle. I like to think it was a family making good on their preparations for urban disaster. I didn't enjoy taking evasive action, but I couldn't expect amateur bikers to maintain much control down such a grade.

The first lone hiker I spied was trying to blend into the scrub, a biker's leather pack slung from one shoulder, his right hand thrust into it as he watched me pass. No doubt he'd heard me coming, and if he'd had more time, I suspect I'd have seen a handgun. Pure defense? A 'jacking? He probably couldn't have controlled the Lotus in ground-effects mode, but when a man's eyes are as wild as his were, you can't expect him to give a whole lot of thought to his actions. More bikers appeared on my skyline, bobbing toward me; then a few single hikers, all with small packs or none at all. I wondered why until I saw the logic of it.

On the other side of the ridge top lay the entire south and east Bay Areas, a series of forested ridges becoming rolling open meadows with farms and, in the valleys, bedroom communities: San Ramon, Danville, Dublin, Pleasanton. To the southwest stretched Oakland and other big population centers that would be feeding terrified throngs into the imagined safety of the hills. The vast nuclear hammer blows had struck forty minutes before—any people fleeing up the highland roads might've abandoned the roads when the great shocks came, especially those who were most highly mobile. And nothing but a baja-rigged sportscar was as mobile as a tough lightweight scrambler bike. No wonder the first wave of evacuees down the fire lane consisted almost wholly of bikers!

More bikers passed. One bike lay in the edge of the scrub, its front wheel fork ruined, and I guessed that the guy who was afoot with the saddlebag and the frightened eyes had abandoned it. Then Spot's attention drew mine to tiny figures that bobbed across open heights; people afoot who had abandoned the fire lane, perhaps fearful of the onrushing bikers. I saw a half-dozen of them in the next few minutes, one squatting over another who lay face-down. I couldn't tell if it was a mugging, but in my work you tend to infer the worst and I figured the rough stuff was only beginning among people who would need each other damned soon.

I topped out on the last ridge near state park property, staring down to locate the road from Livermore, then let my gaze sweep to the cities along San Francisco Bay. I said, "Oh—my—God."

Parking the car just off the fire lane, I made Spot stay as my sentry, retrieving the snub-nose little piece I kept clipped under the dash with its cutaway holster. Twenty miles away, where Oakland fronts the bay, was—had been—Alameda. Now the entire region, miles across, lay half-obscured under a gray pall like dirty fog. Winking through it were literally thousands of fires, some of them running together by now. Black plumes roiled up from oil storage dumps, and as I watched, a white star glared in the bay, hurling debris up and away in all directions. Even faster than the debris, flying away in what seemed a mathematically precise pattern, a ghostly shock wave expanded through the smoke, fading as it spread from its epicenter. In the paths of the debris, spidery white traceries of smoke fattened into a snowy mile-wide chrysanthemum that hid the source of that mighty blast. It looked like one of the old phosphorus shells from an earlier war, but an incredibly enormous one. I guessed it had been a shipload of munitions.

All the smoke over Oakland seemed drawn toward Alameda; in fact, sucked toward the broad foot of the smoke column we'd been taught to call a mushroom cloud. But this mushroom had a ring around it and several heads, the top one so unimaginably high that it seemed nearly above me. The mind-numbing quantity of energy released by that airburst had heated every square inch below it so that the very earth, like incandescent lava, heated the surrounding air and triggered leviathan updrafts that fed the stem of the cloud. I was watching a city consumed by fire, the updrafts creating winds that howled across skeletal buildings and fed flames that would rage until nothing burnable remained.

Nothing could live in or under that hellish heat unless far down in some airtight subbasement. Even after everything on the surface was consumed, the heat, baking down into the earth below fried macadam, would linger for many hours to slowly cook the juices from any organic tissue that might have somehow survived the first hour of firestorm. In a few hours there would not be a child—a tree root—an amoeba—living within miles of ground zero.

Far to the south another deadly column climbed through the stratosphere. Its shape was different, its pedestal and ring of smoke broader, with one well-defined globular head that was beginning to topple, so it seemed, eastward, blown by prevailing high-altitude winds. I wondered if any USAF personnel had bunkers in Sunnyvale deep enough to live through that ground-level wallop. The firestorm raging into San Jose was too distant for me to see flames, but the smoke suggested low-level winds blowing east to west toward Sunnyvale.

Nearer to me, some traffic moved, but for the most part the arterials were simply clotted into stagnation. A faint boom, horn bleats, and beneath it a soft whispering rumble told me of a million lethal scenes being played out below me against a backdrop of Armageddon. A pair of bikes *braapped* past me fifty yards off, and a dozen hikers labored up the slopes, reminding me of a crowd straggling away from the site of some vast sporting event after the fun was all over.

Short stretches of Morgan Road were visible from a promontory some distance away, and I turned to get my stubby 7-by-50 monocular from the glove box only to see a man in a half-crouch trading eye contact with Spot. He hadn't seen me. The man wore a business suit and expensive shoes and he was motionless except for his right hand, which was drawing a medium-caliber automatic, very slowly, from a hip pocket.

"I wouldn't," I said. He jerked his head around, saw me holding my little .38 in approved two-handed police stance, and wisely decided that he wouldn't, either. "Just put it back in your pocket, Jasper, and don't look back. I don't want to kill you—but I don't much want *not* to at the moment."

The handgun disappeared. He tried to smile but his sweat-streaked face wanted to cry instead. "Lotus and cheetah," he enumerated, licking dust-caked lips. "I know you. Can't recall the name, but word gets around. My name's Hollinger; I'm an attorney." And I will be damned if he didn't two-finger a little embossed card from his vest!

I ignored it, watching his hands as I moved to the car and fumbled for my gadgetry. "I haven't time to chat and neither do you, Mr. Hollinger." I waved him away with the revolver as I came up with the monocular, not wanting him near while I peered through it.

"Look, my car's two miles back, on the shoulder. No fuel. Cadillac. I'll sign it over to you for a lift to Santa Rosa."

I chuckled. "Tried to sandbag us, and now you want to plea-bargain. You're a lawyer, all right." I motioned him away.

He wasn't used to summary judgments. "The emerald in this ring is worth five big ones, buddy. It's yours for a lift. You won't get many offers this good."

"In two weeks there may be emeralds available for anybody who likes 'em. God Almighty couldn't get you to Santa Rosa right now; you waited too long. Put the fucking ring in your pocket, stay off the fire lanes, and look for shelter in Antioch." He crossed his arms, threw his head back, and inhaled. "Or I can put you out of your misery right now because you're starting to bug me," I finished, thumbing the hammer.

He turned and ran; limping, cursing, and sobbing, ignoring my free advice. I scratched Spot between the ears as I watched the man scramble down, and stuck my convincer away as a fortyish couple approached. They were both rangy, with small scruffy-looking packs, Aussie hats, and high-top hiking boots; and the man saluted me casually as they passed. They didn't seem panicky and their faces were weathered from many a day in the open. They weren't breathing as hard as I was and I was glad for them, hoping they could translate their readiness into long-term survival. If only Shar and Ern had kept up their daily two-mile runs—one of the many fads she'd badgered him into during the past years—I'd have felt more confident about them. Now, they were probably somewhere below me to the southwest, waiting for a road to unclog or pedaling their second-stage vehicles, or maybe lying in a ditch with bullets in their heads while some business-suited opportunist pedaled away with their survival packs.

I knew my kinfolk; they'd all reach me together or not at all. Scanning the road, I saw that something had blocked it in one of the ravines beyond my view, for a solid line of traffic formed a chain that wound for miles to the south, perhaps to Livermore. Nothing larger than a big bike traversed the road nearby, and for every citizen who headed for my ridge, twenty kept to the roadway. I hoped they didn't expect too much when they got to Concord, and hoped I was wrong about that, though I wasn't. Singletons moved faster than groups, a moving panoply of Americana. One old guy trundled a wheeled golf bag along; not, I hoped, stuffed with putters. Most evacuees carried something and most showed that they hadn't given their evacuation much thought until the last possible moment. When I saw the man, woman, and two kids loping along my heart did a samba stumble-beat, but it wasn't my family after all. I guessed they were active in scouting because they walked fifty paces, trotted fifty, then walked again. They were the only group that overtook most singletons.

Maybe, I thought, I should drive along the ridge, stopping to scan the road from time to time; in for a penny, in for a pound. Then I glanced toward the Travis cloud and saw, slightly to the north of west, the enormous dark thunderhead approaching from Hamilton AFB. It loomed higher than the evening cirrus, curling up and toward me from where San Rafael must have been. Its lower half hid behind the flank of the nearby mountain but it was obviously, lethally, a fallout-laden megacloud heading in my direction.

I might be in for a pound, but not for the full ton. I didn't know how long it would take the dust to fall forty thousand feet.

Not long enough to let me backtrack to Livermore, for damn sure. Ern had brought me a fax copy of a manual that showed how to build an honest-to-God fallout meter, but I hadn't built the effing thing, and in any case it wasn't enough to know you were frying in radiation. You had to get away from it.

I stepped into the car again, sorrowing for all the people who, walking in the shadowed flank of Mount Diablo, could not see that they were moving straight into another shadow that could banish all their future sunshine forever. I started my engine before I saw the youngster hauling his trail-rigged moped upslope.

"If it's broken, leave it," I called to him.

"Just out of gas," he said with a grin, puffing. His moped was one of the good four-cycle, one-horse jobs that didn't need oil mixed with its fuel.

What I did then shamed me, but at least I didn't con the kid. "See that cloud?" I pointed toward the dull gray enormity curving toward us across the heavens. "Fallout. Those people won't know it until too late, unless you tell 'em."

"Me? Mister, my tongue is just about hanging down into my front wheel spokes." Impudence and good humor: I wanted to hug him.

"If you'll do it, I'll fill that little tank of yours. Get somebody to erect a sign or something. Tell 'em"—I glanced at my watch and swallowed hard—"that fallout will be raining down from San Rafael in a few hours. They must find shelter before then. Deal?"

He nodded. I got my spare coil of fuel hose from the tool compartment. One nice thing about an electric fuel pump is that you can quick-disconnect its output line and slip another hose on, then turn on the car's ignition and let it pump a stream of fuel from your fuel line to someone else's tank. The kid had his tank cap off in seconds and tried to stammer his thanks.

"I'm letting you take chances for me," I admitted. "It could cost you."

"My aunt in Walnut Creek has a deep basement," he replied. "With this refill I can stay on the road and get there in an hour."

He was priming his little flitter as I reattached my fuel line. "Is that a real cheetah?"

"Yep, and a good one. I can never catch him cheating."

He laughed and bounced away, refitting his goggles, and didn't look back. Neither did I. If he didn't stop to warn others on the road below me, I didn't want to know. I also did not want to scan the carnage again that stretched across the dying megalopolis. I no longer felt anger; only profound pity for good honest people whose chief transgression lay in thirty years of refusal to prepare for a disaster so monstrous that no government could save them from it. I hadn't felt tears on my cheeks for years, but as I nosed the Lotus downhill toward my place, I decided these didn't count. They were mostly self-pity, in advance, for the loss of my little sis and her family. They were my family, too.

I didn't feel like shooing Spot out to lighten the car's load for another fence-jump. Besides, there was always the chance of a miscalculation, which could snag a tire and throw the Lotus off balance, and I was beginning to consider every screw-up in context of a total moratorium on medical help. So I toggled the automatic gate control. Nothing. Usually at this hour of lengthening shadow—it was past six—I could see distant lights from a few places up and down the road from my place. Not now. The power from Antioch had failed. It was a little late for me to wish I'd installed a wind-powered alternator or even an engine-driven rig. I hadn't.

I unlocked the gate using the manual combination, let Spot in, pushed the damn car through because it was such a chore to get my lardbutt in and out, then relocked the gate, wondering if Ern would recall that combination; wondered if he'd get the chance to. I saw honey-gold hair flying, the girl running to meet me as I scooted for the garage, and thought it was Kate until I remembered Kate's hair was black. Ern wouldn't have to remember any combination because the girl embracing Spot on the shadowed lawn was my niece, Camille!

She gave me a big smack as I left the car. "Scared the heh-heh-*hell* out of us, Uncle Harve," she scolded, starting to sniffle, trying to get an arm all the way across my shoulders as we headed for the root cellar.

"Just taking a look around," I lied as Shar met me on the steps.

I got a quick tearful hug and kiss from my sis, whose dark Rackham hair was tied back from her round, attractively plumpish features. In response Shar had a faint upcurl at one corner of her mouth that tended to make a man check his fly for gaposis. In action she was a doer, an organizer; and I saw that the upcurl was now only part of a thin line. "Ernie and Lance are making a fallout meter in your office," she said and added darkly, "while your cutie-pie tapes around doors and windows upstairs. Harve, I thought you said we wouldn't turn the place into a public shelter."

"So everybody's here, and you've met Kate." I sighed my relief, letting my arms drop, realizing I was already tired and getting hungry. "Sis, we need to bring in everything movable from the garage and smithy storage and stack it in the tunnel."

"Done, thanks to your little flesh," Cammie cracked, and I needed a moment to translate her high-school jargon. She was linking me to Kate.

Before I could protest, Shar put in: "Your friend seemed ready to fight us off until Ernie told her who we were and proved he had your gate combination. That young lady runs a taut ship."

"She's led a rough life," I said and shrugged, then saw the welter of materials where Shar had been working in the root cellar. "What's all this?"

Shar's irritated headshake made her ponytail bounce. Like me, Shar inherited a tendency toward overweight. Unlike me, she had fought it to keep some vestige of a youthful figure, and diets were among her fads. They kept her bod merely on the *zaftig* side but also made her snappish and hyperactive. Now she was both. "I know you kept those outside cellar doors decrepit just for atmosphere," she said, bending in the gloom to choose a strip of plywood. "But they're no seal against fallout. If we intend to use the tunnel, someone has to stretch plastic film over these doors before we tape them shut. As they are now with all those cracks, they're hopeless. Just hopeless," she repeated with a sigh that richly expressed Why Mothers Got Gray.

My root cellar was so crowded with stuff from the garage that there was barely room for my sis to work. Obviously the whole bunch had arrived shortly after I'd left, because they'd done half a day's toting in half an hour. "You'll need light in here," I said in passing.

"You're in the way, Uncle Harve," said Cammie, and I saw that she was perched on her bike at the tunnel mouth. Ern had talked about rigging old-style bike stands, the kind that elevated the rear wheel and swiveled up like a wide rear bumper for riding; but he hadn't built them. Instead someone had taken two of my old folding chairs, put them back to back a foot apart, and strapped wooden sticks between them so that they formed a support frame to elevate the bike's rear wheel. As I stepped aside, Cammie began to pedal and the fist-size headlamp of her bike glowed, then dazzled, illuminating Shar's work. "Sonofabitch," I chortled. "Score one point for cottage industry."

The tiny DC generator on the rear wheel whined quietly, and I noticed that Cammie had removed the red lens from the puny little tail lamp. In the gathering dark of the tunnel, its glow wasn't all that puny. I trotted through the tunnel, every muscle protesting, feeling every ounce of my extra flab.

Soft creaks above me said that someone was hurrying between windows, taping around the edges to keep out the finest dust particles. Since I hadn't told Kate how to do it or showed her where I kept the inch-wide masking tape, I figured Shar had done it for me. The dozen rolls of tape in cool dark storage had been Shar's idea in the first place. I moved around the stone divider that defined my office to find my brother-in-law, his reading glasses halfway down his nose, his light blue eyes peering at the manual he'd left with me long before. His massive red-haired forearms were crossed on my desk top.

Ern McKay's calves and forearms had been designed for a larger man. In other physical details he was medium, with short carroty hair balding in front and stubby fingers that should've been clumsy. They were, in fact, so adroit that Ern made his living with them at Ames. Or had until this day. Ern saved all his clumsiness for social uses; he wasn't the demonstrative sort.

"Hi." He gave me his shy grin over the specs. "Heard you

come in. Lance is upstairs looking for your fishing vest. That where you keep your two-pound filament?"

"As you bloody well know," I said, squeezing his shoulder lightly as I studied the pages before him. That was all the greeting either of us needed. Ern was the tyer of dry flies in the family, but I'm the one who got to use them. Two-pound-test monofilament nylon is very thin stuff, the kind I used for leader on scrappy little trout in Sierra streams.

Ern's stumpy forefinger indicated a passage in the manual. "Says here that thin mono is hard to work with though it's otherwise perfect for the electroscope."

"I thought this was a fallout meter, Ern."

He turned his head, vented a two-grunt chuckle typical of his humor: underplayed. "You've had this damn manual five years and never read it once. Got half a mind to tell Shar on you."

"Christ, Ern, have a heart," I mumbled.

He held up the clean empty eight-ounce tin can from among other junk he had collected on my desk: adhesive bandage, razor blade, an oblong of thin aluminum foil, a bottle cork through which he'd forced a hefty needle. "Some guys doped this out years ago at Union Carbide; even got it published through Oak Ridge National Lab, including pages any newspaper could copy, free of charge! Any high school sophomore can build the thing from stuff lying around in the kitchen. If he can read," Ern qualified it.

I had assumed from the official-looking document number, ORNL-5040, that it wasn't kosher to copy it. Apparently the reverse was true, but I'd never read it carefully. The damned manual was in the public domain!

"Fellow named Kearny ramrodded several projects at Oak Ridge oriented toward nuke survival," Ern said, "and his team deserves top marks. The Kearny Fallout Meter is just a capacitor, a foil electroscope really, that's calibrated by the time it takes to lose its static charge after you feed that little charge to it. It loses that charge in an environment of ionizing radiation—the kind that makes fallout such a killer—and you can recharge it by rubbing a piece of plexiglass with paper to build up another charge."

"I understand only about half of what you just said," I complained.

"That's the point: you don't have to. Follow the instructions, learn to read the simple chart here, and you can use it *without* knowing why it works."

"Is it the kind of thing that only tells you when you're as good as dead? I mean, hell, Ern, it can't have much of a range of sensitivity."

"Take an F in guesswork. It works through four orders of magnitude," Ern replied, flipping pages to a sheet with a chart meant to be glued around that tin can. "From point-oh-three rems per hour—which is hardly worth worrying about—to *forty-three* rems per hour," he said with feeling.

"Which means kiss your ass good-bye," I hazarded.

"That's the layman's phrase," he harrumphed, subtly playing the quarrelsome scientist for me. "At NASA we say 'anus.' Ten hours at forty rems an hour and it's an even bet you won't live long."

"You're a little ray of sunshine."

"Just be glad," he said, tapping the pages, "that Kearny's elves realized nobody would buy expensive radiation counters until it was too late. They engineered this thing so well even you could build it for thirty cents—and why didn't you? And where the devil is Lance? I'm ready for that monofilament line."

"My fishing vest is in the screen porch closet," I said, and trotted upstairs. Only it wasn't in the closet. I called Lance.

From somewhere on the second floor came his muffled eleven-year-old tenor: "Come find me."

Sometimes Lance was eleven going on thirty, and sometimes going on seven. What rankled most was that he looked so much like I did at his age; beefy, shock of black hair, insolent button-black eyes under heavy brows. But mom hadn't spoiled me, hadn't let me hurl tantrums. I'd grown up with due respect for dad's belt. That was where Lance and I differed; my sis had figured her youngest for a genius since he began talking so much, so soon, and ruled against breaking his spirit. In that, at least, she'd succeeded. "We can play later, Lance," I called up. "Bring my fishing vest if you have it."

"I have it," his voice floated tantalizingly down the stairs. "Come find me."

Kate Gallo paused while tearing a strip of tape with her teeth; smiled at me. "Welcome back, boss." The evening light through the film-covered windows was a dusty pink, tinting the gloom in which she worked.

"Some boss," I said and bellowed, "Goddamnit, Lance, this is life and death!"

"I don't think you'll make much of an impression on that one," Kate murmured and continued working.

"Come fi-i-ind meee," quavered in the air.

So I climbed the stairs and found him in the closet of the guest bedroom his parents sometimes used. "You win," he chirruped and held up my many-pocketed, fish-scented old vest. Then, "You better watch out," he wailed.

My vest in one hand, Lance's belt and trouser back in my other, I carried him like a duffel bag to the window. Kate hadn't sealed it yet but had put the plastic over it outside. "You know why the sunset's so red, Lance?"

"Those smoky clouds. You're hurting my stummick."

"Those clouds are full of poison. The poison will be falling on us tonight and for a long time after. It'll kill us if we don't get ready, Lance. Your help could make the difference."

Sullen, short of breath with his belt impeding it: "Better put me down." Then as I did so, he folded his arms and faced me. "I think that's a lot of crap about clouds being poison. How come airplanes fly through 'em all the time?"

I waved him ahead of me down the stairs. "Haven't you paid any attention to what your folks told you about fallout?"

"Some. Mostly I have better things to do. That stuff is dull." I knew what his better things were; I'd found his caches of comics and kidporn. "Anyway, if any poison comes down, the roof'll stop it."

The roof! I pushed him aside and took the rest of the stairs fast, tossing my vest to Ern. "I'd completely forgot," I said to him, trying to recall where I'd stashed my tools. "The central roof beam buckled from concussion. We've got to shore it up, Ern. Could you finish that thing later?"

He tapped the little cork with the needle in it; only the tip of the needle was exposed. He'd made several tiny holes in the tin can that way, following the manual but using amateur model-builders' tricks to do a neater job. "Guess the roof is top priority," he mused, then arose and called into the tunnel. "Shar, when you're finished, will you and Cammie haul mattresses and bedding down here?"

"Another few minutes," Shar's voice echoed.

Cammie, faintly: "Isn't sealing the tunnel more important?"

"Yes," Ern and I chorused. Bedding or no bedding, the tunnel was the safest spot on my place. I'd had it dug with a backhoe as a deep, broad trench years before, a passageway from the old farmhouse to the root cellar. Then, by hand, I had dug a shoulder a foot wide and three feet deep on each side, running the length of the tunnel. Finally I laid cheap discarded railroad ties across that shoulder with a layer of heavy tar paper between the cross-tie roof and the dirt I shoveled onto it.

During one rainy season the tunnel had stood three inches deep in water, thanks to my incompetence. After that I dug a smaller, foot-deep trench along one side of the bottom of the tunnel, laying perforated plastic pipe in the hole with gravel around it before I installed a floor and wall paneling. The perforated pipe took ground water that percolated into the gravel. I had to dig another trench by hand around the old concrete foundation of the house so I could install more drainage pipe to carry ground water downhill from the tunnel and the house—but that kept the basement dryer, too. With that mod, my old place no longer had the dank, musty, moldy basement common to many old homes. I'd be lying if I claimed it was all done for nuclear survival, but my dry tunnel beneath cross ties and three feet of damp soil provided protection you could beat only in a mine shaft. According to Shar's texts, the tunnel had a fallout protection factor several times greater than the basement itself.

In Shar's jargon, the basement under my two-story house was rated at a PF of over 30; that is, over thirty times as much protection as you'd get walking around outside in shirt sleeves, which is no protection to speak of. The PF got better when I blocked off my one basement window with dirt; that's why I did it. It would've been better still had I thrown a ramp of earth up against the exposed concrete foundation, which was visible for a foot or so below the clapboard siding.

Shar estimated that with the window blocked off (and the long, hinged trapdoor lowered over the stairwell so that it became, in best farmhouse tradition, a segment of my kitchen floor), my basement could have a PF of nearly fifty. If fallout radiation got as high as a hundred rems per hour outside, it might be only two rems per hour in the basement.

Of course, two rems an hour weren't good for you. If you absorbed that much radiation steadily for a week, your body would get a total exposure of 336 rems during that time. Chances were one in three that you'd die in a month or so from such a dose.

The operative word there was "steadily": fallout particles radiate so much during the first day or so, they're only emitting ten percent as strongly seven hours after the blast; *one* percent as strongly after two days. After fifteen days that emission rate is only *one tenth of one percent* as much as it was during the first moments of that monstrous fireball.

That dwindling radiation rate was the rationale for staying put awhile—and for optimism. If radiation rose to deadly levels outside, we would experience only a small fraction of it in my basement. Sure, it was still dangerous. We might get sick; we might even contract cancer and die in a few years. In my book a few years beats hell out of a few days.

But Shar's hundred-rem-per-hour estimate had been wildly optimistic. As Ern chased me up to the attic, we had no idea that the particles slowly drifting down toward us from forty-thousand-foot altitude were from the very center of the Hamilton cloud, so ferociously lethal they should've glowed in the dark. They didn't, of course.

Stepping carefully to avoid fiberglass insulation, we still got it in our eyes and cussed it as we worked. Ern had a better understanding of structures than I did; he judged we could make a four-legged pyramid from the A-frame tubes. We used up ten minutes putting the A-frames in place with only my lamp to illuminate us, straddling the tube butts on joists and nailing stubs of two-by-four to keep the butt ends from skating away. Then I braced my legs, put my head and both forearms under the cracked roofbeam, and Ern helped me lift.

A pain like an electric shock banged alongside my spine. I'd half-expected it. Given plenty of time, Ern would've jacked the beam up by an old expedient: a sturdy vertical timber under the roof beam with overlapping hardwood wedges under the vertical piece. By driving the wedges toward each other with a hammer, a slender housewife could elevate that timber by the thickness of both wedges; several inches, in fact. Well, we didn't have the time. We did have a tall, heavy-boned idiot with an old back injury—me.

The joists groaned underfoot. Dust and splinters fell from the roof beam. With a great dry groan the center of the beam rose within an inch or so of horizontal. Ern, standing on different joists, panted, "Can you hold?"

"Do it," I grunted, and he rushed to lean the tops of the tubes into place, apexes nearly together under the roof beam.

"Let down easy," he said, holding the tops of the tubes in place. As I did, the tubes bit a half-inch up into the beam—a good thing, since they wanted to slip aside. Ern saw the problem, grabbed the hammer and nails, and drove nails into the beam so their protruding heads held the tube lips from moving. Then, "I still don't like it, but it'll do," he said, and I staggered back. "We should span the break with plywood and screws, Harve, but we don't have the time."

"What if we nailed chains across the bottom of the beam?"

He saw what I meant. If we stretched a chain across the bottom face of the beam, nailing through several links where the wood wasn't split, the beam couldn't sag again without snapping chain or very sturdy nails. "Smart," he agreed, and we did it in two minutes flat. Now he was happy. Ours was a stronger repair than a simple vertical post resting in the middle of a joist, since that lone joist might give way. I suggested that we clear out.

"Oh hell, we didn't block the attic vents," Ern said then as we collected our tools. The little screened vents weren't large, but a strong updraft under the eaves could sift dust into the attic. Ern saw me kneading the muscles near my kidney, told me to wait, and scrambled downstairs. He was back moments later with newspapers I had put in the bedrooms for atmosphere. The front pages were expensive fakes with historic headlines like FIRE RAVAGING SAN FRANCISCO—an appalling irony now—and LUSITANIA TORPEDOED. We thrust the paper, a dozen thicknesses at each vent, flat against the holes and nailed them in place. Then we abandoned the attic and taped the door edges.

Kate and Cammie were rechecking their tape job around upstairs window edges while Shar, with some help from Lance, wrestled mattresses downstairs to the basement. Ern and I shucked off our clothes in my old-fashioned second-floor bathroom and used perfectly clean water from the toilet tank to sponge-bathe, scrubbing off the itchy insulation as well as we could.

On our way downstairs for fresh clothes, Ern tried joking about the picture we made, two middle-aged naked guys scratching where it itched.

"I'll laugh tomorrow," I promised glumly.

Then while he retrieved a coverall he'd left at my place, Ern called to me. "Who's that outside?"

I paused with one foot in my size 46 jeans. "Beats me; we're all inside."

"Spot isn't," he rejoined.

"Why the hell isn't he," I stormed, and pounded out to the back porch while buttoning a long-sleeve shirt.

The back of my roof overhung the screen porch by three feet, but the faint breeze on my cheeks told me the place wouldn't be safe for long. We hadn't stretched film over the screen. Now I heard, from beyond my perimeter fence, a voice either female or falsetto. "Get down, Richard, *there's a lion in there!*"

This was followed by a male whoop and cries that faded into the distance. I called Spot and waited, peering into a rosy semi-darkness that obscured all but silhouettes of trees and skyline. The glow over the mass of mountain was red on rose. I wondered if fires would spread from Oakland to leap the fire lanes;

to engulf us all before dawn. I wondered if I should've let those poor devils in. And I wondered if Spot was radioactive by now.

I finally got my dumb cheetah inside and made him understand that he was to stay in the tunnel. When I returned to my office and told Ern what I'd heard outside, I was too exhausted to ream anyone out for letting Spot roam loose. It was hard to believe that it was only eight o'clock.

Ern, who had to be more weary than I, sat with my battery lamp and sipped from a glass of my brandy as he trimmed rectangles of aluminum foil. "Another hour and I'll know if this one works," he said as I sat on the edge of my waterbed, twenty feet away in my unpartitioned sleeping area. Then he must've heard me grunt. "Hurt your back up there, didn't you?"

My old vertebra compression fracture was an enemy I had to live with. "Just a muscle spasm," I said, and eased myself onto the floor where I could lie flat on the carpet. Sometimes, by forcing myself to relax while lying full-length, I could feel the flutter-crunch of vertebrae unpopping in the small of my back. I closed my eyes. "We had room for those two out there, you know," I said softly.

"Two? It may have been twenty," he replied. "We made that decision a long time back."

"I know."

"When would we stop, Harve? How many could we take?"

I didn't answer. Ours was the classic crowded-lifeboat dilemma: how to decide when taking one more swimmer meant reducing the odds of the lucky occupants. My cop-out was accidental, but no less an avoidance. I fell asleep the instant those vertebrae unkinked.

I awoke to feel fingers massaging my scalp so I knew it was Cammie bending over me, speaking softly, urgently, ". . . to get up now. We can't carry you."

I peered into almost total darkness; came up on one elbow, flooded with the sudden awareness of where I was, and why. My forty-by-twenty-foot basement was lit by a single candle, its wick trimmed, that squatted on a low bookshelf in my lounging area. "I can walk," I protested, and saw Ern's bulk disappearing into my tunnel, dragging mattresses. "Whatthehell? Another bomb?"

"It's hot in here, Harve," called my sis, who was lugging a tub of water into the tunnel.

"I don't feel very—" I said, then realized what she meant. "Fallout?"

"Yes, and getting heavier," Cammie said. She hurried off to help carry things to the tunnel as I creaked upright.

My watch was still in the clothes I'd discarded. My digital clock didn't glow because the power was off, and if it hadn't been for that candle, that basement would've been dark as Satan's soul. I learned while blundering into people with books and boxes that I'd slept only three hours, but that little bit had done my back lots of good.

"Wish we could get that damn waterbed in here," Ern groused as I swung the tunnel door closed. He busied himself by passing armloads of books to Shar and Kate, who were restacking them on a bookshelf they'd scrounged from my office. Cammie was on her bike, pedaling to provide enough light for our needs. Lance was sitting on a mattress. And what the hell was I doing? Nothing useful. I didn't have to ask why they were making a barrier of books at the foot of the stairs in the root cellar; instead, I hurried back to the basement and lifted my entire small bookcase of *Britannicas*, hauling it through the tunnel to help create the book barrier.

If fallout was intense enough to warrant our moving into the tunnel, the radiation through the puny film-covered doors of my root cellar would be high at that end of the tunnel. Distance alone was some help. The right-angle turn into the tunnel helped, too. But thick, dense stacks of paper make an excellent barrier against ionizing radiation—and a shelf of books, Shar's texts claimed, was better than a steel-faced door. She had begun the book barrier directly in front of the root cellar steps and used scraps of lumber nailed across the wooden stairway framing to keep the rickety barrier from toppling.

I leaned against the bookcase to help Shar and watched as Ern rubbed an antique phonograph record against the fur rim of my old parka. The light in the tunnel was dim enough to reveal the blue crackles of static sparkling in the fur. "Ern, what the hell are you—oh," I subsided as he brought the record disc near a whiskery piece of wire that protruded from the top of the tin can in his other hand. He'd finished his fallout meter.

A small spark jumped to the wire. Ern snapped on my lamp, stared down at the tin can, which now had a clear plastic film cover through which the wire protruded. He moved the wire gently. He glanced at his wristwatch, gnawing his lip—and Ern chews that lip only in extremis.

He glared through the plastic cover into the tin can, holding it in the light as if daring it to do him wrong. After a minute he glanced up at me, and his smile was an act of bravery. "The manual tells you to charge the leaves of foil by rubbing a hunk of plexiglass with paper," he said, trying to sound unconcerned. "I remembered how old vinyl records sometimes took a hellacious static charge from wool or fur and stole one of your old LPs and—sure 'nough," he said and shrugged, squinting down into the can again, checking his watch.

I whispered it: "Don't kid me, Ern: how we doin'?"

His reading glasses gleamed as he muttered, "Lots better here." He pointed down into the tin can to show me. "Those little foil leaves are suspended by nylon monofilament. See the inked paper scale I pasted on the plastic top? You center the scale so its zero mark is exactly between the foil leaves, and then see how far out the bottom of each leaf is from zero." Anxiety infiltrated his low baritone. "No, don't lean so close; your eye must be one foot from the scale to give the right parallax—uh, anyway, after a little practice you can get it pretty close without a ruler."

Though I was older than Ern, my eyes haven't yet gone farsighted on me. I could see that the suspended leaves of foil stood slightly apart, defying gravity since their static charges made them repel each other. "I get a reading of two," I said.

He pulled the can back in a hurry, stared at it, glared at me. "Scare the living shit out of a feller," he grumbled. "Two millimeters for one leaf and nearly three on the other. That makes five, Harve. I started about four minutes ago with readings of seven and eight millimeters on the scale. Now"—he checked his watch and nodded—"I read it as two and three. So the bottom edges of the foil leaves have swung nearer by a total of ten millimeters in four minutes. Look at the paper chart on the side of the can."

I did, knowing Ern was *not* going to tell me how much radiation we were taking because he wanted me to do it myself. "Ten millimeters in four minutes: two rems. In four minutes?"

"Jesus, no! Two rems per *hour*; you read the dose rate in rems per hour, you nik-nik. Why didn't you build one of these years ago?"

"Because I'm an idiot," I concluded. "And you?"

"Built mine so long ago I forgot half the details. But Lance tore it up trying to get at the hunks of desiccant in the bottom of the can. He was only five. Thought it was candy." Ern tried to make it seem a clever ploy by a blameless child, but I knew his disappointment with Lance was marrow-deep even if he rarely showed it.

To realign the topic away from Lance I said, "Those little hunks of rocks in the bottom are desiccant? Where'd you get it?"

"Knocked a corner from a piece of wallboard under your stairwell," he confessed. "The crumbly stuff in wallboard is gypsum. Kate heated the little hunks inside a tin cup over a candle for a half-hour to make sure they were dry before I put 'em in. You can't afford moisture in this can, and dry gypsum is a desiccant—soaks up the water vapor from the air in the can. It's all in the manual."

I watched Shar and Kate finish their work, conscious of the close quarters and of the muffled echoes in the tunnel. Only Spot and Lance seemed capable of sleep. "Hey, a two-rem reading in here is pretty high, isn't it?"

Ern snorted. "Try it on your porch. For the first two hours I didn't notice the foil leaves relaxing. Then when I wasn't looking, they lost their charge in a hurry. When I charged 'em up again, they sagged by twelve millimeters in one minute flat, which is nearly ten rems an hour. Just to check, I took your lamp and wore your parka out to the porch with a handkerchief over my mouth, and tried to get a reading." His long single headshake was eloquent. "I could actually *see* the damn aluminum leaves wilting down, and the best spark I can make gives about a sixteen-millimeter reading to start with, and the static charge decayed to zilch, buddy—*zero*—in just a few seconds."

I stared at the chart pasted on his fallout meter. "That's completely off scale, Ern. Over fifty rems per hour on my porch! Any chance the meter is wrong?"

"Sure there's a chance. You feel like taking that chance?"

"Maybe some other time," I husked. "What do you think the dose rate would be for anyone out in the open?"

"If the protection factors we estimated are any guide, Harve," and now he was whispering, "they could be taking hundreds."

"And their chances after an hour or so—"

"No chance, buddy. Maybe a ghost of one if they got to shelter right after that. But they'd probably be the walking dead, and not walking for long."

I glanced at that steel-faced door, then down the tunnel as Shar moved toward us. "I'm wondering if we'd get a different reading right up against that door, or by the book barrier," I said.

"What could we do about it?"

"If there's a radiation gradient along the tunnel, we could stay in the safest part of it."

"I'm getting stupid with exhaustion," Ern admitted. "You're right." He started past Shar; kissed her forehead.

She was too preoccupied to respond. "All right, girls," she said, "now we must lie down and relax. There's only so much air in here, and the less we exercise, the less we foul the air." Kate had a snippish reply on her face but glanced at me, shrugged, and chose a mattress.

"Until we get our flashlights it's gonna be dark, mom," said Cammie, and slowed her pedaling to prove it.

"Your father has Harve's lamp," my sis replied, and saw Ern nod in confirmation. Moments later the only source of light was my lamp, which Ern conserved as much as possible. The women settled quietly among blankets they didn't really need, and I sat almost as quietly, avoiding exertion.

Ern took readings at the book barrier, then backtracked down the tunnel to the basement door. It took him quite a while because the longer he waited for a reading, the more accurate it was. When he finished at the basement door, I was nearly asleep on the mattress I shared with Kate, who was snoring gently, and no wonder.

He walked to us, roughly midway down the tunnel, and switched off the lamp as he sat next to Shar. "Looks like we did something right by sheerest intuition. Hon? Harve? You awake?"

My sis and I acknowledged it.

Softly he asked, "You awake, Kate?" Silence, if you discounted the mezzo-soprano of her snores. "Cammie?" No answer. "Lance?" No answer. "Okay, team, it's midnight; time for a progress report."

In his travels down the tunnel, Ern had also made sure our food and water were not only present but out of the way. The root cellar was a jumble that we would have to straighten out, because we might be living in these cramped quarters for quite a while.

Near the steel-faced door, he said, the reading was roughly three rems per hour. At the book barrier it was over four. At the midpoint of the tunnel it was only two, maybe a shade less. Without any question, my half-assed root-cellar-door arrangement could have killed us all—might still be killing us, depending on how much dust might get through the sealing job Shar had done with such desperate speed. "The good news is, the radiation level must be dropping," he reminded us. "At least it *should* be. We'll know for sure in an hour or so." He stopped, listening. Rain drummed against the plastic that covered the root cellar doors, reminding me of a stampede of small animals. Those drops must've been as big as marbles. To my relief, it didn't last long.

"I wonder how fast we're using up the air in here," Shar muttered in the darkness. "Harve, how many cubic feet of air are in the tunnel?"

I made a rough calculation. Seven feet high, four and a half wide, sixty from end to end, plus the volume of the root cellar itself. "Maybe two thousand," I said.

"Not enough," she said with a catch in her voice. "Not even half enough. We're exhaling carbon dioxide into it, fouling what we have, and we need three or four hundred cubic feet an hour *each.* I'm trying not to panic, but if we fall asleep now, it's possible we'd never wake up."

I could hear their movements and imagined Ern trying, in his diffident way, to comfort my sis. Finally he said, "So we pump fresh air in here somehow."

"My hand-cranked blower in the smithy might do it," I said.

"It might as well be at the North Pole," he rejoined. "It'd take you an hour to detach it and bring it back. You'd be dead in a few days, so forget it. Hold on: your forced-draft furnace blower in the basement has a filter, doesn't it?"

Not much use, I said, when the power was off.

"But we could tap into the air source if we had an air pump. Look, team, I'm having a brainstorm. If we can locate a big sturdy cardboard box, I think I could build a bellows pump with it. A bellows will suck air through a filter better than a squirrel-cage blower does."

Shar said, "It's dangerous, hon. Who's going to stand in the basement and pump it all night?"

But Ern was already up, groaning with fatigue, the lamp shining toward the disorder of the root cellar. "We can run a pipe from the filter box to the tunnel and pump from in here," he insisted, starting to rummage between the bikes. "If either of you has a better idea or can figure where we'll get—um—thirty feet of pipe as wide as your fist, let me know. We need it for an air conduit."

My modern forced-air furnace system sat under the stairs in the basement, linked to sheet-metal conduits. I had no pipe and no ideas. For a long moment I considered just relaxing, taking my chances. Which weren't good, and I'd be whittling away at the chances of three young sleepers and Spot as well. I grunted to my feet and followed Shar, who'd already had a lifesaving idea.

Ern chose a corrugated carton big as a two-drawer file cabinet and worked without visible blueprints. He thought Shar's pipe might be too flimsy but had no better answer, and I helped her when I saw what my sis had in mind. Shar just took a stack of old newspaper and started rolling tubes, each tube made from a dozen sheets. I taped the seams. Ern suggested we cover the paper tubes with latex paint to seal the pores in the paper, then countermanded his own idea; it'd take too long to dry. Instead we unrolled my thin two-mil roll of plastic film and sheathed each paper tube with it, taped on the seam. The first two were pretty sorry specimens, wrinkled and repaired with too much tape, but we got better at it. By the time I noticed the muggy, oppressive atmosphere, Shar and I had finished over a dozen knee-high lengths of air pipe made from newsprint.

Ern muttered, "We're going to have to open that basement door soon." Sweat stood on his face. He was breathing a bit too quickly, and so was I. "Shar, you remember how to read the fallout meter from the one I built before?"

She did, but didn't know how to charge it up. I said I'd show her. It was necessary to align that protruding wire with the foil leaves, then move the wire away again after its spark charged the foil. We crowded near my lamp—all hail to the guy who invented rechargeable dry cells—and after a few tries we got it right.

"I'm still getting three rems an hour here in the root cellar," she announced softly after timing it with her watch, then fumbled in the bag strapped to her bike. She withdrew a two-cell flashlight, reminding me that those little second-stage evacuation kits contained everything from raisins to razor blades. I still had no idea what problems they'd had getting to my place—but there'd be plenty of time for those stories in the next week. Assuming we lived that long. Judging from the way our bodies were laboring in that clammy air, I couldn't assume we'd pull through.

Shar went into the basement and closed the door again to take fresh readings; not that we had much choice about them. We would have to go in there and punch into my sheet-metal furnace filter box and insert the air pipe whether we liked the readings or not. Meanwhile I held a heavy polyfilm trapezoid in place while Ern double-taped it onto the big cardboard box.

The box was now cut away so it had a steep wedge shape in side view, with thick polyfilm replacing the trapezoid of cardboard he had cut away. He had cut two holes through the rectangular back of the box, cut a thin-walled mailing tube into two shorter pieces, and taped them firmly into the holes. As we taped polyfilm on, I could see through it into the box. A hastily cut rectangle of cardboard was taped over the mouth of one segment of mailing tube, but only at the top so that the rectangle could flap loose. "You didn't find any more mailing tubes, did you?" I asked.

"Nope. Wish I had. The partial vacuum when I lift this bellows will probably collapse Shar's air pipe—no it won't, either!" He put down the big box and upended another smaller cardboard carton, letting food cans spill onto shelves in the root cellar. "Harve, you cut this box into strips, maybe three inches wide—just so they'll slip into the airpipe. We'll need twice as many inches of cardboard strip as we have of pipe."

I grabbed tin snips, a shitty tool but better than nothing, and began cutting without knowing what Ern had in mind. I saw, though, while cutting the third strip. Ern grabbed the two I had cut, used his keen-edged pocketknife to cut slits lengthwise halfway down the center of each, then forced the slit wider by prying and reversed one strip so the mouths of the slits matched. Then he merely shoved them together so that, seen from the end, the two strips had an X shape. "There, damnit. Shove that down the air pipe and it won't collapse." It was good to hear the satisfaction in his tone. It said he wasn't licked yet.

Shar returned with guarded optimism as Ern attacked his project again. He was making a handle from the folded widths of cardboard but looked up expectantly. "What reading did you get in the basement, honey?"

"About fifteen rems an hour at the desk."

"That's a shade less than I got."

"Funny thing, though: I get about eight at the stairwell, and the same at the other end of the room near the waterbed."

We considered this in silence. Shar cooed in delight when she saw how my cardboard strips stiffened her air pipes and began assembling the things as I cut them. Then, "Hon, you're stumbling like a wino," she warned Ern. "And my headache is definitely worse."

Without a word he lifted his bellows pump, tape, and tools; staggered down the tunnel; managed to get the door open. We were gradually asphyxiating in the root cellar's stagnant air, and it wasn't much past midnight.

I grabbed a double armload of air pipe and caromed off the paneling en route to the basement, leaving Shar to bring what I'd left. Ern helped me to the stairwell. Though I was dizzy, I had no headache and said as much.

Ern, breathing deeply in the basement, located the filter intake box of my furnace system and selected the large blade of his bulky Swiss pocketknife, then jabbed hard into the bottom face of the thin sheet-metal box. Using the heel of his hand to hammer the blade in, he glanced at me. "Foul air doesn't affect everyone the same, Harve. Tell me: what's twelve times eleven?"

I blinked, swayed. "Uh—look it up," I said.

"Headache or not, you're rocky. Just keep breathin', and bring the kids to the basement doorway. I can do this without you."

I grabbed mattresses and pulled them, kids and all, toward the basement. I was already recuperating enough to wonder how long the basement air would last when we were sealed in. If only we had a column of clean air to draw from—*the chimney!*

Spot was awake and curious. I settled him with a pat and a "stay," and hurried to where Ern was folding thin metal tabs back on the underside of my furnace air intake box. "I know why the fallout's worse near my desk, Ern," I said, not wanting to say it. "We should've blocked the chimney at the top while we could still get to it."

Shar, holding a segment of air pipe ready, frowned and then understood. "Of course! The dust box at the foot of the chimney is right outside the foundation near your desk. A little fallout is dropping straight down the chimney. It can't be much."

"Enough, though," Ern grunted. "Nothing we can do about it right now except stay away from that part of the basement. Here, hon; try it now."

She thrust the air pipe past the bent tabs; let Ern tape it in place. She said, "Let's hope the furnace filter's a good one."

It wasn't, but we wouldn't learn that for another fifteen minutes.

Our primitive air pipe looked like hell, but lying along the floor from stairwell to tunnel entrance, it looked like salvation, too. Ern finished taping a square of cardboard over the outside "exhaust" piece of mailing tube protruding from the pump and lifted the handle atop the bellows.

The whole thing tried to lift. "Wedge it down for me," he said and pulled again. The box heaved a mighty sigh as its top came up, the polyfilm unwrinkling at its full extension, and then Ern pushed down. I heard a *clack* inside the bellows—that cardboard flapper operating, the simplest kind of valve you can make.

But more important, a solid *whooosh* emerged from the exhaust tube, its flapper flying up until Ern started another intake cycle. He kept lifting and shoving for a minute or more, and squatting there in the tunnel, we could not mistake the change in the air quality.

Ern saw the tears of relief in Shar's eyes. "Hon, get something to wedge this bellows box in place; takes more force to lift it than I thought, but it's farting nearly two cubic feet of fresh air every time it cycles. Where are you going, Harve?"

"Not far, that's for sure," I said instead of telling him. I wanted to use the fallout meter to be sure the air was free of fallout.

It wasn't as easy to get a static charge transferred to the foil leaves as it looked. When I touched the uninsulated end of the charging wire, the foil lost some of its charge. I tried again, and after several fumble-fingered tries I had the foil-leaf capacitor properly charged up.

All these goddamn details! They were driving me around the bend. But my brother-in-law had known details that let him build a high-volume bellows pump from scratch, and in an hour. My flibbertigibbet sis had saved my very considerable bacon with air pipes made from fucking *newspaper*, of all things. But I knew some details I didn't like.

Item: I hadn't changed that furnace filter in a year.

Item: The furnace filter drew air from a standpipe buried in the wall, which poked up through my roof.

Item: Ern's bellows pump sucked so hard you could see the air pipes flexing, even with the cruciform stiffeners inside them. Would it also suck fallout particles in *sideways* under the raincap on my roof?

Item: If it did, would the dirty furnace filter trap them?

I found out a few minutes later, eyeing the fallout meter in front of the bellows exhaust. "Stop the damn pump, Ern," I said.

He'd worked up a sweat. "Gladly. You want to take a turn?"

"No. The meter is reading over thirty rems an hour. We're sucking fallout in past the filter."

"Oh dear God," Shar moaned, and covered the sleeping body of Lance with her own.

In the glow of Shar's flashlight I took another reading just inside the tunnel, aware of Ern's eyes on me and of our mutual exhaustion. From many nights of stakeouts, waiting for some bail jumper to poke his nose up, I knew you felt most like cashing it all in when your body was at its lowest ebb. "Twelve rems now, maybe just residual from what we pulled in through the filter," I said, as chipper as possible. I went to the door, fanned it back and forth a few times, then saw the obvious and untaped the air pipe halfway across the floor. "This damn basement must have six or seven thousand cubic feet of air," I growled. "Try pumping again."

Shar saw her husband trying to rise and pushed him back; knelt at the bellows as if venerating it—and why not?—then cycled it slowly. Noting with regret that the old LP record Ern had chosen to generate a static charge was my rare old ten-inch Tom Lehrer album, I recharged the meter again and waited a long time to get my reading. We were too tired to cheer when I concluded that we were taking only two or three rems an hour lying in the tunnel, its door open only enough to admit the airpipe, drawing air from the basement.

I flicked the flashlight off. "We just may make it through," I said.

Ern, almost dreamily: "I've been thinking. The dose we take is cumulative, but that fallout couldn't have reached us much before eleven or so. Maybe we took ten rems before we got to the tunnel, but we haven't taken over a few more in here. Then another five or so in the basement, another couple while pumping shit through your lousy furnace filter—I'm sorry, Harve, and anyway it was my own idea—and I come up with a grand total of less than twenty rems. We have a fighting chance to pull through."

"Unless we run out of air," I reminded him.

"Bubba," panted Shar in the darkness near me, "I am going to—pull every single hair—out of your body." Thirty-five years before, that had been her darkest threat to a brother twice her size. I started to chuckle and heard Ern's soft laugh warming me, and we squeezed that moment of merriment dry.

Sometime after one A.M. I took over the pumping chores. We hadn't set up any official sequence, but when a cautious whisk of the flashlight beam told me Shar and Ern were both asleep, I decided they needed it. I pumped the bellows every ten seconds and rested in between, and figured after four hundred cycles that an hour had passed. Then I roused Kate, calmed her sudden outbreak of fear; told her we were going to make it if she would do three hundred slow pumps of this bizarre gadget before waking Cammie to take her place.

"And who does Cammie wake?"

"Me," I said.

After a moment's thought in the blackness she said, "That won't do, boss. If anybody plays the sacrificial lamb now, we can all be sorry later. And," she said teasingly but with damning accuracy, "you're the one dude in this menagerie that nobody can lift if he collapses. Now we'll try it again: Cammie wakes who?"

"Her old man," I said, and laid my hand on her shoulder before I thought about it.

I think she said, "Thanks," but I was already drifting away to Lilliput, where, according to my synapses, evil homunculi amused themselves by driving pickaxes between my vertebrae for the next few hours.

## II. Doomsday Plus One

Around six in the morning my sis roused me. Thanks to the work I chose, when awakened by rough handling I tended to come up with elbow sweeps. Of all those dear to me, only Cammie had intuited that a gentle scalp massage defused the reflex that had soured some relationships with ladies over the years. Shar just squatted near my feet and tugged at my trouser legs until I sat up and said something akin to, "Who 'sit?"

"Shar, bubba; can you take over at the pump?"

With my mental cobwebs torn asunder I reckoned that I could, and asked about the radiation level. She lent me her wristwatch; told me it now took four minutes to get a decent reading, which was roughly one rem on the chart.

As I took the little flashlight and sat down before Ern's pump, I noticed that my plastic film was now taped down the slit where the basement door stood open enough to admit the air pipe. I played the flashbeam up and down the new mod. "Trouble, sis?"

"Huh? Oh; no, Ern did it, thinking we could raise the air pressure in here by a smidgin and gradually flush the foul air out past holes in those *despicable* doors above the root cellar."

"Shouldn't be any holes," I said.

"Maybe; but when you pump, you can see the plastic bulge at the doorway, and Ern says the root-cellar air smelled okay to him just before he waked me. Spot was sniffing around in there a few minutes ago. Would he advance into foul air? Well, you two argue about it later, Harve; I'm simply dead." And she curled up and proved it.

I began the hour by worrying about falling asleep but found enough worries to keep me awake. My back still ached; I resented the fact that Lance weighed almost as much as Kate but couldn't be trusted to man the pump; realized that Spot was freeloading in the same way and worried about justifying his presence. Finally I thought about the frozen horsemeat in Spot's automatic feeder in a corner of the root cellar and realized that all my frozen food upstairs would soon be at room temperature; and how the goddamn, et cetera, hell could we avoid all that spoilage?

For one thing, we could avoid opening a freezer door until the moment we needed something. Maybe tape polyfilm over the opening when we opened it, cut a hand-size slit, and minimize the heat transfer every time we opened that compartment.

Spot's feeder could be manually triggered without opening its horsemeat compartment—and it contained thirty pounds or so of ground dobbin in one-pound discs. The stuff might stay frozen three days if we didn't open the top, and by then we might be ready to eat horsemeat. The feeder's defrost coil, of course, no longer would warm the disc. We'd have to cook it somehow, and Spot could damn well eat farina mix.

He could also stink the place up until we were ready to embrace a fallout cloud, or to shoo him outside, which was obviously the more logical answer. I didn't smell cat shit until, halfway through my stint, I toured the tunnel and got to the root cellar. Like most cats, Spot had fastidious ideas about taking his dumps. In the flashbeam I saw clawmarks where he'd tried to get around the book barrier. But it was intact; he hadn't forced the issue. My nose told me he'd done his doodahs somewhere near instead, and since I hadn't spread linolamat under the cellar shelves, it was still packed dirt.

So why couldn't cheetahs defecate like other cats and cover

it up? They don't. They're choosy, yes—but they choose high places.

So voilà, and damn, and cat shit at the back of the top shelf a yard from the ancient timbered ceiling. I scooped it onto a hunk of plastic film, folded the fair-size blivit neatly, and left it nearby.

Back at the pump, doubling the cycle rate to make up for lost time, I thought some more about elimination. Cats weren't the only folks who shat. People who underrate that function as one of life's little pleasures should do without it, and without sex, for a week—and see which one they crave the more. I'd heard that homey observation as a kid and still couldn't fault it. We would have to solve another problem soon.

The best answer was *not* my basement john; it required several gallons of water per flush. My waterbed, the one thing after my tunnel that Shar had praised most as nuclear survival advantage, was as outsize as I was: six feet by seven, eight inches thick. Twenty-eight cubic feet of water was roughly two hundred and thirty gallons.

I reflected on the evenings when we'd sat by my fire upstairs and toyed with the ghastly math of obliteration, comfy and cheerful with our beer and popcorn—Ern's version, corn popped in olive oil and spiced with garlic and oregano. Armed with her texts, my sis knew a lot of disquieting facts. Water, for one: locked in a basement, we might consume nearly a gallon a day each, plus what we cooked with. Plus what we washed in, and that might be a lot. If we needed to decontaminate ourselves after a foray outdoors, we would each use eight or ten gallons per wash. Discounting Spot, the six of us could empty my waterbed in a few days if we weren't careful.

We didn't expect to emerge from the basement in less than a week or so.

There simply wouldn't be enough water for niceties; we would have to skimp. And I hadn't even figured on the water needed to flush the Thomas Crapper. Ern had said once that a porta-potty was a simple rig. I hoped he hadn't forgotten his mental blueprint.

Urination was no real problem if we were willing to do it

in my basement john, because you can pee endlessly into a toilet bowl and it will maintain its fluid level. But as I roused Kate again to take her place at the pump, I felt a familiar abdominal urge. I denied it and let sleep return, knowing that in a few hours we would have to face a problem in, ah, solid-waste management.

It must've been the shock that woke me, about nine-thirty in the morning; whacked me right through the mattress. I sat up, hearing familiar voices under stress in the near distance, peering through the open basement door toward faint illumination. Kate lay at my side, and I managed to get up without waking her. From what I gathered, Master Lance had innocently made use of my toilet before anybody discussed it with him.

With all my muscles tight from the previous day, I still felt vaguely humanoid. In my lounge area Cammie was setting up a cold breakfast. "The kid didn't know," I called as I shambled my way to the candlelit area. "And it's the day after doomsday, and we're still vertical, team."

Ern came out of my john with a "why me" look, asking if I had felt an earth tremor. He added, "Sharp jolt, not the usual shuddery shakes we get in the Bay Area."

"A quake," Kate said and yawned, standing in the doorway. "Goody, just what we need now."

Shar, after explaining the facts of water conservation to Lance, exited my john and went straight to my coffee table to criticize Cammie's choice of food. "Pineapple juice and stewed tomatoes for breakfast?" She lifted her hands in helplessness.

"That's what Uncle Harve had the most of. I thought these big quart-and-a-half cans would be about right for a meal."

Then the second shock hit, the sonic clap that set crockery and nerves ajangle and, judging from the sound of it, blew out one of my windows. "*Goddamn,*" I said.

Lance, jaw stuck out in defiance, voiced for all of us as he latched his belt: "They better not be atom-bombing us again."

Ern: "Roughly two minutes between ground shock and air shock; thirty miles or so. But in which direction?"

Everybody had frozen in place. Into this still-life Shar said,

"If it's south, we may be okay. In any case, we have several hours. The radiation reading in the bathroom is about four rems, but Lord knows what it will be later if that *was* another bomb."

"I suggest we all, uh, tinkle in the john and hold our heavy stuff until we get a portable rig fixed," Ern said as Cammie started toward my john. To me, he said, "We can't keep drawing air from the basement forever, Harve. Got to make a decent filter."

"I don't suppose the Lotus air-intake filter would do."

After a moment, half-listening to Shar arrange a repair party to the upstairs window: "No—but its twelve-volt battery would sure boost the tunnel lights without making us sweat for it. And you just gave me an idea," he added, grabbing up the empty pineapple juice can. "How long would you need to get the battery?"

"Five minutes. It's no biggie, and I know the drill."

"Wear your stream waders, raincoat, hat, gloves, and a scarf to breathe through. Near as I can figure, Harve, there's still a hundred and fifty rems an hour firing away at anybody outside."

I dressed for my mission, dreading it. I would absorb another ten rems in five minutes—maybe less in the garage, if I used the scarf to breathe through and buttoned my rain slicker. The women had already gone upstairs, leaving the trapdoor open so that a gloomy light flooded the basement.

Ern glanced at me at the stairwell. "You're early for Halloween, fella, but that's a great costume."

"Screw you, fumble-fingers," I chortled. In those hip-length rubber waders, with gloves and my wide-brim rain hat as accessories to my slicker, I felt clumsy and absurd; almost as absurd as my brother-in-law, who stood studying a juice can in one hand and a roll of toilet paper in the other.

I stumped upstairs, unsealed the kitchen door, shut it after me, and while crossing the screen porch to the back door, I learned to step lively without scuffing. A thin patina of dust lay on the porch, stuff that had passed through the screen during the night, and I didn't want to breathe it.

The sun's glow on the east ridge fought its way through a grayish yellow haze as I crossed the yard, and I wished I'd dug the tunnel all the way to the garage. A few tiny visible gray flecks drifted down, dislodged from my staunch old sycamores by wisps of breeze, and I tugged the scarf up over my eyes. I had forgotten my sunglasses but could see dimly through the scarf, and I kept an old pair of racing goggles in the Lotus.

Before filching the battery, I tried the Lotus phone, hoping to learn whether we'd been bombed again, feeling sure we had. I couldn't even punch a prefix without a busy signal. Well, what had I expected? In an urban disaster public two-way communication channels are among the surest casualties.

Pliers and screwdrivers are vicious tools, but in ninety seconds I'd used them to wrest the battery terminals loose while trying to identify a putrid odor nearby. I pried the battery up, fearful of the faint dust coat on the car and floor. Then I eased the hood down, lifted the heavy battery, and hurried to get those goggles from the glove box, pausing long enough to pop the glove-box lamp—socket and all—from its niche. Given time, I could've pocketed a dozen twelve-volt bulbs from the car, some with sockets intact.

But I didn't get that time. What I got was a silent thunderclap of emotional shock as I recognized what stood motionless, had stood there while I worked, in a shadowed corner near me.

"You can put the mattock down, son," I managed to say. "Nobody wants to hurt either one of you."

He was a slender seventeen or so, with corn-silk hair falling like a shed roof across his forehead and a wide mouth meant for grinning. His dark windbreaker and jeans were a typical high school uniform; not much protection, yet he was still lively enough to be dangerous. You couldn't say the same for the woman huddled at his feet, draped in a pathetic torn canvas awning. The kid had tucked it around her, unable to find anything in my garage to keep the lethal dust away from himself. "You've gotta help my mom," he croaked, the mattock still on his narrow shoulder.

"We can't do it here," I said, and stared at the mattock. He lowered it in slow suspicion.

"Where, then?"

"In my house," I heard myself say, thrusting aside all the carefully reasoned arguments of an era that had vanished forever under mushroom clouds. "Help me lift her and then take this battery for me."

En route to the house I learned something about masks and goggles; unless they are sealed against your cheeks, goggles quickly fog up when a mask directs your exhalations upward. I had to breathe out through my mouth and still I nearly fell on my ruined back steps, half-blind with my limp burden.

"Only four minutes, Harve," my sis called as she heard us come into the kitchen. "I timed you."

Kate raced down from the second floor, arms loaded with wrapped packs of toilet paper, calling, "I found it, Mr. McKay, in the"—and then she saw the wild eyes of the youth as he pressed himself against the wall, and she gaped at the awning-wrapped woman—"closet, Holy Mary comeseethis," she finished just as loudly. It had the ring of a call to arms.

Kate and the boy regarded each other warily, and I developed a notion that both he and his mother might be so contaminated that, like Rappacini's daughter, their very bodies were poison. Though that was purest fantasy, their clothes might well be a danger.

I made a command decision then, unwrapping the canvas as I said, "Throw this thing outside, kid, then come upstairs," The woman seemed gossamer, very frail in a short housedress and open-toed flat shoes. I took her upstairs as fast as I could, ignoring the outbursts as Shar and Cammie came into view; ignoring also the awful smell of the woman.

The boy—his name was Devon Baird—found us in my upstairs john and was too scared to protest at the sight of his mother being stripped by a clownishly dressed stranger. "You get every stitch off, boy. Toss it in the tub and rinse your hair with water from the toilet tank."

The mother's straight blond hair and breast were streaked with vomit, but the worst was from her diarrhea. I kept my gloves on while sponging Mrs. Baird's sad little bod with a damp towel, propping her up until young Devon stood by, shivering and naked, to help.

He washed her hair out with loving tenderness, talking to her all the while. "We're gonna be all right, mom," he said; and, "It's *my* turn to take care of *you*," and, "These guys have food and water. You'll be okay." His gaze at mine asked whether he was a liar. I didn't want to give him my opinion.

The Baird woman's breathing had been shallow. Momentarily it became stertorous, and then she retched; long trembling dry heaves. What did come forth came from the other end; a thin trickle that soiled the toilet lid. The boy pressed his mother's face to his stomach and beseeched me wordlessly with tear-filled eyes. Maybe my sis had been waiting for something poignant enough to let her accept these strangers gracefully. In any case, she waited no longer but pulled me aside and began to tend the woman.

I said to the boy, perhaps too gruffly, "Have you been sick like this, too?"

He hesitated, started a negative headshake, swallowed hard, glanced away.

"You have to be strong, and truthful, if we're going to help you," my sis said. It had a threat in it. I wished she'd always been this firm with Lancey-pants.

Mumbling, he said, "She made me wear that damn awning in the culvert while she went to find a better place in the middle of the night and wouldn't let me give it to her until we got over your fence about dawn and then she started puking and—and all. I barfed a little just before you found us. I think it was her being sick that made me sick."

Shar said she hoped he was right and asked why the devil I was still wearing contaminated clothes. While I took my scare costume off in an upstairs bedroom, Shar got the fallout meter and set it between Mrs. Baird's thighs while Devon murmured hopeful things and answered Shar's questions. It seems that Mrs. Baird, a divorcee wary of adult male help, had been panicked by a radio warning at roughly ten the night before; had driven wildly from Concord without the least idea where she was taking her son. She simply took the road of least resistance away from the debris of a shattering, flattening blast wave that had freakishly left their apartment whole while sending storefronts screaming like buzz saws through crowded streets, and through the people composing those crowds. By the time the Bairds drove through it, the massacre of innocents was hours old, and the scenes they passed were silent and dead.

When stopped by a wreck, they had run together up the highway, taking refuge in a culvert for a time. Assuming Ern's estimate was close, she must've taken nearly two thousand rems during those first few hours when the fallout was at its most lethal level, showering its gamma radiation in all directions. Devon's dose might have been survivable as he cowered in that culvert, but Shar's single glance at me endorsed my thoughts about the woman; we were in the presence of death momentarily deferred.

"Her reading is about ten rems per hour," my sis said as I handed an old bathrobe to the youth. "That's about the same as it is everywhere on this floor, maybe a bit more—maybe because of all that," she indicated the pile of clothing in the bathtub. "Let's get her to the basement, Harve, and make her—better." We both knew that was a white lie. We could only try to make her comfortable. But Devon perked up a bit, stumbling along in a robe that swallowed his thin frame. Later Shar presented Devon with her old jeans and sweater from my guest bedroom.

Ern, feverishly slashing precise cuts in cardboard boxes he had pirated from the root cellar, stared in glum silence as we made a pallet for Mrs. Baird near my waterbed. The boy hurriedly visited the john and from the sound of it was trying to muffle his dry heaves. Kate had stashed containers of water in the tub, and I figured Devon knew enough to use it as necessary.

I told Ern how I'd found the pair; watched him work, mystified at the juice tins Lance had emptied into my old stewpot. My nephew was now modifying them in accord with the one Ern had made.

Ern made no complaint about the foundlings, no reproof for my weak-minded decision to take charity cases I had sworn not to take. He chose another topic. "I hope you got the battery. It's going to get damn tiresome in the dark when those dry cells run down, 'cause we can't afford to keep somebody pedaling a bike all the time. Uses too much oxygen; gives off too much water vapor and carbon dioxide."

Cammie was making a tinned beef sandwich for Devon. I asked, "Cammie, will you bring that battery down from the kitchen?"

My niece stopped assembling the sandwich, glanced at her dad, made no move to comply until he gave her the slightest of nods in the basement gloom. I dug the glove-box lamp from my pocket and gave it to Ern, who recognized its utility without a word being spoken. And then I sat down with Lance and mimicked the things he was doing with juice cans. I had some thinking to do.

This was *my* place. If I chose to get sticky about it, they were all guests subject to my rules. As I'd warned Kate, democracy couldn't reign unchecked when our lives depended on everyone taking some direction. If I made the rules, couldn't I break them?

Well, I had; first with Kate and now by ushering this desperately sick woman and her teenage son into my shelter after agreeing with Ern and Shar that extra people would overcrowd our "lifeboat." Now I sensed that my kinfolk were realigning their ideas about my leadership. That worried me. Was I or wasn't I the one who ran things in my own home?

I compared my work with Lance's and punched holes in the next juice can more like his. Then I realized I was actually letting a spoiled kid show me what to do. I didn't like that one damn bit.

However, Lance was working in accord with our recognized expert: Ern. I could choose to do things differently for the sheer pleasure of self-determination, or I could do them the right way. Seen in this light, my urge for control looked pretty silly. Any leader who leads primarily for the joy of wielding power is a leader ripe for overthrow, especially if he makes too many bad decisions. I couldn't fault that logic. It had brought about the Magna Carta and the Continental Congresses and the Russian revolution and *goddamn* if I wasn't denying my own right to run things in my own castle, so to speak.

Had I made a bad decision, bringing the hapless Bairds in?

I knew Shar thought so; suspected the others felt the same way. Yet no one had overtly challenged me for it. Maybe they were giving me another chance—or enough rope. And maybe Ern's mystifying work with toilet paper and tin cans would prove faulty, too, but he had a good track record. The least I could do was give him the freedom to keep improvising, even if that meant my temporarily becoming a peon on his tiny assembly line.

In this way I discovered a rationale of leadership that we seemed to be adopting without endless wrangles about it. I knew where things were; had physical strength the others lacked; and in the economic sense we were living in an investment I had made. On the other hand, my brother-in-law brought technical expertise that I lacked, and at this point our survival was chiefly a matter of technology and its applications.

To some extent my sis also knew more of the technology than I did. I'd be suicidally stupid if I failed to let them guide us while we navigated these nuclear shoals. Like it or lump it, I knew I should accept this erosion of my authority, letting it pass to Ern without making a big deal about it. I neglected the fact that Ern was not the authority figure in his household. Shar was:—and she hadn't exercised much authority with Lance.

Kate interrupted my reverie, having taken a sentry position on the second floor. She had used a spatula to pry a few inches of tape loose at several window edges, the better to squint at our horizons without going outside. Anger and dismay filled her voice as she called, "It's another radioactive cloud west of us!"

The Golden Gate bomb needed forty-five minutes to thrust its cloud so high that we could see it over nearby ridges. There's been lots of speculation about the warhead, some claiming it was meant for military reservations near the north end of the bridge, and some insisting it was part of a ragged second-strike volley targeted against cities instead of military sites.

We weren't concerned about strategy but about tactics. That cloud was headed our way, and if we were going to survive another day in the tunnel, we would need something better than the air supply in the house. It might've been adequate for two or three people, but with so much activity by a half-dozen of us, our sealed environment was becoming a hazard.

Shar made herself a poncho from polyfilm and a babushka to match, taping it together with Kate's help. She wasted no time explaining when I protested her trip outside. "The girls can tell you, bubba," she said, mimed a kiss, and went outside.

"You and Mr. McKay have taken the most radiation so far," Kate told me, "so she's the logical one." For what, I asked. "To make a slit in the film over the cellar doors and tape a flap of film over it, leaving the bottom of the flap untaped. It makes a one-way air-exit valve, to encourage flow of air through the tunnel. I volunteered but I'm not sure I know the best way to do it. Shar claims it'll only take a minute or two."

I nodded. If that new fallout cloud dumped on us, it would soon be too late for outside work. "Kate, can you use the fallout meter?"

She smiled almost shyly. "Cammie showed me. Should I start taking readings here in the kitchen?"

"Right. Uh—you getting along with everybody?"

An instant's hesitation before, "Everybody that counts."

"Everybody counts, Kate. You mean Lance?"

A nod.

"He's a problem. But Shar's the one who keeps him in line. Just wanted you to know you're not alone."

Leading the way to the basement, she stopped, looked back. "No, I'm not. It's a good feeling, boss."

"Not 'boss.' You know my name, Kate. This is no time to be stressing who's boss; we have enough problems without that."

"I noticed," she murmured, and collected the meter materials. By now someone had cut a swatch of fur from my parka to make the process simpler.

Mrs. Baird had not improved, but Cammie had rigged a bedpan from a biscuit tray. She and Devon hovered over the woman, trying to get her to accept a sip of water.

"Don't try to force-feed anyone who's unconscious," I cautioned. "She could strangle."

"Mom said we need to replace the fluids she's losing," Cammie said. "Her skin is flushed but she's trembling all over, Uncle Harve. I don't know whether to cover her up or sponge her with cool water."

I didn't know either, but one look at Devon's drawn features warned me against saying so. I felt his mother's pulse—quick and shallow—and despite her reddened skin, she didn't seem warm. If anything, her body temperature might be a bit low. I said, "Cover her lightly and keep trying to get her to swallow. There's instant coffee somewhere and I'd say she could use the stimulant. Better if it was warm. Devon, you might nibble on that sandwich whether you want it or not," I finished, spying the food he hadn't touched. I hoped all my guesswork wouldn't do any harm.

Meanwhile I had another job. Ern heard me out and agreed, with a suggestion I hadn't considered. "If you're going to block the chimney flue from the inside, try lightly stuffing a brown paper sack with newspaper and stick a broom head in with it. Then tape the sack's mouth over the broom handle and push like hell. The handle will give you something to pull the plug out with later," he explained.

Kate went to the second-floor fireplace with me and took a fallout reading while I arranged the plug I'd made. I had broken the broom handle off short enough to get it into the fireplace and was kneeling at the hearth when she gasped, "Wait! Isn't some fallout going to get on you when you go poking into that thing?"

I stopped short with a curse, aware that she had saved me from a dose of contamination. "So how else can I do it?"

She hurtled downstairs without answering. I spent the time checking our attic beam repair, which looked good, and came down as Kate unfolded more of my thin poly film. Hers was a sloppy-looking answer to the problem: film taped completely across the hearth opening, so loose and voluminous that I could grasp my handmade plug through the film. "Don't breathe," Kate warned, and stepped back sensibly as I began to stuff the paper plug up past the flue damper.

We could hear a cascade of small particles falling like sand;

most of it just harmless crud, no doubt, but Kate rushed to retape the edge of film I pulled loose as a puff of dust emerged near me.

The broom head was too wide and I virtually tore it to pieces in thirty breathless seconds, using the handle like a ramrod. When I felt the plug leap upward inside, I knew it was past the damper into the main chimney shaft, and I simply lit out for the stairs. Kate collected our hardware and followed.

My sis had returned from outside. She shooed Cammie away from a very unpleasant moment while Mrs. Baird threw up pale green fluid into a saucepan. Devon himself wasn't having an easy time because I could hear him retching in the john. At least he had something to throw up, having eaten half a sandwich.

Kate reported that her last reading had been twenty-five rems on the second floor. "And we're soaking up too much radiation here in the basement," Shar replied. "Just because it's gradually dropping, we're acting as if we weren't accumulating more damage to our bodies. But we are, and the sooner we return to the tunnel the better off we'll be. Ernest McKay, that means you!"

Ern sighed and agreed. "I can finish this filter arrangement in the tunnel. Kate, will you take readings under the stairs and then in the tunnel?"

I was collecting the hardware for a string of tunnel lights when Kate revealed her findings. The readings were horrific; twenty in the basement, nearly the same in the tunnel.

Ern paused, thunderstruck, his arms full of cardboard and tin cans. "Good God, we're losing the tunnel advantage!"

Then I mentally flashed on the little meter, abandoned near the fireplace upstairs while Kate helped me minimize the leakage of dust through the film. Grabbing a roll of toilet paper, I moistened a few squares of it and wiped the little meter, taking care to clean its entire outer surface. "Try it now, Kate. You may be reading light contamination on the meter itself."

It was true. Dusted by "hot" particles, the meter had given spurious readings. Now, repeating her readings several times to make absolutely sure, Kate got three rems at the stairs, a half-rem in the tunnel. But the low basement reading didn't slow our retreat back to the tunnel. Shar kept reminding us that every additional rem was one too many. Up to a point, a human body repaired its riddled tissues—but who among us wanted to find that point?

Through all these morning antics Spot had stayed out of the way, but with all of us milling around on our hurried errands, he began to pace the length of the tunnel. A cheetah is a great one for pacing when he can't cut loose and run.

I busied myself collecting parts for the portable john, which Ern had explained to me in one breath: "Make a seat by cutting a big hole through several thicknesses of heavy cardboard, tape them together over the mouth of a plastic trash box, and make a plastic bag to fit inside."

I was astonished to see how much polyfilm we'd used. We had started with a pair of fifty-foot rolls, but now only a little of the ten-mil stuff remained. Of the two-mil film perhaps half the roll was available for toilet baggies or whatever. Those two rolls of polyfilm were among the smartest purchases I ever made.

Then I tripped over a mattress in the dark tunnel and nearly fell on Spot, who marched with feline dignity to the root cellar and sat warily watching Lance. The kid was foraging in the bike kits with my big lamp.

"What're you after, Lance?"

"Getting flashlights for mom," he complained, as if I had accused him of something.

"Good. Don't use the big lamp when a little flash will do," I said as pleasantly as I could while moving away. I didn't hear his reply clearly but my palms itched because it sounded suspiciously like "fuck off" to me. Surely, I reflected, there must be some way to pulp a kid without actually harming him.

The subdued light flooding down the stairwell shed enough illumination for most of our basement operations, but I needed a flashlight to ransack my office for a coil of wire. I asked for a light.

"Coming up," Shar responded, then raised her voice in no-nonsense tones: "Lance, if I don't have a light by the count of ten, you will get *no lunch*!" I filed that one for future reference; Lance was with us, displaying two fresh flashlights, at the count of nine.

During the next few minutes we lined the tunnel with our stuff and pulled Mrs. Baird into it, pallet and all, before sealing the stairwell door and filing into the tunnel. Devon still had little to say, though he made optimistic noises each time his mother managed to sip cool coffee. I suppose she was, at most, half-conscious.

Ern's air filter was a trick he borrowed from oil filtration of an earlier era. During the next hour five of us slaved to get it ready. Ern filled empty juice cans with rolls of toilet paper, plugging off the central tube of each roll and punching holes near the bottom of each can. Then he taped the cans into circular holes in a cardboard box so that, when he connected the bellows pump to the filter box, any air that reached the bellows had to be sucked endwise through the toilet paper rolls from edge to edge. According to Ern, any dust particle that found its way through those layers of paper—between the layers, really—had to be a micron or less in size. So much for the good news.

The bad news was that the bellows had to suck like hell to get any air through a single filter element. That was why Ern used six elements, six rolls in juice cans, for the filter box. He had a second filter box half completed, not knowing how long it might be before the filters became clogged and perhaps heavily contaminated with fallout particles. If one clogged, we'd have another ready.

Before going back into the basement, we discussed the job. Shar felt that she should stay with Mrs. Baird, which left me and Ern as the two most adept at placing that filter box. We needed a fifth hand to hold the flashlight, and Lance and Cammie were the two who had taken the least dosage. Of course we chose Cammie; she could also take meter readings out there.

Kate saw the portajohn I'd been making while we talked and put the plastic trashcan between her knees when I relinquished it. "By the time you're finished with that filter out there, this little throne is going to be very popular," she said with a smile that wouldn't stay on straight.

I showed her my palm and she slapped it lightly, and then I shuffled into the basement to make the filter hookup, wondering if a new Kate Gallo would emerge from all this; and if we would all be changed. *If* we emerged.

The hookup went quickly. First we coupled the air tube we'd already linked to my furnace air intake to the new filter box which had an enclosed front plenum chamber. That way we made sure the filter elements couldn't draw air from the basement. Our next hookup was from the rear plenum chamber of the filter box to the air pipe leading to the pump and took only moments. We secured the connection with tape and went back to the tunnel.

While I sealed up the slit at the tunnel door, Ern was pumping. "Kee-*rist* but it's hard to pump," he muttered. "Cammie, get a reading on the pump exhaust, will you, hon?"

Me: "An obstruction?"

Ern: "No, I checked that. This damn thing just needs a lot of suction, or a little extra time to get through a cycle."

He was understating it. I could see the air pipe trying its best to collapse until he slowed the cycle rate. I counted sixteen cycles a minute and said, "We have two more people but we're pumping at half-speed, and it's harder work. Ungood, Ern."

Cammie knelt with the meter and flashlight, counting sotto voce, and registered pleasure. "I get less than a rem," she said.

"No more than we were taking last night during the worst," said Ern, still pumping, studying his handiwork. "You know, we really should be keeping a journal on radiation versus time."

Farther down the tunnel Spot kibitzed as Kate and Devon lugged Cammie's propped-up bike nearer to us. A good sign: the youth was fit for light duty, or thought he was.

"Here, dad, let me," said Cammie, and she settled herself at the pump. "Lordy, and me already sore from working this thing last night," she said but kept at it.

Ern mumbled, "We've got to do better than this," and motioned me to follow him to the root cellar. We could talk there without auditors except for Spot, whose coarse doggy shoulder ruff I scratched as Ern plied a flashbeam around us.

As though to himself he said, "Here it is, then: the valve Shar made at this end of the tunnel might improve airflow enough to offset the addition of two more people. Or it might not."

"I'm sorry, Ern. If I'd had more time I might have made a different decision out there."

"I doubt it. And I probably would've done just what you did. I guess I just didn't expect you to suddenly turn soft on the human race."

"It could be in short supply a week from now," I explained.

In determination that bordered on anger he grated, "Well, we aren't gonna go under here, by God! We *must* build another front plenum for that spare filter box. But we're out of cardboard."

"Why duplicate the one you built?"

"To put twice as many filter elements into the system, which ought to give us almost twice as much air."

I tried to envision it. "You mean put a second filter box out there and draw air from the basement, too?"

"No, no, goddamnit, we need air that we haven't been breathing. The only restriction is through those rolls of ass wipe. We'll just have to run crossover tubes between the front intake plenums and between the collector plenums—uh, on the suction side. Got it?"

"Yup." When Ern started cussing, he was either drunk or exceedingly worried; and he hadn't taken a nip that day. As he leaned against my thin wall paneling in the tunnel, I recalled nailing the stuff up. It was thin panel board with a watertight plastic facing. I tapped the panel behind him and said, "Well, here's our front plenum."

In two minutes we had the big panel loose and had used the back of the filter box to scribe a pattern. Though Ern's Swiss knife even had a small saw blade, we found it quicker to make repeated scribe lines with a sharp blade and then snap the panel along the lines. Soon we were trimming sides of the new part and double-taping the seams to make them airtight. Ern used the saw blade to cut a circular hole for an air pipe. We taped our new intake plenum onto the spare filter box and found ourselves ready.

I hefted the thing, which weighed no more than ten pounds, and said, "I'll tote it."

Ern's chin went down against his chest. Firmly: "No you won't, Harve. It's only a one-man job, and I—I'd rather you weren't out there."

So: open dissension. I misunderstood his motive. "I'm not *that* klutzy, Ern. And who's going to stop me?"

"Sweet reason, I hope. You and Shar absorbed some heavy stuff outside today. I didn't. Lance can handle a flashlight, and it's time he pulled some weight." Ern's stance was that of a man expecting a backhand, but he planted himself in front of me like a cornerstone waiting for a bulldozer.

Kate disturbed our tableau, moving toward us with the one-holer she and Cammie had finished. It had a taped-together seat of corrugated cardboard over an inch thick, probably in deference to my great arse, and a film-faced cardboard lid with a tape hinge. The lid wasn't airtight, but the film hung down so it could be lightly taped when we weren't using it. Ern's vanwagon had a real chemical toilet, but they had left their first-stage vehicle somewhere en route. Kate's portaprivy would have to serve.

"I'm on the verge of a—ah—breakthrough, fellas. Mind if I test the thing in privacy?"

I grinned at her, stepped aside, handed the unwieldy filter box to Ern, and sighed. "Lance, huh?"

"He's a big help when he wants to be. Don't sell him short."

"Not me, pal." Consumer-protection laws were invented to balk sales of such products as Lance.

But Lance didn't want to. "Why pick on me? Cammie can do it."

"Let him have his breakfast, hon," Shar said. "He's worked very well this morning." Her tone suggested there was nothing more to say.

Ern said something anyway, very softly.

"You wouldn't," said my sis in horror. Lance smiled and slurped pineapple juice. Shar went on. "Ernest McKay, I will not let you bully your own son. Childish bullying, that's all it is," she snorted.

Ern stripped tape from the door slit one-handed, shouldering the filter box. "Coming, Cammie?"

My niece's gaze swept across her mother and brother in silent accusation as she stood up, stretching the muscle kinks from her neck. She took the little flashlight and went into the basement with her father.

I took over at the pump, exchanging stolid glances with my sister. She held my gaze for a long moment and then said to Lance, "Why don't you pedal the bike awhile, hon?"

"Pedals are too far away."

"That hasn't stopped you in the past, lamb. And you *do* want lunch, don't you?"

"There's more than one kind of bully," he observed. But he went.

In the stillness we could identify sounds of survival: breathing; the clack of pump valves and the whoosh of air; the ratchety whir of the bike as Lance pedaled; the whine of a tiny generator. And muffled by distance, the murmur and industry of a new filter emplacement in our primitive little life-support system. Unheard but very much in my mind was the slow-fire hammer of gamma radiation riddling the flesh of Ern and Cammie.

Then we heard Kate in the root cellar, denouncing Spot as a voyeur. I smiled briefly and said to Shar, "Lance is right, you know."

"My bubba siding with Lance! Will wonders never—"

"Don't 'bubba' me; I'm not siding with him. He said there are various kinds of bullying, and he's right. He's an expert at it, Shar; he just uses you as his weapon and his shield."

"Nonsense. Look at the child, pedaling for dear life."

"Bullshit; pedaling for dear lunch, you mean."

"A much better alternative than beating a child," she sniffed.

I considered that, found it apt so long as it worked, then applied the idea to our whole situation—if we were lucky enough to have one—our future. "Maybe the whole country made a mistake by inventing so many alternatives," I mused.

"Lower scores on college entrance exams; middle-class druggies in junior high; professional athletics dominated by minorities. Maybe because the average middle-class kid has too many neat alternatives, a lot of 'em never learn to pitch into a shitty job and get it over with. At worst they can just run away from home and crash at a series of halfway houses. We've let our kids replace self-discipline with alternatives. No goddamn wonder divorce rates are still climbing, sis."

Armed with years of adult-ed jargon, Shar jabbed with a favorite: "Simplistic. Cammie's no druggie and she's on the tennis varsity."

"Yep, and she also got your belt across her bottom when she snotted off. She didn't get pleasant alternatives, as I recall."

Fiercely whispered: "Cammie's not the angel everybody thinks she is. She's subtle; winds you around her finger. When I see that, it makes me want to protect Lance."

I knew Cammie could be a vamp. But she knew how to give freely, even when it interfered with what she wanted. Chuckling in spite of myself, I said, "Cammie has to work to wind us around, and if we like being wound it can't be all bad, sis." Suddenly the pump handle became very much easier to lift, and I figured Ern would be back shortly. "Anyway, think about it. From yesterday forward, for the rest of his life, Lance McKay is going to find himself goddamn short on pleasant alternatives. For his sake, I hope he's not too old to learn discipline."

After a long silence Shar mused, "As far back as I can remember, bubba, you prided yourself on finding alternatives. Nearly drove mother crazy, and got your backside tanned to saddle leather. But you've turned out to be one of those people who have *so much* self-discipline, except for feeding your face, that you tend to think of yourself as judge, jury, and . . ."

I'm sure she was about to add "executioner." Despite my best efforts, somehow my little sis had learned about the heroin wholesaler, years before. I rousted him in Ensenada and brought him back after he jumped bail. I'd been naive then, and he was such a mannerly dude, and I didn't know about short ice picks in homburgs until it glanced off a rib on its way in while I was negotiating a slow curve on the coast highway. As I saw it, Mr. Mannerly had executed himself.

"*Nolo contendere,*" I said to my sister.

"Cute," she said gently. "What I was getting at is, why aren't you one of the irresponsibles?"

I said it was a fair question and mulled it over as I pumped. Finally I replied, "Maybe because we were farm kids, though we moved to town before you had chores to do, sis. Sure, I love alternatives; they're fun! But feeding those stupid chickens and collecting eggs were things for which there simply were *no* alternatives on our farm. They wouldn't stop laying on weekends no matter what I told 'em. On a farm you try a lot of alternatives, but you shovel a lot of shit, too. Maybe there's an ideal balance. And maybe that's what I'm trying to steer you toward."

In the dim light her profile and the way she had of lifting one shoulder while she cocked her head took me back many years, to when my little sis consulted me on matters she wouldn't dare bring to mother. Finally she laid a loving hand on my arm. "I'll think on it," she promised. "It certainly won't do to let Lance defy his father in this dreadful cooped-up situation."

At this juncture Kate padded back to announce that the potty had passed her most exacting test. Shar allowed as how she was simply *bursting* to try it.

"You see," I called as Shar moved away, "indoor plumbing! We've weathered the worst."

Su-u-ure we had . . .

Ern and Cammie returned moments after my exchange with Shar, and they were elated when I showed them how easily the pump operated. They drank some juice, and we agreed for Devon's benefit that his mother seemed better. Obviously her system had rid itself of most available moisture, including bile. There was no point in mentioning an IV with saline solution. We couldn't even boil or distill water, much less get it into her veins. All we could do was urge cold instant coffee down her throat when she was able to swallow. That wasn't often, and her gamma-ravaged body refused to keep it long.

Her reddened skin was perhaps the only thing Shar could

treat, by sponging her body with saltwater into which a bit of baking soda was stirred. I can't swear it helped much, except that it kept the silent, hollow-eyed Devon from dwelling on his own condition. If he had a chance it lay in his desire to stay active, and we stressed that he must eat and drink plenty.

Shar's purse held a note pad and ball-point pen, which she used to begin a tally of events, beginning with the first ground shock. She started it as a running record of radiation versus time, but it soon grew into a series of anecdotes as well. There was something about the sharing of tales that brought our spirits up and drew Kate and Devon into the group. Not that we were idle. We took turns at the honey bucket and the pump, except for Ern. With extension cords and safety pins for test connections, he was busily embarking on an honest-to-God electric power system.

Why hadn't we used the battery-powered radios on hand? Well, we had. Precious little good it had done us.

During the night we'd thought about radio bulletins only when we were in the tunnel, where FM reception was hopeless. I tried to get San Francisco's KGO on the AM dial but found, instead, good ol' XEROK, Juarez, at that frequency. Even with the outrageous transmitter power of the Mexican station, I could hardly make out when they were transmitting in English; a skyful of energetic particles makes hash of most transmissions. From some unidentified station, I heard what may have been a list of local roads still open, but I couldn't spot the locale.

Shar had tried a radio while taping film over my broken window but had quit in a hurry because, she said, the little they did hear was disturbing to the girls. She had gotten KSRO in Santa Rosa, which warned evacuees that the town could not absorb another soul. She got KDFM in Walnut Creek, which begged hysterically for help from a studio buried so deep in rubble that the announcer could not escape. From San Francisco and Oakland she got nothing. And that was when she quit trying.

I decided to try a third time early in the afternoon, and while using the homemade toilet in the root cellar, I poked a little aerial past our book barrier, hoping to tune in and hear something that would make me feel better. I got Santa Rosa's rebroadcast of an EBS bulletin claiming that the Soviet Union had paid with its life for exceeding the parameters of limited nuclear war. The announcer called on Americans to throw open their doors—those who still had doors—to battered victims escaping from target areas. It tried to cheer us with the news that the President was safe, but in my case I'm afraid it failed there. Finally it insisted that many small towns were responding heroically to hordes of evacuees. The Santa Rosa announcer then broke in and reminded all and sundry that Santa Rosa was not one of those towns. Evacuees from the San Francisco bomb were reminded that the Golden Gate spans were now in the bay. I snapped the radio off then. I'd had enough and went back down the tunnel to my little family, hoping to hear something that would make me feel better.

During our first long afternoon in the tunnel, we at last had time to organize and to accept our enforced isolation from the deadly world outside. Shar suggested our rotation schedule for air-pump duties and assembled notes to estimate our individual radiation doses. Meanwhile Ern separated the wires on one end of an extension cord and, drilling pilot holes into the soft metal of my Lotus battery terminals with the awl on his knife, inserted small wood screws as anchors for the bared wire ends. I stapled extension cords for twenty feet along one wall of the tunnel. With spare wire and safety pins, Ern soon had a bike headlamp completing the circuit.

At that point the kids cheered and abandoned Cammie's bike, grateful for a source of light they didn't have to work for. Ern observed dryly, "You kids are lucky; many bike generators are six-volt but these are twelve, so the bulbs are compatible with a car battery." Then he hauled the other two bikes near our cheery little half-amp light and, one by one, stole their generators and headlamps for the tunnel. During all this I heard the McKay family's one-day saga.

Ern had driven to work at Ames that morning, playing a tape album by the twin-piano Paradox duo instead of listening to the radio. The traffic was very light. Small wonder! He had been stunned to find everyone at the shop in a dither over the news reports, and then had tried to telephone Shar. Their line was busy because Shar, by this time, was trying to call *him.*

Long ago they'd agreed that Ern would feign illness and return home if hostilities seemed near. He couldn't at first believe things had deteriorated so far, but the model shop at Ames was operating at less than half-strength that morning. Ern kept quiet, stayed near his phone, and swore he would not run for home on the strength of unconfirmed reports of a tussle with Syria.

He had just began checking sensor holes in a specimen wing section when he overheard his manager on video link talking with his wife, who worked in the nearby Satellite Test Center; whatever American citizens might think, Soviet citizens were streaming into firestorm-proof subways in major cities while our spy satellites watched.

Ern knew that STC, spy master of those satellites, would be a primary target if war came. And STC was only a short walk across Moffett Field from the Ames complex. Ern was not fool enough to wait for some official NASA holiday announcement and was jogging to his car moments later.

At home in their suburb north of San Jose, the kids were nearly off to school before Shar caught the first scarifying bulletins about the capsizing of our leviathan *Nimitz.* Shar called them back, ordered them both into hiking duds, and started trying to contact Ern while she consulted her checklists.

My sis had done everything once: EST, Catholicism, a lover, and a bookkeeping job for a parts supplier in Silicon Gulch. I suspect that each of those activities included a common side effect: a knack for compartmenting and categorizing. In Shar's case it yielded checklists that first became a joke, then a mainstay in the family.

Her crisis-relocation checklist went further than a vacation list. In addition to shutting off the water heater and resetting the thermostat, she included a cleanout of several cabinets that would fill the vanwagon. Ern had the Ford runabout, but their vanwagon, with its cavernous storage space on a sturdy light chassis, squatted in their carport ready to serve as their first-stage booster vehicle. It was roomy enough for boxes of medicine and food, Ern's tool chest, bedrolls, even a pair of bikes and the hand-operated winch that could haul them from a ditch. The other two bikes could fit on racks outside. Each bike had its own wire basket for the individual survival packs Ern had assembled. If they became stymied somehow en route to my place, their plan was to jettison the first-stage (translation: park the vanwagon) and continue using the bikes as second-stage vehicles.

Ern squalled his little Ford into the driveway in time to see Cammie toss the last bedroll into the vanwagon and wasted no time scrounging some extras: shovel, a roll of aircraft-quality tow cable, old bleach bottles he'd filled with drinking water, and the "decorative" blunderbuss from over their mantel.

That funny-looking little period piece had been my gift once upon a time, a purely defensive household item for Shar. A do-it-yourself kit from a gunsmith, it was short stocked, a smoothbore modified from flintlock to percussion cap. Of course it would fire only a single black powder charge and then had to be reloaded. But its bell mouth spread to an inch and a half diameter, and I loaded it with BBs. You needed two adult hands to cock it. You also needed a good grip when you pulled the trigger, because it had a recoil wallop like a baseball bat. Any intruder who was even in the general direction of that bell mouth would find his world suddenly filled with thunder and smoke and steel pellets, and if it didn't blow him into another dimension it would at least give him serious misgivings about wandering into my sis's home without knocking. Nor would folks a block away sleep through it. The blunderbuss was, I thought, just about perfect for one exclusive purpose: point-blank defense within the home. Anyway, Ern stuck it into the vanwagon.

I couldn't help laughing when Lance interrupted his mother's account of the bike argument. "They wouldn't let me bring my bike," he accused, "so I brung the skateboard. Dad thought I was nuts but I wasn't."

Give the little bugger credit—he was good on a urethane-wheeled skateboard and he knew it, and wore his pads into the vanwagon like a gladiator heading for the arena. In a way, he was.

Shar locked their house and fumed while Ern topped off their fuel tank from his Ford, using the electric fuel pump trick he'd shown me. They left the outskirts north of San Jose intending to take freeways to Niles Canyon. It didn't take long to see the futility of that idea.

Traffic on Highway Six-Eighty was already stalled clear back to the off-ramp. Shar folded their local map under her clipboard and directed Ern to a state road, then to a winding county road when their second choice permitted them only a walking pace. They passed under the freeway presently and saw highway patrolmen with bolt cutters nipping a hole in the freeway fence to let cars leave the hopeless logjam up there.

When Ern spotted a pickup running along the sloping ridge of railroad tracks in Fremont, he followed. The right-of-way led them to the little community of Niles, but a highballing freight with hundreds of hangers-on nearly clipped the vanwagon, and Ern decided they'd played on the railroad tracks long enough. They hit Niles Canyon Road then, seeing that traffic toward the distant town of Livermore was bullying its way across all four lanes in escaping the overcrowded bay region.

Of course they saw the wrecks and quickly learned to look away since neither of the adults had special medical training and their first responsibility was to get their own two kids to safety with a minimum of lost time. A few motorists helped others; a delivery truck dragged one car out of the road with a tow cable while other traffic, including Ern, streamed past. Ern didn't stop until forced to, but he was expecting trouble, and when the chain of rear-enders began ahead, he wisely slowed before he had to, gaining ten feet of maneuvering room.

Standing atop the vanwagon, Ern studied the blockage. Two lanes had been stopped for some time after one car, rear-ended, had spun sideways. The other two lanes had continued, drivers in the balked lanes trying vainly to edge into lanes in which cars moved bumper to bumper. No one would give. Someone finally tried to bluff or force his way in, touching off a chain reaction as cars took to the shoulder trying to pass the new obstruction. As Ern watched, two fistfights erupted. One guy with a knife was sent packing by another flailing tire chains.

At that point people began simply to abandon their cars in favor of hoofing it.

"I counted fourteen cars between us and the front of the jam," Ern recalled as he snubbed the third bike generator against Cammie's bike wheel in the tunnel. "I figured with enough people helping, we could get all the wrecks pushed onto the shoulder in fifteen minutes, even if we had to winch some of 'em sideways." Ern figured he was an hour or so from my place if they stuck with the vanwagon but longer if they continued by bike. Besides, they'd be abandoning food, hardware, and protection if they left the vanwagon.

Wearing heavy gloves, winch and tow cable in hand, Ern trotted past other drivers, urging them to help instead of just honking. The owner of the first car in the mess stood at bay with a jack handle, threatening to brain the first guy who touched his car unless they'd help him pull his fender away from his blown-out tire. Someone offered him, instead, a ride in another car, and implied that his most likely alternative was a knot on his head from a dozen determined men.

Ern used the man's jack handle as a pry bar under the crumpled edge of the fender, then hooked his tow cable to the handle. With several men hauling at once, they pulled the fender away from the wheel. The owner drove off very slowly while his blown tire disintegrated on its rim, no longer part of the general problem.

One car, abandoned and locked by its owner, was *hors de combat* simply because the owner had taken his keys. The steering column was locked, so even after smashing a side window, the men couldn't steer the heavy coupe over to the shoulder. Ten men could tip it over on its top to get it out of the way, though, and they did, even while Ern begged them not to. Fuel tanks dribble a lot when a car's wheels are in the air.

The first car to shove its nose past the others was a big sedan, and its driver, a level-headed woman, backed up while others used tire chains as a tow cable from her rear bumper. She pulled two more cars free before charging off down the highway. Ern winched a pair of small cars sideways from the tangle, with help from the owners, anchoring his winch to the base of a steel highway sign. "Played hell with the jack sockets on the cars," Ern said, and grinned, remembering it, "because I had 'em stick their jacks into the chassis sockets to give me something to hook onto." He didn't try that with heavier cars, fearing his winch wouldn't take it.

It took thirty minutes to clear two lanes, and while fifty people struggled to clear other lanes, improvising as they went, Ern sprinted to the vanwagon just as Shar got it started. Soon they overtook the guy riding on his rim. Ern estimated it would've taken the man five minutes to change to his spare, which made that press-on-regardless outlook seem pretty shortsighted.

They left the highway at the outskirts of Livermore, a town experiencing its first-ever taste of terminal traffic constipation. Cammie described it wide-eyed: "Worse than Candlestick Park after a game! You'd see a car go shooting down a side street and then it'd come howling back a few blocks further. People were driving across lawns, pounding on doors, getting stuck in flower beds, you name it."

"Like one of those car movies where they do crazy things," Lance put in. "But in the movies they get away with it." Lance had pegged it nicely; too many citizens imagined they could do the stunts they saw on the screen, and too few realized how much those stunts depended on expertise and hidden preparations.

Once they were across town and headed north toward my place, said Shar, she thought they'd pulled it off. They drove slowly, with frequent horn-toots to warn hikers and bikers who streamed out of Livermore along with many cars. There was some traffic into the town as well, coming down from the hills.

Shortly after the road began its twisting course toward Mount Diablo they saw the other van, a battered relic, its driver approaching with no thought for other traffic but the steady blare of its horn. Ern braked hard. "I didn't think they'd make the turn at the rate they were coming," he said.

They did, but only by taking all the road and forcing a hiker to leap for his life. They didn't make it past Ern, though, sideswiping his left front fender with an impact that threw both vehicles into opposite ditches.

Since all four McKays were harnessed, they sustained nothing worse than the bruise along Ern's muscular forearm. Shar quieted Lance's wails ("I wasn't really scared," he insisted.) and after ascertaining that they weren't injured, Ern found that his door would no longer open. He went out the back of the vanwagon, both kids piling out with him, and then hugged them close in protective reflex. Approaching from the other van was a bruiser in his forties, a semiauto carbine in his hands and murder in his face. Behind him, a younger man limped forward hefting a big crescent wrench.

"Damn fool, didn't you hear me honk? That thing of yours better be drivable," snarled the big one, using his carbine as a deliberate menace.

Ern realized he was being hijacked. "Don't point it at the kids," he pleaded, wondering if either vehicle could be driven. "I'll just get the bikes and—"

"Touch that stuff and you're a dead man," said the bruiser, spying a ten-speed bike in the gloom. "Jimmy, we lucked out."

Jimmy, the younger man, brandished the wrench at Ern, who moved back and started to call a warning to Shar. He never got the chance and in any case he would've been warning the wrong person.

The big man with the carbine stepped up to the vanwagon's open doors and was met in midstride by a thunderous blast. Shar had found the antique fowling piece. The tremendous spread of shot took out a bike spoke, knocked a bedroll out of the cargo area, and snatched the carbine from the man, who cartwheeled end for end. Everyone reeled away from the godawful roar and the smoke that followed like a bomb burst from inside the vanwagon.

Ern looked wildly for something to throw at Jimmy the wrench man but found the wrench available. Yowling, hands in air, young Jimmy raced back to his damaged van and tumbled inside. Shar emerged from the vanwagon coughing and spitting, the little blunderbuss empty but still in her hands.

The big man came to his knees, stared at his arms through torn shirt sleeves. Ern was near enough to see the bluish welts on his hands; raised knots like some disfiguring disease that began to ooze blood as both watched in silent fascination. Then the big fellow saw my sis march into view; saw her cock the harmless thing as if to fire again. He stumbled to his feet then and ran doubled over, holding his arms across his body and crooning with pain. Ern ran a few paces after him until he saw that the man had no intention of retrieving his weapon. Obviously the old van was drivable, because in seconds the ex-rough type was spewing gravel in it.

The vanwagon was another matter. Its radiator torn loose, steering rod hopelessly bent, it could not be navigated another hundred feet, much less the twenty miles to my place. Ern managed to start it and got it far off the macadam while water poured from ruptured hoses. The McKays then traded relieved kisses all around and started rigging for their second-stage flight. It was then half past two in the afternoon.

That was about the same time, said Kate Gallo, that she first noticed the burly black-haired gonzo at the racetrack. I let her tell it, making me the heavy in her waggish way. She explained she'd been running from a check-kiting spree and I said nothing to contradict her. But when she tried to describe our open-water crossing as literally floating across, I started to hum "It Ain't Necessarily So" and got my laugh before moving over to help Ern.

He was wiring all three tiny bike generators together, positive to positive and negative to negative. That was when I admitted that Ern McKay had truly found a way to *recharge my damn battery!* The output of a single generator was too puny to feed a whopping big car battery, but three generators in parallel? Still a trickle-charge, but a significant trickle.

I thought it might be hard work to pedal with three generators riding against a bike wheel but I was wrong. Ern insisted that we connect the generator's positive terminal to that of the battery only while someone was pedaling. If that circuit was intact while no one pedaled, he said, the battery's energy might trickle *out* through those generators. As it was, we could recharge the battery with about four hours of pedaling and have twelve hours of light without draining the battery at all. I could've kissed him for that. Kate did it for me, squarely on his forehead.

At length Kate reached the point in her tale where I "abandoned" her to search for my family, and I filled them in with a brief account of my trip along the mountain ridge. "If you had any illusions about the flatlanders around the bay pulling through this," I concluded, "forget 'em. The burn cases in Oakland alone would overload burn-unit facilities from coast to coast."

With a glance toward the comatose Mrs. Baird, Shar muttered, "You might try for a bit of optimism."

"I *am* optimistic, sis. I'm assuming a lot of burn victims will survive the firestorm and fallout long enough to profit from medical treatment. If you've read about the quake and fire in San Francisco back in 1906, you'll recall it was the fire that caused the most casualties. Volunteer crews came from as far as Fresno to help. Trainloads of food and volunteers in, trainloads of refugees out.

"It's not as though there were no precedent for this," I went on, mostly for the benefit of our younger members. "Europeans saw great cities destroyed, whole populations decimated or worse, forty years ago. London, Dresden, Berlin—and don't forget how Japan was plastered. I know it wasn't on such a scale as this, but they did find ways to rebuild."

"It took 'em years," Ern reminded me. "And they had American help."

I nodded. "You're mighty right there, pal. And that's all we can expect, too: American help."

Kate asked in disbelief, "From where? Fresno?"

"No, from us! And millions more like us. Damnit, think! There must be two hundred thousand people schlepping around in Santa Rosa right now, and if the fallout missed 'em they'll probably be outside in shirt sleeves."

"Sure—grubbing for roots," said Cammie. "And I've heard mom talk about the radiation that's spread all over the world now."

"Can't deny that," I said. "We'll probably have higher infant mortality and ten times the cancer we've had in the past. I grant you all that, much as I loathe it. But don't tell me we lack the guts people had in Stalingrad and Texas City and Nagasaki!"

"I wanted to be a golf pro," said young Devon softly. "Looks like I'll be a carpenter or a bricklayer."

Ern: "Could be. Or a cancer researcher. Harve's not promising fun and games, Devon; only hope. We'll all have to bust our butts for a few years, and we have no assurance that we'll ever see things back to normal. Whatever that is," he said and chuckled. "It doesn't take a professor of sociology to predict a sudden change in the American way of life. On the other hand, it might not be so noticeable to farmers in Oregon or a dentist in Napa."

"Oh God," Kate breathed almost inaudibly and quit cycling the air pump.

Cammie asked for us all: "Trouble with the pump?"

Kate took a long shuddering breath, shook her head, began to pump again. "My father has a summer home near Napa. Little acreage just outside of Yountville, which nobody ever heard of. Just a statusy thing. They rarely go there."

"Maybe they're there now," I offered.

Another headshake. "Not them; that's what hurts. You don't know my father. All his clout is in connections with people in the city." No matter where you lived around the bay, when you said "the city" you meant metropolitan San Francisco. "It's just about the only place where he doesn't carry a gun. No, my family will play out their hand right smack in the city."

Of course I'd told them what the Santa Rosa broadcast had said. We knew the approaching fallout was coming from San Francisco itself. Most hands being played out in Baghdad-by-the-Bay were losing hands. It was one thing to reject your family's ways but quite another to envision them all dead in a miles-wide funeral pyre.

"Maybe your folks had a cellar," Cammie said.

Kate brightened. "Wine cellar. Part of the mystique."

"You don't mean *those* Gallos," Lance said in awe.

"No"—Kate managed a wan smile—"but I could lie about it if you insist."

Ern said he didn't care which Gallo she was if she could

produce a bottle of sherry, and that reminded me of the stuff in my liquor cabinet. I said to Shar, "We need to take another reading in the basement for that graph you're making. I'll just nip out and do it and bring back a bottle to celebrate our new electric light plant."

It was around four in the afternoon. Shar consulted her graph and calculated that the outside reading should be around a hundred rems, while the basement should read about two or three—if the fallout cloud had missed us. Five minutes in the basement would be a twelfth of that dosage, which laid only a small fraction of a rem on the meter reader. "It's your hide, bubba," said my sis.

I took the meter hardware and fed several sparks to the meter, then chose a half-empty bottle of brandy and some cream sherry the kids could sip with us. I rummaged and found two decks of cards.

The basement stank like an outhouse. We needed the forty gallons of water in the tunnel for drinking, but my waterbed was available so I sloshed some water from the mattress into a pan and filled the toilet tank in three trips. The damned thing had to be flushed of its barf and never-you-mind.

Then, after nearly four minutes, I checked the meter.

The leaves of foil were completely relaxed together.

Fighting jitters, I charged the meter again and took a one-minute reading. Meanwhile I cursed myself for assuming that the reading wouldn't be off scale in four minutes. I got a one-minute reading of over four rems an hour and hightailed it into the tunnel.

Though abashed by my stupid error, I described it to the others, determined that they could profit by my dumbfuckery. Shar's conclusion was simple and direct; the only smart way to read the meter was to watch it closely for the first minute. If you didn't have a useful reading by that time, ambient radiation was roughly one rem or less.

Her second conclusion was borne out as we took readings in the tunnel. Shortly before I'd gone out to the basement, heavy fallout had begun to irradiate my little place.

* * *

For the next hour the tunnel was a hotbed of projects. I was urged to do nothing that even smacked of exercise because my great bulk would use up twice as much air as, say, Lance—and I'd give off more cee-oh-two and water vapor. So I sat near the little six-watt bike headlamp and took several long readings on the meter.

Shar turned over the sponge-bath chore to Devon and went to use our temporary john. She sprinkled a shotglassful of bleach into the hole after using it, carefully extracted the half-full bag, and placed it into a big brown paper grocery bag. The taped seams of the plastic bag might give way, but it wouldn't come apart with heavy kraft paper around it. She installed the next plastic bag with the paper sack already surrounding it in the plastic trashcan, and I wondered why Ern hadn't thought of that. It is truly amazing how fast we get smart when faced with a dribble of dookey.

Especially somebody else's.

I also understood how farm and ranch people earn their penchant for earthy humor. Dealing with natural functions like evacuation on such a grand scale, you're often faced with side effects that could outrage a saint. But you can always joke about them, robbing them of their power to beat you down. Maybe that explains the rough jokes we shared while in the tunnel.

Ern read my sister's notes and found little to criticize. At a quarter till five we were reading almost exactly two rems per hour in the tunnel, which scared the hell out of us until we found it subsiding soon afterward. We didn't talk about it to the kids, who were fixing a simulacrum of supper and pedaling the bike.

By six o'clock Shar had a radiation-versus-time graph and an estimate of the total dosage for each of us. For Mrs. Baird, who continued her heaves and diarrhea without losing much fluid, Shar simply put a question mark. I knew the answer in total rems had to be in four figures.

Next to Devon Baird's name she wrote four hundred, with another question mark after it. He seemed to be perking up, even insisting on pedaling the bike and pumping air. Best of all, he was retaining food and liquids now. His question mark was the only valid one, but who was so cruel as to tell him that?

I was next on the list with an estimated forty rems because I'd been in the attic and outside, too. Shar and Ern came next with thirty-five; Kate had taken five less. And below Cammie's twenty-five came Lance with twenty or so. Maybe Lance was young enough at eleven to be one of the "very young" who, like the aged, were supposed to be more vulnerable. I tried not to begrudge him the advantage. In any case it was an arguable set of estimates—in Ern's jargon, strictly paper empiricism.

My sis didn't mention lethal doses in front of Devon Baird. Instead she dwelt on the positive side. "In class we studied the *Lucky Dragon* incident," she said, spooning a portion of tuna and green peas that was not—couldn't possibly be!—half as bad as it sounds. "The entire crew of this Japanese fishing boat was accidentally dosed in 1954; they even ate contaminated food. They took gamma doses of around a hundred and seventy-five rems, and *all of them survived it!* I think one man died months later from some medication, but the rest made it. And they took much higher doses than we're taking here."

Devon, listlessly: "What if they keep dropping bombs near us every day?"

Ern said, "I can't believe there's much more to shoot at around here."

"I hope not," Devon replied, and dubiously addressed his tuna salad.

Presently we finished our meal, and though Spot made overtures to the leftovers, I steered him firmly to his farina mix. A tally of our food told us we'd have enough for two meals a day through ten days without resorting to horsemeat. By then we might be eating farina mix ourselves. At least we wouldn't have to cook it.

Shar urged Kate to be dealer, referee, and sergeant-at-arms for a card game among the younger members, and as soon as Devon got engrossed in the game, my sis motioned me nearer to Ern, who was seated at the air pump. "Let's talk about what we'll have to do next month," she said loudly enough to be overheard, and then much more softly, "Mrs. Baird seems to have a new problem."

The woman was semiconscious now but never spoke and could barely swallow. Shar had noticed the gradual, steady appearance of clear blisters on the woman's skin. Though some blisters were forming on her torso, they predominated in a sprinkle of raised glossy patches on her lower legs, arms, neck, and face. To Devon's query, Shar had only smiled and said we'd have to wait and see. To Ern and me, she said, "I'm afraid it means severe radiation burns, probably direct skin contact with particles only a few hours from the fireball. The blisters are on all sides of her body, so there's no way we can make her comfortable unless—but I guess the waterbed is out of the question."

"In more ways than one," I admitted. "I hate to bring it up, but while stealing some water from it to flush the toilet, I realized that that water will not be drinkable."

They both gaped at me in the gloom. "But we've only got maybe twenty gallons left in the tunnel, Harve," said Ern. "And about the same in your bathroom. What's wrong with waterbed stuff?"

"The chemicals I put in to prevent algae," I said and sighed. "It's not just bleach, guys. Bleach slowly deteriorates a vinyl mattress, so I used a pint of a commercial chemical. It's poison. I'm sorry."

We fell silent for a time. The kids didn't notice because they were talking louder, making noise for noise's sake. I understood why when I heard the Baird kid's spasms from the root cellar. He was losing his dinner into our jury-rigged john. I'd spent years rooting out soured curds of the milk of human kindness from my system because of the work I'd chosen; yet the quiet courage of this slender kid forced a tightening in my throat. I knew why I hadn't befriended him more: I didn't want to mourn if we lost him. That didn't say much for *my* courage.

"That poor boy," Shar murmured, "has diarrhea too. I wish we had some plug-you-uptate."

That was our childhood phrase for diarrhea medicine. I said, "Mom used to have a natural remedy. You remember what it was?"

"Well, she started with an enema of salt and baking soda, but that was to replace lost salt and to clean out the microbes. This isn't the same thing. If anything the Bairds probably don't have *enough* intestinal flora. Anyway, mom also gave us pectin and salty bouillon."

"Why the hell didn't you say so," asked Ern. "We've got a half-dozen bouillon cubes in each bike kit."

I put in, "If it's pectin you need, I doodled around with quince preserves from all those quinces falling off my bushes. There's so much pectin in a quince, you can jell other fruit preserves just by adding diced quince."

"I'd forgotten you make a hobby of food. God knows *how* I could forget, you great lump of bubba."

"Beat your wife, Ern," I begged.

"Just washed her and can't do a thing with her," he said.

As soon as Devon returned to the card game, Ern took a flashlight and went to find the bouillon cubes. Our carefully nurtured good spirits took a dip when he returned with only one tiny foil-wrapped bouillon cube. "I know I put 'em in," he complained, tossing the single cube to Shar.

Lance saw the gleam of foil. "Dibs," he shouted. "I saw it first, mother!" My nephew's tone suggested that he could be severe on infractions of fair play.

Shar regarded him silently for a moment, knowing as we all did that Lance had retrieved flashlights from the bike kits. Mildly: "Lance, you must've eaten at least fifty already."

In extracting confessions my sis had only to exaggerate the offense to have Lance set her straight. "Fifty? Naw, there was only a few."

"How many do you have left?"

"All of 'em. Right here," he said and patted his belly. In the ensuing quiet his grin began to slide into limbo.

"Aw, he's all right, Miz McKay," Devon said in the boy's support.

The point was that Devon himself was *not*, and bouillon could have helped him. Inwardly we writhed with an irony that we must not share with Devon. "Thank you, Devon, but I'll decide that. Lance, come here a minute," said Shar.

Mumbled: "Don't wanta."

"Two meals tomorrow, Lance."

He came bearing the word "Bully."

Shar indicated that he should sit between his parents. Then, in tones of muted mildness, my sis composed music for my ears; a menacing sonata, a brilliant *bel canto* that struck my nephew dumb.

Did Lance recall his father's threat? Shar was ready, even eager now, to endorse it. Lance would touch no food or drink without asking first. He would perform every job we asked without audible or visible complaint. He would use nothing, take nothing, play with nothing unless he got permission first. It was not up to Lance to decide when an infraction might be harmless.

Of course he had an alternative, said Shar with a calm glance toward me. Lance could elect to do as he pleased. He would then be thrashed on his bare butt by parents *and* his uncle (here I saw the whites of his eyes) and would be bound and gagged if need be for as long as necessary.

"By now, dear, you may have thought of claiming you need to go to the bathroom while tied up. Of course you can. In your pants. Since you have no other clothes and you can't wash the ones you have, you may want to think twice before you do that. But it's up to you, sonny boy," Shar gradually crescendoed.

"Finally, I'm sure you don't really believe what I'm saying. You'll just *have* to try some little thing to see where the real limits are, just to test us as you always do. Believe me, dear, I can hardly wait. I want you to try some little bitty thing I can interpret as a little bitty test, so I can blister your big bitty bottom after your father and Harve are through warming it up for me.

"I can't tell you how many times I've considered this, Lance. I've wanted to do it, but I didn't want to stunt your development. Now it's time we all stunted the direction it has taken. What you consider a harmless prank might kill someone. Because you didn't know and didn't care. Those bouillon cubes, for example, were very very important. It's not important that you know why. What *is* important is that you're going to forget and pop off, sneak a bit of food or tinker with something without asking. And when you do, dear, I am going to make up for ten years of coddling your backside. Ern? Harve? Do you have anything to add?"

We thought she had it covered rather well and said so. A long silence followed. Lance opened his mouth a few times but always closed it again. For the first time in my memory, he was not physically leaning in his mother's direction. At last Shar said, "Would you like to go now?"

"Yes'm." It was almost inaudible.

"I recommend it." A chastened Lance scuttled back to the card game. I wondered if Shar had exaggerated her willingness to whale her darling. No doubt Lance wondered, too, but not enough to check it out right then.

Ern asked, "You cold, Shar?"

"My shakes have nothing to do with the temperature," she said. "The more I said to Lance, the more I realized how true it was. I feel ashamed of myself but I want to go over there right now and—and—"

"And whack on him some," I finished for her. "You're okay, sis, but you're right about letting us tan his hide first. If you took first licks you might hurt him."

"We have casualties already." She laughed a bit shakily. "I wish we could go upstairs and get those quince preserves."

"They're in little jars in the root cellar," I said and went in search of the stuff, which didn't need special sealing when I used only honey as sweetener. For some reason honey seemed to dissuade mold; so much so that the fermenting of mead, a honey wine, was an expensive process. I couldn't even get the damned stuff to ferment with added yeast, and I knew a lot of old-timer tricks.

Returning with two jars of preserves under wax, I thought of using a candle as a food warmer. If we lit a candle in the root cellar, it would be downstream of us. Its heated air and carbon dioxide would tend to drift out through the valve Shar had made. Ern thought it worth a try, using an empty bean can with vents punched around its top and bottom as a chimney. For fondue warmers I had a dozen squat votive candles, which quickly became broad puddles of fluid wax unless you had a close-fitting container to keep the puddle from spreading. Ern made one from several thicknesses of foil.

Mrs. Baird's bedpan needed emptying, and Lance performed the chore with the expression of one who has an unexpected mouthful of green persimmon. Ern went to the root cellar with him and tried our little food warmer, which Shar wanted to use for hot water to make a quince-preserve gruel. If the Baird woman could swallow such warm sweet stuff she might—well, it might help. I'm sure my sis was thinking about the tremendous strain I had added to our survival efforts by bringing in a woman who was perhaps better dead than suffering. And who almost certainly would die regardless of anything medical science could have done.

The evening brought its full share of good and bad news. It was good that by nine o'clock the tunnel reading was down to one rem, since that meant the sizzling ferocity of radiation outside had dropped to "merely" two hundred rems an hour—half its level only a few hours previous. It was also nice that Shar remembered my hot-water heater in its insulated niche near the furnace, so much out of sight that I'd forgotten its fifty-gallon supply of clean water just waiting to be drained from its bottom faucet. Seventy gallons of drinking water might last us two weeks, and we could use the waterbed stuff for washing.

If we absolutely had to, we could boil the mattress water and hope the chemical would lose its potency. Ern guessed that a lot of people would be drinking from waterbeds, and with a dilution of one pint of chemical to two hundred gallons of water, the user only swallowed a few drops of mild poison in each gallon of water. Better than dying of thirst; far worse than drinking from your hot-water heater.

I couldn't decide whether it was good or bad news that, if the eleven o'clock news from Santa Rosa could be believed, our government had removed restrictions against the purchase of weapons by expatriate Cubans in Florida. There was no longer any doubt that Cuba had been a launch site for cruise missiles against Miami, Tampa, Eglin, and other targets. Want an Uzi with full auto fire? Bazooka? A few incendiary bombs? See your friendly dealer in the nearest bayou or yacht club, so long as you can say "*Fidel come mierda sin sal*" three times quickly. Castro's radar scopes were already measled with blips that consisted of every known vintage aircraft and surface craft, mostly crewed by disgruntled Cubans who had scores to settle and machismo to spare.

Later we might regret this response. For the moment Soviet Cuba had too much coastline to worry about to mount any further actions against the US. If many of those itchy-fingered expatriates went ashore and stayed there, Fidel's ass was grass. Put it down as good and bad news. Maybe "crazy news" was a better term.

On the bad-news side, the radio announced that grocery sales were suspended nationwide for the next few days, with certain exceptions. Perishable produce and milk could be sold in limited quantities while the government assessed stocks of food, and if you didn't have enough food to last two or three days, you were going to get pretty hungry. This rationing plan was a long-standing preparation by the feds, a decision that few of us had ever heard about. I gathered from the broadcast that the government had funded many studies on nuclear survival but hadn't published them widely, perhaps because so few of us cared to request them through our congressional reps or the Department of Commerce.

The radio claimed that an Oak Ridge study, *Expedient Shelter Construction,* was good news since surviving newspapers were printing millions of copies to be distributed across the land by every available means, including air drops of stapled copies. Was it such good news? I wished I thought so. The document hadn't reached the public in time. What did we care if five hundred copies gathered dust in emergency-technology libraries for a decade?

One news item was almost certainly *not* a government news release because it suggested that disaster-related documents could be bought in hard copy or microfiche from an address they repeated several times:

National Technical Information Service
U.S. Department of Commerce
5285 Port Royal Road
Springfield, Virginia 22161

I was sure the item was an ill-advised brainstorm by a local reporter, since the postal service couldn't possibly be functioning well enough to respond to millions of suddenly fascinated citizens who'd never heard of the NTIS before. If they'd known and cared years earlier the item might've been of tremendous importance. Now? Much too little, a little too late.

The news of the Bay Area was too awesomely bad for belief if you listened between the lines. From San Mateo to Palo Alto and in most of Fremont, fallout was only a few rems per hour, though unofficial traffic in those areas would be by bike or on foot. Mill Valley, too, had escaped the brunt of nuke hammer blows. The main population centers were discussed only as a list of places declared off limits and subject to martial law, where deputized crews probed into the debris as far as they dared: San Rafael, San Francisco, Burlingame, Mountain View, Sunnyvale, San Jose, Hayward, Oakland, Vallejo.

Shar jotted down all the details we could recall from the broadcasts, on the theory that we didn't yet know which detail might save our collective skin in the long run. We'd have plenty of time to cobble up notes on the area maps in my office long before we risked going outside.

Within our own tiny subterranean world we made our own bad news. Though Devon managed to get his mother to swallow some lukewarm quince gruel, she couldn't keep it down. He drank a half-pint of it only after Shar insisted that there would be plenty for both of them. When Shar brought up the question of the solitary bouillon cube it seemed a small thing, but it forced a decision none of us wanted to make.

Despite her youth, Kate Gallo was adult in every practical sense. That's why, when Shar demanded a committee decision on which of the Bairds would get the pitiful antidiarrhea dose of clear bouillon broth, I insisted that Kate have her say in it. I had to wake her. By then the kids were asleep.

After fifteen minutes of "yes-but," Ern said with a sigh, "It boils down to one likely fact, one agreement, and a hundred conjectures. Probable fact: Mrs. Baird won't be with us much longer, no matter what we do. Anybody disagree with that?" Nobody did. "And we seem to be agreed that if one cup of broth is barely enough to matter, splitting it between them would probably make it a pointless gesture.

"But the boy may be in the same fix as his mother. I've noticed a few blisters on his hands and neck. Still, he may pull through in spite of that. I think it's time for a vote," he finished.

In a small voice Kate asked, "Couldn't we have a secret ballot?"

"Why didn't I think of that," Shar said with a smile and quickly tore four small squares of paper, writing "M" and "F" on each before folding them. "Just circle which should get the broth, male or female," she said, handing the ballots out. Perhaps my sis was trying to make us more objective with this abstraction from names to simple symbols. If so, it didn't work.

Ern took the pen, did something with it in shadow, handed the pen to Kate. I had no doubt with his engineering-determinist's mind, he favored Devon, who had a fighting chance.

Kate needed lots of time. I figured her for the one most likely to favor Mrs. Baird, since the woman, like Kate herself had been, was an underdog.

Shar took the pen and turned away for only a moment before passing the instrument to me. I needed only a moment, too.

Then Shar took the folded squares, shook them between cupped hands, and opened them.

On three of them, neither letter was circled. On the fourth was a circle around the "M." "Three abstentions," Kate snorted. "That's totally unfair!"

"It does provide a decision," said Shar.

"Forced on one of us alone," said Kate, her voice rising until she caught herself. Of course only one of us knew which three had abstained. Kate went on, "If this is to be a committee decision, we should all take part."

The slow precision with which she fashioned another ballot told me that Shar was affronted by this snip of a girl. "Very well, we'll try again," said my sis, her mouth set primly.

We all took longer the second time. When Shar counted the ballots there was no longer any question; there was still one abstention, but the other three votes favored Devon. We all breathed more easily. No one said anything about that abstention, since the abstainer could not have changed the consensus.

Before settling back to sleep Kate muttered, "One lousy bouillon cube. I wish Lance had eaten it."

"No you don't, Kate," Shar said gently. "It may be the tiny nudge that saves a life."

"I hope so. You'll have to claim we found another one and gave it to Mrs. Baird."

"I intended to. Good night, Kate," spoken with respect.

I padded back to the root cellar and warmed some instant coffee that tasted of quince preserves. It was my first warm brew in days, a scent of ripe summer fruit that deepened my anguish over the decisions we had made; unknown decisions we would have to make later; the millions who were no longer alive to puzzle over decisions. Presently the tepid coffee began to taste of salt and I drained it, brewing more for Ern.

But my brother-in-law slumped snoring at the air pump he had contrived, the brandy bottle empty beside him. I roused him and took his place, unwilling to blame him for the dereliction. I had known Ern's mild dependence on booze for a long time, and I'd brought the stuff to him myself.

## III. Doomsday Plus Two

It was Devon Baird who woke me before seven in the morning, and he was barely able to shake me after working at the pump. Someone had set the coffee warmer in the open where the candle's glow penetrated the tunnel. You could tell which of us was which but little more than that, since Ern had disconnected my car battery to prevent trickle losses.

Devon fought tears as he admitted, "It's not your time yet, Mr. Rackham, but my arms won't pull that thing anymore. I'm just not worth a durn for anything."

I took Shar's watch from him, hit its glow stud, and saw Devon stumble as I stood up. "You've brought your mother out of an annex of hell," I said gruffly, "and you're doing more than your body can handle. You want a criticism?"

Snuffling, but determined: "Say it."

"We all think you're going to be a great help if you'll take it easy and give your innards a chance to recuperate. You're pushing yourself too hard." I settled down at the air pump and added, "The sooner you get your strength back, the sooner you can do hard work."

His tears began to flow then. He asked if he could sit with me, and I said truthfully that I was honored. Five minutes later he was sleeping, his fuzzy cheek still damp against my back, one slender arm draped over my shoulder so that his hand brushed my face as I moved to operate the pump. Ern was right: Devon was developing blisters on his hands.

Near the end of my shift, Lance awoke and tried to talk to Cammie. "Give her a break," I whispered. "She's been working the pump, Lance. But as long as you're up, you might as well take over for me."

"I'm not up," he said, and then he must have remembered something because he did as I asked while I carried the sleeping Devon to his makeshift place near his mother. Then I returned and sat near Lance, who squelched his singsong cadence as he worked the pump. Something about, "Columbus had a cabin boy, the dirty little nipper . . ."

I patted his back the way I used to do when he played outside on the swing set. "How many verses do you know, pal?"

Long silence to prove I wasn't his pal. "Of what?"

"There must be a hundred verses of 'Sonofabitch Columbo.' At your age I knew most of 'em."

"I've heard a few," he acknowledged, softly humming the tune. He didn't sing the words anymore and made sure we didn't touch. Clearly my nephew had changed only to the extent that he was wary of punishment, protecting his flanks. When Lance had worked for a half-hour, I suggested he wake his dad. He was happy enough to do it, happier still to snuggle down against Cammie. As Ern took over at the pump, I settled back near Kate, and as I drifted into sleep, I reflected that I could depend on Lance. He wouldn't be trying to wake the others again if he knew it would earn him an extra stint at the pump.

I don't know whose idea it was to dump the crapsacks up on my screen porch. By the time I was through yawning and blinking late in the morning, Shar had already done it while Ern monitored radiation levels in the basement. Shar reasoned that, since it took only a half-minute to make the round trip to the porch, she'd take only a fractional rem in the process—and any microbe that survived storage on that porch for a week deserved to live. Because the level outside was still upward of two hundred rems.

Ern found two moderately hot spots in the basement. One, near the fireplace foundation, we knew about. The other was very localized at our air filters.

Obviously the filters were collecting fallout. Just as clearly, judging by the negligible readings at the pump, they were stopping that fallout while passing clean air. Still, they made a hot spot that demanded a fix. I helped Ern lug cans of paint, the jerry can of fuel, and pillowcases full of earth shoveled from the root cellar to make a barrier around the filters. We made a bridge of shelving over the filter boxes and stacked books atop it, which isolated the filter boxes fairly well.

I asked Ern why he poured a gallon of fuel into a double boiler from the jerrycan. "Because we need to cook some food before it spoils," he said, and let me wonder what we'd use for a stove and how we'd get rid of the smoke. I couldn't argue the need for it; we were already tired of canned veggies, and my stock of frozen food was thawing.

Shar had her own solution to the fresh vegetable problem, with the pound of alfalfa seeds I had forgotten in my kitchen. I supposed the stuff was too old to germinate after long storage, but my sis knew better. She dumped a handful of seeds into a one-gallon plastic jug and poured a cupful of water in, then set the jug aside. I would've bet a case of dark Löwenbräu against those seeds sprouting in near-total darkness. And I would've lost.

No matter how stir-crazy we became, the basement reading was still dangerously high—four rems. Shar's graph predicted a flattening out of the radiation curve, and Ern calculated that the radiation in the basement wouldn't drop below one rem for at least another day. During the next twenty-four hours we would absorb a total of ten rems in the tunnel but fifty if we moved into the basement. Enough said. One look at Mrs. Baird was enough to make me shrink from heavy doses.

Kate kept the kids occupied by introducing them to a dreadful card game called *I Doubt It* that reduced her foursome to tears of laughter while they operated the air pump. At the other end of the tunnel, my sis and I squinted at her notes in the light of a naked bike lamp while Ern sketched and rummaged through junk in the root cellar. Shar also tended the tiny candle stove while it warmed a cup of water for that paltry serving of broth.

"How long do you think the woman has?" We no longer used her name, as though by that means we could depersonalize her.

"She could go anytime, Harve. Her bedpan is showing blood, and the poor thing has lost so much fluid she weighs next to nothing. If only—"

To keep her from saying it, I broke in, "If only I hadn't—"

"If only she'd get it over with!" By voicing assumed guilt, I'd made her say something worse. "It's only a question of *when.* And after that we'll have another problem I don't even want to talk about."

"Telling Devon?"

"No; what do we do with the body?"

It had never crossed my mind. I thought about the way some primitives discarded their dead like so much debris on midden heaps, and our society's equally bizarre rites with embalming fluid and lead-lined caskets. Neither method would serve us, but we couldn't just let a corpse lie in state among us until it began to putrefy. Shallow burial in the tunnel? Removal to the back porch? The—oh, God!—the modest proposal accepted by the Donner party?

Shar crumbled the bouillon cube into hot water and stirred carefully, then called Devon, who weaved with exhaustion as he approached. That kid would have to be mollified with the burial arrangements; desperate as our situation was, we had to demonstrate some difference between our group and mere apes in britches, for the morale of the group itself.

After Shar offered the broth, Devon paused with the pan in his hands, sniffing the exquisite aroma: "My mom needs this more than I do."

Shar busied herself at her notes, unwilling to face him as she replied with her ready lie: his mom had already taken the "other" cupful.

He sipped, sighed, sipped again, then gulped it down. Staring at the empty pan as if it bore an inscription, he said, "Mom isn't going to make it, is she? How could she?"

"I don't know," I said, unsure whether it was better that he be prepared.

In an angry growl: "I think she's made up her mind to die!" He handed the pan to Shar, his glare challenging her to disagree.

It wasn't the first time I'd seen the living rage at the dead for dying. And anger might be a more survival-oriented reaction than hopeless sorrow, I thought. I said, "Whatever she's decided, I can see you've made up your mind to pull through. Join the club." And I stuck my hand out to be shaken.

His grip was as firm as he could make it, his shoulders almost straight as he strode back to the card game. I traded shrugs with Shar; our tunnel contained no experts in the bereavement process.

My voice has a rumble that carries, so I husked it: "One thing we can do is tape up a bodybag, sis. But not until afterward."

"Burial," she said firmly, "is out. A week from now there will still be too much radiation to dig a grave—unless you can do it in a few minutes. Ernie?"

"I'm listening," he muttered, opening a three-pound can of coffee. "Can't think of a good answer, but I'll mull it over."

Dumping the fresh coffee grains into a plastic bag for storage, he cut wide, shallow tabs around a fourth of the can's lip at the open end. In explanation: "Saw a backpacker's wood stove like this once. Swedish baffles, little telescoping stack. This'll be fed by gasoline, and we'll run its exhaust up your water-heater stack."

I pondered that for a moment. "Won't there be some fallout down that stack?"

"Very little in one that narrow, I suspect. Hell, it's just dust. The stove exhaust should drive it up and out anyway. All the same, Harve, remind me to use gloves when I'm rigging the stack."

I said I would. "But damn if I know what you'll use for an exhaust stack; you sure can't use paper, Ern."

"I was snooping around your furnace and water heater before you woke up. The water-heater exhaust and some of your forced-draft pipes are wrapped with fiberglass insulation, and the insulation has a thin aluminum skin that clips around like a sleeve. It's that sleeving I'll use for a stack."

I objected that aluminum wouldn't take the heat either.

He countered with a weird solution: pack raw horsemeat around the lowest part of it, with bread or dough around the meat and a jacket of aluminum foil around the whole mess. The meat would absorb the heat, the bread would absorb the grease, and we could cook twice as much at once. It might, he added with a smile, even be edible.

I said the aluminum sleeves were much too wide.

He said fine, he would narrow them with tin snips and curl the sleeve down to whatever diameter we needed, using wire to hold that diameter.

I said somebody would have to stay with it, taking four rems an hour in the basement.

He said like hell; we could leave the tunnel only to take quick peeks at the stuff we were cooking.

I said if he was so goddamn smart why hadn't he thought of using the aluminum sleeves while we were sweating out the air pump.

He said if he'd been *that* smart, we would've smarted ourselves out of a cookstove because there wouldn't be any aluminum left.

I burst out laughing and took my electric lantern to steal those aluminum sleeves from the house ducting.

Spot was as jumpy as I'd ever seen him, no doubt longing for a sprint around the fence perimeter. Before taking pliers to the aluminum sleeving, I went to my office desk and took the little aspirin tin from the back of the top drawer. The tabs inside weren't aspirin. They were what I called comealongs, not as fast as chloral hydrate but capable of turning a flash-tempered goon into a very mellow fellow. I wasn't sure of their effect on a cheetah, but I could always start with a half-tab and increase the dose if necessary.

It was a rotten trick to pull on my friend. So was keeping him cooped up when he was designed to run. I figured that my problem was common to a million people with dogs too big for house pets. I hoped they were working out better solutions than mine—and I doubted it.

Hustling back to the tunnel, I brought three lengths of aluminum sleeving to Ern. Shar was gently treating Mrs. Baird's blistered skin with baking-soda solution, a task made more onerous by the near-certainty that it would all be futile. The woman's eyes were half-open, her breathing almost imperceptible. She was no longer swallowing much.

I steered my thoughts away from the notion of getting a few of my comealongs dissolved in her water. Had our survival demanded it, I would have done it. Instead, I busied myself slicing strips from a roast taken from my freezer the day before. It was no longer frozen, and one thing we didn't need was tainted meat. I also placed a half-dozen discs of horsemeat, still frozen from Spot's dispenser, atop the candle heater for partial thawing. Spot hovered near, ignoring his farina mix, the furry white tip of his tail signaling the gradual abrasion of his patience.

I showed Ern the half-tab I crumbled into the first thawed hunk of ground meat. "I don't get it," he said.

"Mighty right you don't; he does," I replied and placed the meat before Spot. It was gone in seconds.

Ern paused at his job of making a shallow fuel tray from a cut-down tuna can and twisted wire. "I thought you weren't going to give him . . . whoa. It's not aspirin," he accused.

I told him what it was. "The finicky bastard would never take it in water, I know that. But fool that he is, he trusts me. I intend to keep him half-zonked for the duration, or as long as twenty tabs will last."

Ern nodded, rubbed his temples while squeezing his eyes shut. "Getting a headache—eyestrain, I think. Could the air be going bad on us?"

"I feel clearheaded. I might even tell you what's eleven times twelve, given a calculator and a half-hour start."

"Proof positive," he said with a chuckle and started trimming tabs around the hole he'd made near the flat bottom of the big coffee can. "There's a dozen sure 'nough aspirin in each bike kit, Harve. How about getting me a couple?"

I did, and sniffed out another of Spot's calling cards on the top shelf in the root cellar. Just the thing to shatter an appetite whetted by my rumbling stomach. In any case, Shar had already announced a two-meal day, and if there was one guy alive who could live on his fat for a month, it was yours truly. Well, the more I dieted, the less I'd sweat. Our exhalations had made the tunnel a bit clammy. And that made me think about the moisture in our bodies—which eventually led me to an answer to Shar's unpleasant question about burial.

Ern's little stove became a joke, distinguishable from a comedy of errors only by the fact that no matter how far a comedy goes wrong, it can't kill you. Spot could've been a nuisance when the smell of cooking—yes, and burning—fat began to permeate the tunnel, but the half-tab in his breakfast had made him lackadaisical. Instead of sitting smug and alert like some Egyptian idol, he put his chin on his paws and ignored us. We no longer bothered to seal the door from the basement to the tunnel, since radiation readings were dropping steadily. Besides, we had to run into the basement to adjust the damned stove too often to maintain the seal.

First, the connection between jury-rigged stovepipe and water-heater outlet pipe leaked like a sonofabitch. But Ern's cure was easy: he pulled cottony bits of fiberglass insulation from my air ducts, packed the fluff around the connection, and covered it with kitchen foil lightly bound with wire.

Then the gasoline pan got too hot. We could see fuel boiling just under the flames and hauled the flat pan out to snuff the fire. Then he put dirt into the pan and soaked it with fuel, and covered the little pan with a tuna can through which he punched several holes. That way only a few candlelike flames arose from fumes generated by the heat.

Ern admitted that it was damned dangerous; a nitwit's trick. So was starving or eating raw horsemeat. He finally managed to make the stove work without blowing himself up, but it's not an experiment I recommend.

Under the stove were four inches of dirt we dug from the root cellar, the whole rig sitting in the bottom half of a big turkey baster. Any spattered fuel would soak into the dirt instead of running down onto my carpet. Eventually our noses told us we had managed to include dirt that had soaked up Spot's urine. A male cheetah sprays backward instead of lifting his leg, and some of it had run down the cellar wall into the dirt. Naturally it smelled as though a big cat had peed into a fire. Lovely; just *lovely.*

Then we had a smoke scare when grease managed to find its way out of the foil surrounding the horsemeat we had packed around the base of the smokestack. Ern said that at least we knew the meat was cooking. Shar replied that any housewife knew we could choke the whole place on grease smoke.

Kate had the real solution: she simply made biscuit dough and packed that around the base of the stack with a foil collar. Worked like a champ; sure, the doughnut-shape biscuit blackened on its inner surface, but who the hell cared by that time?

We found that the stove worked best when it was cooking a potful of stuff on its flat top. Over a period of hours we cooked the sliced roast, twelve pounds of horsemeat, and a big pot of stew simmered with finely diced veggies plus a half-pound of bacon. Kate and Cammie seemed to enjoy the slow assembly-line manufacture of biscuits, which we smeared with fruit preserves. Devon got most of the quince preserves; his diarrhea was less, but still a problem. Shar hoped he could build his own personal plug with quince and half-burned biscuit.

After all the damnfoolishness with that stove, most of us had spent an hour in the basement, which was too long for safety. It was late afternoon then, and the others retreated into the tunnel, where Kate promised to read aloud from a collection of Roald Dahl's fiendish little stories. I had something to do upstairs and didn't want to argue about it, so I announced that I intended to find some soup mix that had been overlooked upstairs. The soup mix and some spices were real enough. Only my motive was faked.

I found the mix and spices at the back of a high kitchen shelf, then ran upstairs to get my raincoat and waders. Back in the kitchen, I put on my regalia and unsealed the door to the screen porch, slipping through with a kitchen knife in one gloved hand.

It took me only a minute to saw the long section of screen

from its framing, and I slapped dust from the screen while holding my breath. At first I wondered at the faint, pungent odor, like the stink of a generator with worn brushes. It was ozone, a by-product of gamma rays through the air. Hurriedly I rolled the screen into a tube, but before opening the door into the house again, I paused to gaze outside.

Folded gray quilts of cloud spanned the sky over a gray and green world. It wasn't yet time for my oaks to shed, but their leaves were falling. My grape arbor and quince hedge lay under a light dusting of gray stuff, the color and harbinger of death. No magpie or robin patrolled the weeds, no late-season grasshopper crackled across the open places. No distant automobile moaned down the creek road, no farmer's dog barked, no hawk wheeled beneath the ash-gray clouds. I found it possible, inside my protective clothing, to sweat and raise gooseflesh simultaneously. I had gone to the porch for a makeshift burial shroud, only to find that the world had anticipated me with a shroud of its own.

This time I shucked the coat, gloves, and waders in my dining room with the rolled screen and hurried down to the basement, pausing only to reseal the trapdoor tape. I had not been truly frightened of being alone, or of the dank-smelling dark that fills enclosed basements, for many years; yet I fled to the tunnel. I feared no hobgoblin in the shadows. I felt haunted from within, as though death were trying my body on for size.

At his mother's bidding Lance brought me a cup of strong instant coffee while I rubbed briskly at my arms and chest to banish my internal blizzard. My sis had known me for forty years, so I saw no point in bullshitting her when she softly asked what my trouble was.

I thanked Lance for the coffee; waited until he went back to squat, cross-legged, where he could hear Kate's lively rendition of a story called "Parson's Pleasure." Then I told Shar what I'd done and why.

"I hadn't thought of an elevated burial, but it certainly puts the rest of us at minimum risk," Shar mused. "Didn't the Indians do that?"

"Crow, Sioux, Cheyenne," I said and nodded. "Kept animals

away. We can strap—the package—outside an upstairs window on the roof, when the time comes. The south exposure gets a lot of sun, and a shroud of screen will let moisture out. It's my guess that a body could simply mummify before it decays very much, given enough sunlight and hard radiation."

"Mm-hmm. Ironic, isn't it, bubba? They've finally made a weapon that not only kills you but keeps you from spoiling."

"Take it further, sis. In cities where they have a half-million dead and no bulldozers to bury them, disposal squads may carry bodies to the hottest spot they dare to reach."

She meditated on me while I slurped coffee. Then: "I never dreamed this sort of awful work would affect you so, Harve."

"Me neither. But that wasn't what sent the wind whistling up my hemorrhoids. Sis, I stood on my porch a few minutes ago and looked and listened, and there's nothing alive out there. No—thing. You know how the effing mosquitoes love to cruise the back porch? Well, not now they don't. Not a bug, not a sight or sound of anything. I know insects are supposed to be resistant to radiation. Maybe it's the ozone in the air; I don't know."

Ern had moved nearer to listen. He said, "Pretty much as we expected, Harve."

"I know. But we also talked about what we'd do as soon as we left the basement. Peeling and canning vegetables that might be in season; jerking and storing meat; planting as soon as possible." I drained the last bitter taste of coffee, envying the innocence of the youngsters twenty feet away. "But it isn't going to happen that way, folks. Don't you understand? *It's all dead out there now.*"

"Not permanently. Surely not the plants," Shar argued.

"Okay, goddammit; if not dead then lost to us. It only has to be hot enough out there to screw a few rems an hour into you every hour for several more weeks. And that it will damn well do!"

"Are you trying to tell us you think it's hopeless?"

"Here? Yes. *Christ,* I hate to think of leaving, but figure it out yourselves. Shar, what do your notes predict in two weeks, after we're completely out of food and safe water?"

"You know as well as I do. Four rems an hour, something like that."

"And seven times longer—fourteen weeks—for it to decay to a half-rem. Let's say we take an average of two rems during every hour we're outside scrounging food and trying to filter water. That means four hours a day or more; eight rems a day. In seven weeks that's a lethal dose.

"And half that dose will make us as sick as those Japanese fishermen, who got expert medical attention, whereas we won't. With all of us in Devon's condition, we won't be able to fend for ourselves here."

Ern, utterly disgusted: "Why the miserable fuck didn't we think about this a long time ago?"

"Maybe it was unthinkable," I replied, "but who expected such hellacious fallout here? It isn't unthinkable now. What we must do—we *have* to!—is plan where to go and the best time to do it."

"That time is certainly not now," Shar said firmly, "unless we know someplace that's free of contamination and that we can reach within a couple of hours."

We thrashed that out for a while. We knew from the radio that safe spots existed across the bay, below San Francisco. But we entertained no illusions about finding a way to get there in a hurry. Roads to the south were probably not navigable anyway.

The fallout pattern eliminated any thought of fleeing east. To our west was the big bay itself, and we thought it unlikely we'd find a boat that would take us all. That left Hobson's choice, northwest past Vallejo into a region without target areas. If we could believe the Santa Rosa broadcasts, their problem was people, not radiation. *Our* problem was getting us across a couple of miles of water onto a road leading north, and doing it in a few hours.

That didn't seem possible. I'd made it with Kate in the Lotus, but it was no freighter. "Ern, could you drive my car over open water? It'd take you and both kids in one hop."

Among Ern's greatest virtues was the ability to face his limitations. "Not a chance, Harve. Anyway, I'd have to leave them and come back for another load, and I wouldn't do that without an armed guard for them. Besides, how would we all get from here to Suisun Bay without walking?"

Shar said it could be done. The McKays had three bikes and a skateboard. With Ern towing Lance and Kate riding double with Cammie, I could take Devon in the Lotus. No one mentioned his mother. We might, said Shar, make it to the narrow neck of the little bay in three hours.

I reminded her that I intended to take Spot, too. "He's a sprinter, not a long-distance runner. If I have to kiss him goodbye I will, sis, but ask yourself where we'll find another guard animal to equal him. You don't have to tell me that people are worth more than animals; I just think we can manage to take him along without tipping the lifeboat over.

"Besides, Spot should be able to go the distance to the water on foot if he goes at the pace of a bike."

"How will you feed him?"

"He may have to work that out himself. My corn patch always gets its share of varmints, and he's learned to snag a raven. He's learned to be wary of a 'coon, but if he's hungry enough he'll make out okay, I think."

An ugly trickling noise told us that Mrs. Baird's body was losing more fluid, a purely mechanical response that we found to be blood instead of fecal material. Shar turned away to attend to the duty she had assumed. Ern and I continued to hammer away at the barriers that stood between us and the north side of Suisun Bay.

I couldn't help ruminating on that day at the racetrack. From a purely selfish standpoint I'd have been smarter to head north instead of coming home. I wondered how often kissable Kate cussed herself for not splitting when she had the chance.

Ern studied Shar's little graph and mused, "One thing's clear: wherever we go, we can't risk it while the radiation count is much over ten rems an hour outside, in case we have to come back. That means we have a week to plan before we run for it."

"Unless we take another heavy dose of fallout," I said. "The damned missilemen are still pounding away at—har, har—

'selected targets,' as they put it in the radio bulletins. If we spot another cloud heading for us, we'll have to be ready to jump. Agreed?"

"Shit. Agreed. Boy, could I use a snort."

"Not if it puts you to sleep like it did the other night. Personally I could lay waste to three helpings of abalone supreme. We're just going to have to hobble along without our crutches, Ern."

"Don't remind me." Then he vented a light flutter of laughter, almost a schoolgirl giggle, which I'd learned to identify as delighted surprise. "You know what? We're neglecting the obvious, Harve. If any of the bridges are still spanning Suisun, we can all *walk* across!"

"Well, I'm a dirty sonofabitch."

"Very perceptive," he grinned. Despite the dying woman an arm's reach away, perhaps because laughter was so inapropos, we failed to strangle our mirth. Presently Shar returned with the emptied bedpan, and Ern told her why we were amused.

She perked up, but with a caveat. "Maybe the radio will give us a hint if the bridges can be crossed. If not, one of us may have to risk a solo trip to make sure."

I agreed, no longer amused. The Lotus was the only fast way to make that reconnaissance. And the only one who could drive it well was fat ol' Harve.

## IV. Doomsday Plus Three

Maybe the Plains Indians were more in tune with their psyches using calendar hides than we were using our almanacs. Lacking written language, they made annual decisions on the most memorable event of the year and drew a small picture on a tanned hide adjacent to the last year's picture. In that way a calendar hide became a history of the tribe. The outstanding event for our tiny tribe, on the third day after the initial nuclear strikes, was the death of Mrs. Baird.

None of us could say when her body finally yielded to hopeless odds. It happened during the night, the thread of her life parting as silently as a single strand of cobweb. She was already cold at seven in the morning when Devon awoke for his turn at the pump. He must've mourned through the entire hour, unwilling to wake the rest of us, because he was all cried out by the time I woke up.

Though I could have carried her body out to the basement alone, Devon insisted on helping; his right, his duty. I almost had to fight him to prevent him from going outside to dig a grave.

"She took the chances she did," I reminded him, "because she wanted you to live. Don't make hers a wasted sacrifice, Devon."

Shar convinced him that several hours outside, especially with the dose he had already sustained, would positively kill him. "Anyway, we've got a better way. We can preserve her remains until we can give her a proper burial," she said with a motherly hug.

I didn't dwell on the mechanisms of dehydration or putrefaction; only told him we should follow the ways of early Americans with an elevated burial and claimed a false certainty that the body would be well preserved. Devon Baird honored me by pretending to be wholly convinced.

By midmorning Shar and Devon had done the best they could with the emaciated, stiffening body, sprinkling it with cologne I never used anyway. The most grotesque moment came when we carried the body upstairs to my maple dining table and began to roll it into its shroud of screen. Ern had the presence of mind to take a reading in the dining room—about four rems, a reminder that we must not let our pitiful service become a drawn-out affair—and he had the good sense to stand aside until the precise instant when the body rolled off the table.

Ern kept the body from thumping the floor. Devon reacted quickly enough but was so weak that he sat down hard on the floor, his mother's head in his lap. "I'm sorry, mom," he whispered, and caressed the dead face. He was unable to rise without help. The kid was much closer to total physical collapse than I'd thought, running on sheer guts.

At last we got the screen rolled around the body and snugged it with wire, and while it may seem ludicrous to hold a funeral service over a roll of screen, that's what we did, holding lit candles. Shar had told me it was my job to say the right words. Devon would want a man to do it, and Ernest McKay would've frozen solid trying.

I said: "Lord, You've heard it all before. You must be hearing it from a hundred million throats today. For which we give no thanks."

I saw Shar's startled frown, her silently mouthed "Oh," or maybe it was "no." But I saw Devon nod, eyes closed, knuckles white on the fists at his sides. I continued.

"You gave this good woman the terrible gift of free choice,

Lord, and she exercised it to keep her son alive, knowing it might kill her.

"And it did. Greater love than this hath no man and no woman, and for this alone we would ask You to cherish her. It's said that you can't take it with you, but Mrs. Baird beat the odds. She takes with her our greatest respect, and our hopes for her everlasting grace.

"If I misquote Khayyam, I crave Your understanding:

> O Thou who woman of earth didst make,
> And in her paradise devised the snake,
> For all the freely-chosen horror with which
> the face of mankind is blackened,
> Our forgiveness give. *And take.*

Into-Your-hands-O-Lord-we-commend-her-spirit-Amen," I ended quickly. I half-expected a lightning bolt before I finished. I didn't care.

We persuaded Devon that it wasn't strictly proper for him to act as pallbearer; that Ern and I wanted that honor. That way he didn't have to watch us hauling the screened bundle to an upstairs window, where, after a little cursing and prying, we got the old-fashioned window raised enough to slide our burden onto the gentle slope of the roof. We bound the screen in place with baling wire, working as fast as we could. It would've been more coldly sensible to place Mrs. Baird's body on insulation in the attic, but it seemed necessary, somehow, that we place the dead outside the lair of the living.

And then we resealed the window and went back to the tunnel with a side trip to get a bottle for the wake we held. And yes, I got shit-faced and no, not too shit-faced to take my turn at the pump. Devon got his chance at the bottle, too, and he was more sensible about it than I was.

It seems that I had a meal that day, a soupy stew with half-cooked veggies and more carbonized biscuits. I suppose Shar or the girls cooked more horsemeat, because the following day there was plenty of it, sprinkled with brine and folded in film. My last clear recollection was of Shar draining the water from that jugful of damp alfalfa seeds and putting them away again.

I don't justify getting drunk; I merely record it. If we'd had another emergency that afternoon, I probably would've paid for it with my hide. As it was, the big trouble came later.

# V. Doomsday Plus Four, Five, Six, Seven

My next few days began with a hangover that segued to a powerful thirst, which I tried to slake with tomato juice. Shar said it was fine with her if I drank everything in my liquor cabinet since it kept me from eating much. My head detonated every time the kids whooped during the joke festival Cammie initiated, and my tongue felt like a squirrel's tail. I straggled back to the root cellar and listened to the radio.

The world news was surprising only in its details. Chinese troops had surged across the Sino-Soviet border to the great trans-Siberian railroad and there they had stopped, daring the Russkis to trade nukes. NATO forces were as good as their word; they had stopped Soviet armor before the lumbering red-starred tanks got more than a toehold in West Germany. But not with neutron bombs. They had done it with a bewildering array of small antiarmor missiles; some laser directed, some wire guided, and some with sensors that guided them straight down onto the thin topside armor of the tanks.

The Soviets had staked a lot on that self-propelled artillery of theirs, and they lost the bet. It was a whole lot easier to replace a German infantryman with his brace of cheap, automated, tank-killer missiles than to replace a seventy-ton Soviet tank with its trained crew.

To my surprise, Radio Damascus was still 'casting. They didn't know whose little kiloton-size neutron warheads had depopulated most of their military bases and wasted no breath on it. Instead Damascus called on the Muslim world to defend Syrian honor with instant cessation of oil shipments to the US and its friends. I was willing to bet that every supertanker in existence was hugging a breakwater somewhere.

Our national news comprised remotely fed bulletins from the EBS, carefully upbeat in tone, claiming we had weathered the worst. I nearly failed to catch the implication of one report from Alaska. The Soviet raid on our pipeline had been squashed, with only scattered remnants of the raiders still afoot in Alaska. That meant US soil had been invaded, and since no one mentioned the condition of our petroleum pipeline, I figured it was blown in a dozen places. Those "scattered remnants" of Russkis were probably much better equipped for Arctic warfare than our own people; shortchanging the defense of our largest state is virtually an American tradition.

On Doomsday plus five, we began to move back into the basement. We had a frightening hour when Ern's readings told him we were taking heavy radiation in the tunnel. But the basement reading was roughly the same, which told us something was wrong with the meter.

So Ern did some meter maintenance. He removed the plastic top, fished the little desiccant lumps out, and baked them on our little stove:—while Cammie and Kate made more biscuits. Using cotton swabs, Ern gently wiped the inside of the meter clean, taking special care to remove the dusting of tiny flecks of gypsum that clung to the aluminum leaves and monofilament.

Then he deposited the dried desiccant back in the can, resealed it, and took fresh readings. It said we were taking only two tenths of a rem in the tunnel and slightly under one rem in the basement. That made sense. It also told us the clammy humidity of the tunnel had finally worked its way into the fallout meter, giving high but spurious readings.

By now I was a believer in alfalfa sprouts. Shar merely added a quart of water and swirled it in the jug to wash the growing sprouts once a day, then drained the water for soup and capped the jug again. Long white tendrils extended from the seeds, a growing, spongy mass that thrived even in the gloom of the basement. I wasn't eating a lot, and when my pants got loose, I just tightened my belt a notch.

Shar made a little speech after brunch—Devon had christened our second meal "lunper"—reminding us that when we had no good reason to be in the basement we should creep back to the safety of "Rackham's lair"—another of Devon's phrases. Shar made her point: did we want to absorb twenty rems a day or only four?

Spot made the most of his freedom to pace the tunnel while the rest of us were busy in the basement. We took the rest of the drinking water from the john, partly drained my waterbed, then took sponge baths in my tub. Kate, first to bathe, was stunned at the way the rest of us stank. Of course she had smelled just as ripe a few minutes before. Each of us then shared Kate's dismay, but soon our noses gave up and quit complaining. The whole basement reeked of bodies.

Ern caught a radio broadcast that mentioned bridges. The long span to San Rafael was down; the San Mateo bridge was limited to military traffic and you could get shot or run down trying to walk it. The Carquinez and Benicia bridges would be cleared soon, which told us that they still spanned the narrows of Suisun Bay.

We began to hope that "soon" might mean the bridges would be navigable within a few days. At worst, said Ern, we could clamber around stalled cars and cross the Benicia bridge to the north. That sounded reasonable to me, because neither of us realized how the Corps of Engineers intended to clear those bridges.

On Doomsday plus six we uncelebrated a week of underground exile and Ern volunteered to give us sunlight in the basement. Among the things Cammie had lugged from my garage was my so-called surface plate. A surface plate is just a slab, usually of granite, polished so perfectly flat that you can use it to measure the exact amount of warp on a race car's cylinder head. But I'm cheap. I bought an old jet fighter's front windshield at a surplus shop, knowing that it had to be optically flat, a surface plate of glass.

The thing was two feet long, a foot wide, and two inches thick; heavy as guilt and solid as virtue. Ern surmised that it might stop gamma rays while letting light through.

His scheme was simple. He toted the glass slab outside, galumphing in my protective outfit though it swallowed him whole. Then he shoveled dirt away from the top of my basement window, waving as he heard us cheer the light that burst into the basement. Finally he dropped the glass plate against the window and replaced some of the dirt so that the only light reaching us was through that thick windshield.

While he took another sponge bath, we learned that his scheme was flawed, since the radiation reading jumped a bit near the window. We took more readings and found that my stone divider wall made a big difference. Near my office area the reading, and the light, were highest. In my lounge area behind the stone wall, the radiation level was "normal," less than a rem, and enough light reflected from my walls to make us happy.

That little oblong of light had a beneficial side effect. We no longer needed to pedal the bike as much, and pedaling had released a lot of water vapor and carbon dioxide, which were still a problem.

On D + 7—we had coined enough jargon terms to confuse a linguist by them—we ran out of horsemeat. I used the last pinch of it to hide a half-tab of comealong for Spot, who must've wondered if he was becoming a manic-depressive.

We still had enough food for another two days, and my water heater's drain spigot was still yielding drinkable water. Shar had already started her second batch of alfalfa sprouts in a stainless steel bowl and served up that first batch to the music of general applause. She harvested three pints of sprouts in a few days, from a half-cupful of seed and without direct sunlight. That was our nearest approach to a green salad, very popular with soy sauce.

The same day was marked by the remainder of the McKay family saga. I record it at this point because I didn't hear it until eight days after it happened. The kids were bored by my hunting stories, and the playing cards were so badly creased that they might as well have had faces on both sides. We were sharing raisins and onion soup when I thought to ask Shar how they had got from their wrecked vanwagon to my place.

Their first decision, said my sis, was to travel light. They took maps, cheese, and tinned meat, and wore jackets. Ern locked the vehicle in the vain hope that he might return to it, then mounted his bike and tried towing Lance. He found it rough going uphill and let Lance fend for himself as soon as they passed the overturned truck. The truck, of course, blocked off other cars, so that bikes and pedestrians didn't need to dodge speeders.

Lance, like many kids, often went to and from school on his skateboard. The fat urethane wheels ran amazingly well over macadam, and on the first downslope, Ern found Lance spurting ahead with a few kicks. The skateboard was more maneuverable than an expert's bike, but after a near-collision with a motorcyclist, my nephew went to the rear of the McKay procession to avoid becoming what he termed a "street pizza."

After two hours they neared exhaustion, but their path led chiefly downhill then and they finally reached the road that doubled back toward my place. They were on the safe side of Mount Diablo at last, and Shar coasted to rest at the foot of a short, tree-lined uphill stretch. Panting, they rested and watched a collegiate youth who sat at the roadside with a wheel dismantled from his expensive lightweight bike.

"What's the trouble?" Cammie asked.

"Picked up a nail," said the young man. "Can you believe I didn't think to bring a cold-patch kit?"

Ern had placed one of the tiny cold-patch packages in each bike bag. He saw the tubular pump clipped to the youngster's bike frame and dug the cold-patch kit from the vinyl bag on his bike. "What am I bid for this?"

Big eyed: "A box of chocolate bars?"

Ern: "We'll settle for one apiece." He was making the trade when the first great flash backlit his skyline.

"Don't look! Hide your eyes," Shar screamed, ignoring her own advice as she grabbed for Lance, who stared at the sky in rapt fascination. A biker and several hikers went full-length onto the shoulder, perhaps expecting a heavy concussion.

The second flash seemed nearer, coming as it did from a direction with lower hilltops and less masking of the initial dazzle. The third and fourth flashes were also distinct and they felt the jolts, the sudden bucking of the earth itself, conducting shock for many miles beyond ground zero. Leaves showered around them.

Cammie was first to seize her bike, pedaling past a gas station and grocery store well in advance of her family. The first airborne rumble didn't seem loud. But scarcely had Ern turned onto the road toward my place when he, like the others, felt the solid slap on his back from the second blast, the errant shock wave that crossed the bay to macerate Concord before funneling up the narrow valley to blow my windows out.

By great luck they were headed away from it in a declivity of Marsh Creek Valley and felt only a peppering of grit and twigs. But Ern saw the multipaned front window of the gas station disintegrate as if sucked into the little building, a polychrome implosion more deadly than a high-velocity shower of razor blades.

"You should've seen what it did to Concord," Devon spoke up. "No, I take it back." Shake of the blond tasseled head.

Everyone likes to think he's seen the worst. "Didn't hurt you any," Lance sniffed.

"It killed Concord. I was in a downstairs apartment," said Devon, "and don't ask me why all our windows got sucked out, 'stead of blown in. But later I saw what happened to people who got caught in the open." He glanced guiltily at us, cleared his throat, shrugged. "A glove, with a hand still in it. People with branches sticking out of them. Slabs of marble knocked off a building, one with a little kid's legs poking from under it. Like that," he trailed off in embarrassment.

I think Cammie already had a special soft spot for Devon

by this time. To ward off further memories of that sort she said, "I'm convinced, Devon. We were lucky. After that shock wave all we did was go like crazy for Uncle Harve's place."

"And we were luckier still that we didn't get hit by the cars that passed us," Ern injected. "You could hear an engine winding up from around the bends behind us, and I made Lance ride double with Shar since he couldn't make good time on the shoulder, and those people were driving like maniacs.

"One guy especially, driving a county jail-farm bus full of inmates. I could see a guard in the rear seat, holding a riot gun and staring back at us, looking scareder than I was. I couldn't decide whether he was more afraid of the bombs or the way his driver was smoking his tires."

The Contra Costa County jail farm was only a few miles from my place. I had helped put a couple of scufflers on that work farm. Inmates ranged from hapless schlemiels and harmless dopers to hard-eyed repeaters who, in my opinion, should've been across the bay in Quentin. I empathized with the guard on that bus; if that vehicle turned over, he'd have a score of two-legged bombs to worry about.

"I don't envy him, or the inmates," I said. "The county farm must've taken the same radiation dose we did. But some of the buildings could be pretty good protection. I gather you were pretty near here by then, eh?"

"Half-hour or so. We got here soon after you left, Harve. Thanks for trying to find us. We owe you a lot."

"*Owe* me? Good God, Ern," I fumed, then pointed at the fallout meter. "Think of yourself as an investment that's paid off a thousand percent. Fallout meter, air pump, filters, even a rechargeable light plant! Nobody owes me. You've done too much for me to owe me."

"We've still got a lot to do for each other," said Kate, perhaps for Devon's benefit. "I can't afford to worry about how much I owe, but I'll pay off as well as I can."

"Strange you should mention that," I said, grinning at her. "Because we've been wondering when you'd extend us an invitation."

Blank look from Kate. "For what?"

Ern, softly: "For the use of your summer place in, uh, where is it again?"

"Yountville," she replied. "There's always a chance that my folks got there. If they did, I can't swear they'd take me in, much less the rest of us." After a moment's thought: "And if it's all the same with you guys, I'll stick with you regardless."

Shar smiled indulgently. "We wouldn't hold you to that."

A snort from Kate: "I'm not saying that to be nice! I just don't think my chances would be as good with anybody else. And by the way, I suspect you've been talking it over when I wasn't listening. Isn't it time you let me in on the plans? After all"—she smiled with disarming shyness—"I might be the landlady."

The evening passed with argument and explanation. Of our younger members, only Kate had ever missed two meals in a row. The kids couldn't believe they'd begin to weaken after a day or so without food and thought we could just buy whatever we needed. I was adamant; we'd be crazy to set out for Yountville on bellies that had been empty for two days. And I didn't think a twenty-dollar bill would buy a meal anywhere in California.

Shar's notebook put our exodus on a no-nonsense footing, with figures to support the notion of northerly escape. We knew the fallout extended to Vallejo from radio broadcasts, and the same source said it did not extend as far north as Napa.

Yet we couldn't figure a way to get us from my place to the Napa County line in less than five hours without taking indefensible chances. I meant "indefensible" in more ways than one. We didn't want to make more than one trip in the Lotus, because I'd already seen how readily some folks would knock you over for the shoes on your feet. Leaving two or three of us near the bridge and retracing nearly thirty miles to my place was a clear case of dividing forces. Like Custer. No thanks. I couldn't defend an arrangement that left any of us more vulnerable than necessary.

It was possible that I was exaggerating the lawlessness we'd be dealing with. But whatever the state of the union, it didn't seem healthy enough in our locale for us to count on anything like business as usual. If we found a place to buy fuel and food, fine. I had a stock of pennies—coppers, at that—and quarters for just such a contingency. But another contingency forced itself on us, heralded as Ern outlined some of the preparations we would have to make. He stopped in midsentence to listen.

In the distance we heard a car pass, the unmistakable *thrumm* of a husky V-eight prowling the creek road. The event took twelve seconds or so, and we strained at the echoes like music lovers catching the faint final overtones of a lute. Such a familiar, homey racket; and now such an anomaly that we fantasized about it. We agreed at last that it must've been some official vehicle checking the road, its driver marvelously tricked out in some kind of space suit, invulnerable to the silent, invisible hail of gamma rays that sought his soft tissues.

A half-hour later Devon interrupted Shar to comment on the backfires he heard far away. Even government cars, he joked, got out of tune.

I laughed because I didn't want to break his mood. I'd heard that brief rattle too. From such a distance, muffled by earth, I might've chosen to think of it as backfires. But it had been a sudden, steady series of sharp reports; perhaps on one of the dairy farms nearby. I hoped it was a farmer killing moribund livestock. Sure as hell it was no backfire.

Shar must have caught the pensive look on my face and she continued outlining the proposed trip with a brief aside. We would have to travel at the pace of the slowest, all together, and we mustn't expect any help—in fact, must be ready for trouble without asking for it, she said.

She figured the bike group could get to the bridge in three hours, Kate and Devon riding with me, and Spot (she sighed) loping alongside the bikes. Then we'd need a half-hour to cross the bridge, strapping the bikes on my Lotus so I could ferry them across the water if necessary. Another hour or two getting around the mess we expected in Vallejo. The best we could hope for was a full five hours in gamma country.

Kate saw the crucial variable immediately. "What does that amount to in rems?"

"If we go tomorrow morning, about sixty. If we spend

tomorrow in the tunnel and go the next day, maybe fifty. The day after that, forty-two or so. Of course we absorb a few rems daily in the tunnel. There's a point of diminishing returns, but it's after we run out of food and water."

"I just want to do the safest thing," Cammie wailed. She had taken her lumps with few complaints, but my niece was distraught to find her decision makers unsure on a vital decision.

"I say we eat our last meal three mornings from now and run for it on full stomachs," Kate said. I agreed with her.

Ern wanted to go in two days, taking our last tins of juice and beef.

Lance wanted to go now, now, now. He was fed up with toeing a tight line in a hole with no chewing gum.

Shar sided with Ern; Cammie didn't know what she wanted; and Devon just looked at us, blinking, fighting a resurgence of stomach cramps. Of course we ended by taking another secret ballot. I figured Cammie would do what she thought her parents wanted.

We counted one vote for leaving the next day, two for leaving in three days, and four for leaving in two days. So it was settled: we'd spend the following day getting the bikes fixed up with their generators and any other maintenance they needed, and I would replace the battery in the Lotus, taking a half-dozen rems while getting it fueled and ready.

We would be all set to run for the border, so to speak, on the morning of D + 9.

And we would have been, if the decision hadn't been snatched from our hands.

# VI. Doomsday Plus Eight

I waited until after brunch—Lord God, how I learned to loathe noodles and tomato paste!—to dress for my trip to the garage to prepare the Lotus. Ern knew I would be packing heavy heat, the twelve-gauge, when I drove away as their escort. To conserve fuel I intended to drive behind them, catching up and then coasting until they were well ahead before I eased ahead again. But none of them left the tunnel to watch me collect my hardware and spare ammo. I made a second trip for the battery and the jerrycan with the remainder of my fuel.

Fully dressed in my Halloween outfit, I hauled the second load across my lawn in bright sunshine, through an ankle-deep layer of dead leaves, to the garage. Here and there I saw the fresh green of tender young weeds, prodded into unseasonal growth by irradiation. The twelve-gauge wouldn't fit under the Lotus's dash so I stashed it more or less out of sight in the foot well, where my left thigh would keep it company.

The fuel went in quickly; the battery, not so quickly. My damned rubber gloves and the fogging of my goggles made me a prize klutz.

I was afraid I'd have to push-start my little bolide, but eventually it coughed, cleared its throat in a healthy rasp, then began to purr. I let it idle and knelt with my tire gauge to see if pressures were okay. I'd been outside about ten minutes, two rems' worth, and figured on running back in another minute or so if the right rear tire was as healthy as the others. Kneeling with my head near the exhaust pipe, I heard muffled staccato reports and simultaneous metallic clangs, and I fell back on my keester. With the scarf over my ears I didn't interpret the sounds correctly; I thought the engine had munched a valve.

But my Lotus continued its quiet purr. I scrambled up, leaned over the doorsill, shut off the ignition. That's when I heard the throb of a big V-eight heading toward the house.

For the space of a heartbeat I felt the joy of unexpected good fortune; and then remembered that my gate had been locked, and reassessed the sounds I'd thought were engine trouble. Someone had used an automatic weapon on my gate.

I stepped near the window, I let my goggles hang at my throat, and picked up the mattock Devon had shouldered a week before. A mattock handle fits loosely into the steel head, unlike an ax. I slipped the hickory shaft from the head, watching through a crack in the old garage door while the pickup followed my gravel drive and stopped near the garage. The pickup had a Contra Costa County logo on the driver's door, but it also had several indented holes through the side panels. They were just about the size of rifle slugs. One headlight had been shattered.

Four men were crammed in the cab. The first to get out was obviously the man in charge, a big sturdy loafer wearing khakis that were too small for him and a shiny badge that looked wrong on him. He carried a pump shotgun in one hand and a long-barreled police .38 in a holster.

The man who emerged after him wore khakis and badge too; a tall, slow-moving fellow without a sidearm. The leader commanded, "Move it, Ellis, and this time remember not to point this thing until you're ready to use it." With that he handed the shotgun to Ellis. Both men swept my acreage with their eyes as the third man scrambled out. The driver stayed put. Someone had taped around the windows, and the three dudes who got out all wore gloves and sunglasses. No respirators or masks of any kind; if these guys were sheriff's deputies, I was a teenage werewolf.

The third man out wore slacks and pullover and carried one of the little vintage Air Force carbines. Not much of a threat at two hundred yards, but closer in on auto fire it could rattle you full of thirty-caliber holes. He glanced toward the Lotus, then said, "You want me for backup, Dennison?"

Dennison, the leader, waved an arm in my general direction. "Look for fuel, whatever you can boost in there. Then come to the door and give us a roust. Hell, you know the procedure, Riley; the smoke from the standpipe says there's somebody in the house. If we can make this sweep without wasting any ammo, that's ammo we won't have to replace later."

"Got it," said Riley, the carbine toter. He moved in my direction. In the cab the fourth man was rolling himself a cigarette. Not many jail-farm employees rolled their own—maybe because so many inmates *did*.

I knew my clownish garb made a lot of noise when I moved, and there was no place to hide and no time to reach into the car for my artillery because I would have to do it in full view of the approaching Riley. I did the only thing I could, an ancient time-honored ploy: I stepped as quietly as possible to the near wall next to the open door and raised my hunk of hickory on high. If he glanced my way, it could be all over for ol' Uncle Harve.

Then a soft pop, no louder than the snap of a fingernail, spanged from the cooling guts of the Lotus. I saw the man's shadow jerk and shorten as he crouched, intent on my car, peering hard into the gloom of my garage.

Another snap of cooling metal. He kept the carbine aimed into the shadow one-handed and knelt to feel my exhaust pipe, and he must have heard the rustle of my clothes because he began to swing the little carbine toward me as I connected with the mattock handle against his receiver mechanism with an impact that bashed the weapon completely from his grasp and knocked it clattering against a wall.

I took three fast steps. The first brought my right foot into range of his belly; the second was a kick just under his sternum to paralyze his hollering apparatus; and the third was a hop to regain my balance as I crossed the doorway in full view of anyone who might be looking toward the garage. He had time to declaim one wordless syllable, ending in a plosive grunt.

Riley, knees drawn up, clutched his belly and rolled to face me, mouth gaping like a carp. I squatted low and menaced him with the mattock handle while risking a peek outside. Dennison and Ellis were approaching my seldom-used front door as coolly and confidently as if on official business. The driver addressed a paperback, still in the pickup. I grabbed the hapless Riley by one ankle and jerked him into shadow so hard his head bumped concrete.

A solid kick to the solar plexus can render a professional athlete helpless for a half-minute. While Riley groveled and gasped, I circled around the front of the Lotus, keeping in shadow, and slung my twelve-gauge on my back by its sling before returning to stand over the man who now lay on his back, eyes rolling at me.

I gave him a quick pat-down and found the five-inch switchblade thrust down the inside of his high-top boot. I let the blade flick open. "Nice and quiet," I growled, placing the flat of the blade under his jaw. "I won't even have to pull a trigger if you try anything louder than a whisper, Master Riley. Now: down on your face if you want to live. Arms and legs spread."

He needed help to roll over, uttering croupy wheezes as his diaphragm muscles began to unkink. Ever since the ice-pick routine years ago, I've had a loathing for knives. I wasn't about to let Riley know that because then he might make me shoot him. And my twelve-gauge announces itself like a multiple boiler explosion, and I didn't want to alert those two on my front porch. Now, I wish I had.

Spread-eagled on his face, he couldn't help but feel the prick of his own stiletto near his carotid artery. I asked it softly: "What is Dennison after?"

"Food. Guns. Booze. Jewelry," he wheezed. Then, "Broads. He's a deputy sheriff. If you're smart you'll let me—"

I raised his head by the hair and whacked it lightly against concrete. "Try again, Riley. He's a scuffler from the rock-hockey farm. If I'm *really* smart, I'll just slit your throat and take out your buddy in the pickup and drive away whistling. Or just wait for your pals. Each lie earns you a fresh headache. Now: what's Dennison's procedure here? Quickly," I added, grasping him by his hair again.

A long breath, a short curse. "Dennison and Ellis go in—very polite, asking—who needs help. Then they say—they're searching for escapees—from the county farm. Sorry, citizen, but that's—how it is, and—whoever looks like trouble—gets asked to lead the way—to search the rest of the house. And then down comes the sap—on the back of his head, and strapping tape—to hogtie him while we—shake the place down. Anybody gets antsy, we—mention we've got a hostage."

Slick; too slick by a damned sight. But he'd left a loose end, and it dangled in the back of my mind. "Why did he want you to give him a roust?"

Pause; sigh. "So I can call him Deputy Dennison. It's supposed to make everybody—sure we're legit."

I took a chance. "Didn't work too well last night, did it?"

Riley stiffened, then shrugged. "Not very. Are you The Man?" If he thought I was a cop, he probably figured I knew something about what his bunch had already done. Which, I suspected, included homicide within a half-mile of my place.

I said I was The Man, all right. "Sit up, facing away from me, and strip out your bootlaces. If I have to speed you up, I'll brain you and do it myself." Still working just to breathe, he tugged the heavy laces from his boots. I leaned the mattock handle against the wall without taking my gaze from Riley.

"Your driver's name," I prompted when I had the laces.

"Oliver."

I could see the two men on my front porch, and at that point I probably could still have averted a tragedy. Then I saw Shar inviting them in, and the moment passed into the oblivion reserved for wasted chances. I wondered how long it would be before Shar called to me, canceling my hope of surprise.

I unslung my terrible hole card and held it ready. To Riley I said, "Your life depends on suckering Oliver in here without making a fuss. I'm just itching to blow you away and I've got as many rounds of double-ought buck here as you had in that carbine. Turn around and see for yourself."

He did, gulping as he saw the fat magazine and stubby barrel of my weapon. "What the fuck is *that*?"

"Enough death to go around, little man. Now stand up and call Oliver in here. Bear in mind that if you can't get him in here or if you take one step toward the outside, you get your ticket canceled."

I could see his arms and legs trembling as he stood. I stepped up next to the mattock handle with my back to the wall near the open door; gestured with my gun barrel for him to move near the Lotus.

He nearly fell, but leaned against the rear fender; licked his lips; gave a low hoarse call. No response. He called again.

I heard a door open. A bored tenor called a sullen, "Yeah?"

The briefest of pauses. I clicked the safety. Riley called urgently, "I never seen a stash like this in my life! You wanta take your cut now, before Dennison hogs it?" Riley was trying to keep from glancing my way; trying so hard his eyelids fluttered.

The door slammed. I didn't risk a glance as I heard footsteps approach. I used the gun barrel to urge Riley away from my car and he stumbled back, both arms jerking as he started to raise them and then thought better of it.

A few yards away, approaching: "What the hell's with you, man? You on a bad trip?" And then Riley essayed the sickest smile I ever witnessed and a silent, palms-out gesture of helplessness, and Oliver stepped into view, frowning intently at Riley. He took two more steps into the garage before he saw me, and for all I know he didn't even notice the twelve-gauge in the hands of what must've seemed like a towering bogeyman in the shadows.

"Sweet*shit*," Oliver screamed, leaping sideways to rebound from a fender.

"No no no," Riley begged me, arms thrust high as he squeezed his eyes shut in anticipation of death. It saved his life. I snatched up the mattock handle and brought it humming in a sidearm swoop as Oliver whirled, and it took him flush across the bridge of his nose and swept on over his forehead as his head snapped back. Another second and he would've been outside, and I would've been obliged to bisect him instead of just giving him the great-grandsire of all concussions. He fell on his back, legs twitching, blood beginning to rivulet from his nostrils.

"Like you said, Riley," I breathed. "No. Keep this up and you may get a reduced sentence." That was bullshit, of course, but I wanted him to see a carrot as well as a stick.

Riley spread-eagled himself again while I trussed Oliver's ankles and wrists with bootlaces, bound behind him so that he lay on his side out of sight. He bled a lot and breathed in snorts. I took a long-barreled revolver from his belt and snapped the blade off his sheath knife between the jaws of my blacksmith's vise. I could claim I hoped I hadn't killed Oliver, but I wasn't even thinking about him. I was furiously considering my next move.

I retrieved the little carbine, pocketed all its ammo, jacked out the chambered round, and reinserted the empty clip. Then I took the second full clip from Riley's hip pocket and gave him another frisk to make sure he hadn't hidden a singleton round on him. I'd heard about a hit man who used to carry one round each of twenty-two long, parabellum, and forty-five ACP in his change pocket, just in case. Riley wasn't that farsighted. He accepted the carbine, blinking nervously.

"That's just window dressing," I told him. "Keep it in view. You'll have an alarm signal—maybe several. Shots? What? And while you're wondering if you should lie about it, think about this: if anybody in that house gets hurt, you get the same."

He licked dry lips. "The horn. One toot for an alert. Two means stay put. Three means haul ass. That was Oliver's job." Enough scorn leaked into that last phrase to make me believe him.

I nodded, considering an assault past the root cellar stairs, which meant bulling through the book barrier. But I wouldn't be able to see into there and I'd be impossible to miss by anyone standing in the cellar. Or I could just wait behind the pickup, or go into the house with Riley. Better still, *behind* Riley.

But too many things could go wrong, and those badged

bastards thought in terms of hostages. Besides, they might spot me coming across the yard from a window while they separated Ern from the others. I wondered if I could make use of the unconscious Oliver, then noticed that his hair was nearly black. Scrunched down while I—literally!—rode shotgun, my head might look like his from the back. That was important, because now I decided to draw those bogus lawmen from the house toward me. My place was infected, and I sought to draw the pus to the surface.

The county pickup was parked so that with a ten-yard sprint, I could put it between me and the house. I gave Riley his orders and made sure he knew I'd be only a pace behind, then whacked his shoulder. He scuttled for the passenger's side, the harmless carbine in one hand, and piled into the pickup while I squatted, my twelve-gauge at ready, and let him slide behind the steering wheel. Only then did I ease into the cab with him, sliding down, stuffing my rain hat in my belt. "Okay, Riley," I said. "Roll down your window, give one toot, and start the engine."

He did it, no longer shaking as he stripped tape from the side window, his face impassive. I liked him shaky so I said, "Did I mention that this thing is semiauto? With sixteen rounds?" He blinked, whispered something to himself, shook his head. "Now give one toot again." He did. I thought I saw movement at one of the upstairs windows. "Aim the carbine up the slope toward the garden," I said.

He did it. I heard him mutter, "Bang bang; this ain't gonna fool anybody."

"Hand me the carbine slowly and burn rubber for the gate," I replied, "and give three toots on the way." I snatched the little weapon as he swung it into the cab, wondering if he entertained ideas of using it as a club. But he did a fine job of spewing gravel as I braced myself, leaning against the far door, aiming my persuader at his middle while we accelerated away.

I called for three more toots and got them, then told Riley to stop at the gate. "No panic braking! You don't want *me* to panic, do you?"

The pickup stopped. I made Riley give another three toots,

had him gun the engine a few times. Nothing—at least nothing I had hoped to see.

I opened my door and eased out, keeping the cab between me and my house. My adrenal pump insisted that hours were whistling past me in a gale of confusion, so I spoke with deliberation. "Don't open your door but lean out and wave and shout," I told Riley. "As if a posse were coming from up the hill. I'm going to fire for effect."

Mine was a delicate problem in personnel management; if Riley thought I was shooting at him without provocation, sure as hell he'd panic. As Riley waved and hollered, I reached in and shifted the gear lever to neutral, then took the revolver from my raincoat and squeezed off three rounds toward my garden plot three hundred yards distant.

Almost immediately the lank Ellis appeared on my porch, swiveling his head and his scattergun, seeking the source of Riley's excitement. "Get 'em here on the double," I snarled.

"They're coming," Riley shouted, waving and pointing. "Let's go, let's go!" He pounded on the side of his door and gunned the engine, darting a glance at me, getting my nod. I should've expected that, in doing a little more than the minimum, the little scuffler was conning me, awaiting a lapse on my part. "Let's *go*," he repeated.

Ellis shouted something in reply, ducked into my house, and reappeared a moment later with Dennison right behind him. My heart pounded against my throat as I saw what Dennison dragged with him.

Naturally he would choose the hostage who seemed most likely to be manageable, but Dennison had made a mistake. He held Lance McKay by the hair with one hand, his sidearm drawn in the other. Both men began to run toward me crabwise, searching behind them, scanning for enemies as they came. Half-squatting, I thrust the revolver into my belt as Ellis came into range of my twelve-gauge. Dennison lagged behind, wrenching my nephew's head, Lance stumbling behind him as a shield against an imagined enemy. Squalling and cursing, Lance was anything but tractable.

I suppose Riley was waiting until he knew my attention was

focused on Ellis, for without warning he gunned the pickup hard and let the clutch pedal thump upward. But Riley hadn't seen me snick the gear lever into neutral and of course the pickup didn't budge. I did, in a half-pivot toward Riley, who tumbled out the other side of the cab and hit running.

"Get 'im, Ellis, he's behind the cab!" Riley sang it over his shoulder as he loped down my access road toward distant blacktop. Ellis stared at him in astonishment, then caught sight of me as I peered over the side of the pickup. He made a stutter-step sideways, heading for a sycamore ten paces from me, and brought up his pumpgun.

My first round of double-ought buck took Ellis just above the belt buckle at a range of ten yards and jerked him backward like a marionette. Recoil aimed my second round higher, partly deflected by the airborne pumpgun, but the rest of the big pellets left him with no skull above the eyebrows. Ellis was already dead as he slid across the carpet of sycamore leaves.

Dennison had struggled within extreme range of my scattergun by now, but the twin thunderclaps of my twelve-gauge and Ellis's rag-doll collapse sent him scurrying behind the largest of my nearby sycamores. I had no confidence in a handgun I'd never sighted in and no time to cram the full clip into the carbine that lay on the floor of the pickup. Lacking pinpoint accuracy, I couldn't risk a shot while Lance screeched and flailed against his tormentor; at twenty-five yards a sawed-off shotgun's pattern is much too broad for precision shooting.

Dennison tried to quell Lance by shouting at him. I knew I had the bastard stopped if I could only get a moment to ransom his freedom for Lance's. "Lance!" I put every decibel I had behind it, making the same mistake as Dennison. "Lance, it's Uncle Harve! Calm down; you'll be okay!"

"Come beat him up! Owww, you better—" replied my nephew before Dennison whacked him with his pistol barrel. Lance heard me, all right; it was his tragedy that he never truly believed in ultimate control or ultimate punishment. But he believed in that pistol barrel and grabbed his head in both hands while screaming his head off.

Dennison's arms were possible targets. So was Lance. Then

my nephew slumped, still squalling. From behind the tree came Dennison's voice, harsh with command: "You try for me and the kid gets it!" His muscular forearm clamped under Lance's chin, the pistol held to the boy's head.

"Stop it, Lance," I shouted and added, "Dennison, you won't outlive him by five seconds."

"Settle him down, then," the man responded, and it was as much a plea as demand. I felt an instant of hope, realizing that Dennison wanted to negotiate.

But only for that instant. Maybe Lance saw his father leap from my front porch, silver shreds of duct tape flapping at his ankles, jacking the slide of my big .45 Colt as he ran for the cover of a walnut tree. Or maybe Lance was only getting his second wind. I'll say this, with a lump in my throat: the little bugger never gave up. I think he bit down on Dennison's wrist.

The man snarled and jerked his left arm up, and then Lance was on all fours, slipping on leaves, and whether Dennison intended to merely wing my nephew or not, he fired from a range of ten feet. Shot through the back, Lance fell heavily and lay still.

I needed a clear shot, but as I stepped away from the safety of the pickup, Dennison backpedaled fast, keeping the sycamore between us, angling for a middle-size oak farther from me. There was a sizable chance that he'd make it until he heard the heavy bark of the Colt in Ern's hands.

Dennison turned toward the sound—a very long shot for a handgun; no wonder Ern missed—and I pulled my trigger again. It didn't nail Dennison but it sent him sprinting away. Ern advanced firing two-handed, each blast of the Colt a second after the last.

Dennison knew his weapons, all right. He managed to get thirty yards from my scattergun and then made a desperate lunge for the top of my eight-foot fence, snapping a shot at Ern before tossing his revolver aside. Ern did not flinch but raced forward. He had already fired five rounds without a strike, but number six caught Dennison just at the base of his neck as he struggled at the top of my fence. Dennison jerked, fell, then hung facing us with one sleeve caught on the top of the wire. Ern, eyes wide in a face whitened by rage, ran without hesitation to point-blank range and put his last round squarely into Dennison's heart.

By this time I had Lance in my arms, and as I ran to the house, I called, "Leave that garbage, Ern! Lance may not be hurt too badly."

My twelve-gauge slapping my back as I ran, I got Lance to the house, where Shar met me wailing. I relinquished her son to her and stood aside for Ern, who ran several paces behind me, sobbing.

Kate stood ashen-faced, my little target pistol in her hand, just inside my front door. The added weapon made me think of Riley, whose defection might not last. "Kate, we'll have to get Lance to a doctor," I said, breathing hard. "Can you tear down the book barrier double-quick?"

"I can try. Is Lance hurt badly?"

"Moaning and breathing. That's all I know," I said and wheeled back toward the pickup, checking the target pistol as I ran. I fairly clanked with my arsenal, but weapons weren't the items of hardware that concerned me most. I wanted that pickup.

The engine was still bumbling along, waiting for whoever got there first. I backed it furiously past two deaders, wondering how much radiation I'd taken during the attack.

When I ripped the plastic cover from my root cellar doors, I found Kate and Devon toppling a bookcase. Devon claimed he could shoot, so I stationed him in the pickup two paces from the root cellar entrance with the carbine, its full clip, and orders to fire one warning round if he saw anything suspicious. Then I hotfooted through my tunnel to the basement and to the keening little group of McKays surrounding my waterbed.

Lance lay on his back, breathing but glassy-eyed with shock. Midway up his naked breast on the right was a small purplish crater, trickling crimson, which Cammie kept wiping away with facial tissue while Shar tore at a roll of adhesive tape. It was good to know that the bullet wasn't lodged in Lance's body. It was very bad that the exit wound was bubbling as he breathed.

✧ ✧ ✧

Lance's punctured lung canceled any thoughts I'd had of sealing my place up. In fifteen minutes we had all dressed as thoroughly as possible with our food in slender blanket rolls and a few other necessaries thrown into my old backpack. At my request, Kate scribbled directions to her place at Yountville, which I pocketed knowing I might never get that far.

The pickup had room for all the McKays, Devon, and the bikes as well. Devon kept the carbine in sight for the edification of any lurking 'jackers. Before backing the Lotus out I cut the bonds of Oliver, who lay still unconscious on my garage floor. Maybe I should've dumped him into the pickup, but on my list of priorities he was as expendable as a hangnail.

Kate didn't like sharing my passenger seat with two shovels, a backpack, and a hundred pounds of Spot—but then neither did he. I led the way past my gate, Ern driving the pickup while Shar cradled Lance in the cab. Poor kid was coughing some blood. Our plan, or more accurately Shar's decision, was for me to lead the way to Kaiser Hospital in Antioch in the forlorn hope that we would find it open. If not, Martinez also had a Kaiser Hospital. Wherever we found medical help, Shar would stay there with Lance while Ern and the rest of us headed for Yountville.

But those plans proved fruitless. I wasted five minutes trying to find a route to the hospital in Antioch, and it seemed to me that the number of wrecks and abandoned vehicles increased as we got within a mile of the place, as if they were deliberately aligned as roadblocks. It *would* look that way, of course, after fifty thousand people converged on the same point with life-threatening emergencies.

I might've got to the hospital by some judicious hops in the Lotus, but not with Lance and Shar both. And since I couldn't raise Kaiser/Antioch on the phone, we didn't know whether it still offered any hope.

We lit out for Martinez, using sidewalks and road shoulders when necessary and trying steadily to get the Martinez hospital on the phone. Kate said all she got was interference. Then we tried emergency numbers and got multiple busy signals. Ditto with police numbers. That was strange because we saw nobody on the streets, and it seemed unlikely that police circuits would be overloaded in a dead township. We finally got through to an emergency fire number, an exchange now manned by army engineers.

"Kaiser/Martinez was evacuated to Petaluma yesterday," said the sergeant, ready to break the connection.

I tried to picture that in my head; it would've been a big operation. "What route did they take, sergeant?"

"Staging area in Martinez just south of the railroad bridge. We ran a bunch of boxcars in and hauled everything movable in one load. There's another train scheduled late today into Concord, but with all those burn cases it's gonna be late. Don't expect to find any medical staff; we had to forcibly evacuate some. Can't risk losing trained people to fallout residuals."

I said, "We're in a pickup. Can we get across at Martinez? Ferry boat? Anything?"

"Not a chance. We're clearing the traffic bridges with 'dozers and wheel-loaders, just dumping vehicles into the bay, and with all that heavy equipment thrashing around, we can't allow any foot traffic. You get conscripted to a work detail for trying." His brusque rumble lowered slightly. "Off the record, I hear they're allowing foot traffic and bikes over the railroad bridge except when there's rolling stock on it. But if you try that with a car you'll wind up on a work detail. Just 'cause you don't see a sentry don't mean he don't see *you.* Signing off," he said, and the line went dead.

I waved Ern to a stop and told him what I'd learned. We could get to the railroad tracks near the bridge, but Lance would have to be my solitary passenger as I wave-hopped across Suisun Bay in the Lotus. Assuming I made it across, I would await the rest of the group on the Vallejo side, then take Shar and Lance to Napa at all possible speed.

Before leaving my place, I had buckled Spot's heavy ID collar on him, more as a mark of his domesticity than anything else. I didn't want him shot as a zoo runaway. Now I saw that the collar would come in handy, because Spot might not take kindly to seeing me drive away without him. True enough, Spot was a watchcat, not an attack cat. But if Cammie's soothing hands and voice weren't enough, he might put clawmarks on somebody when he saw me drive away. I gave that a lot of thought while seeking the nearest approach to the railroad bridge, that great greasy black steel span running parallel to the freeway bridge out of Martinez.

Our little convoy stopped about a mile short of the bridge near a welter of abandoned cars, clothing, even bedding and kitchenware. We saw not one human form—only a few rats, seemingly unaffected by fallout. No doubt they lived far down in sewers; theirs was a holocaust lifestyle. Ern judged that the place looked like the aftermath of a railroad staging area but intended to keep going as near as possible to the railroad bridge before abandoning the pickup.

While Cammie and Shar placed Lance into my passenger seat, I borrowed belts from Devon and Ern, passing them through Spot's collar and looping them through tie-downs on the pickup. I didn't want to use my own belt because my pants would've been at half-mast in an instant. That's how much weight I'd lost in nine days.

I said, "Cammie, try and keep him calm, but if he gets out of control, stand away until I'm out of sight. Ern, you start off for the bridge first. Spot might not get antsy if he's the one who's moving instead of me."

Kate, darkly: "And what if he won't follow us over the bridge?"

"Just don't leave him tied up," I sighed. "I can't ask you to waste a second worrying about him." I wasn't prepared for the lingering hug she gave me; I was too intent on leaving. My sister's eyes were wet but steady on me as I slipped into the car.

"I love you, bubba," she said, her chin quivering as she nodded toward her son. "Get him across for me; okay?"

I gave her our old childhood horsewink because I didn't want to cry, then waved her away. I watched my rearview as Ern steered, jouncing, over tracks and headed toward the bridge. Cammie knelt near Spot, scratching him and talking, and though he yipped and watched me with what may have been yearning, he didn't try to break free. I had underestimated his liking for Cammie—or maybe I'd just underrated my quadruped pal.

With a look at Lance, I squirted the Lotus away in search of boat ramps. My nephew drooled bloody spit into a towel, and his normally ruddy color had faded to pallor. I tried to minimize bumps without using the fans; a Cellular's fans are notoriously short-lived if used for more than momentary jumping, and I'd already made one open-water crossing on them.

From Waterfront Road I turned toward the bay at my first chance, resolved to find a ramp westward, to my left. To my right lay the Naval Weapons Station, and new signs warned that I could expect to be shot if I continued in that direction. Would the sentries be adequately protected against radiation? I doubted it. Would they be at their posts? That I did not doubt. But I saw no one in the open. Martinez lay silent and dusty and dead around me.

A mile of fruitless driving took me past warehouses and loading docks, but finally, almost in the shadow of the railroad bridge, I found a small boat ramp. The fans eased us up and shrilled a song of short life as I studied the opposite shore.

The ramp I aimed for was clogged by a deep-keeled sloop which had somehow rolled off its trailer and now lay like a beached whale, mast thrusting into the water. I continued to within a few yards of shore—if the fans packed up now, I could tow Lance to dry land—and scooted toward the little state park where I'd gone skimming with Kate a week, and an era, before. The keening of fans and wail of my little engine masked the distant bang-clatter of Caterpillar diesels high overhead, and I never thought to look up as I skimmed under the high bridges. Until, of course, the Pontiac hurtled into the bay fifty yards in front of me.

The Army Corps of Engineers was as good as its word, using huge log-fork-equipped behemoths to toss everything off the bridge. No, I didn't wallop the damned sedan, but I passed it two seconds after it struck and its splash nearly swamped us. By some miracle my fans digested the spray without complaint and then I could see the park to my right, and three minutes later I plopped the Lotus down on dry land, grateful for the chance to disengage the fans.

I needed the fans again to jump a fence and a jam of cars

before finding a route through Benicia's waterfront to the railroad tracks. Then I drove slowly back toward the bridge and shut my engine down a few yards from the tracks. My nephew's breath sounded rattly to me but I didn't know what to do about it. Cradling my twelve-gauge, staring down the tracks, I could barely make out the bobbing of tiny figures nearly a mile away. Nearer, on the freeway bridge, I could see a white-clad man in the enclosed cab of an enormous D-10 bulldozer, maneuvering a semi trailer over the rail with his front blade. He was the first stranger I'd seen who spelled "help" instead of "trouble."

Ern needed a car and I had ten minutes to kill, so I spent it inspecting the dozen vehicles nearby. Three of them still had keys in the ignition but none would run. Someone had drained their tanks, just as I would've done. I pondered transferring a gallon of my fuel to a VW transporter that was surely old enough to vote. Then I squinted toward the bridge again and waved a circled thumb and forefinger. My brother-in-law stumbled as he thrust his bike over the cinders, but filling his cargo basket was a hefty fuel can he'd taken from the pickup. What I'd forgotten, Ern had remembered, and vice versa. Spot heard my hail and briefly proved that he was the world's fastest sprinter.

I hugged the fool, ran toward my struggling little group, grabbed the fuel can from the exhausted Ern, and hoofed it toward that old transporter, cursing Spot as he gamboled beside me. Lucky for us, the old VW had no siphon-proof inlet pipe; the fuel thief hadn't needed to cut its fuel line. I got a gallon of fuel into it before the others arrived panting, Devon far in arrears. Ern got it running while I tossed backpack and shovels from the Lotus.

We were breathless from our labors but: "There'll be message centers in Napa and Yountville," Ern husked, pouring the rest of his fuel into the transporter. His eyes flicked toward Shar, who tenderly eased into the Lotus with Lance. "We'll be in touch."

Cammie urged Spot into the VW as I slid into my car. We wasted no time in farewells, and a moment later I chirped rubber heading north. I patted my sis on the knee after circling one barricade. "We'll get there," I reassured her over the engine's snarl, and saw her nod before I drifted the Lotus through a curve. That was the extent of our conversation en route to Napa; if I was quick enough with the Lotus, maybe we wouldn't lose my nephew.

Life is hard, but death is easy. For bullheaded, valiant little Lance it was as easy as slipping away from us in a game of permanent hookey from the school of hard knocks. He was still with us when the police shunted me to Napa State Hospital, a facility near the town now crammed with thousands of trauma cases and not enough medical staff.

Lance seemed to rally, they said, after a third-year med student drained all that blood from his lung cavity and rigged Shar for a whole-blood transfusion. But Dennison's slug had ruptured too much lung tissue; shocked his system too hard; and we had no thoracic surgeon on call. The hospital had no remaining supply of oxygen or adrenalin and goddammit, the kid never had a chance. . . .

My sis and I wept quietly that afternoon, holding each other as we had when mom died, in a basement hall filled with others whose own miseries insulated them from ours. Eventually I left Shar long enough to send a brief message from the emergency comm center to Napa's message center. I agonized over the content of that message but finally spoke for my allotted twenty seconds. Past the lump in my larynx I said, "They're doing all they can here at Napa State Hospital but it doesn't look good, Ern. Shar is coping." Then I added, "No great hurry; he can't have visitors." That way Ern might prepare himself for what I already knew without his hearing it all at once. And maybe he wouldn't take crazy chances driving to us if he knew he couldn't literally race to Lance's side.

After midnight Ern arrived with Cammie, already suspecting the truth. They let me handle the burial arrangements through a massive graves registration system—one of those horrendous details the Surgeon General's Office had worked out long before as a public health measure.

While waiting in line I learned that the almost negligible

radiation in Napa was marginally rising, no thanks to vagrant winds that swept up and borrowed fallout particles from San Rafael. I calculated that we had spent less than two hours between my place and Napa and hoped that the gradual rise in background count would not extend to Yountville. Kate and Devon waited for us there with Spot, working their buns off to get the Gallo house ready for long-term occupation. By "long-term" I was thinking about several weeks. I missed it by a bunch.

# VII. Doomsday Plus One Hundred and Seventy-six

I may as well put the bad news first: Devon Baird didn't make it through the winter. Cammie took it hardest, though she, like the rest of us, knew what was coming after his hair fell out and the chelate medicine wasn't available to the public until after his bone marrow had quit producing red corpuscles. It seemed that I wasn't destined to have a foster son after all.

But "destiny," I believe, is a word we use to hide incompetence. I may have a son or daughter one day, because in Kate I've found one hell of a wife.

It hadn't occurred to me that I might ring any chimes for a young woman until early December when I was in Napa, registering the old VW transporter in case its prewar owner showed up. I recognized Dana Martin instantly as she slid the forms to me. She had been an FBI intermediary cutout years before, but sleek and sharp as she was, Dana didn't recognize me at first.

When she did: "Good Lord, Harve," she marveled. "You're a hell of a specimen—and ten years younger, minus the beard and thirty kilos of suet." Same old Dana; even her compliments came with a built-in backhand.

"Living off the land isn't easy even in a mild winter," I reminded her. She seemed interested in prolonging our chance encounter and wondered out loud how often I got into Napa. I said not often, and she constructed an ingenue's pout for me, and I bugged out feeling like an escapee from a small predator—which was more truth than fancy. I kidded myself that I was only in a hurry to barter my three bushels of processed acorns for seed and a plow attachment for our third-hand garden tractor. But on my way back to our place near Yountville, I thought about Dana Martin some more and the comparison with Kate came unbidden, and from that moment forward I was a lapsed bachelor.

I said as much to Kate that evening. She only smiled and said, "I was beginning to wonder about you," and her mouth was warm and hungry. We legalized it in January.

Why a woman of Kate's youth and vitality would want to make such a commitment to me was a mystery until the night she asked me what I knew about the bouillon ballot.

"You might not want to know," I said.

"Which means that you *do.* I thought as much. That lonesome vote for Devon the first time; that was you, wasn't it?"

I cocked an eyebrow, enjoying her quest and the way she went about it. "That would be telling on Ern and Shar."

"Screw the tenants, buster. I'm dead sure it was you. You're not the kind to weasel out of a tough decision—but I wanted to hear it from you."

"All right. It was me; but the way you hollered afterward, the others must've thought it was you."

"I don't care. It wasn't right that three of us placed the burden on one. But I damn sure voted the second time, Harve. Not that it matters, but I bet the second abstention was Ern's."

"You lose."

"Then Shar—"

"Shar, nothing. It was mine."

For once Kate was astonished. "Do you mean to sit here under my fanny and tell me you abstained just to teach us a lesson? That's petty!"

"Not to teach anything," I protested. How the hell did I let myself get into these things? "Kate, after your protest, I saw shame on three faces. I felt sure you would all toughen yourselves on the next ballot—and if you felt tough, chances were you'd vote for tough logic. For Devon. But if all four were the same there'd be no secret to the ballot, and you three were obviously touchy about making your decisions known. So . . ."

"So you gave us something to hide behind." Her head was wagging sideways, but on her face was loving acceptance.

"If you wanted it," I shrugged.

"I want it still. Very few men realize how much a woman will do for a man she can depend on. Long legs and a tight gut are nice, but give me a man I can depend on. Fortunately I can have it all unless you start eating too much again." And then she found my mouth and used it mercilessly, I'm happy to say.

We—not only three surviving McKays and two Rackhams but the surviving eighty million Americans—aren't out of trouble yet, though the armistice is a month old now and the radiation count is slowly receding from a small fraction of a rem in many regions. The chance of bone tumors, leukemia, and other long-term damage has leaped by an order of magnitude, which means we have a small chance of dying that way within the next twenty years. Compared to life expectancy when this republic was young, those odds look bearable. Since the depletion of stored blood, accident victims get whole-blood transfusions or none at all. That's why a blood-group tattoo on the inner forearm is becoming popular. During the past winter there was a shortage of protein, and we see very few cats or dogs these days. Spot is one of those few, because he doesn't solo very far from our designated turf.

You could say with too much justification that Spot is a perfect example of the kind of luxury nobody can afford in this postwar world. If I'd expected the war, perhaps I'd have turned him over to the people at Oregon's Wildlife Safari.

Well, I didn't; and I won't. In the past few months he has learned to maul an intruder and to dodge strangers with sticks that go bang, and he patrols our tender new crops to bag the beasties that would otherwise damage them. That's the only protein supplement he gets, and if he doesn't like living on cereal grains, well, tough; neither do the rest of us. But soybeans will grow here, and by this fall we may not need to boil acorns or find new ways to flavor alfalfa sprouts.

Do I feel defensive about Spot? Yes. Does he pull his weight? Probably not, but maybe so. Gaunt as he is, he submits to the small saddlebags Cammie sewed for him. They'll hold the seine and the fish when we hike to the reservoir, or twenty pounds of whatever else we don't want to tote when one of us goes foraging. Besides, he's becoming known. Anyone who has seen him cover a hundred yards in three seconds will tend to be circumspect at double that distance.

High-tech luxuries like holovision and many medicines will be in short supply for a long time, and as Bay Area suburbs cool down, they become vast junkyards ripe for reckless foragers. City stripping can be downright foolhardy even in some places the bombs missed. Like Milwaukee, where typhus ran its course; and Lexington, where typhoid began in a public shelter and swept the county. I suspect we're through building beehive cities, those great complex organisms that proved so dreadfully vulnerable. If the current plans are any guide, the feds and state officials will rebuild many sites as ring cities surrounding the ruins.

The federal gummint doesn't interfere much with a state's regional decisions now, and since the rural population pulled through in such good shape, the political climate is just what you'd guess: conservative. Kate and I persuaded the McKays to stay on here at the Gallo acreage because that makes us all one household, and taxes are easier on us this way. Currently we're required to pay twenty-four hours of labor into the skills bank every seven days—two twelve-hour days each week. If you think I put my time in as a part-time cop, think again; I cussed and cajoled a wood stove for years, and on the days when I cook for Napa County nabobs, they look forward to gourmet meals. Of *course* I always bring some of it home! Why should a planning commissioner eat better than my wife does?

As for the McKays? Cammie's in school again, training in radiology, which is going to be a crucial skill. Shar is a lab technician in the nearby hospital that used to be a veteran's home and now manufactures its own coarse penicillin. So we don't lack for some basic pharmaceuticals. And Ern, when he isn't engineering the new water-purification plant, is scrounging materials on his own to convert timber by-products into fuel and lubricants. If any one of us becomes a plutocrat during reconstruction, it'll be Ern McKay. I figure he's earned it.

When anyone asks Kate what she does, she says she's my physical therapist; keeps me skinny. God knows that's true enough, and no complaint, but she has a very special talent with little kids. Anyone who thinks a Yountville first-grader can't be adept at postwar survival skills simply hasn't watched her students dress out a chicken, or repair a bike, or create sandals from worn-out tire casings. An intriguing progression of skills there: Kate got some of it from counterculture folks, who got it from travels among the Mexicans, who learned it by rummaging among the castoffs of the rich yanquis.

So it's my wife Kate, more than any of us, who'll be the key to the future of this country. We adults are survivors by definition; our first priority now is to make our next generations expert at pulling through.

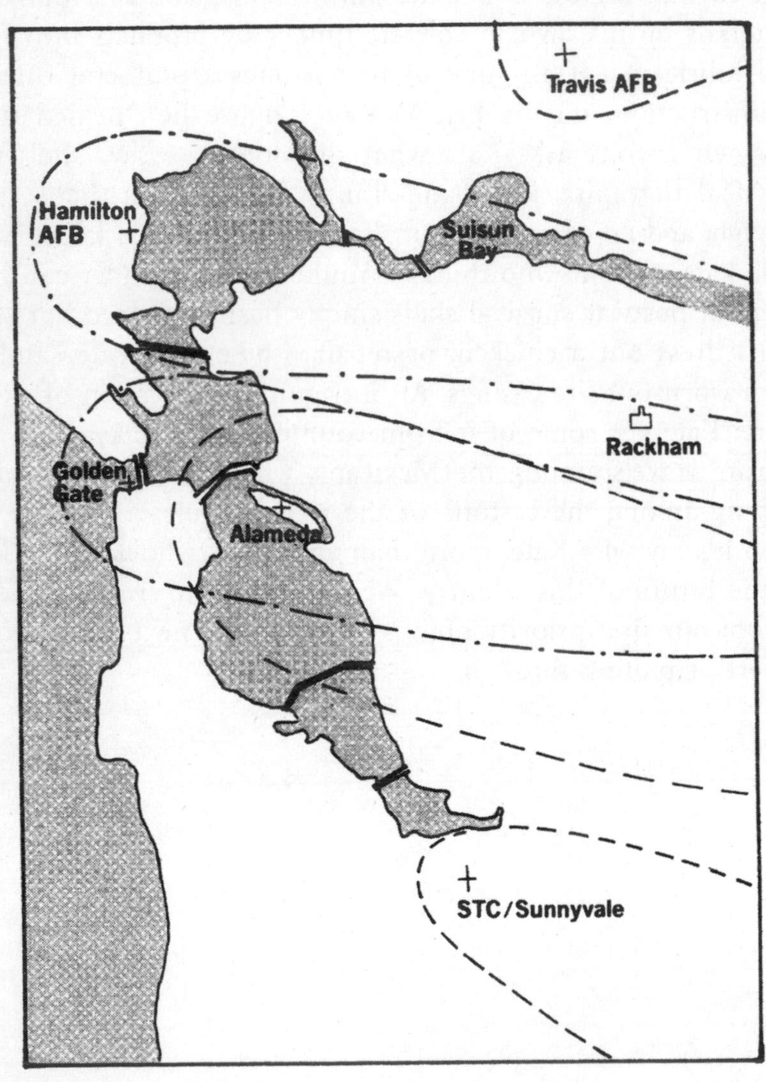
Travis AFB
Hamilton AFB
Suisun Bay
Rackham
Golden Gate
Alameda
STC/Sunnyvale

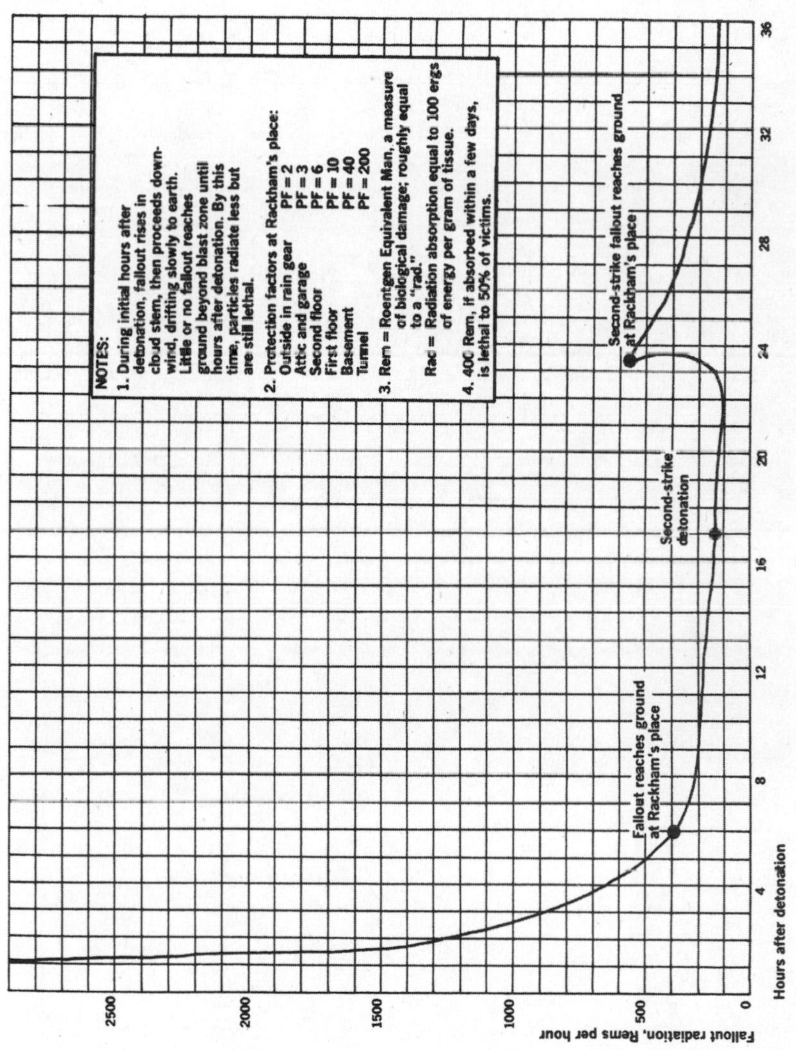
NOTES:
1. During initial hours after detonation, fallout rises in cloud stem, then proceeds down-wind, drifting slowly to earth. Little or no fallout reaches ground beyond blast zone until hours after detonation. By this time, particles radiate less but are still lethal.
2. Protection factors at Rackham's place:
Outside in rain gear PF = 2
Attic and garage PF = 3
Second floor PF = 6
First floor PF = 10
Basement PF = 40
Tunnel PF = 200
3. Rem = Roentgen Equivalent Man, a measure of biological damage; roughly equal to a "rad."
Rad = Radiation absorption equal to 100 ergs of energy per gram of tissue.
4. 400 Rem, if absorbed within a few days, is lethal to 50% of victims.
Fallout reaches ground at Rackham's place
Second-strike detonation
Second-strike fallout reaches ground at Rackham's place
Fallout radiation, Rems per hour
0
500
1000
1500
2000
2500
Hours after detonation
4
8
12
16
20
24
28
32
36